DOGS OF CATHERINE TOWN

TO ZAIDA —
HAPPY READING!

George

DOGS OF CATHERINE TOWN

GEORGE GUESS

PALMETTO
PUBLISHING

Charleston, SC
www.PalmettoPublishing.com

Dogs of Catherine Town
Copyright © 2020 by George Guess

ISBN-13: 978-1-64990-325-9
ISBN-10: 1-64990-325-1

CONTENTS

1   THE TRANSSIB

Just then, I spotted something from the window moving fast across the steppe. Maybe a deer or lynx by the speed … Rather, it was a boy wearing a loose cap running ahead with a surprised almost fearful expression on his face. It was as if a train was something he had never seen before. Yet his disheveled dress, ragged looks, and long strides expressed strength and the confidence of youth. I caught the beginning of a defiant grin in that expression of fearful surprise. Likely a tough one … maybe a Cossack or Chechen brave out for a run. His strides floated him ahead; it was more than a run. Perhaps he did this for a rush beside every passing train. Behind him a few paces back ran his black and white shaggy dog, a ruddy country type that was obviously used to these escapades with him. The peasant boy, if that was what he was, must have stepped in a ditch and fallen, as I could no longer see him though I pressed my face to the far corner of the window. The track was curving away, and the last thing I saw was the dog that probably had stopped to sniff around the scene until his master picked himself back up. It was late in the day, and the austere, dismal plain was covered here and there with withered grass and low reeds. The sunset was deep red as it always was in these parts, and the painted landscape darkened. Farther away, I could see forks of lightning strike the plains—zigzags that ran down to the ground. There must have been thunder but with the din of the train as it jolted along, I heard nothing. I was seeing something significant here. What was it? I had often applied the "what-ness" test to my students. Now I tried it on myself with little to show for it.

Pelts of rain streaked the window, and it darkened further. It was getting late. It was summer, and as we approached the Urals, the heavy forests of silver birches had turned to steppe. I didn't see any more magpies fluttering about or hopping along the ground. As dismal as plains can be, now they were covered by plants and flowers, and the different shadows from the clouds varied by sunlight made them quite stunning. I took a swig from my Soviet-era military flask and noticed how hot and humid it was inside my compartment. From all the booze and lack of food on this long trip, my stomach growled. It had to be time for dinner.

Going through the seven or eight coaches to the dining car was quite the cultural and sociological journey. I had taken the long hike for breakfast and knew the drill. I said "hi" to the lady called Natasha who was in charge of the car and the official *gorgon*. In Soviet times, every hotel floor and railway car had gorgons, who handled cleaning, sold beer, cigarettes, and candy. Most importantly, they watched who came and went and reported suspicious characters at the desk, who spoke immediately to the Party rep usually hanging around the lobby. Natasha was hefty and loud, bellowing at many of the passengers and ordering them around. Much of it was blow-hard bluster of the kind common in Brooklyn and West Side Manhattan. Her aggressive hand gestures and facial expressions suggested she could have been from the Bronx. I could see most of the passengers treated her bluster as light-hearted banter, the kind of friendly abuse you get from the working poor. So, we hit it off that morning. She wanted to know where I had gotten my reading glasses, which I showed her. Trying them on for size, she asked me to get her a pair. I agreed, of course, and told her on my next trip through I would bring her a pair from the U.S. and gave her a roll from the dining car as a down payment. She let out a loud laugh and gave me a friendly punch on the shoulder.

Moving to the next car, the passengers seemed more imprisoned than relaxed. This car began the "hard" class, which was easily distinguishable from the "soft" class where I was. Some in hard were on for the 6,000-mile, 10-day Trans-Siberian Express (or Transsib) journey from Moscow through Siberia to Vladivostok. Not me. I started in Moscow yesterday but was getting off at Perm tomorrow morning. I stayed In Moscow for a few nights then got the Transsib to Yekaterinburg. That was quite enough for me … I could smell the boiled cabbage, body odor, and stale tobacco already. Several were playing dominoes and drinking yellowish, sticky-looking Georgian wine and perhaps lemon vodka. Some were sipping tea from the electric samovar at the end of the car and dipping slices of dark bread into it. There was someone in a white, roughly-stitched peasant coat strumming out tunes on a four-string balalaika and singing a mournful ballad about an outlaw on the run. This lively scene of singing, drinking, and clapping was familiar to me from traveling second class on Mexican railways. In the next car I walked through, there were several others, probably Kazaks from their colorful shirts, singing as one of them played a two-stringed *domras*. Despite the often mournful ballads (which usually ended badly for everyone involved), the voices were throaty and full of gusto. It all mixed in nicely with the vodka from my flask, and got me in the mood for dinner. Some of us exchanged polite nods as I moved on towards the dining car.

The dining car was filling up, but I spotted an almost empty table. The car reminded me of the worn elegance of Russian subway cars from the 1980s that I'd seen in Moscow and Kyiv. Some had chandeliers with burned-out bulbs, gaudy curtains, and the atmosphere of an upscale bordello overall. I sat down at the table that was occupied by a man nervously looking around and gnawing his thumb. I ordered a carafe of Hungarian *bikaver* red and went right to work on it. Unlike in the 1980s when the Soviets collectivized the wineries and destroyed all semblance of quality, the available bikaver was quite smooth. Perhaps a bit giddy from all the vodka, I splashed some into the glass and threw it down in a few gulps. My thumb-gnawing neighbor was working on a glass of the yellow wine I had seen earlier that really looked foul. He chugged his glass down and ordered another. The waitress, a rotund woman similar in physique to Natasha in my car, looked him over menacingly and gave his shoulder a hard slap. Then she applied a tight grip to his arm; he was being sentenced back to hard class. The waitress must have sensed that I had come from soft class. She was bossy and often rude to other patrons such as the thumb-gnawer but polite and attentive with me. She even gave me some bread to wash the superb Hungarian red down with. Then another couple sat down across from me. They looked me over, trying to size me up, I suppose; there was no telling how bad I actually looked to someone. The couple had the over-polished appearance to me of tourists so I tried to stay with Russian, talking to the waitress in hopes they would leave me alone. It didn't work.

On cue, the middle-aged man with wig-like snowy, clipped hair said out loud, "Hi! We're from Centralia, Illinois. I'm Phil and this is my wife, Ethel. Do you speak some English?"

I hesitated, looking for an out, but finally said, "Well yes, I live and work in upstate New York."

"So we're compatriots," she said with an oily smile. Her face was badly made up and smelled of cheap powder. "We've been here attending an agricultural products fair in Moscow. And my husband, Phil, and I are celebrating the good news by taking the train to Siberia."

"Great! And what are you celebrating?"

"Phil's been promoted to Assistant Vice President for this region. He's sold more U.S. products than anyone, and he's been only working here for a few years."

"Why that's good news!" I said trying to appear politely enthusiastic. "So, why go to Siberia for the occasion?"

"We've read so much about it. It was apparently once a frontier just like the U.S. West."

"Something like that ... My grandparents were sentenced to hard labor there and died under Stalin. I doubt he vacationed there much before they were sent over on a free excursion in a boxcar."

"Why were they sentenced?"

"They complained while standing in a bread line and were reported. It might have been the length of the queue, bread quality, or just about life in general."

"They should have been more cautious," counseled Phil.

The waitress arrived and announced the one-item menu. It was borscht, chicken, and potatoes. I told her I would take it.

I told the couple what was on offer, and, looking at each other in surprise at the austere menu, they ordered it.

"So now that you've been promoted, what will you and your firm be doing in Russia?" I asked.

"Our plan is to sell more U.S. agricultural products—seeds, tractors, fertilizer, and the like. They want to increase farm productivity and prevent another famine, and we want to help them."

"The famine was actually in Ukraine in the '40s, and Russian farm productivity has been increasing dramatically. Don't they make many of their own tractors and farm implements? And don't they have plenty of labor to boot? Just wondering …"

I've always had this problem. Seems I can only be politely enthusiastic for a few moments, then my critical faculties kick in.

"We sell them U.S. products financed by the firm and covered with loan guarantees by the U.S. government," Phil explained.

"Still can't imagine why they would need U.S. farm machinery or supplies," I said. "Russia is still the leading exporter of wheat in the world. Western sanctions of Russia haven't increased any interest in negotiation on the other issues. In fact, they increased local self-sufficiency in poultry and pork. Local producers are increasing in number and growing in scale. At current rates, they will substitute most imports with local supplies. I mean, I'm no expert but it's just Econ 101, where we all covered, "import substitution industrialization.""

"Russia still imports more food than it exports," Phil said.

"What a dumb program! You get them to buy imported U.S. products when they already make their own and get them to pay you interest and profits to boot. Seems to me a cruel and moronic thing to do…" I burst out laughing uncontrollably and almost choked on a bite of the overcooked chicken. Luckily, I had some *bikaver* left. I threw down a large glass of it to clear out my passages. Much better …

"We don't have to take this from you," they said, as they rose suddenly. Phil grabbed Ethel by her chubby arm and led her out of the dining car in a huff.

Laughing foolishly, I threw this at them on their way out: "I bet you don't even tend a garden in Central City or wherever the hell you're from! How would you know what they need?" I realized I was drunk.

After the meal of cold, brown chicken meat that tasted like cardboard surrounded by inedible rock-like potatoes, I headed back to my compartment. The potatoes looked like turds.

Realizing I had to take a giant piss, I headed quickly out of the dining car, oblivious of the two men sitting at the next table who were following right behind me. I was feeling the effects of all the drinking and had let my guard down—not the first time this had happened. I often forgot about the many muggers and thieves who lurked and watched foreigners, particularly Americans who were usually flush with cash. I knew how to behave but forgot my lessons. This crew was dressed in khaki-styled clothes and sported patches and badges that tried to signal they were security forces. If you knew anything about modern Russia, these were red flags. Both were stocky and a bit shorter than me. The taller one wore a jeweled earring and featured the peculiar absence of a full nose. Where the nose should have been, there was a smooth, flattened area of scar tissue from which protruded two nostril holes, probably from a knife fight. A distinctive wart in the middle of his forehead looked like a third eye. The shorter one's beady eyes sparkled brightly as they darted around evasively. Built like a bulldog, he had a comic protruding nose and receding chin. When combined with his sloped brow, his face was like that of a rat. A bulldog with a rat face! The two of them looked like most plain-clothed security types in Russia on the make. A tourist would likely be impressed and terrified at what such "officials" could do to them with all that implied authority.

I moved on through to the end of the next coach where there was a free head or WC as they are called. I pushed open the WC door and entered. After tossing some water on my face from the sink to get rid of the accumulated grime and feel a bit refreshed, I opened the door to find the two men waiting. They were decked out in leather jackets, and I suspected that they were either there to use the bathroom or to block my path. I held the door open.

"All yours," I said in Russian.

Almost on cue, they both flashed security IDs. "Your identification please; we are from the state security forces RSA," the tall one said.

"My ID is at my seat. What do you want? I am a U.S. citizen traveling on a 90-day tourist visa to work at a university here."

"Why were you speaking Russian at your table? Why does it seem to us that you didn't pick up Russian at a Berlitz School?"

I looked the two over and tried to slow things down and get ready for trouble, which seemed to be brewing. They both had hard stares and weren't the polite types one might expect from law enforcement people.

"Lot of questions today, no? Say, I like your hairdo. Do you use a Turkish barber? I use one because they burn the hairs out of my nose and ears and use straight razors. But I see that yours left a lot of hairs in your nose ... Must have been a cheap cut, right?"

The nostrils of the taller one flared, and his flattened-out nose pulsated like that of an angry wolf. He was getting pissed.

"I said show me your ID," growled the short, stocky one whose reddish nose belonged on a clown.

"OK, fair enough. But let me see your IDs again first. The light's poor here, and I couldn't get a clear look at them before."

They had no intention of showing me their phony IDs again. Anyone can make these things up at a print shop. Beyond having them made and using them regularly in high school to hit bars and buy liquor, I once had one made up for myself while here in Russia on a Fulbright to give me some gravitas beyond desk-warmer and lecturer at the university for two months. Neither the Fulbright people nor the university provided us with anything so I did a status upgrade. It worked; people snapped to. The problem now was I had nothing but my U.S. passport. I was on a university research grant from Bonaduz College in Elmira, NY. Who the hell had ever heard of that place? Nobody!

"You were trying to sell dollars to the man at your table whom the waitress sent back to hard class. He informed us of this, and that is a serious offense."

"That's a good one, officer. Why would I sell dollars when I need the ones I have? The fact is I didn't say anything to the guy who was sitting at my table when I got there. Both you and he are quite wrong."

There was a brief standoff between the two shabbily uniformed goons and me. Luckily, no one else was passing through the cars or needed to use the head. The two of them probably didn't mug me on the spot because my appearance might cause toughs to hesitate just a bit. I was medium-build, six feet, forty-five years old, and though not what I used to be at twenty, I was still in quite good shape. I had steely, grayish hair, was foreign-enough looking and sounding, squared-jawed (or so I've been told), and had an appropriately pocked-up face, hinting of past battles. So they paused.

The shorter one with the whiskered, rat-like snout, boxer's flattened nose, and crunched up cauliflower ears whipped out what looked like a toy radio from his belt and switched it on. Almost comically, it had blinking, colored lights to add to its symbolic importance. This had to be a must for any kid who wanted to play cop.

Rat face actually talked into his toy phone, saying they had a suspect they were bringing in now who was trying to sell dollars. His voice had a dark, gravelly tenor, which added to the impression of raw, feral animality he conveyed. I was waiting for the deep voice of Willy the Walrus to answer the phone, but to no avail. This must have been a cheaper version.

The taller one with the strange red pimple on his forehead reached down for his handcuffs while the other one was playing with his toy phone. Braving the strong fumes of onions and tobacco hovering around his mouth, I got Cyclops with a quick uppercut hard into his chin and down he went. Before Rat Face could move, I retracted my fist hitting him with my elbow in about the same place. Down he went to join his friend. To finish the job, I pulled them both up and hit their heads against the metal walls a few times, then pushed them into the WC and closed the door.

I made it back to my compartment a few coaches ahead, trying not to walk too fast or to draw attention. Despite all the wine, I had become razor focused and cold sober. I was actually shaking and upset that a good buzz had gone to waste because of these two punks. At least the wine was good enough to kill the taste and memory of what was really a disgusting meal. Time for a good think … I was less worried about Cyclops and Rat face, the two toy cops, than the fact that I had been naïve and off guard in a place famous for hustlers and muggers. Maybe the two would go off and find some more pliant tourists next time. Maybe they would look for me instead. This kind of careless lack of anticipation would never have happened in my old Brooklyn neighborhood. There I dealt with toughs all the time. They tried to take my lunch money on my way to school, pawing my younger sister whom I often accompanied, jeering at me because I didn't hang out with them to shoplift and steal, and so on. I had flattened several of them individually, and when they joined forces, I could usually take on two of them. I had learned that for larger groups, I needed to size things up fast and run from them. Based largely on my street experience, I was a pretty good boxer and wrestler in high school, making the school teams in both sports. And I had learned to fend for myself early on. The Bronx neighborhood was tough, and I faced problems all the time. All of us growing up there faced them—some cowered in fear, others sought the cover of their parents, still others like me had little or no support beyond occasional advice from friendly neighborhood cops. That's the way it was. But years of academic life, fighting people with wits and intellect instead of fists, had caused me to go soft, despite the time I still puffed away in gyms.

To the continuous beating rhythm of the wheels, I finally fell asleep. This time the dream was from an old Hitchcock movie. The locomotive sent long piercing screams into the night. Then I could hear the silent roar of the darkness. But the wheels kept rolling onwards and ever onwards. I woke up occasionally and gazed out the window. I stared into the night. Dead towns drifted by with forgotten lights. Iron bridges slapped the wheels with a thunderous rhythm; I heard another scream pierce the night from the engine.

I woke early after sleeping badly. Somehow, I had to get off the train without attracting attention. I hoped that the two toughs were simply the frauds I suspected, but in Russia, they could still be paid informants. I had run across many such types on previous research stints here. I was still shaken and looked forward to getting coffee in Perm. The announcement said about a half hour remained, and it was just getting light out. As the train approached, I could see a few flaming tall stacks above a vast plain of cement blocks of maybe twenty stories each where workers lived. I knew about them indirectly as my grandparents lived in one of these in Smolensk, south west of Moscow. It wasn't just the brutalist rows of raw concrete flats or the steel fences that made these cities still seem like concentration camps—even nearly thirty years after the "transition." It was the glare of lamps fixed to poles and searchlights. The people looked like prisoners in an exercise yard. As the sun continued to rise, the place started to look better. The shadows disappeared, and the floodlights gradually were extinguished all over town. There were trees and children playing in parks. My mood improved, and I was ready for a new day—perhaps a new life. A few minutes later, on the way out I said goodbye to Natasha who was waiting at the end of the car. I gave her a peanut butter granola bar that I brought along for precisely such occasions, and sealing it all with a big hug, stepped down from the train.

2 PERM

Without looking back, I headed for the *trefpunkt* or meeting place under the station clock. Looking ahead I saw Perm Station II, which was a brutalist structure in the center of this large city of about one million people. The city was an industrial center that apparently made steamboats and produced pulp and paper from the surrounding forests. Every railway station in Europe and the Russian federation had similarly monstrous designs and meeting places. Some of the larger European stations, such as Zurich, were elegant and often included the best restaurants in town. And the meeting places at least saved you from wandering around looking for people—especially if you hadn't actually met them before.

It was around eight in the morning, and no one was in the meeting point area. Where was he? Previous letters he had received from Gyorgy described a grim, quiet town, filled mostly with officials and office workers. He cynically described a place full of little men, like beleaguered and bullied lower-level civil servants and army officers. Gyorgy described the glacial, hidebound, and socially oppressive place where he lived, but which he somehow saw as a refuge from cities like Yekaterinburg (where he taught) and a convenient place to escape to their dacha for some rural authenticity. He often went to their dacha to get in touch with his soul again, he had said repeatedly. I was expecting the worst. I had never been this far east into Russia, into the Ural mountain area. I knew that the Ural region was the source of old legends about witches, warlocks, and mighty warriors who drew their strength from the peaks of the mountains. I also knew that the place was big and had become an industrial center since the coming of the railway in the 1890s, linking it with Moscow. The town sat on the left bank of the Kama River and besides machine building, wood processing, oil mining, it had a famous opera and ballet theatre. So, it didn't sound that bad, and the pictures I saw of it were enticing.

About a half hour later, I spotted a slim, elderly, distinguished looking and balding man with side whiskers and a trim beard was walking fast towards me. The man smiled at me and said in Russian: "You must be Nikolay Krylov! Kolya!"

"Hello Gyorgy! Call me Kolya if you must. But in the states I am known simply as 'Nicholas' or 'Nick'. So please, call me either one!"

"Welcome to Perm!" he said.

We kissed three times, right, left and right cheeks as the ancient Russian tradition required for greeting. The Swiss do this too—but usually not the men. Gyorgy seemed to be about 70, but in these countries one couldn't tell: maybe he was younger and looked old, like the many who had endured the Communist famines and scourges.

We walked briskly from the station to a path along the Kama River where we walked on for about another half hour. The river was wide and had a fine wide walkway along the banks into which many of its streets fed. Little cafes with outdoor seating lined the river at certain places, and the atmosphere was festive. The city was called Molotov from 1940 to 1970 in honor of the famous bomber namesake and party security apparatchik. Occasionally, Molotov 'cocktails' were used locally as in 2013 when several were tossed into a Jewish Community Center. The pogroms still lived on for some. Otherwise, it looked like a large, well-kept city on a scenic river.

Gyorgy motioned us ahead with sweeping waves of his large hands. "I hope you don't mind. I take walks along this path almost every day. It clears my head." The river flowed along past us quickly, and everywhere there were flowers and trees. Joggers passed, and children played in the parks nearby. The only hint of industry was an acidic smell in the air and a noticeable trace of soot, probably from paper mills and tall stacks, which were not visible from here. We came finally to his house, a modest sized place in an older, leafy neighborhood. As I well knew, professors liked these kinds of places, where they could write, think in solitude, and take refuge from university duties. I had the same kind of cozy place in Elmira, where I had lived with my now ex-wife Laurie and my boys for over twenty years.

"I thought you might be hungry, so let's have tea and some breakfast."

"Thank you! Yes, the food on the train was very tolerable, but I might be tempted by a bit more."

"Of better quality, too, I would imagine. Most of it is still disgusting."

A woman who must have been his wife suddenly entered the room and held out her hand to him. Was he supposed to kiss it—or her three times? He opted for shaking it. She appeared to have a man's grip and pumped his arm vigorously. A large yellow dog sauntered over from the corner and sat quietly as if listening to us.

"I am Nadezhda, Gyorgy's spiritual and intellectual advisor," she said with an attempt at irony. She was muscular, not fat, but large-boned and wore a black dress, which was unflattering yet somehow extravagant. The black dress fit with the home décor of dark curtains, bookshelves full of dark, leather-bound books, and darkened rooms. The house was rather stuffy, like a museum, and was gloomy. It was something I imagined that had survived and probably gotten them through the worst of Stalin's Russia—the food shortages, secret police shakedowns, and the daily personal insecurities. It was almost comic that some wanted such good old days back now. Even Khrushchev had decided in 1962 that he had seen enough and catalogued dozens of Stalin's crimes before the Party Congress. But the current longing among some people for the imaginary good old days was also predict-able—a movement by small-minded, resentful, envious people hoping that a regime of neo-Stalinists would allow them to get back at their enemies. Reflecting on her small town elegance at eight in the morn-ing, the thought came to me: all dressed up and no place to go, often a joke related to those lying in coffins. Then again, she might simply have dressed up for my arrival. . . .

I often thought about the neo-Stalinists here, as my Bonaduz College students would gush on about the return of social collectivism as a way of sharing and building community. An ordinary man would have gotten upset. What shit! The reality in all these countries had been rule by humorless, meddlesome bureaucratic thugs. State socialism demonstrated with all of the misery it caused that it did not represent the idealism of Marxian classlessness. No, it was rule by the equivalent of the New York State Motor Vehicle Department on a countrywide basis—endless lines, surly staff, and a zeal to treat applicants as potential criminals. It was the MVD and the state police all in one. Someone had said back in the early 1900s, "Lenin is here! There will be no more Tsars. It will be a workers state." Most Russians now know what that really meant—permanent insecurity and terror at the hands of a pervasive, unaccountable faceless bureaucracy.

Gyorgy guffawed as he spat out, "And she's also the most modest member of the family."

The dog quietly blinked as if trying to remember something he wanted to add. I patted him on the head a few times to let him know he was appreciated.

"You've met Pavel. I hope you like senile dogs. He's a good sort, but he's unpredictable, especially in the kitchen. Please, let's sit down and get acquainted. Your Russian is quite good for a member of the diaspora. So we can talk in either English or Russian," she said.

"Either one is fine for me. I should have the practice while here. Otherwise, I will still walk around using old Russian phases from thirty years ago! I need an update."

They served up tea from a samovar boiling nearby, along with rolls, meats, and breads. I knew most of the food as I made sure to eat ethnic Russian at home as often as possible—with students, family, anyone interested in Russian culture and history. Just looking at it all made me realize how hungry I was. The cause—well I couldn't exactly risk going back to the dining car for breakfast. ...

"Gyorgy has told me all about you. I believe your grandfather once emigrated from Smolensk to New York State where you were eventually born."

"That's right. 'Uncle' Gyorgy here, as I call him, has been writing occasional letters, and we spoke by phone eight years ago when I was on a research grant to Moscow."

"I've been keeping up with Nick's research and writings over the internet," he said.

"Wouldn't they be censored here?" she asked.

"They're hardly controversial. Planning methodologies and the like—something the authorities here eat up given their long tradition of attempting to plan out cities, industries, and people's lives. I expect a lively interest from any students he meets this summer," said Gyorgy.

Nadezdha seemed visibly bored by this talk of students and university research. She made a strange sound through her nose and shifted topics. "We can talk about your stay here later. Right now, here's what we have planned for today. You can tell us if you want to do something different."

I thought I was mistaken at first. Nobody makes noises when you talk. Little children might. Pet birds do. What I heard were audible snorts after most of Gyorgy's remarks. It wasn't him or Pavel or a bird; it was her. Maybe she had a cold? A clogged nose? Soon, I figured it out; they were snorts of contempt.

Gyorgy looked at his watch a few times then announced, "Right! We have to go to the vet for Pavel. He has some ailments of old age—worms, stiff joints, gout—just like an old wife."

"You've been pained your whole life," she said quickly.

"But like Pavel, and unlike an old wife, I rarely complain."

"Afterwards, if you are up to it, we're going to visit a pageant in the afternoon. It's the 150th anniversary of Perm's opera house. Lots of food and fruit vendors—we can eat there."

"Sounds great!" I said.

After more tea and coffee, Gyorgy and I walked into the old section of town and up a narrow, winding, cobbled street to the vet's office. Their house was close to the center of town so it took only minutes to get there. The waiting room was filled with all the usual dogs in a vet's office. Some were barking loudly, wagging their tales nervously, jumping up on things in the office, lying sick and miserable on the floor surrounded by others hungry-looking and eager for additional attention and maybe a few treats. It was a normal vet's office, and Pavel had clearly been there before. He came in with us obediently, just like a regular, and sat down by us awaiting his turn. He knew the drill. As we sat there, I noticed that Gyorgy talked to Pavel as if he were an old colleague. He whispered to him, gave him treats, brushed him off, and gave him little pats as we sat there. In contrast with the conversation at home where Pavel followed Gyorgy's every word, I noticed that his wife rarely looked at him when they spoke. Bad sign ... and I knew it well. At home, Pavel sat there modestly, an expression of endearing shyness on his face and blinked along as if he understood the lack of intimacy. He appeared at times to catch some of the monologue. But it was obvious that his mind was failing. Gyorgy patted him on the head and several times told him not to worry. Just as they had once survived Stalin, perhaps he was watching over Pavel as the embodiment of another tough survivor.

More to the point, I figured that Pavel was somehow serving as a refuge from Gyorgy's wife. Gyorgy often spoke sadly and seemed lonely to me even for the short time I'd watched him since this morning at the railway station. I knew he had lived through tough times during the Stalin era and subsequent dictators. He and his family had to scrape and behave very carefully to avoid the ire of the KGB. For my classes, I had read extensively about the Ceausescu era in Romania and what he did to the people there. The guy was a standard power-hungry tyrant, of course, but this one had knocked down whole neighborhoods in Bucharest. He is known for his megalomaniac building projects, like *Casa Populari* and the bizarre 2/3-scale mock-up of the Champs Elysees in Paris. The crackpot building projects that forced people to move often turned pets into urban vagabonds. Many residents could no longer live with their dogs, but that didn't mean they couldn't go outside to play with them and feed them. So many did, and police and lower-level public officials, understanding the irrational origins of the whole business, stood aside sympathetically and watched it happen—in some cases protecting and facilitating this petty fascist drama. Romanian stray dogs soon became receptacles for the projection of human frustrations. They were respected for their tenacity and boldness; dogs were everything symbolically that the average Romanians were not during this brutal period—heroic, fearless, nimble, and, above all, free.

Thus before, during, and after the Communist epoch in Romania and for the rest of Mitteleuropa, it had been normal for dogs to be the canine equivalents of the wily rascal *Flashman* of the late George MacDonald Fraser: They somehow turned up in every major event in history, or if they did not turn up as needed, people invented stories in which they did. The writer Gyorgy Dragoman once described his communist teachers as joyless, strict, and prone to shrieking; his football coach too, he wrote, conducted regular beatings during sadistic morning practices. Dogs, Dragoman pointed out, avoided such treatment and so occupied a special place in the minds of human sufferers. Some people began to wish they were dogs and wishing hard enough made some act like dogs. I was sure my Uncle Gyorgy lived like this under the petty tyranny of his wife and wished he could run away and start over someplace else with Pavel.

The fact was that not just Romanians, but other East Europeans used dogs as metaphorical foils during the Communist era. As anyone who has ever had a dog for a friend knows, dogs prefer to live with their human families and generally dislike change. In *The Unbearable Lightness of Being*, Milan Kundera described how his dog, Karenin, would be disturbed even by the arrival of a new chair, or by the movement of a flowerpot. The insane policies of Communist (and formerly, fascist) regimes in these countries disturbed dog rituals. Dog time, according to Kundera, moved in a circle like the hands of a clock; not like human time in a straight line. This was the romantic attraction of dogs to humans who were being uprooted and forced into a life that circled around from lies and moral compromises to interrogations, labor camps, and even executions. In *My Happy Days in Hell*, too, the Hungarian poet George Faludy recounted that in his early 1950s labor camp near Recsk, inmates shared scarce food with camp strays and protected them from the sadism of the AVO state security officers. The dogs were superior to the scum of humanity running the camps that tortured dogs and inmates alike; feeding them was an act of trans-human solidarity.

In Elmira, until a year ago when she cleared out, my lab, Gus, was a happy refuge from my wife and all the other crap going on with my job and family at the time. It looked like this was a Russian repeat: Gyorgy admired Pavel's independence and daily routine, while his wife appeared only to complain and then retire someplace else in the darkened house to putter around. She didn't even come along to the vet's office. Some people have dogs to push them around, browbeat them,, and show them who's boss. Some train them to fight in order to enhance their own imagined prowess. I recalled seeing regularly an elderly gent who walked his dog in my neighborhood near the college as I walked to work. His dog was a black terrier-type who accompanied him on his little red leash as the man heaped verbal shit on him. I couldn't make out what he said, but his face was full of hatred and scorn for this dog. Occasionally the man would whine at him—randomly, peevishly. He was a cruel son of a bitch. One day I overtook them on my walk and listened in.

"I came down the stairs to the living room this morning and where were you? You were on the couch, weren't you? (Here his face reddened as he worked up his temper.) What have I told you repeatedly, you worthless cur? You piece of absolute shit! For the last time! Stay off the couch!"

His little brown terrier wore the quiet, stoic expression of a dog that had suffered much verbal abuse and knew for certain that it was going to be another really bad day. I could almost see tears of sweat flying off of him. He was stressed and worried, probably a reflection of the problems of his owner who reflexively projected his own plight onto the dog and blamed him for it all. Still others have dogs simply because they follow them around and do useful tasks—eating scraps off the floor, getting rid of mice and other pests. That's a major reason I liked Gus. He did the cleaning up for me. But most people, I like to think, have them because they need their companionship. And dogs reciprocate with permanent trust and guardianship. It was clear to me that Gyorgy had Pavel because he needed to talk to him now and then, to explain things, and to tell him his troubles. Dogs for such people are very much like children: they are lent to us for a time after which they can reciprocate our trust and love, run away and get lost, get sick, stolen, or involved in an accident and die. Then we grieve for them.

We sat in a small waiting room fittingly adorned with oil portraits of dogs. It was probably a collection of the most famous Permian dogs. More likely, the dogs had been patients here as evidenced from the brass nametags below them. And they were all ruddy, country dogs, Russian all the way—some of them looked like forest wolves, maybe wild pack dogs or sled team dogs of the kind used regularly near Archangel. Perhaps the owners had donated them to their favorite vet who saw them through to the end. The dogs looked distinguished and thoughtful as if they could break out in speech in praise of their fine care here. There were none of the usual happy mutts carrying flowers or happily chasing sticks that one finds on calendars in vets offices. The problem was that these portraits were hung on olive and charcoal-grey striped wallpaper. Without a contrast, it looked like a funeral parlor. That effect was avoided by making every second portrait light-hearted: here was a black spaniel taking a dump on the sidewalk; there was a Dalmatian pissing on a hydrant; there was a black and white rat terrier chasing a truck; and finally, a black lab standing on its hind legs at a kitchen counter eating a leg of lamb. By contrast, the unimaginative vet for my dog, Gus, in Elmira had only cheap photographs of show dogs plastered around his tacky, sterile waiting room.

Soon, Gyorgy and Pavel were called by the vet himself. A very tall, disheveled man of about fifty in a white coat came out to greet us and to offer Pavel a treat. Pavel sidled right up to him, and it was clear that he knew the routine and trusted the vet. Pavel trotted ahead leading the way as the three of us followed him back to his favorite treatment room. Pavel then found his favorite examination platform and sat down on it while the vet glanced over his records.

"OK, Pavel, today we give you some more joint pills and a few shots." He felt around for tumors and signs of joint problems while he spoke to us.

"So, how are you doing Gyorgy? Is this your new assistant?" he said nodding to me with a wink.

"This is Nicholas Krylov, a relative of mine from the U.S. He is headed to Yekaterinburg to do some research at what was called Sverdlovsk Polytechnic for the summer. As we know, it is now called Urals State University. Nick, this is Dr. Vasily Timofeev."

He held out his hand, placing mine in a vice-grip until I could no longer feel it.

"Pleased to meet you," I said.

"What branch of engineering do you work in?" he asked me.

"I'm actually a planner and will teach some courses on U.S. city planning methods. I'll also try to do some research on municipal planning for the World Cup games there."

He brightened up. "Excellent! Maybe you can show them how to really plan. You do know that they still write plans as edicts, just like in the Soviet days. But no Kremlin official up there has any concept of risk and uncertainty, or the opportunity costs of doing different things. That summarizes the simplistic, command and control thinking behind Soviet planning for 70 years!"

"Hey, you should be doing this not me, Doctor!" I said.

"It's simply how I plan my office. Most professional managers plan things from the ground up to ensure supplies and make sure they get the obvious things done. It's common sense. Look around; I need to know the basics of supply and demand, costs and expenses before I do my financial plan for the next quarter and year. That's obvious to anyone except a Soviet planner and maybe some of their younger underlings in government. For now, the underlings have to keep their heads down and mouths shut. The officials harass us in small commercial operations like mine with tax audits and useless inventory inspections. That's why the country is a basket case. The country produces oil and nothing much else!"

He continued to feel around Pavel's stomach and shook his head while looking at Gyorgy.

"A few tumors here around the joints that are probably benign. We should watch them, and you tell me if he shows pain."

Gyorgy nodded and gave Pavel a pat on the head.

"There's something else going on that may interest you as a city planner looking at the upcoming World Cup games," he said while putting some pills in Pavel's mouth and closing his snout around them.

"Listen up," he tells Pavel, whose ears fluttered about in response. "How many street dogs are there in Russia? Some of them are probably your relatives? That's right, around two million. And what's the plan for the World Cup games? 'Removal' of all street and stray dogs… Do you like the sound of that Pavel?"

"Hell no, he doesn't!" I said. "What will the authorities do?"

"'Removal' means killing on the spot or by incineration. Or it could lead to incarceration in 'temporary shelters' where eventually they will be weeded out and killed for lack of space," said Timofeev. "The idea is to look good before the world, to put on a theatrical show of force and concern, just like we did in Sochi a few years ago!"

"That was a public relations fiasco as I recall. Animal rights volunteers came from all over the world to protect dogs against the poisoned darts. Everyone was discredited—the World Cup, the regime, and the city," I said.

Pavel was getting interested in all this and his eyes moved back and forth from one speaker to another. I was getting into it as well. I hadn't thought about the plight of dogs anywhere really. Like most professors, I had read a few articles about the issues and largely forgotten about them. I had been attacked a few times in Bucharest once on a research stay there years ago, but soon forgot about it. Dogs remained invisible beyond my own pet dogs from my past that I always cared for and naively assumed everyone cared for the rest of them! Clearly, I had no premonition of how local dog issues would draw me into a strange, dangerous and exiting new world just down the tracks of the Transsib at the next stop!

"I also recall the Romanian fiasco in the early 2000s as they tried to eliminate street dogs in order to qualify for accession to the E.U. They finally lied their way into the club in 2007, but the stray dog problem still exists. People are getting attacked all the time."

"That's right," said Timofeev with a loud laugh. "They really made a mess of things. The cities were plagued by hundreds of thousands of strays, some of them rabid and vicious, attacking people. The dogs filled up the sidewalks and parks that they took over to live in. Left to their own in feral packs, they bred and multiplied quickly. In desperation, the authorities tried to kill them all, far too late. Right on cue, the animal rights people started campaigns of terror to protect them— including hitting on the animal control hit squads with murder and sabotage."

"We still have time and probably can avoid all that this time," said Gyorgy.

"Maybe that's where Nick can help" said Timofeev. "Officialdom could use a little common sense in dealing with the complexities of the dog problem. A lot is at stake here. But they usually ignore festering public issues until it's too late."

The three of us bid goodbye to Dr. Timofeev, and Pavel got a treat for quietly listening to his advice and taking pills. We then headed out for the pageant in front of the nearby opera house. Like all cities in this region, the Soviets had planned out the basics of services and utilities quite well. The weather was brutal, and the industrial work grim and dangerous. So plans had to work at the operational level every season. Perm was classified as a third-tier city with only electric trolley-buses as the premier means of getting around. Lush parks, riverside walkways, and recently refurbished buildings and streets gave the town a sleek, warm feel. Soviet planners carefully separated the workplaces and factories from living areas. Trolley-buses herded workers to and from factories each day quietly and efficiently. The pre-Soviet wealthy had lived in nice homes on leafy streets under the tsars. In the 1920s and '30s, the Soviets collectivized these places, but after their collapse and the transition to a more open economy and state in the late 1990s, many flats and homes reverted to private owners as single-family dwellings. As before, the working classes lived in high-rise buildings of flats, some of which were now condos. Even Stalin's brutalist styles had been softened by remodeling and more play and park spaces.

The old opera house in Perm had been refurbished for its 150th anniversary, and its golden domes and white marble facades gleamed in the sunlight of a fine summer day. The wafting odors of grilled meat from stands set up all around the opera square made us all hungry so we sat down at one of the long tables for a snack. Gyorgy got us some locally-crafted beers, which he explained were an effort to stop people from killing themselves on vodka binges. They were superb, as good as any Czech or German beer, perhaps better because they were cold drafts, and it was hot and humid outside. The grilled pork and beef sausages were also excellent, almost as good as their smell. The blood sausage reminded me of the popular dish in Romania, which I became fond of when I had once done research there. Naturally, we gave small tidbits to Pavel who sat by the table expectant and alert to any food handling mistake by us at the table. Enjoying our grill and beer, Gyorgy pointed to the opera house.

"You might know that Perm opened a famous choreography school in 1945. That school gave the world Nadezhda Pavlova, who was later to become the prima ballerina of the Bolshoi. The Perm opera was then called the 'laboratory of Soviet opera.' Who knows—my wife was probably named after her, along with hundreds of other newly-born girls in the 1940s. But the name didn't produce any more primas. For instance, my wife often cries and howls theatrically too," he said with the trace of a sad grin across his face. "But something's missing. It's not music—it's the murder of silence!" I found out later why he pointed this out.

"Ah, there she is!" Gyorgy got up and waved vigorously to a woman carrying several bags. "Natasha, over here."

She came over and greeted us warmly. "Natasha, this is our relative from the US, Nicholas. I wanted you two to meet for a practical reason.

Nick, Natasha's husband teaches at Polytechnic in Yekaterinburg, now known as USU."

She sat down next to me and gave us each an apple from her bag. "Yes, Gyorgy tells me you will be in Yekaterinburg for the summer. Do you have a place to stay yet?"

"I do not. I was hoping the university or the city could find me a room."

"That won't happen, I'm sad to say. USU lacks any kind of housing service so students have to find what they can in town. As it happens, I have a small flat near the university, which I will not need for the next several months as I plan to be around here. My husband is also away for the summer in Moscow. So, it's empty. Would you like to stay there?"

I was elated. "It would be my honor—and thank you," I said. "Let me know what I can pay you. I have a research grant that covers rent."

"Since you offered, how about $500 for the time you're here? That should cover my needs and expenses."

"Sold! I'll look the place over, and if all is well, leave the cash for you in a place you can designate later."

"Perfect!" she said. "You can leave it with Sveta, one of my borders who sometimes handles repair and finance tasks for me. Thank you, Nicholas, and thank you, Gyorgy."

She then asked about life in the U.S., and we chatted about life at Bonaduz College as well as upstate New York. "When you work in a university, it becomes your world," I said, "as you must know with a university husband. And your world constantly expands—faculty drift around the planet, picking up data, ideas, contacts, and friends. It's a dream existence, as indicated by the fact that I'm here and not stuck in Elmira, NY, where nothing happens in the summers! I'm also lucky in that I'm of Russian extract so I can come over here and enter another world that isn't entirely alien."

What a break! Things were falling into place nicely. Natasha then told us about the schedule of performances at the pageant and what would happen that evening in front of the opera house. Apparently, there was to be an outdoor performance of several scenes from

"Carmen," which was my favorite opera. But I was starting to tire, as the train journey had been long and stressful. I wasn't going to make any opera. After further exchanges of pleasantries, we left for home about four in the afternoon. Gyorgy could see that I was fading fast so he let me nap a few hours before dinner. I fell on the first bed I saw in my room and faded instantly into a long, deep sleep. I awoke in the dark and saw by my watch that it was nine and was dark outside.

It may have been the silence of the room or the sudden claps of shouting that I heard which woke me up. Shrieks, apparently from Nadezhda, were making the most noise. I could also make out muffled screams. Weird … Occasional wounded animal-like whimpers came in response to the shrieks, probably from Gyorgy. It was apparent to me that they were having a nice solid row since I grew up in a household that shouted at each other a lot. My father and mother regularly fought and threw things at each other. Other families in our building in the Bronx section of New York City in those days often expressed themselves in the same ways of a primitive animal kingdom. The building was like a large animal cage with steel outdoor fire escapes as the only way to get some peace from it all. The tenants all worked hard, long hours in crap jobs and drank off their frustrations at home, often by taking it out on their spouses. If there were kids, they often got the brunt of it all. So I didn't feel out of place here—just surprised.

I emerged cautiously, going down the hall, then slowly into the living room. There was Pavel curled up in the corner with an expression of both disgust and fear in his eyes. He saw me come in and gave his tail a nervous little wag at the end. Next to him sat Gyorgy in a large easy chair of dark wood and dark leather upholstery. He looked down at Pavel and stroked him nervously. They were not strokes of endearment.

"You worm, the place is filthy, and you haven't cooked a thing for dinner!"

"Of course not … I can't cook. Didn't you notice that over forty long years?" he said wearily with a slight laugh. His eyes were bloodshot, and his faced was puffy and red. It looked like he had been crying. All the while I had been asleep.

"You've never noticed any of the filth of this place either." Suddenly, she saw me and was startled.

"Oh! It's Nicholas!" she said, slightly surprised to see me standing there in front of all of them—as if I had never been there before.

"Hello, Nicholas, come in and join the fun," she said. I hadn't noticed before, but her front teeth were all crooked, like tombstones in an unkempt graveyard. Now they looked more like fangs. She threw out this forced, tight little smile between gritted teeth as she spoke.

"Listen to these lies!" she threw out as a general command.

Ignoring all this, I said: "Is there anything I can do to help?" I casually scanned the place for spirit bottles and empty glasses, assuming it was a drunken spat. But I didn't see any. Something organic, deeper and probably routine, was going on here.

"We're set up on the patio. Why not go out and fix yourself a drink?" Gyorgy asked, wiping away a tear as he started to get out of his chair near Pavel.

Without being asked twice, I walked alone out to the lit patio in the back. It was a lush backyard family orchard with plum, apple, pear, and, as always, lime trees, typical of middle class homes in Eastern Europe and the former Soviet Union. They were stylish and deliberately unkempt to serve as miniature forest preserves for birds and animals, along with a small vegetable garden and a few fruit trees. There were a several grape vines on trellises, which I presumed Gyorgy made into wine. It struck me at the time that I could never figure out how lime trees survived Russian winters. In Crimea they easily do it, but not near the Urals ... Nevertheless, they adapted to the climate and here they were. And I learned long ago that everyone in Russia and Eastern Europe was born knowing how to make excellent wines at home. Generations of family words of mouth somehow became encoded into their genes. There was also the family garden with the usual range of lettuce, tomatoes, carrots, sunflowers, and other vegetables. Having no green thumb, I always admired those who tended gardens and orchards. I found a beer in a pail over in the corner and sat down. It was one of the newish Russian beers, replacing the rot-gut imported from East Germany in the past. Then "drinking" mostly meant vodka, but I had never taken to the vodka. I had big plans—I would live until at least sixty.

The shouting and whining seemed to have abated behind me in the house, and I enjoyed the solace of looking up at the stars on a clear night, surrounded by a lush garden with fruit maturing in mid-summer. Homes in this region seemed designed to provide safe spaces away from the uncertainties of the political world, where a nighttime knock on the door in the past might mean a trip to some re-education camp because one had been denounced. Denouncement was a favorite pastime of neighbors or ex-friends who had been insulted or felt slighted—there were more denouncers in flats because there were more opportunities for personal slights. This home probably served Gyorgy as a refuge from his wife. Who knows, maybe the other way around as well. . . . I decided then it was time to leave tomorrow and get going in Yekaterinburg. Besides, I now had a place to stay.

The brick grill was smoking in the corner of the patio so someone must have planned ahead. Both of them emerged from the house.

"Gyorgy is grilling lamb, and I made up some salad from the garden if that is ok. It's all we have here."

Here she began a rather pointless monologue of her life from their marriage years ago to the present. She seemed to expect that I was curious and wanted to hear all about it. I sat there in silence, bored but afraid of appearing impolite for not hanging on her every word. Her well-rehearsed monologue seemed to me largely a catalogue of small annoyances, many of which, in her view, Gyorgy had somehow caused.

"The grill plan sounds superb," I interjected. "Can I get you both drinks?"

"We'll have a taste of our homemade red for dinner." I noticed most of the bottles on the portable bar were vodka. Maybe she meant red vodka?

"I thought we would. Everyone knows how to make wine here. I wish I could. I've tried to do it. But somehow, I always get the timing or ingredients wrong, and it comes out awful."

No response on this one. I'll try again in a minute. My image of these people was of flat beer. Neither of them displayed any levity or humor, and light banter was not part of their repertoire. I vowed to push on nevertheless.

"In your letter to me, Gyorgy, you mentioned that you might be out of town at your dacha. Is that close by? Perhaps I could see it someday."

Gyorgy tossed some slabs of lamb on the grill, and in the kitchen Nadezdha silently made up the salads for all of us.

"When your father visited here shortly before his death more than twenty years ago, we went out there. It is far from here in a place called Novomlinsk. That's a Cossack village south of Perm near Ukraine, close to where the Kama River meets the Volga. Beautiful area! It's hundreds of miles away by tertiary road or slow rail service So we decided not to make this trip while you were here as the roads and rail service have not improved between here and there," he said.

"Did Gyorgy tell you what kind of family you come from?" Nadezdha asked.

"He's not interested in your fanciful theories of inherited behavior. Just tell him about the dacha," he said in a voice that was almost a cry for help.

"Of course he cares about his Russian family," she said firmly. "Go get the meat off the grill."

I noticed Pavel got up and followed him over to the grill. Probably scared …

"Your father had a dumb sister who came from that village and did the labor of a man. Did you know that?" he asked.

"No, this is the first time I've heard it."

"I met her several times. Her name was Maryanka. She was a loveable little girl, but couldn't really communicate with anyone. When she became excited, often because she was given meat or gingerbread, her faced flushed with joy, and she made weird noises to signify she was happy. She would smack her lips and sway her head and press her hands to her breast to let you know she was happy," he said.

"She must have been a great person," I said. "What happened to her?"

Nadezdha was getting impatient and began drumming her fingers on the table. "He doesn't give a damn about a dumb sister. Tell him about the dacha."

Gyorgy absorbed the abuse quietly, out of habit. I could tell this was a nightly drama, only with different themes. His eyes watered again, and he continued. "You might be surprised to know that Novomlinsk was a Cossack village. Your family probably came from there, which means you have Cossack blood. At least some of your family respected the Chechens and rather hated the Russians. That's probably why the Russians produced the first Muslim Cossack unit and stationed it here for security back in 2004. A futile attempt at cultural assimilation."

"I've never heard any of this. I'm shocked at my ignorance."

"In fact, I can see it in your eyes. They laugh—just like your father's. That means you have a rebellious streak in you. You probably have had trouble with authority all your life, but you've probably kept your responses measured."

"Sounds about right," I said, thinking of getting through endless, repetitive faculty meetings where I could barely refrain from throwing things, punching someone, or in one case at least, strangling a guy. He was right about the self-control part. One of my colleagues at Bonaduz College did strangle someone in a meeting; we had to pull him off before he killed his victim, a faculty colleague in the next office. He argued self-defense because the victim packed a throwing dagger behind his collar and was going to throw it at him during the meeting. It was proven that he practiced intensely at home on the walls. They actually found the knife on him so his argument won the day. Amazingly, the assailant was promoted anyway because publications counted more than homicidal tendencies. I had had quite enough of the petty turf, ego, and power games all leading supposedly up the imaginary hierarchy of academe. But the insight into my family background made me wonder if I deserved what I got. I often thought I was being controlled by something from off-stage! Now it turns out it was genetics!

Gyorgy laughed and held his glass up in a toast.

"Do you keep a diary?" I asked him. "When going through hard times—sicknesses, job problems, personal crises, angry arguments, even loneliness—I've found that recording my thoughts can help me endure them better. Sometimes the mental and spiritual discipline of writing things down is useful—it might help you when lonely to connect with what is real and more profound, for instance. It's even a good means of catharsis."

"I've heard our astronauts do this, recording their thoughts and dreams to help them endure the loneliness of space," he said.

"Exactly. I even try to fictionalize the events in hopes that the efforts to order my thoughts and turn them into fiction can provide additional clarity. I once wrote a short story about a hen-pecked husband with a nasty, overbearing wife. He endured years of shit before killing her and then stuffing her down the kitchen garbage disposal."

"Must have taken a long time!" he said getting curious.

"He was determined and very meticulous. Ran a clock repair shop. So after a week of telling friends that she had gone on a long vacation to some islands, he invited his friends over to play poker. They played and drank through the night until one of them got up to get a drink out of the kitchen sink. Unfortunately, the husband knew nothing about plumbing and had screwed up the pipe job. So out came his wife into the man's glass in bloody globs of red membranes and flesh!"

"What happened then?"

"They were horrified of course. But the irony of the story is that the one who reported him was the worst cheater at cards among them. Otherwise he might have gotten away with it."

"Good story!"

"But bad ending... My wife, Laurie, came across it in the journal I published it in which I had foolishly left lying around the house. She read it, and I'm certain it contributed to the downfall of my marriage. We've been divorced for almost a year now."

"Maybe it was for the best." he said, giving my tale some more thought.

"I think you may be right."

My hunches about Gyorgy and his wife were not so fanciful. I knew from reading and talking to people that nearly all families in Russia, no matter how ordinary, had lived through tough times. Even loyal party members with secure places in the state bureaucracy and reliable ideologies could make small mistakes, get reported, and lose everything almost overnight. One person I met ran a brewery in rural Russia and had made the mistake of selling a car outside official channels. He spent thirteen years in a Siberian prison. On release, it took several more years before he worked back to a position where he could buy a car again. Everyone had tough stories of personal upheavals, suffering, and survival. They had to navigate party experiments, betrayals by colleagues, and random thuggery from people like Putin's "little green men" who could plausibly deny any links with the state or party. And yet they survived … I mean it wasn't simply a story of downtrodden people in a totalitarian state, though that made for good press. Russians were brutal but also kind, compassionate, and lively: living lives unscathed by much of the morbid history one read about in this region.

"What Gyorgy is trying to tell you is that with that kind of rebellious background, you should be careful here. It may be 2018, but that's not so distant from the 1950s," said Nadezdha.

"We agree for once!" said he. "You have another relative in Yekaterinburg, Boris Krylovsky, who is a bit of a rogue. A mischievous character and much appreciated by all the ladies in town. Apparently, a wily animal rights advocate and always in the news so you should be careful."

"What's his story?"

"I've met him. Nice man and quite the celebrity. But he's rather like listening to a one-note horn. He filters the brutality of Russian history through the odd lens of a long collection and disposal of stray dogs. 'Contrasting despotisms" as he has described them to me. Naturally, I play along, but he's an extremist and apt to rant and fly into rages. Again, it all must be genetic, meaning there's your Cossack blood in action! You must have the same problem."

"I wouldn't be surprised.

I nodded, trying to get them off this obvious flaw of mine. "So tell me about your academic work at Polytechnic," I asked him.

As he began, I thought the sound was the radio from the next room playing classical pieces. A long, low chord on a violin . . . No, it was Nadezdha, emitting what seemed to be a low moan at the table. Was the meat bad? Then she started rocking back and forth uncontrollably.

She interrupted him at one point in his discourse on research. "He does no work at all. He's a wimp, a waste of space, a meek retiree to this museum," she hissed through her crooked teeth. She looked at me strangely, then down at the plate and continued moaning and shaking her head back and forth as if doing a funeral dirge.

"You ungrateful bitch," he said quietly, politely but with a fierce smile at her. "I've supported you for 35 years and listened to your complaints. All of us have suffered, but you thought you were special through all this? What selfish arrogance!"

The expression in her eyes was that of an old, martyred dog, which had been beaten a lot and given little to eat. It was a strange, disturbing look, and I was just glad to be getting out of there tomorrow.

"Have I ever beaten you from spite? No! I've beaten you on occasion because I felt like it and for no other reason at all! I'm sorry for you, and I'm taking you to the hospital," he said.

"You'll never be able to do that!" she hissed.

"And Pavel stays here," he said to rub it in.

"I've lived with her for almost forty years as in a funk, a debilitating mental fog. With all the poverty, drinking, and fighting, I haven't noticed how fast life has passed. Listen to her complaints: wimp, wimp, and worm, that's all I am!" he said, teardrops sliding down his reddened cheeks.

"Nadezdha, you called Gyorgy a wimp?" I asked, trying to cool things down. "Many of us who teach in universities are called 'wimps.' It's what the places turn us into. Feckless, yes men ... My ex-wife called me a wimp all the time because I often came home a beaten man. What did you mean by that label?"

"Doesn't she call you that anymore?" she asked.

"No, she left me last year for a younger, wealthier man!"

"I bet Nicholas knows how to be entrepreneurial. I'm sure he takes risks and gets ahead, don't you Nick?"

"Well I . . . "

"Exactly, you see he moves; he acts. He doesn't sit around and complain like you do. Nicholas, I've been letting Gyorgy in on money-making opportunities for years that he has spurned."

"Is that a fact?" I asked trying to navigate all this.

"It is. For example, tomatoes don't grow in the winter here, do they? That's why we had no salads for years here. But if we had indoor greenhouses, coupled with processing plants, we could grow tomatoes and make jars of tomato paste!" she exclaimed, her whole body shaking with ripples of enthusiasm.

Gyorgy grimaced. "You know that's crap, Nedy! You had to buy these places from the state, and they would be in partnership with you. We'd be in bed with criminals, oligarchs, and chancers! That's not being an entrepreneur; it's called being a sucker. That just wouldn't work. As for building new greenhouses, that would be with money we didn't have, and no bank would lend us."

"Because of your rotten salary."

"Another of her plans was to buy a winery. They made wines in the Soviet days that were about 20 percent drinkable. But the place she had in mind lacked ventilation, and several workers had died from CO_2 releases during the fermentation process. You know that, Nedy? Yeast transforms the sugars or carbohydrates in the grapes into alcohol, releasing CO_2 in the process. In fermentation, the yeast eats the sugar and breathes out CO_2. When you breathe it, it kills you. A cheap high but a costly waste of time. You ignored basic science, which could have cost us our house. To modify the winery buildings would have cost a fortune. Great ideas, but always a minor design flaw." he said.

"What do you think, Nicholas?" she asked me.

"For starters, I'd have to ask if Russians drink much wine? Then I'd ask where the grapes were coming from? Can't be many in Siberia and shipping from Crimea would be expensive, driving up the cost per bot-tle. Finally, do Russians have much money to spend on wine?" I said.

This rehash was all clearly upsetting to Gyorgy, who moved impa-tiently in his chair, threw down a small glass of vodka or schnapps, and cried: "I'm not a small-time business hustler or what used to be called petty bourgeoisie. I am an engineering scientist, teacher, and orator who can uniquely translate complex theories into practical use. My 1½ hour lectures are exciting, as I have been told by many students over the years. I know nothing about business and could care less about it."

Another moan from her, and we continued down the dismal track.

Here I noticed he seemed to have an incurable tic. His face con-vulsed a bit, and his mouth twisted slightly to one side as he spoke.

"I can even make puns if my lectures start to wane."

He was cut off by a loud cackle from Nadezdha. She was throwing down drinks now as she sputtered and sneered at him.

"His colleagues laugh at him because he is a pathetic joke. They keep him around to clean up the place and teach humdrum routine introductory courses. Why have you had the same salary for 25 years?" she bellowed in a whining, high-pitched falsetto.

By contrast, Gyorgy did have that richly authoritative baritone voice that was perfect for university lectures. He also had some style— moving with prissy, intellectual airs and showing his fondness for par-adoxes, wherein all intellectuals thrive.

"Should I have confronted my superiors?" he asked. "It would have just spread more contamination and hatred. Everyone would have been worse off," he chuckled.

Waving her giant spider hands around, she let out a full-throat-ed bellow. "You're nothing but a coward, hiding behind fancy words. Don't recycle your third-rate lectures to me around here! I'm sick of it!"

Pavel had perched himself between Gyorgy and myself. He had that worried look of an about to be abandoned dog that I'd seen be-fore. People in the U.S. disposed of dogs almost as they did their used laptops and other solid waste. They just took them to an institution or let them out of the car far away from home and that was it. But dogs in this region had mostly been uprooted by collective state housing policies and dysfunctional families. Different methods but same result for the dog: misery. I could see he was worried about his future.

If only I'd learned to read and had a marketable skill, like a seeing-eye dog or drug sniffer at the airport. Just think where I would have ended up! Pavel might have been thinking this right now. I recalled reading about Mr. Bones, the dog in Paul Auster's novel *Timbuktu*. He had precisely these worries as he contemplated the deterioration of his drunken, homeless master. When his master dropped dead on him, like many abandoned dogs, he was left to fend for himself on the mean streets of the city.

She slammed down her glass and shouted out in our direction. "I don't have to take any more of this, Gyorgy. You are a sanctimonious bigot, and you know that. I could leave here tomorrow."

People have often compared women to cats bearing their claws. What they meant to me was becoming clearer.

I patted Pavel on the head as I said to her, "It can't be that bad. Look what you have. A nice house, and he has a solid teaching position. I know many who would gladly exchange places with you."

"That's easy for you to say. You don't have to live with him and listen to his complaints!" she cried. "His colleagues are always conspiring against him, he says. He says they have kept him down and that he should have been recognized long ago for his talents. He reviews all of them each evening with always the same conclusion: he's claims to be right and that they are all wrong. Usually one drink per faculty member. It's a cesspit, a sewer full of poisonous snakes. They are silver-tongued phonies, and he alone is the authentic one who sees through their blow-dried hair, suave airs, and bad theatrics. I prod him along, "Who's the shaggy one who thinks he's Aristotle that you fight with all the time?" In addition, his imagined enemies are often minorities, such as Chechens from Ukraine and Asians from the Russian far east. Don't you prattle on about the cretin Pamirs and Yakutians on the faculty almost every night? I couldn't make this crap up if I tried. It's always the same. Like a bad soap opera. What nonsense!"

"Why don't you give your mouth a rest?" he responded with growing anger. "Go do your nails somewhere and leave us alone in peace!"

"I know many, including myself, who have had the same thoughts about their colleagues. Their fanciful conspiracies are confirmed all the time. Maybe universities breed paranoia." I tried to explain to them to lower the temperature a bit.

She went over to pour herself another one, and I figured that was my cue.

"In any case, it's a bit late for me," I said. "I am still tired and want to thank both of you for everything. If you don't mind, I'm going to bed now as I plan to leave on the early morning train to Yekaterinburg."

With a pat for Pavel, who sat stationary through all this—and probably many scenes like it—I got up and slipped out, walking briskly down the hall to my room and out of range. I wrote out a note of thanks, left them some dollars, said the appropriate farewells to all of them, and put it on my desk. I slipped out of there early. I didn't see them, but Pavel was waiting for me, and I gave him a big hug. He wagged his tail rapidly in response.

Good luck to you, old boy: you'll need it!

3   ON TO CATHERINE TOWN

The next morning, I got on a *regio* train or local shuttle from Perm which ran the 50 miles across the Urals to Yekaterinburg on an hourly basis. I deliberately avoided getting back on the Transsib Vostok run from Moscow going east for my next leg. I also tried to avoid running into Gyorgy or Nady by tiptoeing out of the house and practically jogging to the station. There, attracted by the smell of freshly baked bread at the train station, I grabbed a pastry and quick coffee before boarding. Rehashing the weird night at Gyorgy's, I wondered if he might take up plumbing now. From Perm, I took a *regio* since I figured there was no point in attracting any more thugs posing as cops or cops playing thugs to shake me down in their off time. I wanted to make a clean start of it if possible in this magical new land. And Sverdlovsk, now known as Yekaterinburg, is on the border with Siberia—the Russian frontier! I felt a sense of release, as I got deeper into Russia than I had ever been before. Buoyant and optimistic, I felt I was headed into the heart of lightness rather than darkness. Forward into broader, sunlit uplands as Churchill must have said.

I got on in second class and found an empty seat that faced another chair. Shortly afterwards, two stocky men got in and sat down facing me. Would I be having company again? They were stocky guys clad in leather jackets with pockmarked faces. They both looked like they could put their fists though a cement wall with little problem. I nodded and grinned at one of them, and they grinned back. They chatted about a few women they had met the night before and then moved on to something about a local soccer player. I took out my Russian cigarettes and offered them one as I lit up. I hadn't smoked since the last time I was in Russia eight years ago. But I lit up the end without dropping the match or burning my fingers, the dead giveaway of a nervous amateur. I also don't drink vodka in the U.S. but now carried a flask of it for just such encounters as these.

"You guys live in Yekaterinburg?"

"We work there on construction but live in Perm. They are having a building boom because of the World Cup games, and we are making extra money."

"Always comes in handy," I said.

"How about you?"

"I teach at USU and was here visiting a relative. I'm helping the city plan for the Games."

"Who you rooting for...?"

"Well us of course! I follow Ural Yekaterinburg during the regular season, and I hear several of their players are on the national team for these Games," I said with a laugh. "But Uruguay looks good. With legalized pot now they might have extra fuel in them!"

They both laughed at the lame joke and then went back to chatting among themselves. I had passed the first test. They thought I was a local. At least they didn't say anything about my accent. The fact is that most Russians look tough—stocky, leather jackets, mostly black, and pockmarked faces. In some Russian towns, all the men wear black leather coats or jackets, which makes it tough retrieving coats in a bar or restaurant. Russians are tough people who have been through tough times, personally or with their families. Everyone has some relative that died under the hard line Communism at the hands of the KGB security services or related institutions during those seventy or so years around 1917 to the transition in 1991. Before that, the Tsars were just as autocratic but were only amateur autocrats. They lacked proper dictatorial organizational skills to control most of the population, and the state was quite weak—to the advantage of those living beyond big cities in Siberia or Yekaterinburg. But if there were still Tsars in the 1920s, they probably would have tried absolute social control using the more modern methods of the Party.

I looked out of the window as we started to pass through the Urals, which were not very high (around 700 feet in this area) but stretched for about 1,200 miles between north and south. They are full of wildlife, forests, and streams—real scenic beauty for anyone needing a bit of mental peace and are trying to get their heads back together. On the Siberian side, *Yekaterinburg* was the eastern-most city selected for World Cup games. Reflecting on its history and location, I recalled from the Insight Guide that it was founded in 1723 as Yekaterinburg or Ekaterinburg by German and Austrian settlers who named it after Catherine II (the Great), who was trying then to open Russia to Europe. Its name was changed to Sverdlovsk under Stalin in 1924, then back to Yekaterinburg (or Catherine Town) in 1991 by none other than USU alum Boris Yeltsin. Yekaterinburg was considered Russia's window into Asia just as St. Petersburg was its window to Europe. Among other things, it is famous for the murder of the last Tsar Nicholas II and his family of Romanovs in 1918 during the Bolshevik revolution. It is also noted for the construction of Peter the Great's first merchant fleet, the invention of the Russian bicycle by Artamonov, and the birthplace of local boy-made-great leaders such as Boris Yeltsin. It was also the main city east of the Urals that brought in the Siberian gold rush in the 1700s. But the mines and deposits were too small. To diversify from mining, as Perm had done, Yekaterinburg became a heavy industrial center that was now trying to soften its image to the outside world, believing that spectacles such as the World Cup Games would help do that. And it would! As we crossed the bridge into the city, I could see the Iset River embankment, which was slick and modern, an invitation for normal families and strollers. All over it was clear that new sports structures had been erected around Yekaterinburg, probably by sturdy people such as the two guys that were sitting across from me on the *regio*.

From what I had seen so far, there was no visible evidence that the Games had disfigured this Russian town in the least. Coming into the city, I saw the standard pre-modern homes and buildings of those living away from the center. They were huddled together, cowering structures, shrunken down from the elements. They were also built to withstand the awful Russian winters. After all, the winters helped defeat Napoleon and Hitler. The elements here could destroy anyone if one let them. Local designers had no such defeatist intentions then or now. Here, city planners intended to use existing structures in the center, such as the upgraded Central Stadium, for the Games and afterwards. That practical approach was quite unlike the bad state planning that had pushed massively useless vanity projects. The vanity project fetish had driven construction for the Games in many places like Sochi, Tokyo, Beijing, Brasilia, and Rio. I recalled that planning for the 2020 games, the Japanese wiped out the giant Shitamachi fish market in Tokyo called Tsukiji where 600,000 people made their livelihood. The Chinese destroyed whole areas of ancient urban fabric to erect mammoth structures amounting to no more than worship of faceless Party power. It already looked different here; I could see the newly refurbished stadium and several spruced up boulevards. Could it be another Seoul 1988, where students and others took to the streets and ended the brutal dictatorship of Chun Doo-hwan and demanded constitutional government? The Koreans got an accountable, democratic government—much due to the Olympics, which was not that regime's plan at all. At best, regional revivalism could get a massive boost, but probably the Kremlin would experience no major unintended changes.

I was now in Siberia. Siberia! The Russian frontier! In imagination and historical experience, it was like the U.S. Wild West only more exotic. Riding along, peering at the sights, I recalled that the Transsib railway was a tsarist development project. The idea was to spread modernity on the landscape between newly thriving cities and settlements. It began in Vladivostok in 1891 and was originally financed with Russian, British, and American investments. After it began operation in 1903, the Americans offered to build a connector railroad from Alaska under the Bering Strait, across Eastern Siberia for free in exchange for a concession along the line to develop the area, The Russians said "nyet" for probably good reason but lost the opportunity to have their richest region developed for nothing. It might have modernized the Russian economy, moving beyond simple extraction of riches mainly from Siberia to sophisticated manufactures and exports. It might also have softened the autocracy and reduced reliance on state monopolies as well. How things might have turned out! Musing further into geopolitics because it was a nice morning and the pastry had been good, I imagined that the Americans would have developed the region. They probably would have flooded the cities with Sears catalogues in Russian. More realistically, the Soviets would probably have nationalized everything leading to an early geopolitical conflict. Or maybe the Soviets would have been prevented from the takeover of the Kremlin by the British (using such spy aces as Sam Neil aka Reilly), and the Americans intervening using an early manifest destiny justification; President Taft, following Theodore Roosevelt, might have responded with more "manifest destiny," running us up against Germany, Japan, and Russia at the same time. Recall that the U.S. had a miniscule military and virtually non-existent Navy in the early 1900s even after WWI. What language would the Americans be speaking now?

I arrived in Yekaterinburg at the busiest time of the morning. The crush of people through the railway station was surprising but really like any big city rush hour. I was pushed here and there by hurrying commuters and hardly had time to gaze at the huge old station built in 1878, which was upgraded in 1915 and now sported a new whitewash and polish job for the Games. The stunning building was a columned palace in the old style of great buildings during the era of the Tsars and Emperors. The station now served seven train lines including the Transsib, which accounted for the masses of people, together with tourists coming in for the games from all over the world, many from America despite the frosty relations between Putin and Trump. The atmosphere was festive, people carrying team flags, some wearing country flag hats, many just trying to get through and commute to their jobs but smiling and waving as well. I heard a few local girls speaking Russian on the platform, probably waiting around for their boyfriends, and asked them for directions to Natasha's address.

There was a tram out front, but I felt like walking to stretch my legs after sitting on the train. It was another fine summer day which one had to appreciate given the apparently two months of warmth per year around here. Nevertheless, to celebrate my arrival and new sense of freedom, I sat down again and had a coffee at the first local place I spotted. I relaxed in the sun and took in the mixed salad of languages that I could hear at neighboring tables and among the passersby. This café served Turkish-styled coffee, which was rough and had to be drunk fast before it hardened in the cup. So I drank two of them to get my juices flowing. Amply fortified, I proceeded to Natasha's place.

Her place was off the main drag called Sverdlova Street leading from the station and several blocks into a neighborhood of large, old, tsarist-era homes, many of which had been converted into flats. The neighborhood featured hundred-year-old homes, some of which had the delicate, classic nineteenth century ornamentation of the Urals and Siberian regions—wooden Art Nouveau that to me looked very elegant. Some like Natasha's even had back yards. The homes had survived decades of Soviet collectivization during which the places had been chopped up inside and compartmentalized to create small rooms allowing boarders to be added. That provided the worthy communist experience of egalitarian poverty. As is known, all that ended when the Soviet system collapsed from: Party corruption, complexity of the illogical rules, and the inability to provide basic goods and services to the people. Neighborhoods such as this went to seed as the homes fell into disrepair. What were left were funky mansions with airs of shabby gentility that wouldn't look out of place in Cambridge, MA or Berkeley, CA. I know; I had rented rooms in places like this when I was a student and loved them.

I walked up the front stairs carrying my suitcase and backpack and saw someone putting something in a mailbox, which ironically was Natasha's. I introduced myself, and it turned out she was none other than Natasha's landlord, Svetlana.

"Welcome!" she said, "Gyorgy told me you were coming and here you are. I am Svetlana, your new landlady for a few months." Here I was expecting an old biddy like the landlords I had had in my youth. It was my image of landlords. Instead, here was someone who instantly radiated sexual energy—a libido stimulus if there ever was one! Shapely, maybe late thirties, she wore a loose, cotton print dress and had lively eyes and a vivacious manner. I could tell she was intellectually alive and clearly used to dealing with university types—also, as I say, in fine shape! The lack of makeup and apparent trips to the beauty parlor added to her raw energy. She had a quick, inviting smile and was nicely tanned, as most women were around then, in order to take advantage of the short annual sun season. As we talked, I felt she had been a real looker in her past, maybe even one or two years ago, or perhaps just last week with a different outfit on. Accompanying us was her white terrier with a few black spots named Leo, wagging its tail, panting for perhaps good reason, and looking me over in anticipation of perhaps better treats and longer walks.

"Let me show you Natasha's room. It's upstairs," she said, pointing to the living room and dining room downstairs. "You can also sit around here or use the kitchen and dining room if you like." I followed her upstairs and couldn't help notice how she walked with an effortless sway. She combined hip and body twisting exercises with mere walking. This was both efficient and erotic for someone presently in a severe female sexual drought such as I had found myself since last year.

"Also, please call me Sveta; Svetlana is too old-fashioned."

Upstairs, she led me down the hall to my room. It was spacious enough with a desk and a small kitchen for tea and breakfast.

"Here is the key; if you need anything, call on me in #4 downstairs." Giving me a card with her number on it, she said, "This is my phone number for downstairs." I noticed that she had tattoos on the back of her smooth, hot little hand, mainly moons and stars. Could be a whim or perhaps a secret sign for a local student new-wave cult ... Not your usual landlady…

"OK, thanks. I'm sure I will be bothering you for information at some time in the near future."

"Anytime," she said, flashing an inviting little grin and glance back at me, after which she quietly closed the door.

Alone now, I dropped my suitcase on the bed. I was pretty beat but determined not to waste a fine day like this sleeping it off. So I gathered up my backpack with the local maps, a water bottle, and a copy of my passport in it. Sveta then told me the way to USU and how to get to the river walkway from here. USU was a few miles away in another part of town, best reached by tram. With that I shook her hand again. She had a firm but sensuous, pulsating grip that tightened and relaxed as I held it. I then nodded, and we parted, giving the dog a pat on the head for good measure. Could be an interesting stay…

I started my walkabout, heading through the center and toward the Iset River. The city was much bigger than I expected. It is the fourth largest in Russia with 1.4 million people and 50-story skyscrapers, giving it a Manhattan-type feel. It was also the first industrial city in Russia and had that rustbelt aura to it, as well as the tinge of soot in the air common to all such places with large machinery and metal factories. Clearly, it was not a backwater university town like Elmira. And it reminded me now of my youth in the Bronx, which may have accounted for my sudden rush of emotional buoyancy. It was like starting over again … Fleshy landladies working up a sweat in cramped flats, earthy local types uncaring about their shaggy appearances or odd behavior, and homey apartment dogs. They were all there and reminded me of when I was a kid. I still recall getting bitten by one of the homey dogs that turned vicious when I was about three-years-old after I grabbed some food out of his dish. Hey, I got over it. That was the Bronx where dogs ate dogs and maybe a small kid or two in the process, if they got in the way. The only thing missing were the rusty, steel girders of the old "el." subway line I was getting pumped up, and I hadn't even started.

I headed out, trying to recall what Sveta said about directions. I just wanted to take in the sounds, smells, and sites of my new town. It was spread out like all large cities, the downtown area with its skyscrapers, high-rise flats, and offices, and its flashy signs leading to the Weir embankment along the Iset River. In the center there were even signs warning about "drunk people," which, because of the historic tradition of turning slogans into art, featured bright red circles with lines drawn across passed out human figures. Not bad! Graphic and quite like the circular signs in Vienna of dogs squatting to take dumps also with red warning lines through them with the command "No!" written on them. Along the Iset riverwalk, brightly clothed skateboarders flitted in and out of walkers, showing their skills and reminding all that they owned that space. There was a tourist poster reminding readers that one could hike in the birch forests and rock climb 50 miles to the south in Oleny Park. Another sign pointed to "airport," meaning the refurbished "Koltsovo," which recently got a second runway for the Games. That was just fine with me as I was flying home from here in a few months, which should prevent any more shakedowns on the Transsib. Spotting a café along the riverwalk, I sat down for another morning coffee in the sun. Almost immediately, my eyes focused on the many tanned, athletic, and shapely women passing by walking, jogging, and skateboarding.

I had the sudden impulse that it was all too perfect, and that I was being watched. I suppose that comes from being Russian and from faculty paranoia nursed over decades (Bellow's old saw, "I may be paranoid my dear friends, but that doesn't stop people from conspiring against me!"). In any case, my antennae went up between watching bodies and a new sight. What did I see? A quick movement out of the corner of one eye and a rustling sound as a hand grabbed my pack right alongside my chair. I made a low sweep with my left arm and threw him off balance. Still holding on, he rebounded and was about to run off again when I tripped him and pushed him over. A waiter saw all this and yelled at the high-energy urchin who then scampered off to look for another distracted tourist.

He was just a shaggy kid, probably 11–15 years old, a street urchin of the kind I knew about from doing fieldwork in these parts before. Like in most big cities, there were young toughs, street urchins, working for pimps or principals. You could see them sitting in cafes sometimes, drinking schnapps and smoking just like their adult pimps. The urchins were all over the place, and they were on call. They moved more quickly and nimbly than the usual aids victims, begging for money, the emaciated drug addicts, and the desiccated drunks lying around on sidewalks and streets. For Russian visits, I kept a pocket full of small denomination Russian rubles for appeasement purposes—to spread the good will around and perhaps build up a useful security network. In former Soviet states like Albania or Bulgaria, the number of unemployed and disaffected kids grew in cities during the long "transition" period when the state collapsed and there was no authority or municipal services. The kids panhandled for older pimps who took part of their cut typically in exchange for giving them room and board. Like fathers looking after their family flocks, the pimps would take them to key locations where there were tourists and people with deep pockets full of money. The pimps dressed them up in appropriate garb, e.g. often colorful, Dickensian-styled beggar costumes, and collected them later after ten-hour shifts. Other pimps used their wards for crime such as sex-trafficking, burglary, and pickpocketing. As Roma or gypsies were social outcasts in these countries, they were unemployed and readily available for all these purposes. Looked at from the street angle though, the system had its uses. Support from urchins and even their pimps had come in handy several times as I was about to be mugged, then saved by the timely intervention of a tough urchin who I had tipped previously while walking about. It paid off. The cost in virtually worthless local currency was minimal. I had been dealing with "intellectual muggers" for the past few years at the university. They stole your self-respect and ideas but not your belongings. I had forgotten what the real ones could do if you relaxed and let your guard down. Recalling all this now, I moved the pack under my seat, finished off my coffee, and left.

The day was still young and given this wake-up call, I was getting a rush on for the city and its surprises. I decided to take a short hike away from the river and see what the back streets of the town had to offer. Was it all newish skyscrapers, or was there something less touristy and more down to earth and authentic about this place? I walked about six blocks to get the blood flowing again and entered an area of new high-rise apartment construction and vacant lots. It looked pretty much like any big city with grey high-rise apartment complexes and leftover Soviet cement monstrosities. Some of them went up thirty stories and stretched like accordion folds for blocks. They probably housed thousands of people in each wing of the complex.

I was about to cross a street when I noticed something moving to my left. Another thief? ... No... It was a large, brownish dog walking slowly ahead but eyeing me closely; I had attracted his curiosity. Following behind him was a group of about 15-20 more dogs. He was apparently the alfa male and leader of a neighborhood pack. Now this was interesting. No one around, just the dogs and me. I could tell that a few of the large furry white and brown ones with longer snouts were Borzois or Russian wolfhounds, weighing in around 80 pounds. Now why would anyone abandon such fine animals I wondered!? Maybe life was better with the stray packs than with the families at their previous homes! Too bad I didn't have a box of treats in my pack. I certainly had nothing to fight them off with except a small pepper spray canister. That might work on one of them for a few minutes before the others moved in, if that was their intention. I clearly couldn't run which would have been the dumbest option of all. So I stood still and looked straight at him. I had to try and impress him that, 'if you don't touch me, I won't touch you.' I played the "game of stares" with him for a few minutes. I was alone with these dogs as there was still no one around—probably all in parks or down by the river. He looked at me intently now, more curious, sizing me up. I looked at him like I was not to be trifled with. The standoff seemed like hours. Then he inexplicably looked away from me and ahead down the road again. He then yawned and trotted off in his original direction. The others obediently followed him not even throwing a passing glance my way. After they had gone, I walked over to the side and took a long piss. During the standoff, I had already pissed a bit in my pants, and now the rest came out fast. Enough excitement for one day. I decided to head back to the river after that . . .

That evening, I was eager to try out my new kitchenette and cooked up some *pelmeni* dumplings, which I found at a nearby greengrocer. I also had a small fridge, which served to keep beer and milk cold; that was all I needed. As I was getting things ready for the big feast, I heard some raps on the door. It was a friendly knock—not like those of alien thumps, which presaged bad news. It was none other than Sveta and Leo.

"Come in, glad to see you."

"We just stopped by to see how you were." I did like that pink flush that came over her face as she talked enthusiastically. Now I was putting my emotional guard down. The place seemed to shut down the defenses.! First go the instinctive security guards, then the intellectual ones, and now the emotional guardrails … What next?

"I wondered if you could take Leo for a walk around the neighborhood. I have to go out and won't be back until much later. I've been invited to dinner at my boyfriend's parents," she said, "and they don't like dogs."

Leo sat there with his long tongue out panting and expectantly waiting for an answer as we talked. "And suppose I had plans? I said. "Am I to cover for you every night?"

She squinted a bit and focused on me, trying to read my intentions. "I'm sorry, if it's too much, I can just take him along."

I let out a clap of laugher and held out my hand. "Just kidding! Give me his leash. You can leave him with me, and I'll bring him by in the morning if you are not around later this evening."

Sveta smiled in relief, handed me the end of Leo's leash, and off she went. "I owe you one," she said.

I pondered that one. All this, and I've only been here a day. Later on that evening, it began to rain pretty hard so I grabbed an umbrella from the stand by the door.

"Let's go Leo; you know the drill apparently," I must have been the latest in a long line of boarders doing her bidding on this. But I liked dogs, and it was the least I could do for both of them. Out the door we went.

We moved down the street, Leo doing what dogs do, pissing in strategic places all over to remind rivals of his territory and that he still claimed it. With his little metered spray, he hit tires of parked cars, stones by sidewalks, telephone poles, even a statue of a cat (hating cats, I gave him a pat on the head for his good work). Sometimes he just pissed in the air for the thrill of it. No wonder we admired dogs for their free spirits!

We went several blocks into the neighborhood and came to an intersection with a tram stop in front of us. The rain drummed the pavement loudly and pelted the metal shutters nearby. Through this all, I heard what sounded like screams. We stopped and listened. More screams. I saw movement up ahead which appeared to be someone being attacked. The attackers were dogs, which made low growls as they charged their target.

I ran forward, leaving Leo behind perched in some bushes, and struck out at what appeared to be about three large dogs, taking turns lunging at someone in a rain parka trying to fend them off with waves of their hands and arms. In the driving rain the patchy visibility made it hard to see what exactly was going on. But it reminded me of the popular British game where packs of hounds attack bears. Only this one was clearly a human. There was a dim street lamp so I could make out what was going on pretty well, even in the darkness and rain. I closed my umbrella now and got ready to attack. The heavy umbrella served its purpose as it was mostly metal, and the wooden handle packed a nice wallop. I got a few hits in, after which they quickly turned on me. That worked to my advantage as I could now hit them head on and deal a few decisive blows to the lead dog. There was always a lead dog, whether it was a pack of hounds or a human gang. With either head, you just didn't have much time to explain things to him or to negotiate an exit.

Right around the time I had that brilliant thought, I felt a sharp pain in the back of my leg. One of them had attacked me from behind and got his teeth into my leg through the pants. I did a backhand shot and got him with the handle, which was enough to throw him off balance for a second and get him to back off. I followed through, swinging around to get in another close-in shot (just like at the tennis net—knees bent read to go), and nailed what turned out to be the head dog. Once this lead dog whimpered and started to retreat, the others followed suit. The alpha male was wounded, and his mates quickly lost their courage. The three of them moved off now without looking back.

Since packs of street dogs often regroup and attack suddenly again, I quickly turned back to the victim. I helped up from the sidewalk what turned out to be a woman carrying a shopping bag.

She got up slowly and limped along. So, I walked her under my umbrella slowly through the rain to my room a few blocks away. All this time, Leo had been hiding in the bushes, scared and shivering from the cold rain. I held onto his leash as she held on to my arm loosely, tightening up suddenly as she stumbled over ruptures in the sidewalks. We inched forward, hoping there would not be any more surprises on the way home. She said she lived a few blocks down one of the streets we passed. Entering the flat, I told her to sit at the kitchen table and got my travel first-aid kit from the backpack to see what could be done. She was bleeding in several places on her arms, and her blouse was torn in at least one place, which meant probably she had been bitten in the back or stomach. She was wet as well as she had no umbrella and was only wearing a parka, which didn't appear to even be waterproof.

"Thanks for getting them off me. I like dogs myself, but those were a bit much, don't you think? I mean they just came at me as I got off the tram. What nerve!" she exclaimed.

I wondered if she was hyperventilating from shock or just liked to talk freely. It turned out to be the latter. I tried to keep her talking and applied antiseptic cream and bandages where there were cuts. I asked her about the holey blouse, and she lifted it, showing me her stomach. I tried to focus on the wound and not the tight package of shapely brown flesh in front of me. There were several cuts, one on her hip and another in the middle, possibly from claws and not teeth. The ones on her stomach were near a colored tattoo of a Russian doll. Another cut was on her arm, also next to a small doll tattoo. Though intriguing, I was worried that if these were teeth marks, there could be a risk of rabies. At the same time, I went into the bathroom to inspect my leg. It had teeth marks in it and was bleeding. So I put cream and bandages on it, hoping for the best.

I came back out. "Well Doctor, what do you think? Am I going to live?" she asked playfully. "Do you have something liquid to lower my shock levels? I'm about to faint."

"You could use a scrub. You must have hit the dirt and rolled around in the mud as they attacked."

"Brilliant deduction!" she said looking hard at me.

I poured a glass of Ukrainian *gorilka,* or pepper vodka, for her, which I had wisely picked up at the corner today. Unforgettable, great name! Easily associated with Gorilla Glue. She threw it down quickly and asked for another.

"Listen, I get attacked by dogs regularly. We all do around here. We're used to the torn skin and leaking blood staining our clothes. No one is in shock after them. The shock is that the attacks aren't worse."

Her facial expressions, body language, and gaze all triggered flashbacks. It seemed to me that I had known her once before, somewhere and at some time, and had seen these features, perhaps in the days of my immemorial childhood—some old flame?

"I have heard about the strays here," I said. "Also, you should get yourself tested for rabies as there are several deeper wounds from claws or fangs."

"I will, of course, thanks for the tip! As you noticed, there are lots of strays, and it's more than hearsay .... Just look around. Those are not friendly pet dogs, like yours there. They are scared, hungry dogs in packs that have become vicious by being in an urban state of nature. I usually carry pepper spray or an umbrella. It's what most people do to fight them off."

"Does that work?"

"Sometimes ..."

"Do any of them have rabies?"

"Unfortunately, yes. Animal control seems to have gotten most of the obvious rabies cases off the streets. They are obvious—foaming mouths and permanently aggressive."

"What about tonight's brood?"

"Probably not; they just wanted food or maybe our wallets."

"Wily bastards, aren't they! Would you like something more to drink?"

"Thanks, but I should get home to my husband."

"Well, at least take my umbrella. They or their associates may be still out there."

"No, there are probably not any more of them around here. I'd wager they are probably part of a nomadic tribe. Once they had homes, but now homeless, they fend for themselves. As a pack, they've likely moved on to a new neighborhood with better pickings. And thanks again for the offer, but I have my pepper spray. Rain check on the additional drink . . ."

"OK, but take out your pepper spray now and put it in your hand."

"As you suggest, Doctor. A sensible plan . . . My name is Anna. I haven't seen you around here."

"I just moved in here. I'm Nicholas. Hope to see you around the neighborhood under less exciting circumstances."

"Why less exciting?" she asked, looking at me with surprised curiosity. She straightened out her torn blouse and stood up. "Excitement gives me a rush. Very healthy, don't you think? Thanks again for patching me up."

The image that came to mind was of dynamite. She held out her hand for what turned out to be a muscular, but erotically pulsating shake—something like Sveta's, but more decisive. And with that, out the door she went, tattered clothes and all.

It had been a long day. I spent a few moments puttering around my room getting papers together for tomorrow, filling up Leo's water dish, getting ready for bed, and trying to establish a routine. But a strange thing happened when she left. My mind was thrown into a state of feverish excitement the likes of which I had not experienced for a long time. My thoughts had become rusty and sluggish, as if my brain awaited a new thought to push the old one out, and it was a long time coming. I had been in a long funk of mindless sloth. Now my thoughts became active and restless, as ideas turned up everywhere and pecked their way into my head. It was as if I had been in a long, rip van winkle slumber and had now emerged from an emotional and intellectual cave.

4　THE NEW COLLEAGUES

The next morning, I dropped off Leo downstairs. He had slept quietly and unobtrusively in the corner all night. At least that was my theory. I fell into a deep sleep after hitting the bed so he might have been all over the place, and I wouldn't have heard anything. Clearly, I was the latest in a long line of temp dog walkers who doubled as boarders. Sveta gave me directions to USU, which turned out to be from the same tram stop as Anna had emerged from last night to the surprise feral attack.

It looked like the usual crowd one would see on an early city tram. It could have been the morning run to any big-city university district. Two heavily tattooed girls sat smoking and laughing it up across from me; one had a purple butch haircut, and her pal had long white hair. They had lots of colored nose rings and necklaces with colors that matched the tattoos. Both were on something, which was perhaps not surprising even though the day was young. So why not get the day going with a hardcore breakfast of meth or something stronger? I noticed that the larger one had a nose stud in the shape of what appeared to be a silver flower. There was a youngish guy sitting across from me in a leather jacket whose large, unblinking eyes glued onto me with a fixed, almost catatonic stare. Wild! He seemed to be trying to focus on something with razor clarity. Perhaps a complex math problem ... Good for him if it helps. I noticed that someone else nearby was hanging on a pole in the mid-car, twirling around it in rhythm with the jolts and curves taken by the car we were in. He was really moving now, almost like break-dancing. He must have enjoyed this and probably had a lot of practice at it. He wore a merry grin, and his eyes whirled around in circles like a kid's toy store doll. He began to sing out loudly but was cut short when he hit the floor after collapsing. I went over to see if he was conscious and looked around to see if anyone had a solution to someone lying on the floor. What that might be, smelling salts or something else, I had no idea. But no one even looked at us. Moving back to my seat, an older man ordered me to go around his outstretched legs. He abruptly shouted out something and pointed at me to keep moving.

Despite all this I sat back down and rummaged through my pack to see if I had the necessary intro letters and campus maps to find my way around. Suddenly, I heard tapping amidst the din of the car. The riders not singing or dancing sat immobile, looking forward, leaving their rings and umbrellas available to tap the metal frames of the seats and the stand-up poles in the car. They were obviously practiced at this. The young ones looked at their iPhones and wailed out songs; the older riders concentrated on tapping choruses. I had forgotten that this was the way riders responded to suspected fare evaders. In the old days, everyone was suspected of some crime. It gave people something to do—pry and de-nounce! To avoid the whole drama, I had punched my ticket in the little machine, but apparently several others had not. The watchful eyes of tram riders, honed from generations of being police informants as land-ladies and other types of snitches that had cut deals with the intelligence services such as SMERSH, CHEKA, and KGB, made sure of that. The snitches saw and recorded every move you made. So, many riders still engaged in tapping their umbrellas under the seat to alert the on-board, usually plain-clothes controllers that would now issue fines.

But in the good old days (ten years ago), it might have meant an extended stay in an exile village or just a trip straight to prison. Official control didn't always work anymore. Their Nazi armbands from the local transit authority featuring ominous designs similar to the SS were simply laughed at by most people now. Fear of the once powerful tran-sit controllers who could send you off to prison has diminished greatly. Once, in Sofia I saw the modern response in action. It might even have been the result of all the civil society training the locals had received from aid programs of the Brits and Americans. Then, a plain-clothes controller grabbed someone by the arm whom he suspected hadn't paid and started to push him toward the exit. Surrounded by a rush-hour crowd of commuters, I was holding onto a pole in mid-car just like the guy lying on the floor here. But in Sofia, a large, hairy arm reached over my shoulder and grabbed the controller by the neck. Others joined in the little rebellion, grabbing the controller by the arms and legs, and they threw him to the floor. At the next stop, several of them rolled him down the stairs and off the tram altogether. They then let out a good collective howl of laughter. A nice growl and spring at the authorities was a good way to end a hard day of monotonous work.

Through my window on the tram, I could see the usual mix of classic old shops and buildings mixed with brutalist Soviet architecture and gleaming building of glass and marble. There were some stately old homes that had been transformed into functioning businesses, schools, shops, and cafes. Probably built during the pre-Soviet tsarist times, some looked like Victorian Gothic structures with elaborate turrets and flying buttresses, Alongside, many of them were still the gray dull buildings of old. They all appeared to have a discreet shabbiness to them as if they had been built and ignored with peeling paintwork on the gutters, rusting scaffolding here and there. The scene could be anywhere ... Budapest, St. Louis, parts of Berlin. We lurched along nearer to the university, and the type of riders morphed. After a few more stops, new-wave styles were thinning out, and a more elegant class of conscious down-dressers began arriving. Their shabby dress was designer, with carefully distressed and torn jeans and peasant dresses, complete with labels on the outside, often with websites listed in fine print so you could order one for yourself with just one click after spotting it on a tram. Their designer packs now contained iPads and books instead of clothes and toothbrushes. In the space of just a few blocks, we had entered the student intellectual quarter, assuming such a place existed here. Some of the new arrivals actually conversed, which seemed a rarity these days, temporarily looking away from their screens for actual human exchange and contact. What boldness!

I got off at the university stop with the rest of the student hoard headed to classes and other engagements on campus. The campus was about a block from the stop, and it was a nice day so I strolled forward pulled along by the throng of students. For this time of the day, I figured that there was the normal level of stray dogs in the university neighborhood. Many of them were sitting on their hind legs alertly with their ears pointed. They were not lounging around or sleeping, as they would usually do in the hot afternoon sun. These were hearty street dogs—clever and always underfed. Domesticated dogs trusted naturally in human goodwill—guileless puppies wondering why you have tied a tin can to their tails. Those were the owned dogs of pedigree—the middle and upper class dogs of Yekaterinburg canine society like Borzoi house dogs. I noticed how the street dogs, the stray, and the mixed breeds viewed the pedigree dogs and their owners. Some were jealous and attacked; others seemed visibly ashamed and looked away as they passed by, ashamed that they had been abandoned and had once been just as well cared for as the one walking by with its proud owner. Could jealous rage explain some of their vicious anger? Was humiliation the hidden reason they often attacked people? Was it a form of generalized payback? Was it projected frustration and contempt directed at the humans who had abandoned them to the streets? Was it from these misunderstood motives that the authorities now treated dogs as no better than fornicators or murderers?

Continuing down the sidewalk, I heard a lot of dogs barking in the distance above the standard city din of car alarms and radios blaring in the streets. I noticed that some of the strays around me didn't move. They stayed where they were, wailing and howling, distinctly but not very loudly—was this some kind of warning? Calls of recognition? I had no clue. The sounds of barking got louder. It was a large fight—I could hear the chorus of yelps and cries accompanied by growls and barks of maybe twenty dogs going at it. From a distance, it looked like a canine gang war, the type I had seen in gangster films of the U.S. in the 1920s' battles between Al Capone and rival gangs in Chicago. I saw a group of dogs led by a large black one moving toward a group of several people, perhaps students. The black dog moved close to one of them, snapped and quickly lunged forward knocking him backwards. The little group of bystanders was suddenly surrounded by at least four more large, angry dogs. One of them swung his leather notebook at them and hit one in the head. As he did this, the dog bit into his notebook and, shaking his head violently back and forth, came at him over the top. One of the students, an obvious veteran of encounters like this, got off some shots of pepper spray into the faces of several of the dogs. They howled in surprise and screamed in pain, then retreated backwards, looking over their shoulders at him. The same man nailed the last dog charging them, and the rest of the pack retreated. As if nothing had happened, the neighborhood was suddenly quiet again, no louder than normal, and the pack was gone. There were still a few dogs lying around here and there, but not part of the invading pack at least. The surprising fact to me was that nobody had noticed any of this. No one came to the aid of the victims. It was simply another unreported incident. How many of these incidents were there? What happened when they had no pepper spray, which was technically illegal to possess even though it was the only effective means of warding of attacking dogs?

I was about to find out the answer. On the other side of the street, I heard more barking and saw what appeared to be a dust devil churning around, throwing trash and boxes in the air and depositing them far away. On closer inspection, it was another dogfight. In the middle of about fifteen angry dogs that were busy fighting and chewing on each other, a man was trying to fend them off with a stick as his own dog lay nearby in a heap. He threw away his dog's leash that he was holding onto and swung the stick at them with amazing vigor. He was putting up quite a battle against obviously bad stakes. He tried to reach for something in his pants as one of the dogs jumped and bit into his arm. He dropped the stick, which appeared to be what was left of a rug-beater, and was now defenseless against the pack, angrily waving his arms around at them. He finally got his pepper spray canister out between lunges and sprayed them, one at a time as close to their noses as he could get without being bitten again. This produced even more canine rage. They attacked him more ferociously now, and one of them got him from behind on the lower back. He wheeled around and nailed the dog with his spray, producing a loud shrieking wail from the dog, which retreated with expressive shakes of his head looking quite confused. After a few more minutes of this, some of the dogs began to flee, leaving the man bent over in his torn shirt and pants attending to his bloodied dog lying on the sidewalk. Again, nobody came forward to help them.

I was pretty shaken up after witnessing all this. It was already a hell of a morning rush—no need for any double espressos today. I walked ahead, stepping carefully between the regular dogs that were controlling parts of the sidewalks, as they lay there quietly reclining and hoping for handouts of food. After asking several likely students for directions, I finally found the Politology Department, known as political science, or simply politics, outside Europe, in a large old Gothic structure with the obligatory white columns behind imposing marble statues. One of them was a USU hero, Boris Yeltsin, an alumnus who played volleyball here on his way to becoming president. There was another statue of Molotov who apparently studied here as well, though the engraving didn't say what he had studied.

Feeling I was close to the place but still lost, I asked a nerdish-type lad of about twenty wearing a pair of tiny, wire-rimmed, pink-colored glasses where the department was. He spoke with a permanent little grin, but so fast I could barely understand him. Nevertheless, he understood me and led me with a few expansive gestures to the office of Dr. Yeveny Risanovsky on the third floor of a large building. I could see that this student must have been on his fifth cup of something already and was headed for a charged up day if he could keep his feet on the ground. Inside the departmental office, several students were milling around the desk of a woman who appeared to be the department secretary. I introduced myself to the woman of about 35 with dyed copper-colored hair, sitting behind a large desk adorned with the usual computers, phones, and papers randomly piled here and there. She was stocky and displayed body language that was belligerent, slamming cups down and shoving files around with muscular abandon. Sizing her up too quickly, I'm sure, I figured she could have driven tractors on a collective before taking the job. The message to students and all time-wasters was "don't mess with me!" I showed her my letter, which she studied briefly and then changed her expression from hardened resistance to a broad, transformative smile in an instant. "Welcome to USU!" she said, "Dr, Risanovsky will be right with you." Her instant smile was warm, but diminished somewhat by the many gold fillings inside her mouth.

Russians in this region, like Slavs everywhere, were tough straight-talkers. They could also be warm and intimate if they liked you, and it didn't take them long to size you up. Growing up in the Bronx borough of New York, familiarity with split personality characters like this was baked into my genes. My neighbors were all colorful characters like the secretary—tough types dressed in black, muscles outwardly bulging through their torso t-shirts, sleeves rolled up, but incongruously walking white poodles. Mobsters, who when not making a hit would give you directions or help old ladies across streets. I remembered a story about Whitey Bulger, who was recently beaten to death in his cell. The story went on about how as a well-mannered boy from the housing projects in South Boston he regularly took on local bullies with threats and his lightening fists. He had eyes as cold as marble and a hair-trigger violent streak for which he was famous. When he wasn't roughing rivals up, he bought turkeys for the poor at Thanksgiving and held doors open for women. People clawing their way up from the bottom in the mean streets needed defense systems from the other punks so they couldn't help but put on good fronts, addressing you as "youse" between quick chews of their gum. Just keep them friendly and smiling. As someone said about dealing with the renegade killers floating around the former Yugoslavia during the wars in the late 1990s: "always smile at the men with the guns." The secretary here gave me a good feeling. Like any faculty member, I knew that the departmental secretary is the most powerful member of any university department.

Titles, countries, cultures, political parties, rank, class—all these didn't matter. It was the institutional role. She (usually) could make things happen for grad students and faculty. She was the Sherman tank or the facilitator, depending on her whim. She could slam on the brakes in innumerable procedural and bureaucratic ways that even seasoned faculty didn't know about.

While waiting, I milled about looking at the announcements on the boards for jobs, assistantships, possible employment, and internship opportunities—none of which was any different from our bulletin boards in Elmira. A man appeared next to me holding my letter and gave me a polite nudge.

"You must be our Visiting Scholar from the U.S.," he said. "I am Dr. Yeveny Risanovsky. Please come in."

"Welcome to our little department. Tell me how you're settling in and all about what your plans are for the summer. If you need anything, Irina, our departmental secretary, can help you as well as me of course."

"I've settled in nearby in a flat," I told him. "Bit of excitement outside this morning that surprised me."

"Oh, yes?'

"Several large dog fights out front of here. One man at least was attacked, and the dog he was walking was probably killed."

"Yes," he said wearily, "I'm not surprised. Sorry you had to witness this. I can only advise you to make sure you protect yourself with the usual pepper spray canisters or a good hard stick. They seem to be getting worse. We, of course, have complained repeatedly to the local authorities about threats to the students. Not much action so far. At USU we have volunteers keeping the dogs away or at least controlled to protect the university community. They hit them with their books and briefcases or use pepper spray if they can get it out of their pants in time. It's about all we can do."

"I watched a few students try fending them off with their books; only the pepper spray had any effect."

"Correct! It is often said that the books lack enough substance to do any lasting benefit or damage to them. The pepper spray has been empirically proven many times as the best method. The second best is a good wooden club."

Risanovsky had an amiable face to match his droll humor and wore large, owlish aviator style glasses that added to his mystique. His hair was jet black and combed tightly around his head, then disappeared down the back of his collar. The more we chatted, the more I realized he was a Russian version of my old boss, Jack Marshall, at the New York Port Authority where I worked for a summer. The trigger was owls. He, too, had owls all over his office: on his desk, on bookshelves, made of wood, metal, and ceramic. They were all sizes and colors and came from all over the world.

"A fine collection of owls …" I said. "I had one for a pet once, but he flew away one day and returned to the wilds, I assume. Too bad, as we had a nice relationship."

"These are presents from colleagues who know my eclectic tastes. Do you still collect owls as well?"

"I moved on to pigeons when I was young. Many of us had pigeons on the rooftops of our apartment houses in the Bronx where I grew up—rooftop cages. Pigeons were pets, but they were exotic to us. Several decades before I was born, they still used them to carry messages around town. My pigeon was just a pet—a respite from the gritty life down in the streets."

"At least I don't have to feed these owls!" he said. He had a relaxed smile that invited trust, and he seemed like a potential friend here as well as a colleague.

"I see from your letter that you are related to Gyorgy Krylov in the engineering school. A fine man with many years of teaching and service here at USU."

"Yes, they very graciously put me up in Perm for a night, and we caught up on old family history."

"So now you are teaching at Bonaduz College, or I should say, have been for years. I've read over your CV, and we hope you can help us with some up-to-date city planning methods for the World Cup Games and other municipal services; provide us with some joint research avenues, and maybe do some teaching while you are here. How does that sound? We also have close ties with the city administration, especially now that the Games are coming."

"Great! I'd like to do all three if possible. I've worked with officials in the City of Elmira to do training and develop decision analysis methods as part of my work at the College there."

"Let me fill you in about USU and then we can see who's around. You must have a lot of questions. In general, the original university was founded in 1920 as Urals State Technical School of Economics," he went on as he rubbed a large, porcelain owl between his hands. "One of the founders was Maxim Gorky, whose statue is outside the building."

"One of my favorite authors!" I said.

"The latest iteration of USU was established in 1936. It is one of 16 universities in Yekaterinburg. Politology is one of its 14 departments. It's a big place with 95 endowed chairs. That's it in a nutshell," he said, putting the owl back in precisely the same spot on the corner of his desk. I noticed he had a slight tic that moved his aviator glasses off center. He had to re-center them several times as he explained things to me. He probably had a lot of hidden tension buried under his relaxed demeanor, as is the case with most people who end up as faculty chairs. From experience I knew that they got blamed for everything and had no real power to change anything.

"What kind of practical programs do you have with the city and the larger oblast for students?" It was the usual softball question anyone would ask coming to work here.

"Almost all of our programs link in with city and oblast institutions, private, state, and even non-profit organizations like charities. This is where you might help strengthen our ties—with the city officials planning for the Games." Now he was massaging gel into his hands from a dish in the shape of an owl's head, which he also kept on his desk.

"Great! That's exactly what I would like to do, though I have little experience planning for such a large public event."

We headed out of the office and down the hall to the first room, which turned out to be a set of shared offices full of advanced doctoral student types.

Several of them yawned and slowly turned as we entered. Probably an indication of how intimate, respected, and feared Risanovsky actually was. Of course, that was only a first impression ... Risanovsky waved for someone in the back to come forward. "Nicholas," he announced, "meet Andrey Kostov. We thought he could be your assistant for the summer. Andrey, this is Dr. Krylov, about whom we spoke last week. Well, here he is now—all the way from Elmira, New York!"

Up sauntered a scraggly-looking guy of about 6' 2" in a rolled up, long-sleeved shirt. His black and blond streaked hair was like a nest on top, then pushed slightly back like the mane of a lion. Like most of the students there, he sported a neatly trimmed beard. As he quickly took me in, I saw his twinkly, laughing eyes hiding behind tiny, wire-rimmed spectacles.

"How was the trip?" he asked me. "Train made it here on time?" he asked with an almost knowing little grin to top it off. I gathered the trains here were rarely on time.

"Fine, no problem. I'll take the plane back though."

"Faster or safer?"

"Both," I said, getting his points.

"Your Russian is fluent and almost local dialect. That's good. Everyone will trust you at least on that front."

"My family from the last generation was from around this region, near Perm."

"I've read over your research plan. I can help you with appointments at the city planning office, and with the FIFA people locally who are actually organizing the Game events here in Yekaterinburg."

We exchanged contacts, emails, cell phone numbers (mine had a local sim card, which I picked up in Perm), and addresses.

"Let's meet later and discuss all this."

"You know where to find me most of the time—right here."

"We're going to meet the rest of the faculty, and Dr. Kylov can get back to you later," said Risanovsky.

"Nobody's really around," Kostov said. "They are all in classes or preparing to come in this afternoon."

"Right," said Risanovsky impatiently, as if he knew all that and had heard it before.

We pushed off down the hall, and he pointed to some of the names on the doors. "Most of our faculty works on political theory and questions about the evolution of the state," he explained. "For instance, here is Dr. Kaminsky's office. He works on regional development policies in Russia.

"Sounds interesting," I said, "hope to talk with him sometime."

We stopped at the next office, the door of which was slightly ajar. He knocked lightly. "Ah, someone's home!"

A youngish woman opened the door holding a watering can for her flowers on the windowsill. She looked us over quickly with a flat smile, then went over and sat down behind her desk. About mid-30s, she wore tight jeans revealing a well-shaped body that contrasted nicely with her large, cold, and officious spectacles. There was no recognition from either side.

"Nick, this is Anna. Anna, this is Nick Krylov, visiting scholar from Bonaduz College in New York state. As I understand it, I think his project fits into your area of city planning."

She took off her glasses, looked hard at me, and then smiled broadly. Her face came alive in an instant. It was her! Instant mutual awareness! "So Nick's your name. Sorry we didn't exchange names a few nights ago."

"So you've met?"

"Indeed we have. Anna was attacked by dogs in my neighborhood, and I happened to be there to club them off with my umbrella and then try and patch her up."

"Were you injured?"

"Both of us got some minor flesh wounds and torn clothes. I got bitten in the back of the leg a few times."

"You might want to watch that. Rabies has been going around."

"I get bitten all the time by my faculty colleagues—no rabies yet! But if I start to bark, I'll call the health department."

"Up to you ... We have a university doctor and clinic, if you need it. In any case, I wanted you two to connect. Anna's husband, Semyon Irtenev, is on the city council and can probably show you the way around city institutions as well as the vertical command structures emanating from Moscow that will run the Games here."

I shook her hand and again noticed the slight pulsating beat of recognition as she held onto it for just an instant too long. Though I had missed it a few nights ago when she was at my apartment, she was a beautiful, dark-haired woman in her mid-thirties, keenly intelligent sounding and intense about her work. She had those Slavic good looks to me— high cheekbones, full lips, and almond shaped eyes. I also missed that she was voluptuous, as I felt her eyes bore right through me, strolling around inside my head and playfully riffling through the drawers of my mind.

"Why don't you join me for coffee later, and we can exchange pedigree as well as plan out something for you here?" she said, returning to that playful lightness that I had noticed in her before.

"We assigned him Andrey Kostov as an assistant, so why don't you all meet?"

"Great idea!" she said. "Tomorrow here around 10 a.m. then?"

The dim outlines of a new life appeared to be shaping up. I felt a buoyancy that had been absent from me for years, maybe as far back as the daily rushes from my high school escapades, which included chasing a full range of skirts that chased back eagerly. I also now recalled vividly playing pranks and stealing things after school with my delinquent friends who invariably were followed by weekly run-ins with the police. The only thing that broke the youthful rhythms were the occasional obligatory fights after school when someone felt "dissed" by you and wanted to get even. In those days and in that neighborhood, black eyes for us were the equivalent of the dueling scars of old. It was the carefree, fun part of growing up with few constraints and many opportunities. Perhaps now a repeat of all this—right here…

5   GOING TO THE DOGS

The robbery was the best one we had had. We hadn't started the fight. We never did. It was always our enemies, a rival pack of curs that lived a few miles away by some abandoned factory buildings. There were about twenty of them, and they were tough dogs, used to fighting and maiming their opponents. But we were too, and we basked in triumph at all the food we had eaten at their hideout. We even brought some home, which was rare for dogs, as we stupidly liked to eat and not save any for the future.

Our problem was exactly that, a lack of pack wisdom. We barked at strangers, howled at the moon, scraped with each other all the time when we weren't sleeping. But we lacked any future. Our pack leader simply was a fighter, and we respected him for his prowess. At eighty pounds, he was all muscle and grit, and none of us gainsaid what he wanted to do. So we mostly followed his lead. We had a clownish neighbor who wandered around on his own and used to visit us. Sometimes we offered him a bite, but mostly he just wanted to talk. He was a worrier and a newsmonger, with the latest gossip to share with us from neighboring packs. Not a bad mutt!

Recently, he said to us that he was worried about the young pups that no longer wanted to move in packs and scrounge for food. He worried about where all the fighting among packs for territory and food was getting us. We told him to calm down, and taking the hint, he left us. But he did say that some of the pups were trying new things that we might think about. Most of us listening were bored, and all the talk of food was making us hungry again. But he had said that some of the young had been adopted by people and were happy. They trusted humans and were living happy lives.

We found this disturbing because we we had been livingthere in these gutted urban surroundings. We were living on the streets precisely because humans had betrayed us and pushed us out into there to fend for ourselves. Even more disturbing, the neighbor told us he had seen some pups standing on their hind legs and walking, just like humans! At that, we growled and called these post-pack degenerates subversive. They betrayed our very way of life, and we had heard enough. Still, the tiny worm of doubt persisted among several of us, especially me. What if our top dogs were wrong? What if all the robberies, raids, and food slaughters led to nothing, and we had to fend for ourselves? Apparently, our neighbor, Yevgeny, for that was his name, was making it on his own. But he was only one dog. A loose pack of dogs with mavericks like him would not share food or be given food by other packs.

The lower dogs wanted to continue fighting and scavenging for food and territory. They were emotional and not open to the free interchange of ideas. They were hungry, and hunger sharpens the mind as well as the claws and fangs. But what if we could persuade some of our leaders, the alpha males, to cooperate and share with other packs? What if we learned to make peace with other packs and form a confederation of sorts that would benefit all of us? What if we could find a human ally that would guide us in this?

Several of us talked with a leader who listened with a cocked ear to our plan. He thought it might work and suggested we talk to another pack leader that he knew. We hoped to gain peace from our discussions with the new pack leader and also to preserve our canine dignity as beings that walked on all fours. We wanted to keep barking and chasing cars, but we wanted to stop all the killing and end the scarcity from which we suffered. Only the toughest packs avoided this, but even they were vulnerable when their leaders died off and some of their best fighters were killed in battle. So we talked to the rebel leader despite the opposition of some of our lower dogs who wanted to kill him on the spot. They saw him as a pansy-assed house dog, which sat on the couch and watched TV all day. He was hardly a model for a new type of dog or strong partner who could enforce a working peace.

The day came for the ceremony. The slogans we barked ceaselessly were: "An End to Food Robberies!" "Long Live Our Canine Brothers!" and "To Each According to His Needs!" A few minutes into the ceremony, an event occurred which filled us with horror. Taking advantage of our serenity, a large dog burst through and shouted, "Fraud!"—We can hear you grinding your fangs and sharpening your teeth. We can even hear your low growls! This is a trick! And with that he and a few of his mates attacked us. There were many more of us than them, and we immediately set upon them. But they fought skillfully and laid out almost half of our pack. And we saw that they stood upright like humans and fought with their claws holding clubs and sticks. They had a new kind of spirit that drove them onward with ferocity and almost scientific, tactical skill. We wondered whether the others in this pack had these skills. Our top dog came forward to see the bloodied and panting rebel leader lying there in a pool of blood. He was missing a lot of hair on his backside, and his tail was much shorter than ours. It looked like a newly-evolved form of dog, a dog man? At this, our brows furrowed and we had to give this matter a serious think ...

———

It's a busy Saturday night at the city animal control lab. Housed in a large brick structure with no windows, few people were likely to stumble across the place by accident. The lab was located in a back alley of a run-down industrial section of Yekaterinburg amidst steel assembly plants and abandoned factories that manufactured locomotives in the last century. Several grayish vans were parked outside. Inside the lab, several figures in white coats went about their business. A radio tuned to a local classical music station quietly played guitar music to soften the mood around what was going on. Dr. Krastov liked to hear light stuff like Chopin waltzes and upbeat Brahms Hungarian pieces to loosen him up while working. The music helped him concentrate and see things more clearly.

"Dmitry," said the older gentleman with the white coat on, sporting a pocket full of cheap pens, "have you gone through the checklist for tonight?" he asked the younger man.

"I can't seem to find the tongs," Dmitry said, staring hard at Ivan Krastov, the head of the office and senior vet. Fear, dread, and hatred were mixed in his tentative but fixed stare back at the vet.

"Have you checked in the shop?" said Dr. Krastov. For emphasis, he directed Dmitry with nods of his bald, elongated, head, which was like that of a tortoise toward the shop in the next room. The large tongs were an essential tool of their trade to grasp reclining dogs by the neck so that they could leverage them airborne easily and flip them in the van or one of the locked cages.

"You have the dart and machine guns as well I take it?"

"They're in the van. We probably won't be needing the dart guns, will we?"

"Why not? We usually have to dart some of the runners and toss them in the back with the others."

"Right chief, but the machine guns are really for the day shift, not us."

Krastov turned wearily toward Dmitry. "Let me explain this again to you, Dmitry. I've told you: we need to be ready for anything out there. Do you think that the dogs sort themselves nicely into patrician and plebian dog packs for our benefit? Do you think they hit the streets in neat cohorts of classy, well-trained dogs, partially tame mutts, and others viciously crazed by dangerous diseases?"

Krastov was unusually peevish and quick-tempered today. He couldn't believe how dumb this guy was after five long years of service here. Brains…? This guy was as thick as shit in a bottle! But Krastov rarely bore grudges, especially against the many thickheads that surrounded him, and often, he felt, impeded his daily work.

"No chief, they don't," Dmitry said, clearly miffed at being talked down to by this moronic egghead. He had been there for only five years, and Krastov for thirty. But the vet was a crank workaholic and out of touch with the staff here in his view. Dmitry knew what Krastov thought of him—a plebian slob, a lowlife just like the dogs the crew encountered on the dayshift. Sure he looked a bit savage, tattooed with matted hair in places around his bald head. But an observer would have to notice his steady, business-like gaze. His greedy little eyes darted around taking in most details that Krastov missed. He missed them because he sensed that Krastov was vulnerable and over-confident. As for the clothes and hair, it was his peculiar style, the determined shabbiness that carried him forward into life. Krastov occasionally looked at him over his wire-rimmed glasses as if he were a pitiful specimen of an inferior race. To Dmitry, the doctor looked positively fierce with his pointed red beard and tufts of red hair sticking out on each side of his bald head. Creepy bastard!

Krastov was a confused crank left over from Soviet times, in Dmitry's view. He was trying to look good to the current batch of authorities while feathering his nest with the big man in Moscow, Putin. His biggest complaint about Krastov was that he was missing out on the big money potential of the work here at the lab. Either way, he acknowledged his own ruthlessness: one day he could put Krastov down just as easy as the dogs he eradicated for the city. The achievement wouldn't even show up in the kill statistics, he mused. A wicked smile came across his face.

All one had to do was look around his office to conclude that Krastov was a grim crank. Dmitry didn't mind having a crank for a boss. He had worked for officials before that were mentally unbalanced. One could almost say that all of them working for the state were corrupt sadists. Good artists and writers were also mostly insane and fun to be around. So no problem there ... There were also plenty of cranks in this town, as could be verified by going into any pub at 7 a.m. to see who drank their breakfasts. And he often went drinking with higher up officials—but not this guy. True, he actually took his shit seriously enough to develop abstract social theories out of the mundane work we did at animal control. But in reality, we were nothing but glorified dog catchers. Lenin himself would have been impressed at first until he realized the guy was full of wrongly wired and confused thoughts and should be sent right to a labor camp to straighten his ass out. He had bad circuits! Take his infamous mind-map for instance.

And it was true that Krastov had developed a bizarre flow chart covering the entire wall behind his desk. The multi-colored chart was a variation on one of the old Stalinist control methods as far as Dmitry could tell. It featured an insane 30-step flow chart called the "mind-map." To help the untutored (or uninterested), it added guiding comments and sub-points to reveal the abstruse ideology behind the technical steps of animal control work. For example, day and night van patrol missions were two sub-points under step eight: "eradication." For team-building, the crew could throw darts at the steps on the chart and score points—a 30 could get them a day off, for example, or maybe just a medal. The mind-map was a crude modification of the old Venn diagram of the management world and a fawning attempt to lick Vladimir Putin's boots. But Krastov wouldn't see it that way. He must have known that the slave workers used by the Soviets were called "volunteers" and that they caught dogs for the abstract end of "state solidarity." In those happy days, doctors, nurses, and teachers all "helped" out. They also helped out with annual harvests of wheat and cotton as well as doing street and sidewalk pavement jobs in town. All of this fit into the wonderful solidarity of collective life then, with happy people just volunteering to help the state. From this nonsense, tiptoeing around the idea one might not want to volunteer (at great risk to one's self and family), it was a short leap into a glorious world of sloganeering mindlessness. Dmitry liked the one reminding: "Remember, mass dog executions are an important tool of the revolution (Lenin)!" So here we were in this city animal control facility doing special neo-revolutionary tasks in the name of the people (i.e., the Putin regime).

It wasn't that all of us disliked Krastov's Elvis Presley music either, thought Dmitry Simovich. Some surgeons played their favorite tunes in operating theatres while they cut people up. It got the team on board and kept everyone alert. Krastov played Elvis' ditties while he worked—such as "Mystery Train," which was one of his favorites for some reason. Perhaps in his mind the long black train was full of dead dogs. He even had a speaker in the van that played this mindless noise while we all hunted for dogs. He thought it served as a nice background to the clamor of loud machine-gunning when the teams encountered packs of wild dogs. It's one of the few times you'd see the bastard grin, even if it were a grin of cruel revenge. When Krastov laughed, it was through jerks of the body, like he was having convulsions. Maybe that would be a good time to put him down. Besides, what had the dogs done to this animal doctor? Maybe he was bitten when he was a kid. So get over it, you moron! No, what he didn't like were his phony ceremonial airs and graces.

Dmitry often mulled over these kinds of muddled thoughts in his brain. He clung on to this "higher" sense of grief exactly as a jealous dog that felt slighted. Like a dog, he wanted to vent his spleen not by more whining but by giving him a good bite in the ass. But his glacial mind worked against him. He was often incapable of pushing one thought out and getting a new one. Thus, he remained in a dysfunctional state unable to make any decisive action until a push came from outside—someone shouting at him to wake up and do something he had forgotten for instance.

"OK, start your engines!" Krastov yelled out. Clearly, the doctor imagined himself as a sea captain ordering his crew to cast off on a historic mission or a heroic grand prix driver racing across the track to leap into his car and peel out ahead of the others toward victory. Other times, he imagined he was a WWII tank commander, ordering the beginning of an assault maybe against the Germans. At such times he grunted engine sounds from his mouth twisted into a fierce grimace. He was of course "too young" then, but would have gone and fought with the best of them. *You bet he would have*, his crew might have retorted. They knew such antics made him feel powerful. The odd thing is that it was catching. They often accompanied his grunts with their own on a different note. Could have been a doo-wop acapella chorus!

"Bestir yourselves mates! We are off!" he cried out with erudite gusto, as they roared away from the animal control building with him at the wheel of the truck. His strong baritone voice added to his informal power over the crew and anyone who came in contact with him. It served well in his stints in Orthodox Church choirs around town with whom he occasionally performed. Heavenly vocal power in action!

The van gunned its engine behind Krastov's steady foot. It was time for another night patrol! Off they roared into the wild back streets of Yekaterinburg on their quasi-secret mission to rid the place of strays and advance the emerging science of canine vivisection. The plan as usual was to patrol the wilderness of old buildings in the industrial areas, many of which were dark and abandoned, near the Iset River. The departmental van, towing its little open trailer in the back, was unmarked to avoid having to answer questions from passersby. Both Krastov and Dmitry Simovich knew what vivisection meant. It was no longer the comic book term used in public parlance to describe mad scientists like Wells' Dr. Moreau and his island of freaks. Not at all ... This was serious modern state business.

The two-man crew in the back consisted of "retrievers" and "logistics experts," who mapped out the best tactics on the ground once the dogs were sighted. The men would then shoot darts or throw nets to try and corner them with whistles and treats, all in order to capture them alive. Back at the lab, they would then be castrated if found to be excessively stupid, as indicated by lack of focus, attention, and ability to follow commands. Or, they could be selected for the elite corps of a future dog corps that could perform basic tasks, like filing, driving cars, and doing errands. It all depended on how smart the dog was. Probably around 2% of all dogs fit this elite description. Repetitive selective breeding after a few minor operations and, with more training, in his experience, could produce this elite corps. Otherwise, their carcasses simply went in the river with the others. Despite the mission secrecy and scientific importance, the crew just took it all in as a nice evening outing for extra pay. A nightly fling with the boys to stretch the legs and joints. And they were half right. The daytime shifts were given orders to eradicate strays by any means, taking no prisoners. They did that with darts, large steel tongs, and skillful tosses of dog carcasses into the back of the van. Or, depending on what the logistics expert recommended, they simply machine-gunned large packs of them to be handled later by the sanitation department on the next day's morning pick up of garbage. Like the animal control crews, sanitation would often dump them in the river, and let the carcasses float away from town. Why? They simply could not put hundreds of dog carcasses on the landfills or leave them to attract predators and spread diseases. That was almost as bad as the rabies the strays were spreading around town. The day shift was less science than sport, and Krastov or Simovich rarely went along during day missions. Instead, by day, they rested and worked in the lab.

"'Everything that is at all must begin at some time,' said Mr. Boffin," quoted Krastov as he pulled the van out in anticipation of a great evening hunt.

Krastov's range of delusions included himself as a stage actor—even Shakespearean. Here he revealed his public side, his bent for theatrics. He had that stealthy, dramatic, even mischievous look of the relentless, booming-voiced, suddenly whispering storyteller. It was his public side, not to be confused with the private, vindictive, autocratic side that his underlings knew all about.

He continued now in a sordid tone, speaking through grinding teeth. "Let us go see what is going on in the world," as he slammed the accelerator down, throwing the truck upwards and forward with a lurch. Here his face became handsome, nearly blank, and he made his blue eyes go very small. "To see if there is anything of interest for us."

"You're in a lyrical mood tonight, Doctor," said Dmitry. "Was that Shakespeare?"

Krastov gave him a quick, condescending glance through his spectacles. "No, you fool. It's Dickens. Don't you read?" he shouted out with a burst of laughter. Krastov often followed pedantry with roars of laughter to confuse listeners as to his seriousness.

Dmitry winced, but felt the power emanating from Krastov: dominating, commanding, even inspiring. He was mostly respectful and timid when in Krastov's radiating presence. As now, Dmitry deferentially inclined his head to one side and even bowed occasionally in his presence when he felt Krastov had made an observation that others might find brilliant or penetrating.

"If I have a minute, sir, I read Pushkin," he said. "But I usually don't have a minute." Still these displays of cordial deference didn't stop Dmitry from ferociously grinding his teeth.

Onward they plodded that night through the streets and back alleys of Yekaterinburg in search of measurable productivity achievements and the happy glory of little victories. The official modern strategy of city dog control had been to neutralize the mutts with darts, capture them, castrate them to prevent further problems, and release them back into society. Krastov knew all about this and supervised that approach for years with only marginal results, given the high number of strays still running around and attacking people. More dogs had more puppies, and the canine population grew out of control. Worse, the recent rabies epidemic reported by the health department to him was classified information. If the FIFA people found out before the games (i.e. now), or if the media got that information, everyone would be in deep shit! The old policy approach was obviously flawed in theory and practice: it would take years for the darted dogs to die, even though the ones darted couldn't procreate anymore; the castrated dogs would take years to die off; there were also no places to store the neutered or castrated until they could be adopted (i.e. pounds); the city had no licensing regime—meaning enforced dog tag requirements that included vaccinations; and the result was that all the strays ended up either in kill pounds or back out on the streets biting people anyway. So building expensive pounds wasn't in the cards; there was no culture of dog adoption; there was no regulatory vaccination and licensing regime; and the dogs would still roam around and bite for years. What could be worse? Under these dire circumstances, the most feasible thing to do was to shoot them, gas them, experiment on the best ones, and dump the rest of them in the river. And so they drove on through the night in hopes of getting off this canine treadmill of disaster with a few spectacular successes.

As a recent mayor put it so nicely to Krastov on hearing about the castration plan, "Don't you understand? Dogs don't bite with their balls. They use their teeth!" So the city political regime and the public sensibly wanted something more effective done right now. Since this was Russia, everyone knew about Trut and Belyaev's successful experiments on fox behavior and evolution into domesticated dogs. Every school kid learned about their wild experiments. But the reality was that their work took 60 years, and Krastov's plan for a new biological creature to solve current problems might not work at all. He knew a big win was required to get the Kremlin regime and wider public behind him. The Games seem to have provided just the right opportunity. He also knew that further complicating Trut and Belyaev's work back then was the Russian Orthodox Church, which found out about the contraception practice and opposed it as a sinful policy. Again, this was Russia, and the intellectually petrified Church opposed anything dealing with science. Krastov pondered all this. How would those frocked assholes know anything about the sex habits of people or dogs? Most of the black-robed freaks were perverts or womanizers themselves, and everyone knew it. Bio-eradication via vivisection was Krastov's idea in response to this ecclesiastical nonsense, and so far it had been a mixed bag with most of the experimental operations a failure. In over a decade of work, the Iset River was full of his failures.

But he had just started. None of his target dogs had learned to talk or walk upright in public. A few had done so in private, but they often relapsed later to walking on all fours or reverting to barks, whines, and growls to communicate. So he was reluctant to try any of them out in front of the media, the public, or the big men in Moscow. Even with all their training and advanced skills, they might well walk upright but still run off after a car in front of the cameras. Nor could the targets so far read or lead discussions on high theory. None of them could get admitted to or study at USU yet. Come to think of it, some of them might pass the crap courses they pass off there as higher education. Nevertheless, lighting another cigarette from his last one, he was determined to get there with the regime's implicit and backdoor support and despite the Church killjoys. With the steady assured supply of stray dogs, we vets will just have to keep on trying! Mental stock-takings like this helped him renew his purpose and gave him a more powerful urge to succeed. He knew he could do it! Trut and Belyaev's eclectic approach had been partly genetics. That was still technically forbidden in the scientific world even though this was 2018. The approach was also part medical experimentation—heavy-duty stuff like organ transplants, which he carried out in the 45-year-old annex lab behind the animal control unit. Nothing dramatic like electric transformers throwing bolts in Dr. Frankenstein's lab. That could attract unfortunate attention. Fortunately, no one supervised him, and if they did sniff around, they probably wouldn't know what he, a trained geneticist and self-upgraded doctor cum vet, was doing.

It might be mentioned here that Krastov had so far failed with one big exception: the large, grayish dog named Fyodor sitting unobtrusively over in the corner watching them all with a sharp eye. His tail wagged with rapid but subtle movements of its tip. The fur was shaggy, and he had a blunt, stupid face, which belied his keen intelligence. He was probably a cross between an Irish wolfhound, lab, and bull terrier. Maybe other breeds as well. Over the past several years of work and training with him after picking him off the mean streets one day, Krastov got to know Fyodor well. One might say that Fyodor was even his best friend. But Dmitry Simovich didn't include this little drama in his big picture of things. He thought Fyodor was just another mutt to which the eccentric Krastov had taken a sudden fancy.

Krastov had always said that, "sometimes you have to get your allies the old-fashioned way—create them from scratch." In Fyodor's case, he did exactly that.

The red light on the ceiling suddenly flashed and cast an eerie glow in the cab of the van. It meant the crew has spotted the evening's first horde of suspected strays. Krastov listened on his cell to guidance from his crew in back.

"Large pack of vagrant dogs at 3 o'clock" …

The large black dog in front pulled well in front of the rest of the pack, which was moving down the street in an organized phalanx. "If we can find out the location of the leadership training school, and round up all the alpha males, we could wipe them out in a week," he mused. But this is more fun!"

But just as they were about to pounce, the leader sensed hostile humans were observing them. The pack started evasive action: some moving in to the left while the others reversed course and went back down the street. The leader had disappeared into the shadows, and Krastov's crew was momentarily disoriented—but not for long . . .

The van screeched to a halt near the pack and from the cab he could hear Boris and Igor piling out of the back. The pack consisted of mixed sizes and shapes, gaunt dogs, furry ones, fat ones, dogs with legs missing, spotted ones, white ones, and black ones. They were spaniels, terriers, hounds, and mixed mutts of all types. The dogs barked in a mad chorus confused, hopeful from all the attention, but afraid of the unknown which awaited them. As experienced crew members, Boris and Igor took all this in, and looking for a bit of fun, ran at them and into the pack beating them with their clubs and kicking them like footballs. Several of the dogs regrouped and began attacking the men and each other in their confusion. This was a sad theatre of idiotic pandemonium, an insight into the depths of human cruelty that was taking place daily on the streets of Yekaterinburg. The next sounds Krastov heard was the rapid-fire machine-gunning by the crew. They had tired of the fun and wanted to get it over with. Several of the dogs were hit and thrown around by the force of the large bore shells. Krastov saw the plaster of nearby buildings being shattering along with windows smashing either from direct hits or the concussion of the shells. As the dust cleared, it appeared that most of the dogs had scampered off, and that the few unlucky ones lying motionless and bleeding on the ground were but a small portion of the pack.

No matter. A rousing cheer went up from the hearty lungs of the crew as they declared another major victory.

"How 'bout them dogs? HBTD! How 'bout them fucking dogs?" they shouted out together.

Dmitry knew that this was a cheer copied from one of Krastov's American college football tapes. His eclectic tastes were entirely unpredictable. The crew put the guns back in the van, and, following protocol, they proceeded to scoop up the carcasses and toss them in the trailer for later deposit in the Iset River.

"Think of all the darts and pound costs we saved from this little maneuver. What do you think Dmitry?"

"Maybe, if I were a dog, I would remember who did this and come looking for them."

"Oh come on … you don't think like a dog, Dmitry. They have short memories of these little tragedies. Unlike humans, they don't hold grudges or carry vendettas, which make them in many ways superior to us."

"Never heard that one before. My dog remembers everything I do or don't do. Sometimes he's pissed at me for days because of some little slight to him I forgot about—like forgetting to give him a walk! But you must know. I hope you're right there, Doc!"

They drove on further, Krastov hard at the wheel. He made more grinding racecar sounds, turning the wheel abruptly for hairpin curves. Then he floored it, racing down his fantasy track for a few blocks. Out of the corner of his eye, he spotted a large, blackish dog lying next to a building. He could never be sure about their color as their fur was so packed with dirt and grime that they might actually have been white. But this dog waited for them and was curious about their arrival. That's a good sign, thought Krastov, suggesting recent abandonment by his former family. They slowed to a stop nearby. The dog didn't have that mangy glare of hopelessness yet, so he had not been obviously abused. He had just been abandoned for whatever reason. The van stopped, allowing Igor and Boris to get out and engage him with the soft approach—treats and nets. They whistled and offered treats to the dog. Really curious now, the dog moved towards them.

There was something about its manner suggesting it had once experienced cruel captivity before and had just begun to try and survive by instincts on the mean streets. Its gait suggested it was accustomed to living by its wits in the open. The dog held its head down and loped forward apparently to obtain the treat. It had that look of an orphan, of a runaway animal likely to hit the streets again because that is what it knew how to do best.

Suddenly the dog lunged and bit Boris on the arm. He had forgotten to put on his gloves and arm pads thinking carelessly that this might be a friendly sort. But he was wrong. Meanwhile, the dog started to run off. Igor thought quickly and whistled again, causing momentary confusion in the dog. He hesitated, showing that he once responded to commands, another good sign. As he cautiously approached, Igor calmly reached behind and pulled out his stun dart gun and fired in one sweeping motion. An urban gunslinger in action.

Boris then closed in and with a few deft moves, strapped a muzzle to his snout.

"All right, you bastard, you got me first. But now look at you! I should put you down for biting me!" he bellowed, frustrated and humiliated at being caught off-guard. "But this time you get a second chance!"

The dog was out cold now, and the two crewmembers simply heaved him into the back of the van to occupy first class seating in doggy lingo. He was a big one, weighed about 80 pounds and was in pretty good shape—good cranial features, eyes, teeth, and paws. Krastov looked him over in eager anticipation of conducting some successful experiments with him.

But with a new candidate in tow, it was back to business. Krastov and his crew piled back in the van and driving furiously, he raced the van through more darkened streets and back alleys in search of prey, or "clients" as the modern animal control management people called them.

"That's right. We're here to serve clients—with kill darts and tongs!" he chortled.

"Stray at 6 o'clock!" came the crackly announcement from Igor.

"Ok, men," said Krastov, narrowing his eyes heroically to brace himself for action. "We're going in!" he said, spitting more engine sounds from the side of his mouth. "Unnnn! Unnnn! This could be it!"

Dmitry could never figure if the guy took himself seriously or not. But at least it wasn't a desk job, and things were never dull.

Tires screeching, he wheeled the van around 180 degrees and parked near a large cluster of reddish fur matted with pieces of refuse, lying next to an abandoned building. It might have been a dog or not. The pile could have been dead for a while, which was often the case. Just then, stirred by the noise of the van, the pile turned into a medium-sized dog and with an astonished look, starred at them. As he walked carefully towards them, it was evident that he had a colored cavity on one side of his body. His glare was confused—a mixture of cunning and friendliness. He had the wistful face of a dog trying to understand what was going on. No matter. They concluded with affirmative nods that it was a defective stray and probably rabid. Plenty of unreported rabies cases around ... so there seemed to be no point in taking chances. Dmitry aimed his gun at the dog.

"Just a minute, Dmitry, hold your fire!"

Krastov thought that Dmitry often got carried away with the heroics of the job, missing chances to capture dogs that could be turned into something much more than what they were: lost and frightened street dogs. It was a problem working for someone with a simple set of motives, mostly trigger-happy and violent, but with seemingly no imagination. He would have to deal with this later ...

Out jumped the boys from the back of the van and fired a kill dart into the dog, which to Krastov had showed promise. Boris got the tongs and put them around his neck. A mournful series of yelps and whines rang out as the dog pleaded for some kind of leniency. With a deft twist of his arm and body, Boris tossed him into the air and onto the other carcasses in the trailer before he knew what had happened to him.

"OK boys, let's go to the beach!" shouted out Krastov with a big smile of satisfaction splashed across his face.

They headed around the edges of the city as much as possible to avoid onlookers and camera bugs.

"Hey Dad, what kind of trailer is that? It's full of dead dogs," some child might say while his father snapped photos.

Krastov didn't want tourists or anyone snapping photos of their activities. Local freaks might even do selfies and make things worse for all of them. So they stayed away from busy sections of town, preferring the industrial sections and especially those areas with abandoned factory and shop buildings. It took about a half hour of weaving and detouring to arrive at a back road paralleling the river. The River Iset flowed southeast down from Lake Iset through Yekaterinburg. They drove to their favorite spot in a mixed forest/industrial area south of town. There was a weir, or dam, surrounded by forest cover and several large pieces of rusting industrial junk lying scattered about in a clearing.

"Could be modern art ... Maybe there's a market for this shit with some dealer online," he mused.

By the dam, they unloaded the trailer with gloved hands and tossed the carcasses into the Iset, helpfully flowing south into someone else's territory—the towns down there can get used to the special meaty taste of the water. He estimated there were at least one hundred carcasses that day that would provide the spicy flavoring.

"Not bad for a hard day's work!" he said to Boris, slapping him on the shoulder.

Too bad about all the bodies crapping up the river though, he mused. Krastov recalled that he once heard an economist talking about "negative externalities" at a conference of vets. "Can't imagine what he meant!" laughed Krastov into his nicely trimmed beard.

Back inside the lab building, Krastov again praised all of them for their fine work. "If I could get the day crew to work as diligently as you, we would have the highest productivity rating in the entire animal control system," he gushed.

"Go home, boys, and get a nice rest."

He laughed wickedly, then winked at them from the corner of his eye.

"I wouldn't trust that guy as far as I could spit!" thought Dmitry.

6 THE GOOD DOG FYODOR

Despite the fact it was directed generally at the crew, Dmitry winced at Krastov's praise. He knew what was coming. There would be more outbursts of Krastov's cruel and malicious side … it was always that way. The next day, he came to work in the afternoon and heard shouting and objects being thrown and smashed against the wall and ceiling. It was Krastov berating the day crew for their incompetence. He railed at them with a particular lack of oratorical flourish for their lack of kills or captures. This was the authentic Krastov, not his put-on intellectual elegance—his split personality revealed in all its cruelty and impulsiveness. It was a somber day covered by pewter-tinted clouds despite being summer, with a low sky as heavy as lead.

"What the fuck do you people do out there? You just drive around and waste gas!" he sputtered between bursts of coughing and laughing. Krastov kept a cigarette going most times as he was an inveterate chain-smoker. He had that strange, twisted expression of cruelty across his face, rounded out by his nasty little grin.

"Come here, all of you!" shouted Krastov. "I have a little exercise for you to serve as a discipline-building lesson."

The four crewmembers headed out back, and Dmitry watched them through a window as they approached the large concrete ditch that ran between the buildings. The ditch was filled with dog shit and rotting animal parts.

"Fall in and line up shoulder to shoulder! When I give the command, right shoulder arms, then take the wooden clubs from your shoulders, raise them up above your heads, and hit the dirt! Got it?"

In his capacious baritone he bellowed out: "OK, animal attack! Here they come! Hit the dirt!"

The four of them fell into the mixture of mud and crap beneath them. He repeated the exercise with them a few more times. From the window of the complex, Dmitry saw the four crewmembers standing in the ditch with their heads bowed in contrition while Krastov taunted them to start their well-known song.

"Sing it out now: 'We are bad dogs and must reform and be good dogs'."

How had he diminished to this level, he wondered? It might have been the thirty years of service in government that produced the cruel arrogance in him that expected underlings to address him in refined fashion by heads of departments. He was used to working with small-minded officials who sized him up by a downward look at the boots or quick inspection of one's coattails. Gogol wrote about the stiff formality and inflexibility of the Russian civil service in "Nevsky Prospekt," Whatever Krastov's qualities were initially, years of being part of this culture of pettiness had had a deleterious effect. Now, Krastov was driven by an illusory pursuit of higher rank as a means to something called happiness. His ambition was power and recognition, and that drove him to crass bullying of his crew. When confronted by those of higher rank, he was often obsequious, bombastic, jovial, and cordial—that is, a boot-licker. There was not much of an inner life to the man. No hint of a tortured psychological conflict between base strivings of his soul and higher spiritual aims that Russians often dealt with in their particular individualistic ways.

So it was, one night alone in his lab. He had permanent red rings around his eyes from working every night there. Often he just slept there rather than trudging home. He was exhausted from the many sleepless nights spent there on his routine work, the same work he had been doing for years. It was the dull routine work of recording stray catches during the day and reporting them to the city health department, which oversaw his animal control facility. He reflected that all his efforts had gotten him precisely nowhere on any career recognition scale for vets. He did some late night training on promising strays; he slated others for destruction as hopeless, while working to tame others and groom them for possible adoption. He did all this without enthusiasm and with the assistance of Dmitry, who sometimes helped out when he needed it with the problem dogs classified as "biters." They rarely talked and knew little about each other. Dmitry viewed him as an overworked eccentric, one who was often hard on himself and cruel to the rest of the crew. By contrast, Krastov saw Dmitry simply as an additional body to assist with the demanding physical work of the lab and routine dog retrieval tasks. It was all quite dreary for both of them.

It was late one night that Krastov was working on a large dog that had been chewed up pretty badly in a fight or two and apparently had been hit by a car. But the dog was tough and showed no signs of internal injuries and had a determined fighting spirit. The dozens of other dogs in the surrounding cages began to bark that night. They often barked, but that night their barks turned into howls, ceaseless wailing and malevolent, plaintive moans that could be heard for blocks despite the thick concrete walls of the animal control building. Nobody could explain this. Some said that it was the bright moonlit night that allowed him to see the nearby buildings outside the windows almost as if it were daytime. Next to the dog that was stretched out on the table were all of his instruments. There were also containers of dog body parts—lungs, vocal chords, brains, and kidneys. All preserved by him just in case he needed them. Usually he didn't.

It came to him in a flash as he saw the mangled dog and the spare body parts that he needed to up his game a notch. He could be doing much more for these creatures and give them the lives they deserved. With that flash of insight and sudden inspiration, he proceeded to sedate the dog and cut into his skull. No one saw any of this. No one paid any attention to the dog's condition on arrival. No one really cared what happened to them. Taking advantage of this freedom, he got right to work on the dog's brain to see if he could induce the dog to make certain basic movements—such as stretching out his legs and standing up. It was all straightforward stuff from the old vet textbooks that he had been consulting from his university days. The trial and errors he experienced all night got him further excited and led to some minor re-arrangements of brain tissues that seemed to be leading the dog into efforts to stand upright—like a biped. Not that this was a great achievement—some trained circus dogs walked around on their hind legs all the time. Still, he was encouraged as whatever this was, it was no terrier or any other circus dog breed. He bandaged up the dog, which he fondly named Tsar and kept him in a separate cage. Every night when the others had gone, Krastov worked with Tsar on standing, vocalizing words from growls, and training to sharpen its eye-paw coordination. Tsar grew to trust him, and they made incredible progress. Krastov was excited for the first time in more than 15 years. Technically, he should notify someone in the health department that he was doing all this with a stray dog. But why talk to people whose job was to say "no"? He was at last doing some radical experimentation, and these small successes incrementally had led to dramatic changes in his view of the facility's worth, the needs of the crew, and especially his own self-esteem. But his changed outlook took a bit of time to manifest itself in other behavioral modification.

"You, Igor, bark out the chorus to their song. Get to it!"

After a few verses of this humiliating spectacle, (*the dogs themselves could probably sing better,* thought Dmitry), he ordered them to stop. *When yelling,* Dmitry noticed, *the wart on his upper forehead reddened. It was like a third expressionless fish eye, which stared lifelessly at you.* Accompanied by more coughing and sputtering, he then told them to roll around like the dogs.

"Whenever possible, dogs like to immerse themselves to feel soft manure on their bellies, so should you!"

Now they lay down in the foul-smelling manure and rolled around inside the ditch until Krastov again yelled at them to stop.

"Have we got the point? You must kill more of them to increase our productivity measures! Now get up and get showered."

"Someday, we'll fix this bugger. Maybe take him to the beach for a long swim," Dmitry mused. Seeing a few of the crew come into the building, he sidled up to them.

"Nice dip in the pool, wasn't it?"

They looked at him and shook their heads. Looking around to see if Krastov was there, one of them said: "We don't have to put up with this. We know he's connected and could have us sacked in a minute. But we still don't have to do this as part of the job!"

"You're right; he probably could," Dmitry agreed. "Care for a smoke and a few puffs?" He offered all of them cigarettes and lit them.

"There are other ways to put a stop to his antics. All of you are cutting a wretched spectacle. Imagine if this got into the media … Or he had an accident in the middle of a botched dog kill."

Dmitry and the speaker exchanged knowing glances.

"There just could be an accident someday. Wouldn't affect our productivity, would it?" Boris said with a grin.

"It might not," said Dmitry Simonvich.

The crew packed up and, after showering, left the building. Dmitry did the same and followed them out. The building was deathly quiet and deserted. The crew had forgotten about the large, shaggy dog named Fyodor, who quietly sat in his cage in the corner and heard the entire conversation. He was perched quietly over in the corner awaiting Krastov's return. His alert, loyal eyes darted around, gauging his surroundings. His bushy tail and brownish mutt-like mottled fur were standard fare. A bit later, Krastov entered the room, an all-purpose area with lockers, TV, easy chairs, and a formal round table used by all of them for dressing, showering, and meetings. In the corner were larger cages for special target dogs. At present, there was only one—Tsar's successor and the prime specimen of Krastov's work to date.

"Well, Fyodor, how has the day been?" as he entered the lab. "Slow, I hope."

"That's right, Doctor, I spent the day reading and practicing penmanship with my paws. It's getting better. I can almost read what I write!"

Krastov had been practicing to get Fyodor's growl into a deep resonating voice, and it had worked. Then he had to work with him on his paws—especially getting the claws to hold the pen and try and coordinate it with his thoughts. After several operations on his vocal chords and brain, linking up his thoughts, speech, and actions, Krastov spent many a night working with him on these basic skills; his successes were beyond all expectation. A problem was that he had to hide all this from outsiders, who might have been stunned, gotten suspicious, and called the media. Worse still, he imagined, there might be competitors out there trying to steal his secrets and methods, such as they were, and to make commercial gains from them. He knew he had to be careful with his discoveries and successes.

"Don't get discouraged. Many humans still can't do that, Fyodor! You are way ahead! Read any good books today?"

"I just finished the Bulgakov book about the dog in Soviet Russia. I didn't like what happened at all. His vet turned him into a lout, a crude thug for the Communist regime. Are you going to do that with me?"

Krastov laughed and roughed up Fyodor' fur. "Come on, Fyodor, I have much bigger and more sensible plans for you. You will be a new class of dog altogether, but only in service to yourself—not any regime or dictator. So let me assure you, we have better things in store for you. If you keep up the pace, we may get you your own government department someday."

"Would I have to sit at a desk all day like Gogol's deathly civil servants?"

"Not necessarily. We are training you for an operations role, out in the field where the work is done, maybe technical safety inspections."

"And you think I could do that?"

"Fyodor, we brought in a special stray from this earlier search mission. He seemed a lot like you, and we put him in the first class cages near the lab. I have been working hard on Tsar, and he has responded well! He is on his way biologically to becoming something far more than he was. He was one of maybe five or six in the annex who, like you, received special cages for further tests and treatment. You passed all my tests with flying colors and here you are ready to exit. And you moved way beyond Tsar's level of development. The plan is that you and others like you, such as Tsar, will become the vanguard of a new canine race that only initially will do routine exercises such as patrolling streets and performing security functions."

"But I don't want to return to the streets. I'm not a wild beast anymore, am I?"

"Certainly not. That's why we are preparing you for a management and supervisory role. We know you can do it. We selected you because, after finding you, luckily, just after your family lost you, we discovered that you were worth far more than scavenging table scraps and doing tricks for treats. That's childish, Pavlovian stuff, and you quickly outgrew all that. You learn complex concepts fast and are able to put them together quickly by making practical decisions using your skills of talking, reading, and writing."

"What happens to those strays which don't make it?"

"I think you know now what the dayshift crews do. They are responsible for eradicating lowly strays; those we deem incorrigible can spread more rabies and attack people randomly. That could ruin the city's reputation during the World Cup Games. The Putin regime won't have it, and neither will city officials. Our day crews are responsible for ensuring that these things don't happen. Putin is a cynical populist and needs these Games to come off well. You recognize, because we have discussed it, that as a dealmaker, he has to keep making good deals or his power would be threatened. The Games are one more magical deal in his bag of tricks to keep impressing the masses and the rapacious entrenched interests that surround him."

"So what happens to them? What happens to the ones you mistakenly don't pick for elite training?'

"I think you already know. We can only feel sorry for those that have to be put down because of where they came from and their currently wretched conditions. And we aren't perfect. We missed a solid candidate today because I was too hasty and wanted to get home. We mistakenly put him down."

"In a hurry to get home…? Are your actions, then, driven by productivity measures, something like the Soviet physical norm ratio system that once governed all Russian public services?"

"You see! That's an excellent question that few humans could ask around here. You are definitely going to be in management! The answer is yes. Our little sub-department of animal control has to achieve certain quotas to be judged as efficient and budget-worthy. The quotas are in the "state orders" we receive, just like the ministries operated before in the Soviet system. Very often the supervisors have no idea what we are faced with in capturing strays or what we have to accomplish because they are inexperienced generalists. They are also afraid of getting numbers reported that make them look bad. So we often game the numbers to make everyone look good. We report that we catch and or kill more than we actually do."

"I would probably do the same thing. Do we, I mean you, have all the equipment you need here to achieve the result you want?"

"You should definitely take over this department now, Fyodor! The short answer is 'yes we do.' In fact, the authorities in the Ministry of Health have constructed us these superb lab facilities in the modern tradition of veterinarian labs all over Europe and the U.S. You could operate comfortably on a human with what we have now in this place. That is more or less what I did with you here. Most importantly, as you probably figured out, our lab is separated physically from the common stray dog cages, and the field offices of the search and kill crews. They have a separate wing of cages and even an area for adoptions, which unfortunately rarely happens in Yekaterinburg or anywhere else in Russia. So we work in absolute privacy and secrecy. The only one partially familiar with my work is Dmitry, who also works with the search and skill crews. As you have probably figured out, Dmitry helps but has never been able to connect the dots as he is distracted by search and destroy missions.

"But Fyodor, I have to keep most of my accomplishments hidden, even from him. I have to avoid publicity at all costs or everything could be ruined for the future of Russia and me as well. Put simply, I can't trust him, and I need you to discuss my ideas with. I need someone who can do first-rate work and who I can trust. That's you. I want someone with whom I can discuss ideas openly, who will tell me I'm wrong, who will debate my ideas with me and provide some better options. Again, that's you. Clear?"

He thus ended his explanation on a high note.

"Got it, chief!"

Fyodor often listened to Krastov, banging on with social theory of the new man. He had heard it all before and knew most of it was nonsense—modified Soviet socialist realist claptrap. It was simply a collection of fatuous slogans masquerading as formal theory, designed to get the workers in collectives to work longer hours. How would that help crops grow faster? Did the plants learn that they had to try harder and grow more? What shit! Regardless, all we had to do here at animal control was to update the rhetoric and produce it on stage with marching dogs and cannons going off amidst swollen banners and drums for added impact. Just feed them back modified slogans that had worked before to provide officials power and legitimacy for their operations. He also knew that Krastov himself thought it was claptrap. But properly modified, it could all be a motivational device.

Worse, both of them knew that Stalin had bought into the teachings of the charlatan Trofim Lysenko and had once banned genetic research. That was more dangerous nonsense because the real scientists of the time in the 1950s were working on improving mink and fox furs for export to generate needed foreign exchange. So Stalin was a cretin as well as a ruthless tyrant, banning what he didn't understand because of an influential fake scientist. Other fakes like Lysenko were behind Stalin's tragicomic agricultural policies that caused attacks of famine and millions of preventable deaths. Luckily, Putin has no such qualms about science and is not beholden to any group of confused ideologues or doctrinaire types. He merely has to stir up sufficient doses of nationalism to keep him in power. There was no danger of him being tossed into a labor camp or being forced to resign or accept a menial position now. Krastov figured that he had a respectable, scientific career and was a well-respected vet in the industry. Still, different types of goons and jealous morons lurked about, and he had to be careful.

Beyond the realm of theory but touching on fantasy speculation, which had always been popular with the public, Krastov also knew that fortunately there had been similarly reported surreal cases which would come in handy in case of premature discovery by the media or officialdom. He could feed the public such sensational incidents as to distract them and get them off the trail. A fish is said to have surfaced in the U.S. and spoken several words in an unintelligible language to some fishermen. A cow apparently entered a shop in India and ordered several pounds of tea. What would you expect coming out of places like the U.S. where UFOs were seen all the time and real facts were considered fake news? Or in India where cows were held as sacred? None of these behaviors had been linked to any medical experiments. And he could always make the pitch that dogs just got tired of walking around on all fours after a few thousand years and decided to stand upright! They evolved. Selected squirrels hung down from tree limbs by one leg, reached down to lift birdhouses and throw them to the ground, sending the seeds flying. Most squirrels couldn't ever figure this out. But special smart ones did all the time!

It might be a stretch to claim that a dog wearing a cardigan and sporting a monocle just evolved one day. But until he thought of a better story, that's what happened with Fyodor, if anyone found out what he was doing here. His only competition in the animal-human vivisection field was on Dr. Moreau's island, which was the fictional testament to a madman who failed spectacularly at his vivisection efforts. Krastov was also aware that Gogol and Bulgakov had written about talking dogs and dogs made into humans by vets. But they were only fiction pieces for the gullible Russian public. Moreau did his wild experiments untroubled by ethical considerations. Bulgakov's Dr. Persikov was more to his liking—a scientific pioneer who was modest and circumspect about his discovery—he, like himself, wanted to ensure that any further experiments with dogs would take place under strictly controlled circumstances. The Soviets had actually domesticated silver foxes into pet dogs in the 1950s starting with the Trut and Belyaev experiments. So Krastov could always deny his experiments and the bio-solutions favored by the police and the city officials and claim it was just another example of a superb training system. They were simply breeding new types of dogs that could work and achieve higher productivity. It was going to be good for Russian business and the Putin regime. And who could object to that? He also knew he had a clear track and green light so long as no one found out what he was doing until he presented the evidence formally to the Russian power people in the Kremlin.

"What happens to elite strays like me who don't make it through your transformational operations?" asked Fyodor.

"I think you know that other candidates were selected before you. Our selection process is obviously inferior—observations on the random streets we patrol, hoping to find the right dogs. We miss so many good candidates because we lack time and resources. Even those dogs that we find to be excellent candidates often fail to survive. Most of this is my fault in that I often use trial and error methods on what I thought were the right dogs. Suppose we had picked from the commoner canines retrieved from the dayshift's catch? If my experimental operations had worked on a common stray as in Bulgakov's book, we might have ended up with a lout similar to what his fictional vet created: a Sharikov. No, not good at all! So we work on the potentially elite dogs and even there have been unsuccessful several times. I feel remorse for this, as I love dogs. Thankfully, you gained the benefit of my earlier mistakes that cost the other dogs the remainder of their rather miserable lives."

"I've been having nightmares lately," said Krastov.

"What kinds?"

"A few nights ago I had a bad one and woke up choking and coughing in a pool of sweat. They had me down on an operating table?"

"Who?"

"Several large dogs dressed in white coats and operating tools such as tongs and giant hypodermic needles. They were cutting off my balls with the tongs after injecting me several times with bright green fluids."

"It hurts me just hearing about it!"

"After they finished, they threw my balls into a trash can and unstrapped me from the table. There was blood and torn flesh everywhere. The dogs were chuckling as they worked and made sounds from their snouts like low growls, which sounded more like engine sounds. Then they grabbed me and pushed me out the door of the operating room into a van. Dmitry was driving the van and smiled at me on arrival. 'Hi doc,' he said. 'Not so smart now are we?'"

"They drove on into an area of warehouses surrounded by packs of wild dogs where he slammed on the brakes, and they threw me out. The dogs came at me and began ripping flesh from my body. I could see the muscles and bones protruding. Oddly enough, there was no blood this time, only what looked like venison or steak meat. I felt them tearing away my flesh, but it oddly felt warm and relaxing—like a massage."

"I think you know what this all means! You are terribly guilty about your treatment of both stray dogs and your own crew!"

Krastov nodded and looked at the floor. "I have to do something about all this," he said.

Just then, there was a knock on the door. Krastov motioned for Fyodor to be quiet, and he opened it to find a technician coming from the kill area still dressed in large trousers and boots with goggles thrown back on his head.

"What's up, Vlad?"

"Nothing, Chief. I thought I heard voices as I was preparing to leave. I had to clean up a rather large mess tonight. We got a lot of them!"

"Good work! That will help our monthly statistical report on productivity."

"Is there someone else here?"

"No, I was reading aloud as I often do for my musical work in the church choir."

"Woof! Woof!" was heard coming from Fyodor's cage where he had quickly decamped before Krastov opened the door.

"OK, Doc, see you tomorrow. Glad all is ok."

"Good night, Vlad."

Krastov came over to Fyodor's cage. "You're going to have to learn how to bark properly! No dog says, "Woof!" Someone's going to get suspicious!"

"Relax… They know I'm in here in first class. They'll just think we enunciate my barks more clearly as is done in the better parts of town."

"Be careful, Fyodor! We don't want to get careless!"

"Doctor, how did I evolve? Was it a smooth process from stray to human?"

Sometimes Krastov was sure that Fyodor was putting him on with his rhetorical questions.

"That's a long story for another time, over a large dog bone and a glass of wine for me. You were trouble to say the least. You moaned and swore into the night, and I had to keep the radio volume up high."

"I swore?" Can't imagine doing that now. Why did I swear?"

"We don't know, but you were obviously pissed about something from your past. Said things like: 'you dirty motherfuckers, leave me alone, or I'll bite off your balls!' And 'what kind of shit is this for food? Do you expect me to eat this? It isn't fit for a dog!' Outbursts like that…"

"I get the idea. Probably how I really felt though!"

"You also bit people. You bared your teeth at us and lunged, snarling viciously at first. You didn't trust us, understandably, so we had to deal with that medically and with sedatives. We knew that you, like the foxes and wolves some of us had worked with in other labs, could bite hard!"

"It won't happen again. Unless I get pissed at something!"

"If you bite me, no food for a month…"

"It's crap food anyway … Keep it!"

Fyodor knew what Krastov had said about his efforts to keep most dogs alive was not quite true. He often heard the sounds of the night crew butchering dogs and torturing them with various treatments. He could tell that a lot of them weren't working. He knew just how bad it was, the howling and weeping of wounded and misbegotten dogs in the nearby annex for common strays. And miserable they were in both the pens here and in Krastov's lab. He could only imagine the surreal interior of the killing machines and knew how seriously they mistreated the common dogs. He had read about chicken lines where chicken killing factories sped the process of converting live chickens to packages of body parts for cooking in just minutes! The same was done with beef cattle—industrial killing machines and processes.

Of course, Fyodor didn't see the outright machine gunning and canine carcass dumps into the river. Inside here was a slight variation on a pig slaughterhouse. At night their howls and shrieks sounded like jackals as the vets worked to inject the poison into them for self-destruction. At other times, the vet technicians would kill them outright in the annex. The technicians wore goggles and earplugs to work. That hid the squealing and gurgling of the dogs, some of which were hung up like pigs to drain them of blood and entrails after their deaths. Like pigs, some of them were placed in boiling water, which accounted for the fog on goggles making it hard for them to see. Sometimes the dogs would look on passively at the last humans they would see or human grunts they would hear as they did their routine jobs of killing their brethren who had the misfortune of being captured in the latest sting. The clattering of equipment and lids banging down was deafening, hence the earplugs for the crew. They really get into it sometimes, smoking cigars while swinging axes and hammers at the dogs to kill them. The cigars added a nice complement to their official garb of trousers and braces. The smooth smell of cigar tobacco also smothered the stench of blood and guts everywhere. He knew from reading about the German war camps, which wiped out masses of Jews, that more than a few of the technicians felt awe and pity for these creatures. But like many of their superiors in the camp killing machines, they had few options to humanize the processes or indeed stop them altogether. Despite the popular heroic tales written for contemporary fiction readers, they couldn't really refuse. So they continued to kill and maim the dogs in their care. The technicians mindlessly logged them in and worked their routines like assassins in an extermination death camp. It was a dirty business, and Krastov was not proud of being part of this. But it had to be done.

"I'm glad I wasn't your first candidate!" said Fyodor.

"I am too. I think we have become real friends and soul mates."

"You hear the one about the talking dog in Tirana?"

"Tell me!"

"The Albanian owner advertised his dog for sale for $50, and a prospective buyer showed up. The seller told him he could talk. In disbelief, the buyer asked the dog to explain his qualities. The dog then launched into a tale about being raised by a very wealthy and cultured family. That family traveled the world and allowed him to learn three languages. The buyer asked: "With all this, why are you giving him away for only $50?" The seller said: "The price is $50 because he is a liar. He's never been out of the back yard!"

"Good one! Where do you learn these things? "

"Sometimes I listen to your radio late at night. The Brahms and Mozart pieces especially help me get in touch with my emotions. They calm down my inner dog and its primitive feral tendencies. I can focus and think more clearly. For instance, you said your work is kept secret from Dmitry."

"That's right, for all the reasons I told you."

"We need to talk about some shop gossip I picked up while you were away today."

"So you do more than just listen to the radio!"

"As I said, the classical pieces stimulate my feelings and thoughts. They allow me to reflect on certain matters."

"And.?"

Now Fyodor was a dog, and dogs and all animals have it in their blood to worry. Certain creatures have worries as in dog-worries-cat, and cat-worries-mouse. He was 25-50 percent human, thanks to Krastov's veterinarian skills, imagination, and risk-taking. And he was a loyal dog to those whom he trusted and therefore felt obliged to serve. The flip side is that he relentlessly pursued humans disloyal to either himself or his master. He might forget a trick or two. But he never forgot the smell of someone he distrusted. Still, being a sensible dog now, he was less prone to the standard feral solution of a growl and spring than working things out rationally. He reflected that he used to have fun, play with his mates, cavort in the streets, steal food and scraps, and after all this still got invited back to the big house where he lived. There he continued to steal scraps until someone kicked him or hit him with a stick. It was all very predictable and rewarding. It was an ok life, and he loved it. He pretended to become disciplined in exchange for treats; his family pretended or at least hoped his behavior would improve. Maybe they just liked him and were tolerant. But deep down they knew how dogs were, and they all got along fine. Then one day about a year and a half ago, Fyodor got loose, went for a spin around town, and here he was!

"I know you did some nasty things to one of the day crews, and they are upset. You humiliated them."

Fyodor was pretty well read by now and knew that the idea of a dog reporting on the behavior of a superior was not outlandish. In Gogol's *Madman*, a minor official relied for information on a dog, Polkan. This amazing dog wrote everything down about the 'Madman's' Director and, most importantly, his mistress Fidele about whom the Madman wanted to know more. And why not? The minor official knew that dogs were more clever than humans and that they were shrewd enough to notice everything and every step their human superiors took. So, Fyodor reasoned, I am simply following in a long line of paw prints by being a loyal observer.

"Yes, I had to humiliate them. As I've explained to you, part of management is to install fear as a means of gaining respect."

"Does that really work?"

"No, probably not. I can tell they don't respect me. It might work in the short run, long enough, hopefully, to keep them away from my experiments and to game the kill and capture statistics enough to keep things going here. But I doubt it sometimes."

"Do you ever wonder how much time you have left to succeed on this?"

"Are the natives restless then?"

"Not just the natives, as you call the crew, but apparently Dmitry is in some kind of league with them. You need to be careful."

"I try to think how you would be cared for if anything happens to me. I knew the risks getting into all this special work—from the regime, the city, the local police, and now my assistant and crews. I'm quite isolated. I have no family to speak of and no real friends."

"What can I do about this? How can I help?"

"I suggest you keep your impressions to yourself."

"What if I talked in my sleep?"

"That could be a problem. I suspect what you say about the crew is correct. All they need is leadership from a higher up, someone who shares their concerns with me. And now they may have Dmitry to organize them. What could Dmitry want? He might want to commercialize my methods and make money. He could do that if I had a sudden accident, and he took over the office. Of course, he's not a trained vet, only an assistant, but that likely wouldn't stop him from getting the job. He might even be able to find a real vet to work under him and do what the job requires while he took all the credit."

"Yikes!" said Fyodor, visibly shaken.

"So you see my predicament here. I've been successful but remain vulnerable. I have no power of any kind except over the crews. And I know my power over them is very weak. I thought that my fiery temper wouldn't hurt anyone. I thought the emotional, verbal, and physical harassment would make them appreciate my praise for them even more. But I was wrong. It only made me look weak and insecure, and they viewed it as simple power harassment."

"Fear not, Doctor! 'That which we are, we are'…quoted Fyodor from something he had read. "You can turn this around. We just have to think it through. Take the high road. If you take the low road, you end up wallowing in manure like your crew. Like pigs in the mud … You get dirty, and the pigs just get mad and eventually will want revenge."

"That's why I need you here as a mate. Steak this evening?"

"Naturally! The first thing you need to do is get the crews back on your side. Stop bullying them and trying to drive a wedge between them and Dmitry. He has no claim on their loyalty other than that he hangs around the kill pens and rides with them on search missions. I know all about him from what I hear."

"Makes me envy your life as a humanized dog in first class. Other than hiring you as my assistant, how can I deal with all this?"

"Who said I want to work for you? It might get me killed! I'd rather read books and chase cars. That's the flaw in your new non-human creature or dog slogan! But back to earth ... We need to think this through clearly to the end."

They sat together in the dimly lit lab and chatted through the night. Krastov sat near his desk drinking tea and smoking cigarettes. Fyodor perched on an easy chair across from him and chewed on a small bone to help him move his thoughts along in a practical manner. The radio quietly played Chopin piano concertos. It was an edifying spectacle. From a distance, it was a normal dog and his master in an office. On closer inspection, they chatted quietly as comrades, trying to work out solutions to a pressing problem.

"Here's how I see it," Dr. Ivan. "You are a serious medical professional thrown into a bureaucratic, public safety job that is beneath your skills and education. You have involuntarily lived like your underlings, driving around in vans shooting and eradicating strays by darting them and coaxing some of them into your clutches for experiments. You have to do this and, in part, enjoy it because it so different from your normal life. Your mind still soars, and you like to put practices into theories, but you also like to ham it up with the boys, racing the van, and making engine sounds like you are in a war. It's fun. Am I right so far?"

"You have figured me out! You are perceptive beyond both your canine and human years!"

"To continue, you would like to do something original as a contribution to vet science and to humanity. You have already done that, and I am living proof of it. But you have to keep it quiet and still get no credit for anything. Now what?"

"Yes, now what? From what you say, both the work and even you could be in jeopardy."

"Let's talk that through. Let's do that away from here. I need a walk! Bring the leash so we will look like a normal dog owner and his pet."

They got in the van and drove across town, parking near the Iset riverwalk. Fyodor rode in front, looking out the window just like a normal dog. It was late, and there was no traffic or people to bother about. They began strolling along the riverwalk pathway. Krastov brought along his signature umbrella with the steel handle and attached pepper spray canister. It literally rained cats and dogs around here, and he needed to be ready for anything.

They headed towards town on the pathway. The lights of town twinkled and were an intoxicating spectacle. It felt free to fill the lungs with real air, not the chemically-treated vapors that typically flooded the lab. The absence of the excessively bright lab lights with their annoying buzz were a luxury as well; he might as well be working in a morgue.

"First, you need to keep doing your job. Nothing physically will change—you still have the same productivity mandates, equipment, staff, and schedules to meet. But you can change your staff relations and thereby your whole job."

"How?"

"Stop bullying them. Treat them as equals because whether you like it or not, they are in this system. So like Pavlov gave out treats to motivate his lab dogs, throw office parties and hand out incentives to them. No more shaming! You need to exude some real, hearty bonhomie with them."

"Sensible."

"I've learned this from your training and the books you have given me. But hold it Doc, I think we have some live ones at 2 o'clock."

Four dogs were approaching them fast in a suspicious phalanx from up ahead. They moved silently and had all the markings of a pack that was used to working together. The group leader moved towards Fyodor. Krastov fumbled with his umbrella, trying unsuccessfully to get it open.

"Shit! It's stuck."

He then grabbed the teargas canister and promptly fired a powerful burst into his own face! He doubled over cursing, trying to wipe the tears away so he could at least see. Fyodor emitted a low growl, moving forward with fur standing on end of his neck. He deftly grabbed the head dog behind his neck, shook him a few times, and threw him to the ground. Amazed, the dog retreated back through his comrades, who then turned and scampered off behind him.

"Here, Doc," said Fyodor handing him a handkerchief from his own pocket. "Wipe it away. It shouldn't last long, unless you try and attack them again."

"Very funny! Damn umbrella!" he swore. "That's the third time I've sprayed myself. Nothing works."

"If the day crews were doing their jobs, we wouldn't have to put up with more vicious strays like that! Just kidding ... Are you ok now, Doctor?"

"And what about you? I was more worried that they would hurt you; I didn't realize that you could still fight like a real dog."

"I am still 50 percent the street dog you once found. Remember that," he said, perching down and pulling out his bone from Krastov's coat. He proceeded to chew it with one paw like a stick of candy. Then he stood up on his hind legs, leaned against the river wall and chewed the bone with both paws.

"Stop that, Fyodor, don't do that! Someone might snap a photo and then what would I say?"

"Just say that some dogs like chasing cars. Mine likes to stand around and chew bones instead."

"Damn it, Fyodor, be careful!"

Krastov was understandably petulant and testy now. But Fyodor could see that he was more humiliated than hurt by the episode. There was a bond of confidence between them, and Fyodor wouldn't risk it knowingly. He realized he was often reckless due to his remaining doggy instincts that at times ignored risk. After giving him a while to let him cool off, he continued:

"The attack by these lowlife strays underscores the need to get the crews to see their jobs as public services and challenges to improve their own performance. You want them to have more trust and respect for you."

"Indeed," said Krastov, still wiping his eyes and face. "How?"

"Right now your motivational technique is to shame the crew by making them roll in ditches full of manure. That's medieval and cruel! That method needs to be scrapped, and you need new ones, don't you?"

"OK, that's obvious."

"You could start with an afternoon party and let everyone knock off early that day. Then announce the need for motivational songs. The crew could submit song lyrics for prizes. We'll found a local rap group and call them the "Mutt Rappers" to fit with the city and regime's needs for upbeat music. They could sing out the ditties, and you would hand out the prizes. Or, we could sponsor a poster contest—submit the best motivational poster. You know, slogans on them like: 'Let's get going now. Make it more bow, wow, bow, wow! The poster should inspire positive thinking."

"What's in those bones you chew, cocaine?"

"OK, obviously these gimmicks won't work. They're hokey and could encourage backlash and ridicule. So we go to the next steps: financial and non-financial incentives for performance out on the search and removal missions. Except we change the metrics to favor capture, sterilization, adoption, or release over the currently preferred ends of shooting and killing ..."

"Sounds more like it. Might even get the crew to come around."

"Now let's go to the next step: your future.

"I just want to keep working in my lab and achieve more successes like you."

"Those goals are not enough. You will lose all that unless you aim much higher. Didn't Nietzsche say: 'Man is something that must be overcome'? The civil service is a dead end here. Nothing but the usual turf, ego, and power game all the way until retirement—unless you are outplayed beforehand by some power-hungry shirker and lose your retirement. You know that from years of service. The acquisition of power has the greatest attraction for the lowest natures. And you are surrounded by lowly natures. Am I painting an exaggerated picture?" Fyodor said, taking a chomp of his bone.

"No. It may be even worse than that. The city wants measurable results. The public complains no matter what the results are, and I become the point man—the obvious throat to choke. There are deserving and unfortunate citizens who need protection and safety from us."

"That's the spirit. You are audacious, adventurous, and charismatic; use those qualities right now."

"I get it. That could be the departmental motto: 'To protect and to keep us safe!' But worthy publics are often silenced by professional anger merchants who detest us no matter what we do."

"I see this additional predicament for you," said Fyodor. "The civil service is a dead end. I know what you do, but also what you really are—your deeper values and preferences."

"Not bad for a dog! You could also be a shrink as well as a senior manager. Maybe psychological testing by you in the human resources department for recruitment of new employees in a firm or government someplace."

"So we need to think of some new roles for you where you can be more at ease with yourself. Several options: I know you like dogs despite what you say and do. There are now nonprofits around here that want humane treatment of strays, like I used to be. They want to see kennels for domestic violence centers, more pounds for adoption purposes, and sterilization as a longer-term solution. From hearing Dmitry and the crew talk, I know there is someone named Krylovsky who heads an animal rights group here. He apparently wants to stop stray killing before and after the Games so the crew is set against him and his type. Have you heard of him?"

"No. But he is probably part of the professionally angry public that the city complains to me about all the time. The worse thing that could happen for his types is that we eliminate all the strays, and he loses his issue and supporters."

"So what? That's his problem! You said I was like a shrink. Not really... I am loyal to my master, and my master is proud of me. Is he not? We have a confidence pact unlike the relationship between the monstrosity and Dr. Victor Frankenstein, if you've read that one."

Here Krastov eyed him as a dog that might be angling for a bigger bone for himself. Between comments, Fyodor emitted low growls that hinted of hidden anger and ambition. He wondered where all this flattery was leading. Krastov was suddenly suspicious.

"Of course, I've read it. Who hasn't?'

"Then you must know that what you've created in me is something totally different, a new type of race, if you will. Not the 'new man' you've been trumpeting, an army of mindless drones marching off to the factories or to war. Dr. Frankenstein's monster was a creature of id that yielded to disappointment and murders. But as your trusted agent, I have a superego and guilt, duty-bound against violence and killing. Why? Because I know what instincts dogs have: they are inside me, and they must be disciplined by my superego. I know what is wrong and what should be done to do right."

"Does that mean you won't steal food, drink out of toilets, and go through the garbage pails when I'm not looking and not try to chase cars anymore?"

"I'm working on it, Doc!"

"Glad to hear it!" said Krastov, as he motioned for them to sit down on one of the benches overlooking the river.

"Let's get back to your singular greatness, your uniqueness as a scientist and a man. I think I can describe them because as your canine 'creation' I can describe your darkest wishes and deeds. You're not a Frankenstein's monster out to kill your family and friends. But you have negative impulses that need to be harnessed and directed. I think I can help defeat your enemies out of loyalty to you and move you into a position that you should rightfully have by now."

"Go on..."

"You've been thinking of options because you are dissatisfied with the crude methods employed by the regime and the city. You know they can't work because they didn't work most recently in Sochi. Strays ran around biting people during the Winter Olympics, which embarrassed Putin, the city, and Russia before the entire world. The chic FIFA people remained above everything at the ground level. Working in the great Zurich 'hot air machine,' they didn't get their hands dirty and didn't know or care about anything except their next lavish ceremonies and meals where they'd show off their broad grins and hug and con-gratulate each other on pulling off another spectacle. Rabid stray dogs would spoil all that in Yekaterinburg so remember, you are merely their lackey, a hired hand."

"I know what they stand for and what they do. I'd be working for the Russian deep state, which Orwell once said was 'as conscious as ever of the truth, but as wedded as ever to lies.' But I do get a real rush on search and destroy missions!"

"Just like a 12-year-old. But where has it gotten you? Where does it lead you? It's like the dead-end jobs around here flipping burgers for tour-ists that end with the seasons and nothing more. Look at yourself honestly. You understand what it means to explore unknown forces and the need to reveal the deepest mysteries of creation through practical demonstrations. Not through the popular gene-editing of the day and creation of test-tube dog-people to run around loose. You are using your judgment to try and identify and to work with the right dogs to create a humanized version of the original dog. That means only you know what to look for in the target dogs. You avoid the swivel-eyed loons, the ones with foaming mouths, and look out for smiling tame ones. And you find them. I even know you have at least three more promising apprentices in separate cages that you are working on called Tsar, Alexander, and Anton."

Krastov was getting impatient with all this and looked at his watch. "We should be getting back."

"Let me finish, Doc."

"OK, but let's start walking."

"You are a philosopher doing veterinary science—that rare per-son, from what I read, who combines natural philosophy with science. You didn't want to be a freak, trying to animate lifeless matter from a random corpse like Dr. Victor, but, like Dr. Moreau, modifying what already lives. You deliberately avoided playing God with the usual ex-pectation of gratitude by blind religious followers, bowing and scrap-ing in your wake. Instead, you wanted to save strays, get them homes if possible, help them fend for themselves, maybe make them useful but allow them to retain their doggy habits. I still play with toys, chew bones, and chase rubber balls. I can also still fight like a dog. That's the way it should be for all of us!

"By contrast, do you know how we see most of you humans? You are the cruelest creatures on earth. You torture, kill, maim, and taunt us. You run us over with your cars and leave us for dead. You experiment on us in your labs and are unsuccessful most of the time. The failures are discarded like so much rancid meat behind the worst markets. The ones who survive, like me, provide benefits for human health and longevity, but hardly ever for other dogs. At the same time you are the best creatures on earth, providing us love, homes, families, and care, and we protect and care for you in return. We know there are many empathetic veterinarians out there. You are the best example of the two types of humans that we all see. Make up for it and give us strays homes and health. Let us be ourselves and serve you!"

"Nice speech Fyodor! It just means we let you go through the garbage and chase all the cars you want, right?"

"Come on … Deep down you like us to cavort and ham it up. You like to see us express remorse for these bad habits, hanging our heads in shame for capping in your houses and chewing up the furniture. You know we are just begging for another chance! We just like to play all the time—stealing, fetching, and scrapping. Some humans don't get it and think we're serious and need to be re-educated. Clueless bipeds! Think back thousands of years ago. How did our wolf ancestors and you people get together? Of course we liked to steal your food, but you noticed that we also chased sticks and protected you at night with timely barks. That cemented the deal. You liked us to clown around, and your kids especially adopted us as pets. We protected them and helped you with your hunts—procuring food and, of course, getting cuts for ourselves. Pretty clever, eh?"

"Nonsense!"

"You know it's all true. More importantly, you didn't come up with the idea that I needed a bitch for a companion like Dr. Victor's monster. The last thing I or any other self-respecting stud needs is a bitch ordering me around, interrupting my reading and thinking. I serve you and don't need someone else to take orders from."

"Glad to hear it. I'll make sure my candidates are all male. The male dog preference should work as long as the strays are still out there, and I can adopt the right dog. As you noted, Tsar, Alexander, and Anton are males and seem to be learning fast. I may put you to work soon training them—especially in the speech area."

"That's the way to go. You recognize that being a real dog and a fine specimen of humanity are not mutually exclusive. That's why you are unique and have to go forward, out of this constricted little world and this job. I suggest you establish a nonprofit organization right now dedicated to animal welfare. You have the top-level support at official levels to do this. I also suggest you talk to the animal rights people but stay separate from them, as you don't know what they do in the shadows. I hear some of their tactics are pretty brutal—against humans!"

"Not bad, Fyodor. You've been doing some strategic thinking!"

"I further suggest that you put me in charge of that organization as head dog, which we might call something like 'Paws for Russia.' If the city claims you achieved your scientific feats on their time, offer to share profits with them with funds generated going to cover kennel, boarding, licensing, and inoculation expenses for strays and potential adoptees. Don't waste time fighting with them. Just get out. What do you think?"

"It all sounds good, except the part where we suddenly put a dog in charge. You want to be top dog right away. But we will have to do this in stages, maybe introduce you during the establishment process."

"Agreed. Bring on my role later in the circus. We don't want to shock the world all at once, do we?"

"Obviously not. But there's one big flaw in all these fine plans—Dmitry," said Krastov.

"I mentioned how we can pre-empt his authority by getting the crew on your side. The bigger problem is that even then, he might not follow along. He might not just wither away."

"He won't. I can expect that he will engage even in blackmail to get my secrets and worse, which might mean threats to you in the process.

'Give me the secrets plus money, or I expose you and threaten or maybe kill Fyodor'."

Fyodor thought about that one, quietly chewing his bone and looking out at the river. Both of them were silent for a time. His furry brow furrowed in deep concern.

"Remember, I am still only half human. I have my dog instincts as you just saw on the riverwalk, albeit with a superego added for ethical guidance."

"And I am still fully human, but partially guided by my superego. Since we know what they have planned for me, we could try and turn the tables on them," replied Krastov.

Fyodor offered him a bite of his bone with his paw, which he petulantly pushed away.

"Let's see if the crew responds, and Dmitry comes around. Then we have time to ease you out of here. If that doesn't work, Fyodor, accidents do happen. I'm sure Dmitry thinks the same way about me—accidents can be made to happen."

"Woof! Woof!"

"You need to work on that. It sounds like a put on."

7 FIFA

Later that week, Nicholas Krylov was sitting in his new office in the Politology Department at USU looking out the window. The view was onto a quad surrounded by older brick buildings linked together by landscaped paths filled with students coming and going to classes. It could have been a college anywhere, even Elmira, NY.

"Knock, Knock," came from the door. It was Ivan, who in the tradition of the effortless millennial world would rather articulate a knock than make the effort with his knuckles.

"Saw you were in and thought I'd stop by to see what you were doing this morning."

Today Andrey wore a white shirt with rolled-up sleeves, making him look almost like a matchstick with a large shiny bundle of hair on top thrown down his back into a pony-tale. He must not have weighed more than 150 pounds. His little spectacles complemented the merry little grin that he flashed regularly. The impression was of a man who saw things and felt deeply about humanity and its follies, and thought it all was pretty amusing. A perfect portrait of the young modern cynic, a student in no hurry to graduate, who plied his trade at the university.

"Thought I'd hit the library after I finish gazing out the window for another hour or so. It's how I get my thoughts moving in Elmira. I call it the Elmira Method, alternating periods of intense reflection and day-dreaming … should work here too, don't you think?"

"Exactly, I thought that might be what you are doing. Much can be gained from gazing outwards," he said with a casual puff on what seemed to be a permanently lit cigarette.

"I spoke with Yevgeny earlier, and he set me up with a contact at FIFA locally. We could meet him in the Raddison coffee shop at 10 this morning. Up for it?"

"Thanks for doing this."

"I also thought Anna should tag along as we might discuss city goings on that you may not know about and should hear of. Her ladylike presence might encourage the guy to spring for the bill."

"All good …"

We moved down the hall to her office. On the way, Risanovsky walked by, and I nodded to him. "Thanks for the suggestion. We are headed to meet the FIFA man now."

"He's a Brit from some ex-colony I understand. Maybe South African," said Risanovsky. "He goes by the name Greg Gold, which could be his name or one of their football teams. Who knows?"

Anna heard us and came out ready to go. "Let's go play some round football as you Americans call it."

"Remember, I'm at least half Russian, maybe even 25 percent Cossack. And growing up in New York City, I prefer baseball."

"Baseball?" she said with a mocking smile. "Isn't that even more boring than cricket?"

Anna decided they would drive to the hotel, avoiding the crowds on the morning trams and basking in the luxury of being able to direct her own vehicle toward a destination. Life's small victories! I sat in the back of the departmental Lada, known locally as a *Zhiguli*, and listened to them chat, occasionally interrupting to ask what this or that monument or building was. After a few minutes, it was clear who was in charge. She knew the way around town and to the hotel while Ivan clearly wasn't switched on to directions or locations. He had a more languid, circular, non-linear mode of thinking while she was definitely the planner: skillful and polite but moving us toward the objective most efficiently.

"Andrey, watch out for Chekov Street. It should be coming up."

He glanced right. "Nothing around here."

A few minutes later, "Ivan, I need to follow a street behind the hotel. See the hotel? It's at least 50 stories in case you don't notice it."

"OK, but what's the street behind it? Do you mean parallel to it?"

"Never mind... here it is. OK, now I have to park; see anything on the street available?"

Silence as they both darted their heads back and forth while moving the car forward. "Nothing around here." said Ivan at about the same time as she did a U-turn and parked almost in front of the hotel. "Well, maybe one spot," he said, looking back at me with the self-effacing smile of the poorly performing student caught out in front of class.

Despite his delicate air of professional student that expressed complex thoughts in soft whispers, Ivan had that scraggly warrior look. That meant there was probably some Cossack blood in him, something like me. He reminded me of a friend I had at college: intellectually alive, a bit unhinged, merry laughing eyes, a radical critic of all things, cynical, philosophical, and abstract to the point of boredom, but surprisingly practical at times. Like him, Ivan had a keen intellect and spoke in a wry formalistic language. It was like hearing a Nabokov novel being read to you—full of outrageous gallows humor. As we moved towards the front of the hotel, he apologized for his lack of focus to Anna and told her that he was a bit discombobulated because he was almost mugged last night.

"What? You were almost mugged?" I asked, overhearing this.

"It happens all the time around here—surprise attacks by muggers, assaults by packs of wounded and misbegotten dogs, and kidnaps by terrorists. It's a real tourist mecca. If tourists really knew about all this, they most certainly would avoid the Games. You should be careful...."

She stopped in the street and grabbed him by his skinny frame with both hands. "Alright Andrey, stop theorizing and tell us what happened."

"Two guys emerged from the darkened surroundings of my neighborhood to directly confront me. They looked quite persuasive, being of stocky builds and razor cuts that accentuated their shiny, dented skulls. It was otherwise a placid evening, I had to admit. I had just partaken of a modest but hearty meal of rabbit and artichokes with a glass of nice Georgian red."

"All right, Ivan, then what?' she said.

"They seemed to know I would be coming which intrigued me for a millisecond. They may have been in the restaurant and seen me display some ready cash from my carrying case. We were paid by USU last week, you recall. Anyway, there they were."

"Did they hit you?"

"Actually, they didn't get to that phase. They moved forward in a small phalanx," he said in his lyrical, stagey way of expression. "It was an old-fashioned show of force."

"And?"

"Fortunately, I carry this small derringer in the back in my pants," he said, reaching back and showing the faded, silver mini-pistol to us. "It fires two shots, one for each of them, and they knew it. I quietly drew it and took a bead on them. They looked at it in unison like raccoons caught in some headlights. They started to back away, muttering something about being peaceful people out for a walk and that they would report me to the police. I told them to check with Inspector Simon Petrovsky at headquarters, as the gun was a gift from him. I also told them that he taught me how to use it. I didn't tell them that the lessons were a waste of time, as I couldn't hit anything, having deficient eyesight that inhibited my aim. With these words exchanged, they withdrew into the shadows and disappeared down the street. Through the use of intelligence, perfect timing, luck, and a meaningful looking pistol, I narrowly escaped the prowess of my muscular visitors."

"Good work, Andrey!" I said, giving him a pat on the shoulder.

Entering the capacious lobby of the hotel, we were hit with waves of soft background music that was like the chemical tang of an artificial sweetener. It was always there when conversation paused. It filled the silence with bright, inauthentic, and inoffensive tunes picked by some Muzak algorithm, similar probably to what they play in a morgue or the back office of an undertaker's. It droned on, filling the silence while we absorbed Ivan's harrowing story.

"Andrey," I said, "you have to be careful; they will probably return some night. They know about where you live."

"Not likely. They can find far easier pickings in this city. Most of them without derringers."

Towards the back of the lobby inside the five-star hotel, we found the restaurant and sat down at a table in the back after telling the manager whom we were expecting. The hotel was the typical, gaudy, red-curtained palace used by the self-important worldwide for meetings and deals. Not sure how we fit the mold, but here we were.

"Andrey, really, you have to be careful ... If something happens to you, I lose all my contacts at the city!" I said to him, trying to keep a straight face. "I hate dealing with bullies, especially when they are also muggers. I was confronted all the time by thugs like that when growing up in the Bronx and going to college around Spanish Harlem. The younger boys like me were always picked on. It was a kind of natural pecking order in high-density urban slums. You had to live with it. They sometimes roughed me up and took the few cents I had off me. Other times, they just beat the shit out of me for fun."

"What did you do?"

"I had no gun, because in the mean streets in the U.S. that was always a big mistake—someone always had a bigger gun than you. So, I resorted to fisticuffs. I boxed at a local sports club, which helped for self-defense. The problem was they didn't play by ring rules on the streets, and since they were always bigger, I got beaten up a lot anyway. But eventually, I grew bigger and was able to fend off most of them. I only recommend the getting hardware method to simplify matters if you have no other choices. I do like your derringer though. Must be where 'derring-do' comes from!"

"By the way, I want you to meet my police inspector friend, Simon Petrovsky, soon. I told him about you, and he wants to meet."

"Sure, Andrey. I'm clean!" I said, showing him my palms. "Speaking of clean hands, who is this guy we are meeting here from FIFA?"

"I met him last year in the city planning office through my husband. Ivan met him once later," Anna said. "Not to prejudice anyone, but he's full of himself—self-important and wildly overconfident," she added.

"Was he always like that or did the job make him slimy?" asked Ivan.

"In his mind, he's probably a big womanizer. At least he tries to be. He spent a lot of time checking me over and making exaggerated claims about himself to impress me."

"Come on Anna, why would he look at you?" said Andrey.

She made a quick theatric gesture with her shoulders and winked both eyes at us. Then she popped Ivan with her napkin. "Some people still do!" she said with pretend wounded vanity.

"He works for the director of FIFA operations for Sverdlovsk Oblast, Yeveny Kuyvashev, who is in charge of local games here. As you might know, Kuyvashev is a Putin confident. So everything is run from Moscow, and everyone here reports up to them."

"Not surprised that you think he is full of himself, " said Andrey. "The whole FIFA organizational culture is full of itself. Nobody knows what those people do from their swank operations in Zurich. Their cash cow is the annual World Cup where bribes and payoffs are regularly exchanged from top country officials who want their locales selected as the host. Country team managers and even players are often part of the opaque web of corruption. The Zurich police arrested several of their execs over alleged bribery in 2015 at the modest locale of the Baur au Lac hotel. Their headquarters nearby were not swank enough so they frequent another five-star hotel in the neighborhood to do their business. So here we are in Russia where Putin is the real point man. I wonder what is going on with cash flows to and from the Kremlin?"

"Oh nothing suspicious, I imagine," smirked Anna.

An odd blur streaked across behind Ivan, and we suddenly had a new guest at the table. He glided in soundlessly and unobtrusively, perhaps in the style of FIFA. Beaming with a broad smile for all of us, he introduced himself, in English. As he switched on an enameled smile, he deftly held out cards between his fingers on his left hand and extended his right for shaking. A polished man on the move!

"Sorry I'm late. Greg Gold," he said to us, as he quickly handed out the cards. He then shook all our hands vigorously. "Anna, I believe we met here last year, and you're looking fresh as always. Andrey, I think we also met sometime this year in the city offices. And you are?" he asked me.

"This is Dr. Nicholas Krylov from the U.S., who is here at USU for the summer doing research on planning for the Cup games, and also teaching us about American methods for large events planning," said Ivan.

"Wonderful, you must know some English!"

"I'm half Russian," I said in the local dialect."

"Capital!" he said. "I'm sorry, but I have to be at a FIFA gathering nearby in 30 minutes, but I wanted to meet with all of you and answer any questions. If anything further is needed, I am assigning my staff to help you."

"We understand. Given the time constraint, could we ask you about something slightly more pointed ... which are your planning methods for the many stray dogs that we have here. You recall that was a major problem in Sochi," said Anna.

"We've decided to issue thousands of laced treats and send the dogs unconsciously to France so Bridgette Bardot can deal with them in her inimitable ways."

"Oh, that's a good one!" said Anna, with a loud clap of laughter. She clasped her hands with gushing abandon just under the surface. She then winked at him to continue her mimicry of the impressionable maiden.

"What a card!" I thought.

A waiter appeared, and Gold simply ordered an espresso. The rest of us had more espressos and asked for some croissants and jam.

Gold talked fast, filling us in about coordination with city offi-cials, logistics, animal control methods, potential success and failure rates, back-up plans, and finally plans to deal with the pesky media that might want to spoil the party here. In his slick presentation, he had all the answers and few questions. He showed special force when he stressed how he and his people could make the problems go away. He seemed like the usual fixer type as he explained all this to Andrey and Anna. I usually saw types like this on the front pages of tabloids as they were carted off to jail, claiming they were framed. I tried to figure this guy. A stocky man of about 5'5", he wore a double-breasted suit and loud tie to contrast with a mod pink dress shirt. He spoke with a British-Australian accent with traces of cockney. His face was smooth and framed by a large bush of manicured hair. His accent could mean working class origins with efforts to upgrade into the elite class (economy plus?). That was often the channel to acquire the right behavioral and linguistic qualities, that is, careful attention to the codes and nuances of casual conversations. I had met people like that in my overseas work that at first wrong-footed me. I learned of the put-on Oxbridge accent. It was like trying to cover up your Bronx accent and City College education to fit in with the Princeton-type grads and posh officials. In the U.S., we could easily smell these kinds of lame efforts but not in the Commonwealth cultures apparently.

But he talked too fast. He had an annoying motor-mouth and was not a listener at all. Seemed like the standard salesman type, obviously better paid than most. He couldn't stop rolling his eyes around evasively as if hiding something suspicious about himself. My bullshit alarms went off—here was a happy-talker, one of the many high-paid hucksters I'd met over the years. My Bronx pals from high school and college might say that he was the oratorical type, a talking-over stranger. But he still had flaws in his act to the trained eye. For instance, he never looked at any of us intently. He wasn't able to engage our attention and never solicited feedback. He had the word. Instead, he threw around quick glances, eyes darting back and forth between us, winking at us (but at whom?) for emphasis and occasionally blinking both eyes for even more emphasis. He was selling the games, reiterating the official and public complaints about nasty wild dogs of Yekaterinburg, telling us implicitly to fix the stray dog problem (which one?), and finally offering discount meals to us to the other swank hotels and associated five-star restaurants. If this were baseball, he had struck out at least five times in less than an hour!

But it was an entertaining morning for me at least. As he presented his little show, Anna was really getting into it, looking at him approvingly, hamming it up as the awe-struck local with loud giggles and clapping. She seemed to enjoy stringing people like this along, and here it worked to continue his theatrics. He thought she was impressed! Ivan seemed to be struggling with his face to avoid bursting out in spasms of laughter at the wrong time. To avoid that mistake, he timed his laughter to match Gold's attempts at humor. Only the laughs were a bit too loud. One had to be careful about knowing when and when not to laugh if faced by a speaker who was a humorless dolt who relied on sneering mockery of others for laughs.

"So you see the kinds of incompetents I am dealing with in government at the ministries here," he said taking a gulp of his espresso. He must have chugged the whole thing! Do the Brits know what espresso is? To stay wired and on his game, he probably avoided milk tea and chugged shots of espresso.

"Some of the officials even wanted the stray cats picked up... not just all the dogs!" he went on.

"O, that's really rich," shouted out Anna as Ivan doubled over with his bright red face, pulling his chair back from the table and using his napkin to wipe away a profuse flow of tears. They were all over his face. They could tell that I wasn't the demonstrative type, so I got away with smiling and shaking my head on cue.

Gold suddenly threw a large arm skyward allowing him to check his large gold watch. "Sorry, I've really got to run. I'd like to stay for a bit more of this 'chin wag,' but I have to be at a meeting with the mayor at city hall. Thanks for everything. You have my cards now so give me a ring." And as swiftly as he had arrived, like a submarine he silently cruised through the lobby and was gone.

FIFA must specialize in forgettable characters like this. Where do they find these people? Imagine, we had a "chin wag!" What the fuck was that? Maximum trivialized conversation, I suppose. Who was *not* forgettable was Anna. Her refined beauty was on full display, and I watched her mind work with emotional tact in action. She positively beamed with playful energy as she went where her mind drove her. For me, it was her steady emphatic look when we talked that revealed the authentic personage she was. How could I have not noticed any of this when talking with her as I patched up her dog bites at my flat? She had gently made a fool of this guy while he thought she was impressed by his genius as a 'can do' operator plying his trade! To us, he was just another deluded power-hungry pimp. The depressing thing is that he was probably successful at what he did, and FIFA was full of his types—and not just FIFA. Other institutions like universities produced their fair share of deluded misfits, but in that tragi-comedy the stakes were so low that it rarely mattered to the outside world.

The background music played soft rock in the restaurant, fitting for the tacky trimmings of this concrete and brass palace. I would often put on different songs in my head to ward off the murdering of silence by Muzak in elevators, stores, and hotels everywhere. Still, I'd been in shops, fast-food eateries, even drugstores where the Muzak tunes hit me hard. They brought back a childhood incident, an old girlfriend, a cherished dog, even my parents, who I had treated so badly. I wanted the names of them so I could get CDs, tapes, or records. That was usually impossible. How do you describe a tune to someone if you don't even know the artist? The song we heard now burrowed into my head with old associations and flashbacks from bars and restaurants I'd been in years ago.

Turn around go back down back the way you came.
Can't you see that flash of fire ten times brighter than the day?
And behold a mighty city broken in the dust again.
Oh God pride of man broken in the dust again.

Instead of Gordon Lightfoot from the '70s, why wasn't my head filled with Purcell's 'Song for the Funeral of Queen Mary' or Prokofiev's 'Romeo and Juliet'? Some music just made me jump and throw my fists into the air!

"Hey, let's get some food. After that sorry performance, I need to be rejuvenated. My stomach is growling, and they have a nice buffet here. It's on me, or my grant to be more exact. You can thank Bonaduz College!"

We headed over to the long buffet bar and started filling up our plates. Standing next to me was a large man of indeterminately youthful age, but about 6' 4" and wearing a WAXQ Rock New York t-shirt. As he filled up his plate with some kind of eggs, I admired the stylishness of his shiny jet-black hair, slicked back, and wide handlebar mustache. He was right out of a vaudeville show—he had to be Oil Can Harry! Oddly enough, he was dressed in tuxedo pants but no black coat or white shirt and tie. Probably forgot them in the rush to get breakfast.

"Hey, that's my favorite FM station! I grew up in the Bronx waiting to hear what they would play next instead of studying!"

He was stunned, first to hear English, then the New York accent. But he grinned widely and threw out his hand. "Ron Slaton," he said, "I'm here with a small acting crew doing a movie."

"A film! Imagine! We don't meet many actors in our lines of business. Why not join us over there and tell us more about what you're doing?"

So he did. When he arrived at the table, I introduced Slaton to the group as an actor in town doing a movie. Andrey and Anna were at first perplexed, then impressed by his thick New York English. They were both good at English, but were trying to figure out who this guy was and what he was saying. Not a tourist, not a spy, not an academic, and definitely not an embassy type. "Who the hell is he?" they were probably thinking?

He sat down with his pile of food, pushed his mustache back slightly, looked us over with a smile, and took a large chomp of something meaty looking. "We haven't eaten since yesterday. Long shooting schedules... Can't seem to get the scenes right, you know," he mumbled. "I mean we're not Hollywood's best you understand—bit parts as 'consultants' when we can get them. This film sounded good to all of us, and the money is good."

"Ron, tell us about your film." I said.

"The story is the easy part."

Here he hunched down, grimaced to show his large teeth, and threw a large napkin over his head.

"Giff me you neck! I vant your blot!" he said with a cackle. "It's just filming it that's tough. As I say, we're all amateurs working on short-term contracts. The plot is a modern take on Dracula with different historical roots."

"Sounds like my kind of film," said Anna in clipped British English. Listening more carefully to her now, she must have learned her English at a posh local school or abroad. Or she was doing a nice imitation of someone who had.

"In this one, Anton Dracula is a young Russian schizophrenic living right around town here. He's probably Chechen with a name like that … fantasizes about sucking on women's flesh and puncturing them with his sharp teeth, using some neo-vampire flair like his namesake. I play a bespectacled shrink, who plods along explaining his bizarre turns of behavior with rational textbook-like precision in big psychological terms like 'psychotic pervert' and making inane statements like, 'are you certain those are teeth marks on her neck? They look more like mosquito bites to me!' You know the type— the audience urges him onwards, 'Come on you moron, he's a real blood-sucker; do something! Get off your ass and do something!' But nobody does, and the film moves along to its predictable climax."

Slaton was really getting into it now. "Dracula believes he is possessed by the real eighteenth century vampire and that a cure for his own mental problems lies in the text of Shelley's *Dracula* somewhere. But the shrink—that's me—misses the larger picture, and Anton Dracula continues on his rampage, drinking blood from several women, contaminating them like a rabid dog. Great plot, eh? It's another B film, but at least we get paid. As luck would have it, I don't have any more parts once this film is done."

"Then what?" I asked.

"I head back to Marina del Rey to my marina condo and sail around the bay until I get another part. Same for the rest of the crew unless they can find something else in the next weeks. That's the business for minor actors like us. We have no solid careers, but a few skills we can peddle."

"Sounds tough." said Andrey, who followed along his English as best as he could.

"You get used to it. Just like the weekly 'tremors' or minor earthquakes and occasional forest fires we have in LA. This day could be really good or bad. But hell, on the bay you don't feel the flames or tremors, just the sea breezes and sun. Somehow, we survive. To an outsider, the place sounds like an insane place to live."

"It sounds like many of my friends in the foreign aid business who live from one short-term gig to another all over the world," I said. "Unlike you guys, some of them have no permanent homes anywhere. No place to come back to between jobs. No home bases."

The loud sound of a door banging nearby interrupted us, and we were joined by a large burley figure standing by our table wearing what appeared to be colored rags and pieces of burlap. Flashing a big toothy grin, he looked more like a medieval barbarian, unshaven with long shaggy hair worked into a ponytail. His tiny dark shades looked like black pennies on a flimsy wired frame. Barrel-chested, he sported a little beard with colored knots in it. He nodded to all of us and sat down.

"You look like you need a strong double espresso," Slaton said.

"Two of them! Pronto!" he said with a weary grin. "We've been all over town. There must be hundreds of lively bars and hot clubs in this place—hard to take them all in. We should stick around after the film and check them all out. And the music—gypsy ballads, Chechen village songs, pop hits—amazing! The more they sing and play, the thirstier you get. And I've never seen so many fine women ... What ho? Here's another one!" he bellowed, gazing at Anna. "Sorry, madam, I can't help myself around such refined beauties!" he mumbled, flashing a shy grin at her.

"Everyone, this is Bill Roberts, who will be known worldwide for his role in this film as Dracula," said Slaton. "He plays the vampire as an outrageous wild man in the film, which is quite close to his normal character as you see here. He's been out all night drinking with his friends and the rest of the crew, which accounts for the strong smell of cheap booze. Still from instinct, here he's right on time for breakfast."

"Dracula should control himself in public! This is Russia, not Texas!" Anna said to all of us.

"Yes, of course! I will remember that and try my best!"

Ivan was impressed by his theatrics and by the grand entrance of the lead character. "Could I see your glasses?" he asked.

As the three of them chatted, I asked Slaton about his acting work. It seemed intriguing to find American actors doing an off-beat film this far from home.

"Have you been an actor living in LA long?"

"Not exactly," he said. "I'm actually an MBA who decided business was a bore and went into acting. Profit making is boring, but it does have its uses if it makes money. But inside a firm, the routine is stultifying. I had done some acting while in college in at Columbia in New York City and decided to give it a try for money. So I went to USC for the MBA, and after a nice warm winter there where I could study on the beach, decided it was the place to live. If I couldn't pay my bills, I could always go back and sell incomprehensible financial products like everyone else, such as derivatives, hedges, and swaps. I got a few small parts, and then, after a series of lucky breaks, I graduated to larger parts in B films. Have to say, it's fun and provides me personal freedom as well."

"It must have been a big risk to drop a salaried job for short-term contracts. What gave you the confidence to try it?"

"Well, let me show you. You just do it! Briefly explain to me what you are doing here."

I told him about my research on planning methods to improve city services, in particular animal control and specifically how to deal with the many stray dogs that could threaten the World Cup games. He listened with one ear then picked up his spoon.

"Ladies and gentlemen," he said, solemnly rising and banging his water glass with the spoon. There were about 150 people sitting in the restaurant that morning, mostly attracted by the daily breakfast buffet.

People gave him their good-natured attention. He had just a few seconds before they would get back to eating.

"It gives me a great pleasure to introduce you to our honorable guest, Dr. Nicholas Krylov from Bonaduz College in the U.S., who is an expert on city planning methods. He has travelled the globe and is bringing Yekaterinburg the most modern techniques available to improve their municipal services such as: urban transport, sanitation, water and sewerage, and animal control. A recipient of numerous awards for his work, he is here at Urals State University working with both the City and the Politology Faculty to strengthen their knowledge bases in order to provide the best World Cup Games for you, the citizenry of this fine city!"

With that he led a thunderous round of applause that included "Bravos!" and whistles for several minutes. I took a few bows, waved, and sat down as unobtrusively as possible. The remarkable thing is it was all delivered in English. The breakfast crowd either knew some English, or I looked important enough to get a round of applause.

"Is he your agent?" asked Anna.

"It looks that way!"

"Are all Americans as crazy as you people?" asked Andrey.

"No question about it!" I said. "You never know what we will come up with because we don't either!"

I looked back at Slaton, "In any case I see how and why you became an actor! You're really good, self-confident, quick-witted, and smart. And you apply all these qualities with a straight face that can be molded to any role. A real talent!"

"Unfortunately, I'm one of many with those qualities in the acting market, but thanks for the complements."

As Kostov and Slaton began chatting, I looked over at Anna, whose radiant face was a flaming glow. Her greenish eyes, shining with playful mischief, moved about in playful calculation. She was a cheerful spirit, a bright light. With subtle movements of her arms and body she fell into the habit of tempting me, and several times she caught me looking at her. "When are we going to talk about our team class that we might do this summer?" she asked.

"Anytime you like."

"I suggest you come to dinner. Let me talk with my husband, Semyon Irtenev, and arrange an invitation."

Not sure what her husband and a dinner had to do with our class, but I nodded acceptance. I had crowded a good deal into that day, more than any in the past ten years, probably, and was pleased.

————

I got home later, dead tired from all the new experiences of the day. As I walked down the hall of my flat, I heard something that sounded like crying. Maybe it was a cat or Leo whimpering ... I walked back and found the source. It was coming from inside Sveta's flat on the first floor. I knocked, and there was no answer. I kept knocking to see if Leo would whimper again ... But he could smell me and was silent except for a few expectant sounds that he might be in for a late walk. That was certainly not in the cards. The nearby sobbing sounds continued.

"Sveta, it's me, Nicholas. Open the door. Are you ok?"

Still no sound, but also the crying had stopped so I knew it was she. I heard some movement inside.

"Come on, open up. I got you a present."

I heard the latch retract slowly, and the door cracked open.

"Come in," she said and moved back.

I entered the darkened room and found a chair in the corner.

"OK, what's the matter?"

She sat near me in the dark with only the dim light from the kitchen to reveal her face. She had been crying, as I suspected.

"Come on, I'm here now. You can tell me."

She was in her robe curled up on the couch. I sat down in a chair nearby.

"It's nothing. I get depressed sometimes. I have no real friends except Leo, and I am never here for him. You are the only one who walks him."

My past lady friends had consistently accused me of insensitivity and selfishness. I loved them all at one point. I know I did! The ones who didn't dump me outright gave me this message of outrage regularly. They generally said I got tired of them after sex and would push on to the next conquest and source of instant pleasure and passion just like a dog moving from one bitch to the next. They were right, except that I was also loyal to the ones I really liked. Have to give myself some credit there ... So it was a matter of personal taste with men, which I suspected changed when men sensed that long-term relations lay ahead. For short-term women like land-ladies and casual hook-ups, it had to be much less— simple, formal, arm's length relations. Naturally these required that the girl understand and agree to the duration and intensity of the relationship, which rarely happened. That made man-woman relations too rational, formal, and mechanistic, which they rarely were in the real world. Jealousy, resentment, and even revenge were often the result of a miscalculation by either party.

"Hey! That can't be true. Leo's here for you, and he knows that I'm just another short-term guest."

"I have no friends. He is my only solace in life. But I am a nurse all day long and have been going to night school to learn welding."

"That's great, Sveta! Nothing wrong with that! A nurse who can weld! Think of it—industrial stitches! How many nurses can weld or welders who can take care of people who get hurt? Remember that some people have no friends at all, and you have a fine dog, Leo."

"I talk to him every night, and he looks at me like he understands. Someone would think I'm crazy for putting my trust in a dog."

"Not me. I think only dogs can be trusted. You can tell when they trust you by their eyes. Strays for obvious reasons don't trust people, and if rescued by someone, still take a long time to establish any real trust. But long-time housedogs like Leo are here for you and will stay by your side no matter what. I can tell by looking at him. That's a real friend."

"Do you think so?"

"I know it's true. I've always confided in my dog, and I've always owned one."

She sat there in the dark in silence. I went over and gave her a hug. The cold I was getting suddenly erupted into a violent fit of coughing.

"I better not get too close as I think I'm getting something. Sveta, I'm dead tired. Let's talk more sometime. I think we have a lot in common. OK?"

"OK, Nicholas. Get some cold tablets from the shelf over there, and take them before you go to bed."

With that I got up, retrieved a few tablets from her bottle, and gave Leo a pat as I left the room. I sensed that her reasons for crying were not simple and would have to be handled in a more extensive discussion later. It might be a productive talk for both of us.

8 DINNER AT THE IRTENEVS

Thunder rolled in the distance and forked lightning with jagged rents struck the ground as we drove toward her house. Anna was driving the family car away from the city and into the surrounding hills and woods towards their home. It was late in a squally day with driving rain and gusting winds. The summer storm was severe, and waves of rain hit the windows in sheets, driven by the powerful wind gusts. She drove with fierce determination and skill along winding narrow roads, some of which were littered with large branches and chunks of broken limbs. I held on tight to the door handle and hoped for the best.

"Where are we going," I asked to break the silence and ensure that she was alert.

"We are now in Leninskiy rayon, which is one of Yekaterinburg's 29 districts. It's getting dark, but you may be able to make out the thick forests with occasional lodges in them. We have one of them farther up the road. We have been going up into the smaller mountains west of the city, which is why it's colder. You're not cold, are you?"

"Why no, just refreshed," I said, gripping the door tightly as she roared around curves, tires barely clinging to the road. Several times, the car actually skidded, but she skillfully turned into the skid and kept going.

"Are we getting close?"

She glanced quickly at me and flashed me a wry grin: "Not scared, are you?"

Was that the inside of my mouth getting dry just now? I threw a lame smile back at her. I hadn't been with a smooth morsel like this in many years. She was one who drove her car as furiously as she probably drove her life. Conflicting emotions, ready to burst . . . now my mouth went into reverse and was watering. All this had stimulated my senses, especially the ones that could feel the heat from the dangerously voluptuous presence nearby.

After a few more curves of the road going up the mountain, she slowed the car, and we turned into a drive with a large iron gate, there presumably to keep out unwary travelers. The headlights revealed that the drive was covered in torn branches and limbs from the wind-driven rains. She inserted a plastic card into something, and the gates opened, allowing us into the magically gated kingdom of the Irtenevs.

After going up a winding driveway through the woods, we arrived in front of a large mountain chalet-like structure made of dark, heavy pine timber with slanted roofs covered in tiles. There their servant, who I learned was called Anton, met us at the entrance. He took all of our coats and ushered us inside with a restrained smile of welcome. With a loud flourish, someone announced that drinks were being served in the great room. A smiling, confident, rather stocky man wearing a green, corduroy, shooting jacket rushed in from the side door to greet us. Holding out his hands, he announced in a deep bass voice that he was Semyon Irtenev.

"Sorry not to be there to greet you on arrival," he said. "I was cleaning debris away from the back driveway and porch. Nasty storm out there."

His gaze shifted around, then focused on me. He had intense eyes that seemed full of enthusiasm: "And you must be Nicholas Krylov! Anna has told me about you. Welcome, and let me thank you from my soul for saving her from those dogs. We have a place in the city apparently near you, and, as you have noticed, there are a lot of strays around us. Something must be done of course. But now, let us have drinks before dinner and get acquainted."

"Delighted to be of assistance!" I said, "Thanks for inviting me." He talked fast, so fast I almost couldn't follow him. The words came out fast in short bursts, but his jaw hardly moved.

As we headed into the large open room at the front entrance, I noticed that Anna was about four inches taller than he. He made up for his smaller stature with his enthusiasm and ceaseless energy, shaking hands, patting the back, guiding his guests here and there, solicitous of their every need. He walked fast, practically running from one side of the room to the other, asking questions, waving to the servant to fill glasses. Semyon was surprisingly quick for a squat man carrying some weight around in his middle. He was not portly but rather well built, stocky, muscular, in shape, but also well fed which probably accounted for a slight paunch.

A spectacle to behold— a good scene from one of the Victorian fashion dramas from today's media fare—royal guests feasting in a luxurious great room, fed and quenched by loyal servants of long-standing. Semyon's corrugated wavy and heavily-jelled hair almost fluttered in the breeze as he shot across in a blur from here to there. Only this was a Russian drama . . . It was all quite theatrical and amusing to me. I was getting fatigued just watching Semyon dart between and around his guests.

As he scampered about, Anna was suddenly by my side, watching me watch him. "He's quite the social butterfly, isn't he? Let's meet the others while he gets prepared for the evening. Over here is Damir Lebedev. Let me introduce you." The target was a large man standing by the empty stone fireplace whose wife, Natalya, was apparently somewhere else in the room.

"Damir, this is Nick Krylov, who is here for the summer doing research and teaching at USU. We are both on the same Politology faculty. Nick, Damir runs a construction firm that does a lot of business with the City."

"Very pleased to meet you," he said with all the gusto of a flat beer.

I returned Lebedev's intense, deadening stare with an obligatory smile of greeting. But this guy was weird! His eyes looked right through me and hid more than they revealed. Like Semyon's intensity, he looked right through me as if he were reading my mind. It seemed impossible to keep anything from those eyes or to deceive him. No matter ... that didn't stop a good conversation.

"We do our best for the City," Lebedev said.

"And why wouldn't we?" I asked rhetorically.

"My firm built a new runway for the airport, reconstructed some stadiums around town for the Games. We built the Ploshchad Kommunarov metro station near the Central Stadium that will be heavily used for the Games. You may have seen it. We also have done some rehab work on the three metro lines. We have advised the city on ways that preservation and reconstruction of existing structures can be better and cheaper than building new assets. You saw how the new construction worked out in Sochi, right? Bad planning advice there! Lots of unused structures littering the place after the Games that have to be expensively maintained or they deteriorate and become unusable."

"Are you ready for the Games?"

"Of course! The structures like our metro stations and metros are all there, and the City is ready to control crowds and keep the structures in order, just like they do for regular events, even though this a much bigger deal," he said, flashing a confident grin at me. The grin featured several prominent gold teeth in front and on the sides. They were leftover relics from early dentistry where one displayed their wealth through gold teeth. The dentists went along because they didn't know any better, and everyone was happy with the work in the short term. Patients, usually poor ones, had their social status displayed prominently, and dentists sold more teeth.

"The only thing here is that the City has to deal with hooligans. I was a front line hooligan once, so I know it's a problem around here and elsewhere in Russia. We used to travel around in well-organized packs and get in fights at local matches. Those were the days! Before I went straight around eighteen, I was in trouble with the law all the time."

"You, a hooligan?"

"That's right; I myself find soccer boring, but I do like fighting. At a Game there are always gangs of toughs looking for trouble, which is great from my perspective as adviser. The City finds less use for them so they have me advising on mob and gang control as well as preservation of infrastructure. Quite logical, don't you think? But I must say, there's nothing quite like getting drunk and spending a few hours beating the shit out of each other. It's a real rush, if you get my meaning."

I was surprised. Lebedev didn't have the build of a tough or thug. His face was smooth without that punched-up look of past fighters. He probably had lightning fists and knew how to move fast to get out of their way as well.

"To be honest, I also find the game boring and a magnet for distraction and delinquency. You've heard the old one: 'I went to a fight last night, and a hockey game broke out!' That could easily apply to soccer."

Semyon suddenly appeared back in the room again: "Let's all adjourn to the dining chamber and begin our dinner!" announced Irtenev in his commanding baritone.

Anna led me into the large dimly lit high-ceilinged room with heavy curtains and furniture surrounding a long, heavy piece of barn timber used as a table. Likewise, the silverware and plates were large, heavy, and probably of past family origins. In my U.S. experience, they might have been acquired at upscale garage sales or antique stores to give that added touch of elegance and class to dinner gatherings. The table was impressively lit with candelabras holding four candles each. The room was cozy and majestic, like those one reads about in novels of Victorian English manors packed with a cornucopia of fine ladies, squires, and barons. Irtenev was at the head with Anna to his side. I was seated further down on the other side in the middle next to Lebedev and a priest. Risanovsky and his wife were seated on the other side next to Anna.

We sat down and instantly the servant began ladling up a clear soup into dark, hand- made, colored ceramic bowls. The servant, a savage-looking man, possibly Chechen, with a curly beard wearing a loose, greyish shirt, seemed like a multi-task type, probably shooting game for dinners, doing occasional wood-chopping, tinkering with car repairs and plumbing jobs as well as kitchen duties to support the cook. They called him Lukashka, which was more a Cossack name, but he could have been either Chechen or Cossack. To me he came from central casting as a real warrior from the old days. White towel draped over his forearm, he went at his serving tasks with a fine energetic gusto. The clear broth was embellished with vegetables, pearls of fat, and chunks of dark meat. The wine was the best from Georgian, I was told, and there was lots of vodka available for the regulars to supercharge their evening.

Irtenev rose quickly at the end of the table, toasted us all with his glass, and wished us good health. The wine was excellent—I'd been used to the rotgut from upstate New York for so long I had forgotten what good Georgian red could taste like.

I took a few gulps of soup and remarked to no one in particular how good it tasted.

"How do you like the meat?" Lebedev asked, with a smile and knowing nod.

"It's excellent!"

"Venison and a few other animals from Semyon's little estate here," he boasted.

Lebedev didn't laugh through his mouth but by crinkling the skin around his eyes into scratchy lines and showing his teeth. His eyes would become wicked and expectant as he glanced around quickly at his fellow conspirators, ready to spring the great joke on a victim, in this case the American professor.

"So you like horse meat too then?"

I tried to hide my surprise. I had eaten horse lung in Kyrgyzstan, mistaking it for local cheese; I had also eaten boar brain in Macedonia and mistook that for beef. I learned too late that *cutya* was dog meat in Hungary, and that it was eaten regularly there. So that was a surprise! The broiled dog, raw horse lung, and grilled brain though tasted quite nice, especially then when I was hungry—like right now.

"Superb!" I said.

He had a magnetic gaze with eyes that bored right through me, and yet he looked concerned. "But you looked shocked. Remember, it was a nice horse! Nice, but past its prime."

He twitched his nostrils open in a bovine-like manner and smiled with a fierce kind of enjoyment. We both laughed. I was genuinely surprised; I didn't get the source of amusement at first—I thought it was just my culinary stupidity. He then turned to talk with Irtenev, who was already chatting with Risanovsky, probably to line up his next construction contract with the city.

The priest, dressed up in black orthodox garb with several medallions hanging around his neck, had been talking briefly on his cell phone next to me and hung up. A veritable symbol of the modern Orthodox Church. . His robe even had a cell pocket sewed into it! He turned to me and said: "Welcome. I am Father Pavel Petrovich of the Church on the Blood in town. I hope that you can visit us during your stay here."

A large, rotund man, he filled out his robes to the maximum. He sported a black beard, which contrasted nicely with his colored spectacles. He had a friendly face and exuded openness and understanding, I thought, rather than severity and rigid dogma.

"I've read about your Church and have always wanted to visit it. I know it's on the spot where the story of the tsar and his family ended. The killing of the Romanovs in the cellar there marked the end of the Russian monarchy and Tsar Nicholas II, right? I also want to experience a real Orthodox service. I know it has that special and selfless light of mercy associated with not only the highest and richest, but also the lowest and the poorest. I know it's also morbid and typically Russian, right out of a Dostoyevsky novel. But I have to go. I once had that transcendent feeling in the Armenian Orthodox services I've attended, and I'm sure it's the same at your church. I also loved the Orthodox choirs which I heard in Armenia and Bulgaria."

"You are part Russian and an expert on Slavic studies and politics, I understand from Anna. So you would be sensitive to the light of mercy. And we do have a superb choir. You are very perceptive. The Romanovs and that authoritarian clique were murdered by drunken thugs in the name of the vicious dreamers. They took over the regime and spouted off their revolutionary theories while the masses starved at home or in labor camps. "

"Sobering thought . . . Thank you for inviting me."

"I hope you will not be disappointed. Our church is new, rebuilt because the originals were destroyed in World War II. We have pristine replicas of the old structures and icons. They are not new; we are not old. Symbolic, yes! But it is also a strange kind of reality like Disneyland . . . No?"

"I hope not. I've seen rebuilt Old Town Warsaw and been to modern Vienna. They look almost too perfect—better than the originals. And the ancient stone church at Echmiadzin in Armenia has been taken over by marketing hucksters, selling CDs of the choir and glossy tourist books. It's embarrassing and devastating if you had been there before the money-grubbers came as I have. Residents of those countries like Germany and France like to visit earthy places like Budapest, which are still authentically shabby, still sporting bullet holes throughout town in many buildings and walls, letting their ancient trams rumble about, and allowing the classic old buildings to fall apart before your very eyes. It's sad, but at least it's real."

"I know what you are talking about. We see this happening all over Russia. So tell me what you are doing here. I know you are at USU with Anna and Dr. Risanovsky there. Most of us here went there for our degrees. It's a great, well-respected institution. But of course we are prejudiced!"

I explained to him that I came for one purpose: to exchange methods and lessons from running city services and to try and come up with better infrastructure planning systems and techniques for both his cities and ours. Specifically, my goal was to see how systems here will assist or constrain them in planning for the Games this summer. From listening to the vet in Perm, I learned that a real problem was the spate of stray dogs running around in vicious packs biting people in random attacks. So, the public health, fan safety, and predictable media response issues were added to my original study design.

"It's now a more comprehensive dog response problem," I told him. "I'm learning about the options tried elsewhere that could work here as well. Some work and some don't. Some are longer-term. Some aren't adaptable here because of risks and cultural incompatibility. We can't eat up all the dogs, can we? Some options, like sterilization and contraception, are constrained. They would be viewed by the Orthodox Church here as sins, no?"

He gave me a severe look—then his face cracked into a broad smile. "I have two *sobakas* and couldn't live without them. They need me just as much! I want the stray dog problems solved for their benefit as well as for humans. You have an interesting task. No one will be pleased by what you find—or by what must be done."

"What do you mean?"

"I mean there are some tough characters involved with eliminating stray dogs, and you may come across them. Be careful. Also, I've heard rumors of secret experiments going on with bio-solutions to the stray dog problem. Not just the usual contraception, which is an old method."

"Secret experiments? You don't mean turning dogs into humans and sci-fi stuff like that from H. G. Wells, do you?"

We both laughed. "Who knows?" Petrovich said. "But on the subject of the Church, some of their views are ancient and dogmatic, hardly suited to complicated city problems where most people live and have to survive now. It's not a sin to help them in the best way we can, which often just means tolerance, forgiveness, and lightening up. Simple instructions from the Bible. Why is it not a sin to force people to suffer now in order to preserve an abstraction in the future, called a 'life'? Ancient liturgical dogmas often obstruct progress and hurt a lot of people. Burying our heads in the sand in the name of the Church also makes us less popular and more out of touch. It makes it harder for us to connect with the real people in need."

"Hey, if you had been my local priest, I might have gone to Church more often."

"We are often insulted for good reason. Priests try to make the pitch that people insult Christ through them, and they wilt in the process. Nonsense! They become afraid and hide behind Latin liturgy and impersonal confessions and rote mutterings. But some of us in the clergy fight back. We don't wilt. I try to fight against ignorant dogma whether they are nonsensical biblical interpretations by fanatics or simply Church doctrines, which are wrong. Are you aware that some Catholic Churches in countries like Argentina and Guatemala ban the messages of Mary in Luke's gospel, chapter 1, known as the *Magnificat,* which commands that we help others in need with love and mercy? Political regimes fear that message as both subversive and threatening to them, and order their churches to stop repeating it.

The message goes something like this:

He has scattered the proud in the conceit of their heart;
He has put down the mighty from their throne and has exalted the lowly;
He has filled the hungry with great things and the rich he has sent away empty.

"You can see why regimes of a tyrannical bent would have trouble with these lines and delete them from the Gospels. It's the modern way with authoritarian populist leaders. Mary articulated an end to economic structures that are exploitative and unjust. Why should the Church be complicit in banning practical Christianity in service of real need, and go along with enforcement of cruel and literal dogmas? The words simply mean that we should help all living creatures, humans as well as dogs. Why is that so subversive?"

"Couldn't agree more, Father… I certainly will visit the Church and hope to hear a sermon from you! But tell me, based on what you said, what should they do about the dog problem here?"

"Maybe turning everyone into good Christians and trying new bio-solutions wouldn't be a bad idea," he said, laughing again. "Attendance is down!"

I sensed that it was time to listen to Irtenev, who was holding forth at the end of the table. He was telling an old familiar Russian joke.

"So a dozen workers from the Urals around here were visiting Stalin in his office. After they left, Stalin was missing his pipe. He told his aide, Poskrebyshev, to make sure that all the workers were questioned. A few minutes later, Stalin found his pipe in his desk and told Poskrebyshev to release all the workers. 'But Comrade Stalin, they have all confessed.'"

Laugher at this was polite, quiet, and innocuous. Around here, it could have been a joke about the weather.

I ask Father Petrovich how things have changed since Stalin. "Do people still confess things they haven't done? Isn't that simply an old Orthodox Church habit?" I said, flashing him a quick wink.

Irtenev overheard us, which got him to turn serious. "The Putin regime is boxed in by U.S. sanctions that have crimped investment and pushed the ruble down. That means we have fewer funds at the provincial and city levels to engage in construction works. I think Damir Lebedev would agree that we have bid out fewer works contracts these last few years. Our euphoria over the Crimea annexation and the Syrian military escapades has worn off. The public clamors for more funds to be spent here to solve domestic problems."

"What does that mean in specifics?" I asked him.

"That the upcoming Games come off well...."

"Some of us at USU such as Nicholas and I have been trying to reduce the stray dog problem before it gets in the way of this event. We all know that happened in Sochi, and it spoiled the image of other Olympic games," said Anna.

"The running dogs will be eliminated. We have never worried about a few strays. I am reliably informed that our security officials will be able to handle this problem," he announced with a theatrical sweep of his arm, culminating in a powerful thump on the table by one of his large fists.

"Just like that ... can we assume that the dogs are just gone?" said Anna. "Where has that ever happened? That's as simplistic and naïve as the people behaved in Cadiz, Spain who planned to relocate 5,000 pigeons hundreds of miles away to stop them from shitting in the parks and creating health risks for waiters who had to clean it all up. They thought that this was better than contraceptive pills because they were afraid other species might like to try the pills themselves into extinction. Cadiz officials imagined the pigeons were so stupid they wouldn't know how to fly back to Cadiz. You're just as naïve, talking tough as if bluster will eliminate strays before they breed more pups. Why not try napalming them? Any idea how big this city is? Also, Semyon, the animal rights people have been showing films on YouTube of large dog packs that are already ravaging tourists in our city. Don't you remember that I was attacked a few weeks ago in our very neighborhood?"

"Well then, Anna, let's teach the dogs to read leaflets about proper dog behavior in the city limits and around the Games. No fighting around the games! No stealing food either!" scoffed Semyon.

"That's right, leave the hooligans in peace to fight amongst themselves and the strays!" said Lebedev.

"That would make the secret experiments we hear about even more important. We hear that a new, refined race of dogs that behaves properly is being created at this very moment!" laughed Petrovich.

"Anyway Anna, most of what you hear in the media about the dog problem is exaggerated," said Iretenev.

Another clap of laughter from Anna: "Of course! It's fake news!" she said.

The entire table followed with spasms of laughter. "Everything was 'fake' in the Soviet Union, wasn't it? We all know that what the regime didn't want to hear about was 'fake.' Trump and other neo-fascists follow the same method to appeal to the blockhead toughs in their bases," said Anna. Her cheeks glowed bright red, matching the gleeful smile she flashed at each of us.

"No, it's not 'fake.' It's really quite old news that everyone here knows about. These problems have to be addressed now by the authorities. They have nothing to do with the credibility of the journalists."

I noticed that even sitting at the table she was bigger, taller, tougher, and more quick-witted than he. As the night moved on, I also noticed how she quietly responded with deft irony that he often missed or ignored. Next to her, he seemed like a dimwit. From his side, he didn't seem to take her seriously.

"Nicholas must know from living in the U.S. that money can be made selling dogs and dog carcasses," said Semyon.

Before I could think of a response, she lit back into him. "You think that is how U.S. cities deal with stray dogs? Creating and exploiting sales markets? What nonsense!" she said with a screech of laughter. The wine was flowing heavily now as Lukashka kept up the pace filling the rapidly emptying glasses. The audible volume from shouts and laughter was also headed upwards.

"You like making money in business, but your mind is in the vice grip in the reactionary prose of recycled Marxist claptrap," said Anna.

"The stray dog problem is serious everywhere and especially here, given the delicacy of the moment with the Games. In the U.S., cities that want to deal with these problems build pounds, license dogs, support adoption programs, and fine owners who refuse to have their dogs sterilized. Individually, these approaches make some difference. But as a packaged approach, they really help," I threw into the fray. It was futile—like tossing a hat into a flood to stop it from flowing.

"But you still have problems, no?" Irtenev asked.

"Of course. Lots of cities have weak mayors that ignore problems, passing them on to higher levels of government, which plead the usual lack of budget funding as excuses. Special interests, like backyard breeders, sell puppies that are later abandoned, and produce more strays and public expenses. But these are marginal issues and usually don't turn into epidemics or serious problems like rabid packs of dogs foraging for food in cities and biting a lot of people in the process. In some countries that still ignore the stray dog problem, like Romania, they even let the brown bears get rid of the dogs in the cities for them. That is a Darwinian and cheap way of dealing with stray dogs for a time. But the bears became accustomed to city life, and they eventually have bigger problems."

"So you don't have any magic solutions either?" said Lebedev.

"Hardly ...we grasp at workable solutions like city officials everywhere. We still have our city kill pounds, and many dogs are euthanized or put to death because no one adopts them. Anything I could propose after talking with the city people here might help in the future, but probably not now. Your problem is that you have the Games coming up now and need remedial actions not long-term solutions."

My last effort at diplomacy seemed to settle the dust a bit. As he sipped his wine, I glanced behind Irtenev's head to the oil engraving of his great-grandfather, a local landowner with probably vast acreage and many serfs during the Tsarist regimes. As I watched Lukashka running back and forth to the kitchen with silver trays full of more food and extra carafes of wine, I fancied that I had become a part of a local dining circle right out of a Gogol story.

I noticed Semyon staring at me with a puzzled look. "I see you looking at the portrait of my forefather. Just like he did, I hire the nearby small farmers to harvest our modest wheat and fruit orchards while I am away in the city on business." I gathered that meant most of the time.

"Semyon would like the Tsarevich to return. But weren't you telling me that he already has?" said Anna. "The days of the Tsars were bad times for most Russians. We were then and still are a Third World country, but with nuclear weapons and a First World space program."

"Putin would like to have the power of a Tsar but modernize the economy," said Semyon.

"From what I've learned, current laws and customs are still like those of French feudalism 250 years ago. Russia is a neo-feudal system with extremely low agricultural production. Isn't that true?" I said to show I that at least could contribute something about history.

"Not exactly. I work with the provincial governor and the ministries in Moscow on rural and local development and welfare problems," said Semyon, getting a bit defensive. "Critics are wrong to attack officials for the complexity and vastness of our problems."

"Who else is supposed to be accountable if not you officials?" asked Anna. "Nicholas is right about the neo-feudal aspect of our society. Our problems are 250 years old—neither new, nor fake," said Anna.

That one bit hard! Semyon grimaced at this, and his nose twitched in obvious irritation. "Nick wasn't raised here, and he has been away for too long. He learns about Russia from books and the Western media, not by having lived and worked here," said Semyon.

"Semyon is correct about that. I have much to learn, and I am only speculating from afar; I hope you can correct me. The best I can suggest are: treats, dog whistles, and leashes to capture them all before they cause any more trouble," I said, trying to lower the heat.

"Stray dogs—maybe you have nothing new there for us. But there is something in what you say about feudalism," said Pavel Petrovich.

"Feudalism disappeared in France years ago, but here it was only really abolished in 1859. Norms that gave French slaves and serfs European rights didn't make it into Russian Law. And most of us would agree that the regime in Moscow tries to act like royal nobility with lots of glitz and symbolism from Tsarist times. Like the Tsar, Putin relies on multi-layered bureaucratic and military elites to stay in power. And here power has always been centralized. The Praetorian Guard of the FSB tied to the President is the real source of his power. All power emanates from Moscow and his offices. We have a modicum of power here in Sverdlovsk as heads of the district, solid ties to the provincial governor, and even to the FSB that can make or break us all. Note that these are neo-feudal rules and relationships that are known to all and are disobeyed at our peril. We know that they can be abused, ignored, or overstepped by officials up and down the line, and when that happens, the only appeal is to a higher handler. We have a few of those, but they frequently change or are removed suddenly. No one is surprised by loss of cover. That's how it works!"

"So what Anna refers to is neo-feudalism," said Pavel. "There used to be an institutional power war between the Prosecutor General's office and the FSB. Not any longer ... officials in the Prosecutor General office suffered many "accidents," such as being run over by garbage trucks and being forced to commit suicide by various improbable means. The best one can hope for, if he flouts the rules, or goes rogue in a bout of self-righteousness is to make deals. But there you end up in a fix. You have to yield compromising information on the officials harassing you in exchange for cessation of steamrolling from opposing officials."

"Endless petty power games," Anna said, "not much of an organic society or government, if you ask me."

"No, it isn't. And it gets worse," said Pavel Petrovich. "We know that Putin doesn't really control the day to day operations of the cliques and cartels of different armed groups. Many of these have quasi police powers of their own. There are hundreds of irregular authorities ostensibly reporting to Putin, but in fact they do not. They work largely on their own, and he rarely intervenes in specific cases. A classic Hobbesian nightmare where 'might makes right'."

"Politics here is really like Sudan or Algeria," said Anna. "It's only a temporary means of mediating conflict among powerful stakeholders. Then they go right back to armed conflict and make new dirty deals. We don't have a coherent government so much as a shadowy collection of army officers and businessmen negotiating among themselves to raid the treasury. Each stakeholder in the clique has a group of armed followers to protect them in their deal making. In this context, the accumulation of power is critical, but provides only short-term security since the balance can shift quickly against you."

"So any concept of 'good governance' for the future means vesting power in institutions rather than individuals," I said.

"That's right. But the institutions have to be independent, which is not possible here for the foreseeable future in my view," said Petrovich.

"What kind of change are you hoping for Pavel?" asked Semyon.

"Something that would have at least prevented the bust-up of our Church. The Ukrainian Orthodox wing just split off from us, and I don't think that suggests a modern Church responsive to real needs. Both wings of the church do very little social outreach to obvious victims like the many poor or homeless people living on the streets. Do you think that tougher security forces or dissemination of more compromising information on priests could have prevented this, Semyon?"

"Perhaps not Pavel…"

I wondered how much of this was intended for me as a warning. Irtenev's message seemed to be: 'Caution!' I have power enough to inflict menace if you go off the track on your own and play the maverick around here.' Throughout the dinner, he displayed the effortless superiority of a powerful man, self-satisfied, denying there were any dog problems in the city, and finding any contrary suggestions as personal affronts. So, if I were to avoid trouble, I would do my little study and go home quietly.

We drank cognacs and smoked Semyon's fine Havana cigars over dessert for another hour or so. Then Semyon rose at the end of the table and, smiling at each of us, announced:

"Let me thank all of you for coming. I know you have to get going early tomorrow. Let us plan to get together again soon." He waved his wine glass around, and pointing it towards each of us with short toasts according to polite tradition, looked directly into our eyes as we sat around the table. He then bid us good night.

We moved out of the dining hall into the entrance foyer chatting and shaking hands. It was a nice evening, and the Risanovskys fortunately offered to give me a ride back to my apartment. Before leaving and paying my respects to the host couple, Semyon then graciously invited me to go hiking with them the next weekend at a rustic park in the nearby Urals. I was surprised and worried that he was getting irked and jealous of my banter with Anna and our repeated exchange of quick looks during his commentary, which he noticed several times. I still wasn't sure... But I thanked him for the hiking invitation. I then thanked the rest of his friends profusely with several rounds of vigorous handshakes and hugs in the local style. It was an evening of honest discussion, disagreements, and departures without, I hoped, any bruised egos.

9   A HIKE IN THE URALS

The three of us drove out from Yekaterinburg southwards toward the mountains. Semyon drove with Anna riding shotgun, and I sat in the back of their car. As we left town, I saw the tightly cloistered residences and shops webbed together with the city by tram tracks thin out into more greenery. Trees, shrubbery, green fields— some planted with corn and sunflowers—and open sports field-like spaces provided an intoxicating country setting. Children played and threw themselves around flinging rocks and other objects with energetic abandon. I saw a few ponds where the enthusiastic little kids tossed stones and skipped them across to watch the ripples. These people had the luxury of space and better air, but obviously with less money. There were now fewer shops, more cloisters of smaller homes, more run-down buildings, no tram tracks anymore, and just the occasional bus stop signs denoting the infrequent ex-urban services they had to deal with during the working week. It was Saturday so there were fewer commuters and clusters of people going home from their daily labors. But the people outside seemed to have more life and color about them. They wore brightly-dyed scarves and dresses to prove it. I heard the sound of laughter, which made a cheerful impression on me. The laughter spewed forth in natural outpourings, unlike the guttural, sneering, scoffing kinds of jollification I had been exposed to the past years of my life. Their laughter was a release and celebration of another day lived in the country amongst friends and neighbors. Even the fluttering colors of their shopping baskets and packs looked more authentic for their wear and ruddy earthiness.

"Do you hike much?" Semyon asked.

"Quite a bit actually. I teach near the Adirondack Mountains. They consist of hundreds of peaks and foothills in the 4,000-5,000-ft. range (1200-1300 meters). I often go backpacking with groups of students from the college to nearby places like Mt. Marcy and Whiteface Mountain."

"They seem to resemble the Urals in altitudes and immensity," said Anna.

"I think both the Urals and Adirondacks are about the same age. They are old mountain ranges. That also means they aren't too high or steep like our Rockies or the Baikal range here. But that's ok with me. I like a more leisurely stroll."

"Not trying to beat any endurance records are you?" said Semyon.

"Not me, I can assure you!"

We drove through several villages heading up the ridges into mountains. The sky seemed to meet the earth as if there were no space between heaven and the rest of mankind. In one village, I spotted a small pack of several dogs eagerly milling about a butcher shop. Village dogs were always more interested in the doings of humanity than in the affairs of their own species. I noticed a corner pub with benches in front. There, a bearded man was playing a fiddle accompanied by a lean, long-bodied, grayish dog. The dog's head was thrown back, and his snout shaped into a zero as he hit the high notes with good, long howls. He might even have been whistling, but from the car I couldn't hear and only surmised this. After all, if Mother Hubbard's dog smoked, why couldn't a dog whistle too? I could only hope that someone captured these kinds of rustic scenes in bright acrylics and richly-colored oils for posterity.

A short time later, we arrived at the park entrance and pulled into a space. Oleni Rochyi Park was a protected area with wilderness extending hundreds of square miles into the foothills and mountains. Though popular with local hikers and campers, it wasn't crowded that Sunday. We unpacked the car and readied for our hike up the mountain, which according to them was probably a 1,000-foot climb along a winding trail over several hours to the top. The mountains were thick with lush forests of pine, aspen, silver birch, and other hardwoods, such as beech and oak. To round out the picture, they had packed lunches and water bottles to see us through the day's hike.

We started up the trail. Semyon led the way and vigorously pushed ahead up the mountain at a brisk pace. He moved fast, just as he had done at dinner, from rock to rock, jumping over fallen limbs, a man in a hurry and in shape. Anna helpfully pointed out the names of shrubs and trees that were unfamiliar to me. It was mostly Anna who was explaining as Semyon had left us behind several times, and we had to catch up. Along the way, she also noted the various species of birds, some quite exotic. Of course, there were always the magpies to remind me I was back in Russia. They were my favorite, besides being the only ones I could identify. After an hour or so, the sun beat down on us hard, and we were all sweating profusely. We started taking things off and either stuffing them in our backpacks or tying them around us. Semyon had tightly-honed muscles, bred partly in gyms, with the rest a result of his labors around the house chopping wood, mending fences, repairing structures, and carrying objects around on his back or in wheelbarrows. He seemed to be comfortable with the rugged outdoors. Anna took off her trousers down to some short, khaki hiking pants. Her olive-skinned legs with little nuanced muscles, which I noticed undulated with each step, suggested she also spent a lot of time swimming and hiking outdoors. Her curvy, dimpled thighs attracted my notice more than once. I took off my now sweaty shirt and hiked in my jeans and sneakers. Anna launched into a hearty hiking song, probably something local, and she began to sing like a tropical bird as we headed up the trail. She bellowed out tunes with throaty lyrics, smiling and urging us to join her. I hummed along to the tune that from her ecstatic expression seemed full of meaning and gusto to her. Semyon didn't seem to be much into singing, but smiled along to keep up appearances. He seemed to be more into his cell phone than his surroundings. I supposed that went with power—one had to be online and in the loop 24/7 wherever you were, just like driven executives everywhere.

We bounded along up the trail behind Semyon, sweating and singing, but happy finally to reach the top. There we spread out a small blanket in the shade of an oak and had some sandwiches and wine from a bottle they had brought along. From there we could see for many miles, even Yekaterinburg to the north, which could be spotted easily from the industrial haze that engulfed it.

"Don't you wish you could stay here forever?" she suddenly said.

"And start a new life over right here. It all sounds too perfect, doesn't it?"

"Always problems with the details!" said Semyon. "Otherwise, we might decamp to France! Problems with details can often turn into opportunities, can't they? You just have to think around them," he said.

"You'd make a good American-style lawyer. They are school-trained to think how to get around rules creatively. We want to hire lawyers like that and not the average one that can read a rule and say you're stuck. The cynical American writer Ambrose Bierce once defined lawyers as 'professionals skilled in circumventing the law.'"

"Was that supposed to be funny? Rules here are made to be circumvented," said Anna.

The sun passed behind some clouds above us, and we noticed that the sky was darkening to the east.

"I wasn't paying attention," I said. "I suppose the rainstorms come up fast here just like in the Adirondacks or any mountains, no?"

"I think we are soon about to drenched," he said, as he got up and started packing up the gear. "Time to get moving..."

We all took one last swig of wine and started back down the trail again. It had been a refreshing several hours, the most relaxed diversion I had had in years.

Off we went down the mountain again with Semyon in the lead, bounding ahead on his powerful legs, jumping over rocks, and running back and forth. Anna tried to keep up, and I tagged along in the rear in no great hurry to return to earth from this fine afternoon respite.

Semyon passed from view around a bend up ahead and went into a deep patch of forest. I followed along behind Anna, assured that she would keep to the trail and with a naïve hunch that eventually all mountains reach the bottom anyway. Suddenly, I heard her scream.

"Nicholas, he's hurt!"

I caught up with her, and she stood over Semyon, who appeared to be out cold on the ground. His pack had come off, and he lay there looking like he had been mugged. The culprit was a large wet rock that he must have slipped on as he bounded over it. Managing to hit his head on yet another rock before he could put out his hands, he had been hammered.

"Looks bad," I said, seeing some blood coming off his forehead from a cut. "I don't think we can carry him down. Anyway, moving him might cause further problems if he has any serious internal injuries."

"Agreed... Let's try and get someone up here from the station down below at the entrance. They have all kinds of rescue equipment."

"OK, but we should do this fast. Going down and back would take too long. Let's try and find a cell phone signal and call in."

"There should be one lower down the mountain. I saw Semyon stop his cellphone talking further down the trail. I assume now that was because he lost his signal."

"OK, it's worth a try."

"If we had a dog, we could leave him here to watch Semyon while we went for help."

"Let's put a parka over him to shield him from the approaching rains and cold. Put a water bottle by him in case he comes to and is thirsty."

That done, off we both went. As we headed down, I remembered an incident in grade school when a group of us at co-ed scout camp were hiking up in the mountains of Pennsylvania, and one of the kids fell and sprained her ankle. We were all around 12-years-old. Al, the supervisor, decided to go for help and instructed us to stay there. After he left, a furious wind came up, accompanied by hail and explosions of thunder with bolts of lightning hitting nearby. We were scared shit-less, and some of us began to cry and sing to keep up our courage. It helped! We decided to act, and tried to make a stretcher out of wood to carry her down ourselves. Some were pissed at her and suggested leaving her there until Al found her. That is, if he found her at all.

Since we were boy scouts, we threw something together out of sticks and rags and rolled her onto it. It didn't hold, and it collapsed under her weight, sending her tumbling to the ground with accompanying screams and oaths. The problem was that she was a big one! We ended up having her do a slow forced walk with us assisting her. Through all this, some of the more devout kids started in about being meant to die up here, and so on, to which several of us replied: "Shut the fuck up!" After about an hour of this nonsense, eventually Al and a few rangers appeared, and we were all hustled down the mountain to safety.

I started to tell Anna about this as she walked along beside me. The rains were starting to come down, and we heard some thunder, just like in my story.

"You must have been frightened," she said, poking me with a friendly jab.

"I was really scared!"

I continued with the story, and we exchanged a few more pokes and light, emphatic touches. She was quite beautiful in an innocent, unselfconscious way. Perhaps I had been in the routine of marriage too long or sexually numbed by the unisex coeds that permeated the Bonaduz campus to notice her. The gender identity push had somehow erased the powerful sexual attraction of both sexes. I mentioned that she was wearing short hiking pants and a tightly-wound checked blue blouse. What I now noticed were her tanned, smooth, muscular legs that undulated as she skipped over the rocks during our descent. She had a voluptuous torso, which I had missed. I touched her a few more times playfully, and she kept playfully touching back. At first we did this almost accidentally. Then it became more purposeful. My mouth began watering again, and my throat was drying out fast. We looked at each other intensely, and at that point both of us lost all restraint.

The clouds parted, and the sun beat down on us for an instant ahead of the storm. The old Jethro Tull song flashed through my memory.

So when you look into the sun.

See all the things we could have done.

See the words we could have sung.

It's not too late, only begun.

But it had begun. Suddenly a clap of thunder, and the storm hit. I heard a crack nearby from a tree that was probably hit by lightning or just a gust of wind. The rain whistled down like bullets: lightening flashed and the thunder drummed. All around us we felt the hail, the sudden darkness with sluices of light. We were rolling around in the mud and laughing. It was passion—for me, it was partially fear. Fear of what? I wasn't getting any younger. Was I afraid of losing the power to capture objects of my vital passions? Very likely. Here was another chance, a chance that I might never have again. It was the fear that this moment would pass me by forever. So this time, I acted!

I held her around the waist and felt her tight, cool flesh. She grabbed my head, and we kissed long and hard. She reached down and unbuttoned my jeans, and I followed suit with her pants. We moved off the trail under a pine tree nearby that offered a natural bed of needles. On an invisible signal, off came our pants, and we hit the dirt. I stroked her legs then pinched them, and she squealed in delight. I lay on her stomach and slid downwards slowly, licking her stomach and beyond, eventually finding my tongue in her vagina. She groaned, and I could see straight ahead between her smallish, perfectly formed breasts that her eyes were rolling around uncontrollably. What a view! She rolled over and grabbed for my cock. She went at it first with her hand, then her mouth. To avoid exploding, I began stroking her vagina than adding some more heat with my tongue. I entered her, and we went at full force on the ground. Now she groaned more loudly and began shuddering with long orgasmic spasms. I convulsed and came about that time to end this stage of what had to be the best erotic experience I had had since high school days. It was natural, spontaneous, and almost primordial for me, the hit of sex that awakened my passions and zeal for life. Both of us were exhausted, and we lay together for a while longer, breathing hard but in unison. I felt purified and cleansed—emotionally and spiritually renewed.

Some say the ideal sex happens from surprise and gentle aggression, nothing forced, in unison like a concert reaching a crescendo.

Nevertheless, we went at it athletically, rolling around, trying a wide range of different positions until were both exhausted at the end. On our way to that point this afternoon, we enjoyed contortions, animal lust, warmth, and the flow of love—meaning all the passions were exercised. We laughed and hugged tightly to seal the mutual peak experience. Anna combined her fetching schoolgirl fringe and a lovely impudent face with an inviting smile that had slowly melted me, then pushed me to a rapid boil. She had looked me up and down, over and over, I realize it now, and she was pure sauce. Her voice winked even though she didn't. It helped that perhaps neither of us had any shame or conscience. As a girl in high school once told me—lick up the honey, stranger, and ask no questions. In that spirit, Anna and I played the two-backed beast for about an hour on a fine bed of smooth, wet pine needles covered by low hanging pine tree branches.

I helped her up, and we both threw our clothes back on. I knocked off the dirt and needles from her pants and shirt, and she did the same for mine. But anyone could still see there were needles and dirt there that didn't come from the air. But not us; we were both in a euphoric dream state and were oblivious to rational evidence. We tried our cellphones and got through. I told someone at the park station what had happened on the main trail and that we would be waiting with Semyon.

Anna was in the afterglow of a dream state. Nick had brought her back to the old excitement of life. With Semyon, and working at USU for years, she had become tame and used to a routinized boredom. He was never around her much—rarely at home, never invited her anywhere private like a restaurant. He brought her along to his public festivities as a trophy for the media to lap up. When he was around, he droned on about Kremlin power politics and his career. He had no interest in books or music. And in her previous life as a student, a radical at that, she knew she was the kind of woman to whom mad things happened. Well, they were starting to happen again, and she was enthralled.

We hiked back up for about twenty minutes to the spot. And there was Semyon. She ran to him and hugged him as he sat there on the rock. I saw his face. It was emotionally flat—not a welcoming look at all. His eyes were cold, suspicious, and alert to what I feared he sensed as a betrayal on both our parts. His glances at both of us were darting—quick and malicious. I think he could see that we were disheveled, still covered in pine needles and dirt, and obviously in upbeat and stimulated states, despite the absence of alcohol or his presence. I'm certain we both had darkened, reddish faces and probably talked too much. We gave ourselves away.

"Can you walk, Semyon?"

He abruptly waved me away and got up. Packing up his things quietly, I looked at his pack. In an outer pocket was a pair of high-powered binoculars...

10   ACTION PROGRAMS

Several days later, I took Leo for a walk near the campus, and we stopped in for a drink at the Hungry Wolf. That was a civilized thing about Russia—you could bring your dog in with you and no one even batted an eye. The dogs expected it, and they rarely fought or caused any trouble. The public also expected to find dogs sitting below the tables and stools in pubs and restaurants, and that made me feel right at home. We had just emerged from the pub, which was a restaurant-pub across from campus in a rather decrepit building where faculty and students drank tea, beer, and wine and ate home-cooked style meals. Every campus has its main watering hole, and USU had this one. I had been there several times already after work with a few of the faculty members that had put their noses in my office and introduced themselves. After the first one took me there, I had been coming back regularly. The Wolf had a nice, homey feel to it, with flags from universities around the world displayed inside, along with antlers from deer and elk, and a few wolf and fox pelts, all slapped onto dark paneled wood walls. I sensed it had more of a history than these symbols suggested. In fact, Anna told me it was once just a *pivanya* or Soviet beer hole that was later upgraded by students at USU and other nearby universities and their faculties. That accounted for the socialist-realist style posters that were also plastered on the walls alongside the pelts and animal heads. They were in the style of Great War propaganda, with ironic slogans like "Demand a victorious shot of vodka!" to add to the absurdity that was once directed by a grim all-knowing state and now by mere students having a good laugh. The place reflected the kind of regional localism that was growing here and in other provincial places such as Siberia, that felt Moscow and the Kremlin were alien cultures, countries in themselves that had to be resisted at all costs. In the Hungry Wolf, especially at night, the atmosphere was often laced with the shrill, spellbinding tunes of a Roma musician's *zurna* pipe and the quick beat of a large drum. The breakfasts were hearty too, and I often looked forward to their daily fare of local breads and farm fresh eggs.

Sveta had been dropping Leo off with me when I was home, which was rare, and I was always glad to oblige. Leo and I headed out and along the wide Sverdlova Street near the newly rebuilt stadium. He trotted along with me on his little red leash like he had known me for years. As I looked at the buildings on the USU campus, I tried to imagine how Boris Yeltsin could have played volleyball here. He must have weighed less and drunk more moderately in those days. Some said he must have been drunk to resign his office in 2000 and let Putin become acting president. But I bet he spent some good times in the Hungry Wolf, lifting shot glasses of vodka with his pals. I also reflected on what I had hinted to Sveta yesterday about my periodic afternoon mystery guest. Sveta listened with an expression of amused curiosity tinged with wistfulness and something else … jealousy? Was that just my selfish ego in action? She might have been thinking: why her instead of me? Always a good question. Timing … isn't that the usual reason? I asked her to kindly let me know if anyone inquired about either of us. Nothing hidden in that request. More important than my romantic fantasies, I was also convinced the binoculars that were prominently displayed must have been used and that there would be some kind of Semyon-directed payback later.

The sudden screams from a nearby crowd alerted several that something was up as we stood on the corner waiting for a traffic light to cross a street. Loud howls and yelps tipped me off it that it was another dog attack. Leo pricked up his ears and sat down on the curb. He was shaking all over—he knew what to expect. I checked in my back pocket and made sure the pepper spray canister was still there. The sounds grew louder as people came running towards us. This was a major tourist area now that was being spruced up for the Games, and it was absolutely essential that this kind of thing didn't happen in public. But it was… and the media will have a field day. I could see workmen running away from their machines and work sites to get away from an onslaught by at least two large packs of assorted dogs. As usual, the packs contained all sizes and shapes. The cacophony of wails, howls, yelps, and cries from them as they attacked people and each other randomly was excruciating. To me, it was a sad sight. Likely, the dogs had been owned by individuals or families who had released them for whatever reasons. Sometimes, people had to move to new places that prohibited dogs, but the sad part is that these once domestic dogs were undergoing processes of fertilization. That was the opposite of domestication and unlocked their ancient ancestral behaviors. I had heard that wild dingoes in Australia had reverted to being wolves. It could be happening here, if these stray urban dogs were left unchecked. The problem was all over urban cities around the world. There just weren't enough places to keep dogs or families to adopt them.

Meanwhile, some of the curious tourist types, probably from other cities in the U.S. or Europe, were taking all this in stride. They laughed out loud, thinking stupidly that this was a real comedy show. Others, probably from poorer parts of the world such as Eastern Europe, were visibly scared—they see this all the time. They were also closer to the current fray. They had ample experiences of what could go wrong in the way of deaths and rabies from such attacks that in their countries, like Romania, were a daily event. I also saw a few local bystanders who, like me, had been walking their dogs and carried rug-beaters to ward off stray dog attacks and protect their dogs from wild ravaging packs just as these. But rattan rug-beaters would work only up to a point. I made a note to bring my steel-handled umbrella tomorrow. For now, pepper spray would have to do.

As the packs got closer to us, the din grew louder. People were running towards us driven by fear of the dogs that were right behind them. Suddenly, a group of three or four brightly colored trucks sped in from our left and parked in a semi-circle in the middle of the intersection.

The trucks were painted in garish, diagonal red and blue stripes. They sported large black circular logos on each side of cartoonish, drooling brown dogs with large fangs wearing sun-glasses. The doors all banged open simultaneously and out piled several two-man helmeted teams wearing green coveralls, camouflage baseball caps, and large protective gloves. The spiffy crews brandished semi-automatic dart guns and clubs. The drivers carried large tongs, nylon nets, and smaller pistols to deal with the more aggressive biters.

"Look at that, Nicolai! They're mowing them down in droves with darts!" said someone standing on the corner.

"There's another one going after some dogs trying to flee the onslaught. Look! He just shot a few into them!"

Another bystander bellowed: "He's in trouble. The dogs are surrounding him now… Look there, he's clubbing them off by himself. He's all alone!"

"That one seems to be directing operations. He has a clipboard and is checking off actions while pointing and shouting at his crews to move here and there. Pretty slick for a dog eradication operation. Too bad the police aren't this efficient." said another bystander.

The wails and barks had all but ceased, and the crews now concentrated on hauling the sedated dogs into the back of the trucks. Other crews threw the dead ones into the open trailers towed behind several of the trucks. Still other members of the teams had netted certain dogs and put little jackets on them labeled "Special Corps Candidate."

As the crews prepared to leave, three of them stood before the crowd. They bowed in unison, and everyone began to clap. They bounded around in a vigorous Ukrainian squat dance called the *hopak,* while the other two whistled, shouted out, and clapped.

"Hey! Hey! Hey!"

The front dancer hopped up and down to their cadence. He continued to bounce around with his arms folded in the classical style for a few minutes, then all of them, wearing their bright green coveralls piled in the trucks and left, waving to bystanders and throwing small, colored dog dolls to the entranced little kids in the audience on their way out.

Bloody hell! I was exhausted from just watching them! Milling about were clusters of bystanders who had taken photos of the spectacle. Some of these shots would obviously get into the media. It was quite a show, and I had to find out what was going on. Was this a regular city program? I had never seen or heard of anything like this here or anywhere else in the world. It was a lively mix of vaudeville theatre and slick municipal services. In the U.S., local dog-catching crews worked behind the scenes to avoid offending public sensibilities and animal rights advocates who naively wanted dogs liberated from captivity and left free to roam. They worked under the public radar beams like other teams charged with culling animals like deer—a sensitive task fraught with peril given the popularity of Bambi. By contrast, in former Soviet countries such as Armenia, I had seen gangs of burly thugs attacking dog packs with clubs and machine-gunning them with real bullets. The gangs got away with this because the media was weak and had been cowed by the state there into submission. The only thing missing in Yekaterinburg was a dancing bear to take a bow with them as they left. It was all very impressive—relatively humane, efficient, orderly, and with a polished theatrical flair. It could be an off-Broadway musical: "Cometh the Catherine City Dogcatchers!"

"Anton, Boris, make sure the back doors are closed. We don't want any more dogs dropping out in the road in the middle of traffic!" said Dmitry, driving the van and leading the trucks back to base.

"Great work boys! There should be awards and bonuses all around!"

"Rudolf, read us off the stats!"

"We identified three special target dogs that are now in the back of this van. We drugged about 50 with dart guns and had to actually kill around 50 more that were too busy attacking us and themselves to notice we wanted to coax them to be quiet."

"Not bad. But put down that we killed 25 and drugged 75. That figure looks better if the media wants to see our reports. It's quite possible we'll have some publicity, which means they will want statistical performance reports after the show you put on today for the crowds!"

Fired up by the rush from the day's work, Leonid suddenly broke into song in his deep baritone voice. The others picked up the tune.

It's a long way to Tipperary!
It's a long way to go!
It's a long long way to Tipperary!
To the sweetest girl I know!

"Perfect pub voice, Leonid! Resonant, beautiful, and spellbinding! I didn't know you could sing like that. You could make a living as a bar room singer, maybe in a cabaret club!"

"Actually, Dmitry, I sing with an amateur opera group here. I've been at it for about five years."

Like Krastov, Dmitry had been trying to win the crew's favor. Krastov's moves threatened him, and he had been feeling on the outs lately. He had this going for himself. Like Semyon, he was seldom right when he made a judgment. But he was seldom in doubt about himself. He had thought running a tight, efficient ship meant showing a firm, authoritarian hand. By mixing this with frequent use of endearing insults of the crew, he thought all that cemented his management authority by letting them know he was one of the boys. But it wasn't working and he sensed it.

The trucks drove on south of town to the Iset River weir surrounded by thick forests. It was their favorite spot to dump carcasses, So far, no one had noticed or complained.

"OK, men, go to it!" Dmitry bellowed.

With gloved hands, they began grabbing the dogs out of the trailers and throwing them off the weir into the rushing river below. Many of the carcasses were so large that it took both crew members to heave them over. It happened that many of the drugged dogs also went in with the dead ones, revealing the primitive sorting system was slipshod and random. If they went downstream too, good for them—have a nice swim if you wake up. Otherwise, they drowned alongside their already dead mates.

"That one looks like your uncle, Rudolf!"

He grimaced and laughed. "Or is it yours, Dmitry?"

After several hours of this, they drove in a convoy back to the animal control complex. On arrival, Krastov was waiting for them in front, waving to them as they arrived in the parking lot. He greeted them, and they went into the room next to the labs where he had set out a few snacks, bottles of beer, and soda water. There were chairs for them to sit around the table and chat.

"Well, how was it?"

Dmitry shuffled some papers around and gave them all a glowing report, telling Krastov of the squat dances and widespread, on the spot media coverage. His tone was cautiously flat and officious.

"That's just superb! In anticipation of another fine performance, I've prepared a few items for you. For all of you, I have these envelopes in which I have included some financial treats."

"No more tricks for treats?" said Anton.

"We've done enough of those kinds of tricks. Tomorrow you can count on positive media coverage. You're all going to be City stars! I want you to know that both the City and the Putin regime have taken notice of your work here. We are in the forefront by testing what they call a new National City strategy to deal with stray dogs and ensure the safety of important events like the World Cup."

"Someone told me of a rumor out there that we were creating a team of dogs that can secure the Games without any human handlers!" said Leonid.

"Not a bad idea! But crude science fiction, I can assure you, Leonid." Krastov grabbed his shoulder and said with a menacing grin aimed directly into his face:

"But if you come up with something interesting like that which we can develop quickly, you'll get another treat in an even larger envelope!"

In the corner, Fyodor listened to the conversations from his cage. Krastov had purposely designed his lodging so that he could open the door from the inside in case he needed to get out, wander around, borrow books, and find writing materials when no one else was around. He also could change the radio station. The cage kept intruders out and protected him from any who might want to dognap him and sell him to a traveling circus. Listening to Krastov and his crew, he could barely restrain himself from bursts of laughter. Furrowing his brow, he reflected on how Krastov had taken his advice. Krastov had done a lot recently to change the culture of the place as well as his own thinking. From his old school methods of shaming, inducing fear, and maintaining an atmosphere of intimidation, he was gradually shifting the emphasis to psychological safety and rewards for being creative. He was encouraging them to think and to speak out with ideas now as individuals and as part of his team. Fyodor had warned him that the metrics were encouraging excessive killing of dogs, and reluctantly, he had listened.

So Krastov changed the system of rewards so that crude metrics like "kills" or "raw captures" became the least important, and identifying and spotting promising experimental targets now got the most points. He saw that the crews felt safe airing criticism of both their work and his orders. Instead of becoming rigidly defensive, Krastov now responded to onslaughts of criticism with wit, tact, and more financial and non-financial rewards for them. If occasionally he didn't, it was because he was being hit from all sides at once: the City, the regime, and so on. Occasionally, he would even stop the work and tell them why he was frustrated so they could get behind his predicament and make it their own. That gave them fewer incentives to game the productivity system. Both Krastov and they leveled with each other—that any idiot could produce plausible numbers for simplistic categories. Now they engaged in review chats about the plausibility of the numbers and what they really meant. Fyodor noticed all this. He also pointed out to Krastov that during these open sessions with his crews, Dmitry remained conspicuously silent, providing no feedback, positive or negative. Fyodor advised him to watch out for this growing problem of disloyalty.

"Now before you go, I want to unveil another program that may interest you."

"More money?"

"Why not? Indirectly, if we are smart, Anton, we could all get more treats."

"I've seen you dance. I know that most of you can sing and that some of you play instruments. I also know that many of you can read music. I've endured your throaty lyrics, and you've listened to my appalling CDs in the truck. I think we can do better than that, don't you?"

"What do you mean?" asked Anton.

They all nodded anyway, waiting to hear what he would come up with this time. As he spoke, Krastov looked into their faces for reactions. Slowly, several became curious and more alert to his latest idea. They liked his earlier ones, such as the spiffy green uniforms. The colored logos, dancing routines, and ditties had given them local fame, and they were proud to advance from being glorified dogcatchers to public showmen, rescuing a few dogs and protecting the public health. In the past, they had been subject to public ridicule for being cruel to animals, lowly and incompetent. They were everyone's punching bag to blame when a dog bit someone, especially a child. Now with the challenge of the Games and Krastov's zeal, things were looking up—status and more pay! Krastov tried to avoid the silliness of success theatre that modern management gurus often dished out. The minute manager types tried site-gags posing as art to boost morale —it was mostly crap. But Krastov's spirited team–building integrated with working routines was changing their minds and focusing behavior. His crews were now snappy, disciplined, and performed impressive routines. Only Dmitry seemed detached. His eyes darted around behind his glasses as if calculating what this all would mean for him personally, his authority and future. He was not curious, didn't offer any suggestions for improvement, and was clearly just fearful—which Krastov found curiously odd.

"Leonid, a few notes please!"

He sang a short ditty he knew that was used by masters of ceremony entries in popular local theatres and cabaret clubs.

"Here's my idea. I got it by noticing how you worked harder and moved faster when accompanied by my Elvis CDs during our search and eradication missions."

"Come on, Dr. Ivan," smirked Leonid, "no more rolling in shit please!"

"OK, really… here it is: we've got the talent: you! We establish a stray dog choir called The Singing Mutts that will do public appearances. The purpose, if anyone asks what the hell we are doing, is to protect public safety and secure eligible stray dogs a secure future. We do music along with our tough love style law enforcement. Who can disagree with those goals or methods? We turn animal control into street theatre, a kind of masque with singing and dancing. Why not? We sing the lyrics in the face of the reality of the stray dog problem that needs sorting out. Maybe we even try to do an Elvis song with Dog lyrics—did you know that he sang one for his dog Shep?"

"I heard it once. It sounded like shit." said Boris.

"Indeed it did; it got him fired from his first audition. But we can do better."

"You think the insane din we hear all the time around here is music?" said Dmitry. "I can't sleep at night because I keep hearing the barking and howling! I even dream I'm stuck in cages with them, and they are all lunging at me and barking."

The rest of them laughed. "Right! It isn't music to most people, Dmitry. But you must know that dogs do accompany violins and accordions with sing-along howls and moans and have done so for centuries in many countries. There have actually been a few famous dog choirs! I have a friend who is an animal trainer nearby who can help us select a few choice mutts to sing along with us."

"Not sure I can see this yet. So how will the choir and instrumental parts work out?' asked Ivan.

"And here, you can help me. I know Leonid sings baritone. You guys tell me what kind of notes you can hit, and we divide up the roles. I can work with you a bit on this. You can help me work out the sounds since you clearly know more about music than I do. I want to establish a unique choir here. It will be amateur, like music at masques was in the old days. That will make it all the more popular as an authentic local product. It will be a "polyphonious" musical choir, as the musicians call them. One of you will lead it sometimes as in "monophonic" music—without any chords or accompanying harmony. The rest of you will help convert the music to "poly" by interweaving tunes and harmonies. It might sound like a '50s a capella group from the working class slums of American cities. So, we sing as one. We also sing apart in different melodies and styles and come back together as one—we have a vibrant beat. It sounds abstract, but it is actually quite simple. And even a bad harmony in that style will make a big impact on listeners. They will remember the Singing Mutts!"

"That still sounds hard. Do you think we can actually do something like that?" asked Danil.

"We can try. At least it will get us noticed by the City and the Kremlin in Moscow!"

"Who will write the lyrics?"

"You will. And I hand out rewards for the best ones, the ones we use. Here's my idea to move ahead. I will compose something initially, writing a few lyrics. I know you play piano, violin, and accordion, right? That's all we need."

They all nodded and exchanged complements. "I've heard you play a mean violin, Danil. You play the piano too loud, but it gets attention, Boris!"

"That's right; you all can play something. I can even play basic guitar. What about you Dmitry?"

He sat there with his arms folded as if he were someplace else. "Are you with us here? Do you understand? Agree? Disagree? What?"

"It is a risk that could get us negative publicity. They could accuse us of belittling our jobs, maybe even disloyalty to the state."

Dmitry then shrugged. The others looked at him curiously and then back to Krastov. None of them said anything.

"Never mind . . . He'll come around later. OK, I'll grab some songs for us from limericks and other sources on the common themes of dogs—lost dogs, dog memories, odes to favorite dogs, the tragic lives of dogs, and so on. We could even weave in hidden musical messages to remind people who we are: The Singing Mutts Choir. Some musical messages would support the Kremlin's policies to kill strays efficiently for the grand benefit of all. If someone is skeptical and challenges us, our defense is that the Orthodox Church likes sacred choral music and *missas* like this. I'll hunt around for a priest who supports our work and have him show up in his robes to bless us. I've talked with Father Pavel Petrovich at the Church on Blood about this, and he likes the idea. Now how would that look! Other compositions could be more subversive or sentimental. To show you how this might work, I wrote some lyrics last night."

Handing them to Leonid, he said: "See what you can do with this just looking at my words. Change them as you see fit."

Leonid concentrated on the paper for a few moments and then closed his eyes in deep thought. His mighty baritone voice threw out lyrics that almost rattled the windows:

Dreamt Daisy left home one day
Could tell from her look back that way
Back to the wilds she ran
If I could change her mind I can
O to the forests she ran!
Her look said nothing I can!

He sang it slow and deeply. It was sad, and Krastov saw that its power hit the crews with its sentimental masculinity. They were amazed. He had put musical rhythm to poetic words just off the top of his head! They began clapping and whistling.

"Perfect Leonid! If you can do something like that, we should be in business!" said Krastov. "Maybe practice together over vodka and beer some evenings, on me. How does that sound?"

Clapping and cheering the idea, they pumped their fists high in the air.

Krastov reviewed his ideas with them because he thought it could be a tribute to both music and their fieldwork. He was tired of years of blame for every conceivable health problem that corrupt officials and the lazy media tied to stray animals. His crew was frustrated, and he recognized that he had not given them enough support. They all needed their dignity back. But he had to be careful. What Fyodor described to him seemed to be moving too fast—they liked the idea of a radical upheaval in the culture and new ways of doing their jobs. It could come off as "virtue-signaling," which he knew some managers did with office parties and feasts to relieve pressure. Such tactics were mostly bullshit and had only short-term effects—like a good evening's drinking binge. Stories abounded of people being sacked the next day after office parties, despite all the hearty bonhomie created the night before. It had been such a nice atmosphere, just like a pot high, wearing off with the reality that work continued the next day surrounded by the same assholes and their petty power games. Somehow, he would have to do something different here to prevent that from happening.

Dmitry endured Krastov's discourse with a strained, grimaced expression that he tried unsuccessfully to stretch into a smile. He had been grinding his teeth unconsciously throughout, and Fyodor, watching all this from his cage in the corner, couldn't help but notice the growing red coloration of his face and the tightening of his jaw muscles. In Fyodor's view, Dmitry had been a good servant of Krastov and to the cause of humane animal control. He was a bit overdressed when he came to work, oddly sporting a plaid frock coat to convey perhaps an exaggerated majestic bearing to the others. He tried to inspire the crew's respect and even instill fear, but with little effect . . . and that bothered him. In front of Krastov, his body language was far too obsequious, leaving anyone with the impression that he was an accomplished boot-licker. His exaggerated bowing in front of Krastov and sudden deferential tilts of the head to one side were all simply too much for Fyodor. Fyodor watched in amazement as he sometimes bent his body in a fraudulent show of loyalty to Krastov and his causes. In Fyodor's view, the guy was a suspicious phony. He had told Krastov of these observations several times, but it was never clear if he noticed them himself or even cared. Though Krastov thought he was a bit odd, to him, Dmitry was simply another member of the crew holding the lofty title of Assistant. But now even his transparent show of deference was hard to continue. Krastov had learned to expect eccentric behavior of his crew. He almost admired that quality and thought it essential for the task. To Fyodor, Dmitry was merely a jealous ingrate and needed to be watched.

———

I got up early the next day and walked the few blocks from my flat to the nearby tram stop. No attack dogs out today so I put the pepper spray back in my pocket and enjoyed the cool summer morning air. Ivan wanted to show me something "terribly important" he said, so I was on my way to meet him. Not sure what he meant, but it sounded intriguing so I cautiously agreed, reminding him that I would really rather just sleep in. The tram rumbled to a stop, and I joined a crowd of people that I gathered from bits of conversation seemed to be working week-end shifts at places like restaurants, laundries, hotels, repair shops, and construction jobs. They were far different from the usual group of weekday urban professionals that I sat with on the way to USU. We lurched and bumped forward a few more stops to the Central Stadium where I hopped off and looked around for Ivan. I heard his voice nearby. He was with a group of people in a heated discussion with several of them and didn't notice me. It had to do with Putin's tenure and when Russia could make the transition to a European style democracy. Ivan wanted Russia to become an EU member, which I gather was not popular among the other students.

"You're a hopeless dreamer, Andrey!" I heard one of them shout.

He turned his back theatrically to the group and waved in frustration. Then he saw me and kept walking away from them.

"Good morning, Andrey! It sounds like you are fully awake!"

"Greetings Nicholas! Welcome to the Central Stadium. As you can tell, I like to get my intellectual juices flowing with a good political argument. I've been discussing issues with them for years. We never change each other's mind, but it's fun anyway. We remain civil in spite of our differences."

"An important issue is why you lured me out here this early? What are we doing?"

"Follow me; we are off to see the good Dr. Krastov. I'm not certain what he wants, but it sounded important. I'm sure you're curious?"

I shook my head affirmatively. "Lead on."

We took a nearby escalator down to the platforms of the Ploshchad Kommunarov metro station in the "1905" neighborhood near the Stadium. It had that familiar, refreshing smell (to me) of older metros that were heavily used. It reminded me fondly of the subway stations in New York City and Philadelphia, which over the years I had spent a lot of time in. I missed the steel girders full of giant rivets of the "Eles" that still cover many streets in the old U.S. cities. I liked the heavy industrial structures that reminded you of your ultimate insignificance to both history and to present events. You were one of many down there, standing between the pale darkness below and the redemptive sunlight above. But to yourself, perhaps, you were among the select allowed into these hallowed temples to experience the deafening roar of heavy trains, ploughing through at top speed on their express runs or, in rare cases, stopping to allow you to board. And that was it . . . Nevertheless, instinctively, I looked down at the rails as I always did in the U.S. No rats! I knew something was missing.

"You look surprised," Andrey said to me.

"I am. Can't see any rats! In New York subway stations, they lumber around between the rails, in and out of the tunnels as if they were coming to catch the trains."

"Why don't they exterminate them?"

"Too many of the buggers... They live off the garbage, much of which is created by the beggars and hobos that live in the tunnels. There's a whole city of poor beggars and tramps living down there. The stations are warm in the winter and cooler than outside in the summer. They feed the rats unintentionally from scraps and leftovers, and the rats grow to the size of groundhogs! Some can hardly walk they are so fat!"

"Sounds like a delightful place!"

"Hard to believe, but you get used to it and see the comic side. Tourists point them out and laugh. Commuters point out the regulars that frequent their stations. As long as the rats are well fed and don't attack any of the commuters and tourists, everyone is happy."

Andrey shook his head and gave me that skeptical look. But he wasn't a New Yorker—how could he know?"

We entered the Ploshchad Kommunarov station, which was like going into an elegant old mansion. The grand entrance was adorned with dark red floors lit by chandeliers from a marble ceiling. The art nouveau station had heavy marble pillars and walls to make you feel at home in this vast living room. I wanted an oil painting of the interior and, barring that, to remember every detail in it, down to the aged Russian soldier with a lengthy but trim beard standing nearby. He had a chest full of colored medals and ribbons from WWII hanging from his bright green military greatcoat and held tightly to the hand of his proudly smiling little granddaughter with blond pigtails. The front of his green dress hat soared upwards in almost comic fashion. The Soviets who built stations like this wanted to make them look better, a little grander than they were. So they used architects as well as engineers and geologists to design and build them.

Still, one might think the metros were older than 27 years. The Yekaterinburg system opened in 1991 with nine stations over almost eight miles. It was the last and most recent metro opened in the Soviet Union. While it has three lines now and is 16 miles long, the Kremlin said they ran out of funds and tried to stop further development. None other than USU alum Boris Yeltsin deftly moved money around the state budget, and it was completed in 1995.

As if to underscore the contrast between the sartorial elegance of the station and the utilitarian present dominated by large cement structures, a deafening roar came from the tunnel as the train exploded through and began to brake with loud screeches and sparks flying off the steel wheels. The train was a string of older dark and rusty green cars with a bright red star in the center of the first one. "Long live the Soviet Union!" and "Never forget!" it seemed to shout to the patrons waiting on the platform.

Expecting a cheer but hearing no one shout "hurrah," Ivan gave me a nudge back to consciousness: "Come on, wake up! This is our train."

We got on and rode a few stops to the Ural'Skaya station in what is called the Railway neighborhood. Without even knowing where you were, the loud, whirring screams of the electric subway motors gave it away. They filled the stations with their sounds on departure and arrival. The older U.S. subways from the 20th century sounded the same, but they are gone now, replaced by the sleek, quiet aerospace type cars for maximum comfort. Russian subway cars in some systems, such as Prague, were modern now, but for most Russian cities and former "colony cities" like Kyiv or "Little Moscow" in Ukraine, they were still ancient. No matter. I liked them and was always glad to be back riding them as they reminded me of just who I was and where I came from.

We passed through the grand salon of the station, heavy on Tsarist nostalgia with large glassy chandeliers and gray granite floors. At both Ploshchad Kommunarov and Ural'Skaya stations, the otherwise elegant platforms were permeated by dogs of all sizes and shapes, lying around, sitting patiently, scratching, yawning and looking around in no particular hurry to move on.

"What are all these dogs doing here? They don't look like their begging for food."

"They usually aren't. Many are abandoned and are here waiting for their masters to return. They knew where the stations were from walks when they were owned dogs and now expect to see them. But most have moved on and live in high rise flats where dogs are not allowed so they just abandoned their pets."

"They couldn't get them adopted or take them to humane societies?"

"Not here. Those kinds of services exist only on paper. You take them to the city or get the state involved, and they are usually put down," said Ivan.

As we walked out, I noticed an alert-looking dwarf bulldog mix following alongside us. About thirty pounds and fit, he seemed to be enjoying our conversation and looked up at us every few feet. We moved along with Andrey explaining in slow detail the history of the neighborhood and what went on there. As he pointed upwards to a statue in a nearby park, he suddenly yelled out.

"Damn dogs, get off me you bastard!"

Another dog had come from behind us and bit into the back of his leg through his pants. He reached down carefully as the dog chewed on him, grabbed the dog by the neck with one hand, and deftly squeezed the dog's nose between the thumb and finger of his other hand. The dog snorted and immediately opened its jaws, allowing Ivan to get in a solid kick that sent him a few feet from us. The dog squealed and retreated, barking hysterically. The bulldog mix darted forward and attacked the other dog and held him to the ground while chewing roughly into its neck. Despite all the violence and action, and the latest fit of barking, there was very little noise, hardly any growling or barking. It was all quite efficient.

"You all right, Andrey? Show me the leg."

"Shit, it looks bad, like the one on my leg that is now just healing. We need to get that looked at."

"Not important today. The weather is too refreshing to waste time on small setbacks such as this. I'm certainly not going to see a doctor about it. What the hell do they know?" he asked, with the cynical grin of someone who knew the health system.

Off Andrey went, leading the way again in even higher spirits than before. Maybe he was in shock . . . The bulldog looked up at us for praise, which we both gave him in ample quantities—pats on the head, accompanied by approving hugs and compliments.

"Let's buy him something from that *shashlik* stand over there as a reward," I said.

As we munched our grilled sausages, or *shashliks*, and gave tidbits to the bulldog, I said: "Andrey, where did you learn that trick to get a dog's jaws open?"

"No trick at all. I learned it from my dad, who had a problem with dogs. I find it almost 100 percent effective, day or night, when I get attacked."

"Which seems to be all the time."

"Might be fewer times than before. At least, that what Dr. Krastov would tell us."

"Here, let's see what this dog can do." He was alertly watching us talk at the sausage seller.

"Down …" I said. He promptly got down on all fours and waited for the next command. I handed him a bit of sausage. "OK, sit." He got up on his haunches and looked at us. "Good lad!" and I handed him another piece of meat.

Just about that time, a green truck roared up with two men in it and parked next to us. Out jumped Boris and Leonid in their spiffy green coveralls.

"Morning, you guys!" shouted Leonid enthusiastically. "And what have we here, a willing stray? Or is it a pet of yours?"

"Not ours. We just met him fifteen minutes ago by the station. He intervened when we were attacked there by another dog," said Andrey. "I think he believes we owe him something for saving us!"

"OK! He gets to ride in first class to the doc's lab. He might get a free brain operation! Otherwise, I'm sure he will be interviewed and signed up quickly for his advanced training in human non-canine be-havior." said Leonid, patting him on the head. "Hop in, boy!" The dog jumped right in without further need for any prodding.

"Boris, get us two *shashliks* to go, will you? Take this change."

We drove through the back streets of the industrial and warehouse section of town to the animal control facility. We entered a building I had not seen before which turned out to be the hospital for sick dogs. These were strays that were not put down, not tossed into the river, or incinerated, but dogs that had potential. The word was that Krastov's staff tried to bring them back to a reasonable state of good health so they could be trained further or even adopted. Most of them didn't make it.

We went inside and found the rest of the crew there gathered around Krastov. There was a large, wounded dog lying on a blanket with bandages all over it. Krastov was talking to them, and they were listening in respectful silence. Standing next to him was Fyodor. It was the first time I saw him stand up. He had a slight stoop forward but otherwise looked like a regular biped. Krastov's face was taut, and he spoke deeply with a rasp in his voice. He had tears in his eyes, and he was clearly angry. I had never seen him in this state.

"I had to search for him around here this morning. Thought he had run off someplace, maybe back to the streets. But I found him hiding in the storeroom. He was ashamed, you see. Didn't want me to see him dying like this... It's what dogs do, don't they? They are humiliated by their own weakness and want to stay hidden from those they love."

"They do that, Doctor. Much more courage and dignity than humans, I think. My dog did exactly what Tsar did, last year. I cried for two whole days," said Boris.

"Thank you Boris. For the past several months, you and I have worked with Tsar. Fyodor helped us in communicating with him and translating for us, as only he can understand the non-verbal language of dogs. I fully planned for him to become Fyodor's assistant and serve as the next model of our efforts here. He was a brilliant dog, and I had every hope for him. But I failed. His cancer has spread all over his insides, and I can do nothing to stop it. How can I perfect dogs and create a new non-human species when I cannot even cure what ails them now?"

Boris stepped forward and put his arm on Krastov's shoulder. "You tried, Doctor. That's all anyone can do. We loved Tsar as much as you, and we were all pulling for him."

"That's right Boris," said Leonid. "Nothing can stop cancer once it gets going inside you. It kills humans; it kills dogs too. All we can do is keep trying to find a cure that works on future dogs that will help humanity."

"Hear! Hear!" the group chorused. "This can only make us work harder to deal with the many problems that dogs face," said Leonid.

"And let us give thanks to Dr. Krastov for his efforts. He developed me, and fortunately, at least for now, I have no cancer to set us back," said Fyodor to the group.

Krastov hugged Fyodor and was now crying like a baby. Tears were all over his face and pouring onto the floor. They bent down to Tsar, who was trying to follow what was going on but had that confused look of the aged or sick dog—they struggle to focus, but can't.

Tsar whimpered and voiced syllables quietly to Fyodor, and he translated: "Tsar thanks all of you for trying to nurse him back to health."

At that moment, the bulldog stray that had been listening attentively to all this, came forward and licked Tsar's face with little squeals and whimpers of sympathy. He was communicating concern to the dog in their silent, non-verbal tongue. He suddenly scampered off and returned with a colored piece of rope that the dogs used as a toy. He put it next to Tsar, who was too weak to notice. But we all did.

Then Krastov bellowed out: "I don't know if I can take this job anymore. The guilt from killing innocent dogs, the failures with dogs like Tsar ... I shouldn't continue at this," he sobbed.

I watched Tsar's expression—a wistful look of sadness that it couldn't continue down its master's path, or its own either. I remembered particularly a lab that I had for over ten years that I found collapsed on the floor in the back of the kitchen out of sight. It was ashamed that it couldn't continue and had the same look as Tsar when I found it. I took it to the vet who told me it was over, and there was nothing that could be done. The vet and nurses left the room with my dog lying on the rug I brought him in on. I hugged him tightly, trying to find something to say, something that meant this was goodbye. He looked at me finally with that saddened expression I will never forget. I got up, went to the door, and looked back. His ears perked up. Was it time for a walk then? I stared at him and began crying uncontrollably. He looked at me. Then he looked away and put his head down on his front paws. I left and went out into the hall, bawling out loud like a baby.

Krastov's crew was stunned. No one said anything but all eyes shifted to Dmitry, who smiled at each of them and nodded. His anticipation of something big was as obvious as his swollen head.

"No!" shouted Leonid. "You must continue, and we will support you whatever happens." The rest of them shouted, "Hear! Hear!"

"We may have found a new candidate for you, Doc," said Andrey. "He saved us from being attacked on the way here, and he's sharp as a blade. Sign him up!"

Krastov bent down and gave the bulldog a few pats on the head, then hugged him uncontrollably. "He looks promising, Andrey. Thanks." Then he shouted out to us, "And thanks to all of you for your support and advice in this matter and all others here at the facility. I owe all this to you!"

Then a bit of high church drama took place. Besides Andrey and myself, there were about ten others in the room: lab workers, staff assistants, as well as members of the several stray retrieval crews. There were several women who worked in the lab I hadn't seen before. All of us came forward and put our hands on Krastov's shoulder as if he were being formally baptized into a congregation. In a way he had been. Over the brief time I had known him, I noticed that Krastov had the attention of his staff and crews—for better or worse. But now he had their respect and favorable attention as well. This suggested a new era of camaraderie between them all—with great things about to be accomplished. While the others clapped along during the little ceremony for Tsar, I did notice that Dmitry had not hugged Krastov, Tsar, or anyone else.

11   TEACHING AND TRAINING IN THE TRENCHES

For the next several days, the electricity of sudden sex in that mountain storm with Anna had brought the fire back and had renewed a sense of life in me. Entire days I spent replaying the scenes in my mind, both in daydreams and at night. I regained the reckless abandon of my teenage years again. The dreams merged into reality as Anna and I met repeatedly and got into bed at my place several afternoons a week. Nobody, not even Sveta I imagined, seemed to notice her comings and goings, and we were never interrupted. Both of us were ecstatic, happy and completely at ease in each other's presence. After a few weeks, the afternoon generation of mutual sparks at my apartment morphed into the regularity of a professional relationship. We were still on fire, and there was no loss of passion between us. Semyon, according to her, was evidently colder towards her, but she was used to his moods and to sparring with him regularly over petty matters. So in her view, there was nothing to be concerned about there, at least not yet. With me, she was still a new item, and we both enjoyed our times in passionate love-making as well as working together on the Politology faculty at USU.

As planned, we began the team teaching effort after developing a module that, we thought, might be replicated elsewhere if we were successful. Ivan accompanied us to help with logistics and to observe how it worked in a live setting. The training room at the City of Yekaterinburg complex was modern and had an integrated computer system in front that operated our slide files for the remote camera hanging from the ceiling. As with such systems at good U.S. universities (even Bonaduz

College finally installed them), it showed the slides to the class on a large screen behind us. We had personally met with the mayor and the heads of city services including the police and animal control. I especially wanted to see these people to gauge if they could trust me enough to work with and to visit their field operations. I was in luck as once the mayor tuned into me, the rest followed by formal or informal directive. It worked that way for me in several countries of this region at the city level, and it seemed to be working here. The feedback was predictably instant—either they liked and trusted you, or they didn't. In the past, I had been told to leave several cities of the Former Soviet Union on the spot where I was attempting to do research. Such was the life of the unsponsored academic! I had the advantage of being of Russian parentage, but the disadvantage of being raised in the historic Cold War era. Since some of the officials had lived through the Cold War, they responded with surprised looks at meeting me, and in other cases were visibly crusty. I expected that and met the occasional jibes with a few attempts at humor, some forced grins, or just shrugs of indifference.

It was during one class that some of this underlying animosity erupted. Perhaps it was just an expression of genuine anger. But anger from what? Family problems? Wife-husband problems? Money problems? Who knows? Maybe they had just had a bad day. They could have been sacked or given notice to clear off by an abusive boss. That happened all the time around here. Maybe I was taking it all too personally, but their anger seemed directed at me. For several days, Anna, Ivan, and I had been doing team teaching of planning methods for about fifteen city staff from various departments. The idea was to present the latest planning models then shift to service operational problems and remedies. Along the way, we hoped to develop a few instructional cases that could be used in future classes here—especially on the biggest current "messy" problem of dog catching.

Anna and I traded off presenting modules all that morning. I sat to the side and listened to her. She was witty, authoritative, and engaging—just what a professional teacher should be. We had just finished teaching our modules on development planning: the usual topics, such as analysis of current and emerging conditions, and making action programs that would include a financial plan and a land acquisition program. We presented other implementation tools that were used in the U.S. like tax increment financing or TIFs, where poorer neighborhoods could be fixed up with small capital works using city bonds and repayments from land appreciation. From student comments, it turned out that they were the same tools mostly used here except cities were not big on community inputs into planning processes from mass publics, other than core stakeholders like property developers. Or often city planners knew the tools but were blocked from presenting their recommendations based on them by local and provincial leaders that were opposed to their implications. Unsurprisingly, city planning and political processes were typically closed, secretive processes—top-down operations just like the Kremlin itself.

As we began, I realized that I was far more wired up and alert than from my usual morning coffees. The cups of bitter fuel provided powerful jolts to me that pulsated throughout my body and mind, all ramped up by tobacco fumes. Stupidly, I had forgotten that everyone in these parts smoked. The ashtrays were all full of stubbed-out cigarette butts. They had been pushed into them in disgust as a prelude to the standard ritual of lighting more of them. And what didn't end up in the ashtrays ended up on the floor. The rest seeped into your clothing so that you had a portable cigarette going at all times, even without one. You could smoke vicariously by inhaling the permanently thick clouds of fumes. I knew then that all my clothes would have to go into the trash bin on leaving the place before going back to the U.S. Bonaduz College had a strict no smoking policy and just wearing my clothes would violate it.

"We're tired of hearing about vision statements and plans. This is Russia; we know how to plan here," one of the participants said out loud from his desk.

That brought a round of well-deserved laughter from the others. "That you do! And your name is?"

"I am Yevgeny from the Planning Department. Let me tell you what is missing from your presentations. When we at the city produce model land acquisition programs like those you have suggested, we try and accommodate our poorer citizens with affordable housing. But then the poor citizens mysteriously disappear in the final phase of decision-making. How could that happen? Because vanity projects and insider land trading are common practices here and in every Russian city."

"So why is that?"

"Why?" Why do you think?" he replied with a smirk, as his classmates laughed along. "Everyone here knows that the processes are corrupt, and that our version of what you call an eminent domain process is used as a tool by developers to toss out tenants. The developers force the city to drive out tenants by first letting their apartments or homes go to seed. Then they make sure that the 'takings' in the glorious name of the larger privatization programs provide the tenants with very few funds to go elsewhere. In other words, community redevelopment here and elsewhere in Russia is a euphemism for tenant eviction. There are no ordinances requiring that the city provide affordable housing for this newly created class of displaced tenants to buy or rent. It's a cruel boondoggle!" he said, and others nodded their heads and hummed affirmatively.

"My family and I live in one of the homes recently taken by my employer, the city," said a voice from the back.

"Your name, please sir?"

"I am Nicolai from the Public Works Department. Tell us what remedies you can offer for these standard problems?"

I sensed that this was not the kind of group I had faced in places like Norway or Estonia. They were polite and respectful there, a reflection of their peaceful worlds and the cultural values that went with them. These people were switched-on, cynical, aggressive, and challenging. A tough bunch! And they were justifiably pissed at the naivety of our model planning process and the corrupt distortions of their housing system. Worse, as city officials, they got blamed for systems and processes that were put in place by a distant Kremlin regime.

"We have the same problems in the U.S," I said. "Developers game the system and distort city planning, leading to large clusters of brutalist, high-rise ghettos with miserable tenants who suffer bad services. The owners received public subsidies to evict the previous tenants or owners and then profit again at public expense. Not the way it should work, is it?"

"Sounds like you describe ideal and model systems that fail in practice because the wrong people profit from it. Is that what you are teaching then? You're not defending the kinds of technical methods that ruin people's lives, are you?" asked Nicolai.

"Not if I we help it. There are options—none of them perfect at all. Sometimes we recommend higher height limits, as they do in Europe, but that often leads to more profits for corrupt builders who obtain permits via bribes. Our most common recommendation is to allow more stakeholders into the planning process to make their views known. Then through public comment and media coverage others can learn from their ideas, and we think the overall plan will be better for everyone, not just the big builders. On that note, let's take a short break."

I left the room and went out to the head, thinking I hadn't convinced anyone. Least of all myself . . . On my way back, I found Nicolai was waiting for me in the hall. He looked determined, but his face twitched a few times as if he were building up his courage.

"Your words in there ... you know what you said was total bullshit, don't you? I do technical plans like the rest of us, and they are always ignored by the corrupt city administration. We've been reading about "opportunity zones" in the U.S. for years. They don't target the poor or provide affordable housing. They give tax break to banks, investors, and real estate developers. It's a sham, and you know it!"

"Ok! Ok! But, Nicolai, isn't that a bit unfair? My understanding is the City is engaged in modern planning and so far doing a great job preparing for the Games. And economic opportunity zones do provide some affordable housing, if defined properly and targeted. If the cities limit rental and sales prices, they mostly work. Some do; some don't. It's not your fault. It's not ours either since we are not elected or appointed by anyone high enough to make a difference."

"The Games . . . The Games . . ." he ranted. "What do they have to do with us? We live here. The Games are for Putin and his cronies and, of course, the tourists/ Always the tourists, who spend money and fall for his crap PR that this is a paradise . . ."

Nicolai was about my height at six feet, albeit younger, probably around thirty. He was obviously in shape and had that confident, aggressive air of a professional athlete, maybe a footballer or runner. As he spoke, he moved closer and seemed even more nervously frustrated now. He flashed a crocodile grin at me, but it thinly masked deeper insecurities and personal problems. He had mentioned his family was living in a rundown place and were about to be evicted so that was probably it. I also watched some of them in class, including Nicolai, when Anna taught her modules. The way she moved around up front exuded sex. Lecturing in tight jeans, her well-rounded pear-shaped ass undulated back and forth as she wrote on the board. Her olive-skinned hips and stomach showed as she frequently bent over the desk to get marking pens. She aroused some, if not all, of them; some like Nicolai may have been jealous of her. Who knows? From my end, I hadn't been sleeping well lately. I often broke out in feverish sweats at night, only to be back in form by morning. Whatever the problem, I was getting short-tempered, and I was tired of taking crap from morons, the same kind I sometimes had to put up with in my Elmira classes and that had filed nonsense complaints about my attitudes and comments.

But I still was in control of myself. "These are good points, Nicolai. Why don't you raise some of them in the class then?"

"Because I'm raising them with you now. Why don't you say something I haven't heard before, you shithead?"

He hit me so fast I was caught completely off guard. Standing just a few feet from me as he said this, I was suddenly propelled backwards into the wall by the quick force of his powerful, one-handed shove to the chest. I bounced back off the wall and held out my palms to try and get him to be reasonable.

"Come on, Nicolai, I quit doing petty scraps like this after secondary school. Let's go back to the classroom."

Not convinced, he moved towards me again. This time I saw his fist coming and parried it. I followed with a quick right to the jaw, which floored him. Same one I used rather effectively on the Transsib. It only works if I connect. Otherwise, most assailants are in better shape and younger than me. This time it worked. Down he went and didn't get up. As he was temporarily dazed, I went back to the classroom to find Andrey to see if I could get some help. Entering the room, I signaled to Andrey, who was talking with Anna, and he followed me to the head where Nicolai was still on the floor but trying to get up.

"Looks like one of the students tripped over his shoelaces," he said with his wry grin.

"That's right, help him up."

He was silent as we escorted him back to the classroom. Unexpectedly, he sat quietly in his chair for the next module. His eyes were vacant, and his face was completely pale. He seemed spacey and didn't utter a peep. When he wasn't starring glassy-eyed around the room, he looked down at his lap and his hands, folded between his legs like a scolded child. I thought at one point he might pass out and fall onto the floor.

In the afternoon, Anna and I did a team teaching routine covering improved planning and delivery of municipal services. It was the usual stuff about better management control made more appealing by tossing in standard New Public Management concepts like devolution of authority to line managers and rewards for achieving performance targets—basically, a to-do list of modern management concepts since the 1970s. They were equally successful in public as well as commercial management, including state enterprises. The officials warmed to these ideas and asked a lot of questions, which renewed my faith in the value of fiscal and management decentralization for greater local government autonomy. Often students think they are all abstract nonsense, and I couldn't blame them. Such concepts and ideas could actually make a difference to service results, even if the regime was centralized and authoritarian, but not as ambitious as the old-fashioned Soviet totalitarian system. Maybe just a bit "illiberal." I worked all this around to the case of dealing with stray dogs. I approached it as a health issue since there had been reported rabies cases from attacks by strays, and then to the broader political and media issue of how the city has prepared to stage the World Cup Games shortly. That seemed to get their juices flowing.

My part of the module covered efficiency of service operations, performance reporting to improve management oversight, New Public Management concepts like greater managerial discretion to dispense rewards and punishments, and devolution of authority to line units. More of them seemed to like this because it was about their jobs and how they could get more rewards for doing a better job. They were open enough to give examples from their own departments and managerial contexts. Again, I tried to tie this into the stray dog problem that could threaten the Games and for which changes in management authority and incentives had to be made right now. But they had a big problem with the decentralization idea.

"Aren't you just spreading corruption from the central government to local special interests? Are you aware that devolving more power to local authorities plays right into the hands of the entrenched families and their official connections? Do you know that they control virtual fiefs?"

"And you are, sir?" I asked.

"I am Yevgeny," the burly man sitting to the side answered. "I am head of public works here at the City."

"Thank you, and I should add all of you, for the candor of your questions, criticisms, and examples from your work. I can assure you that not all training exercises benefit from such experiences as yours. Yevgeny, you are absolutely right. The concerns you raise have been a problem with decentralization programs all over the world. The way to deal with that is stronger independent, local, internal audit institutions that report to independent authorities. They must be overseen by similar institutions that root out fraud, waste, and abuse at higher provincial levels and, ultimately the Kremlin in Moscow."

"But of course, they don't exist, do they? If they do, they aren't independent and report only what is politically convenient in the short term. Isn't that so?"

"Right again," I said. "No magic solutions there either in the U.S. or elsewhere. But what we are talking about really is municipal services. You would like to have more financial and management discretion and authority in your position, would you not?"

"Yes, I would."

"That's what I am talking about, devolving fiscal and management authority to managers at the local level. Of course, the decision to allow local authorities such as Yekaterinburg to keep more of the revenues that it collects depends on Kremlin decisions. I know that. What you want are not more Kremlin fiscal transfers but permanent fiscal autonomy to raise and spend money as you see fit here for local needs when there are no public spectaculars such as World Cup Games. I'm talking about real structural changes for cities like yours. I think that will happen as you demonstrate your skills in spending the extra funds they are now providing from Moscow to identify and solve local problems. It's a big opportunity.

"Agreed." he said.

"So let's start at the beginning," I said. "How do we know there's a real problem with stray dogs?"

"Reported dog attacks and rabies cases," someone answered.

"Right! That makes the problem actionable and tangible. It gives us a baseline from which to gauge performance. Do we know how many pet owners there are around here? Does the City have data on dog attacks and rabies cases?

"We have most of that data," said the head of the department, sitting in with the rest of the staff.

"What options can you think of to deal with the problem as you defined it?"

"More pounds and dog catchers," said another.

"Excellent!"

"Regulate the pet-owners and fine them," said still another.

"How?"

"The Chinese use a point system. Owners lose points for failing to register or vaccinate their dogs. They lose more points for letting dogs off leads. If one gets away and becomes a stray, they lose even more points until eventually the dog is confiscated."

"Then what?"

"They have them put down."

"Isn't that a bit extreme to blame the dog for the owner? Why not just put the strays in pounds in the first place and get them adopted?"

"Pounds cost a lot of money and take too long to build," someone noted. "Capital projects have to be approved by Provincial and Kremlin officials. More to the point, the City doesn't have the money."

"That's where you can use fines and registration fee revenue to pay off bonds for pounds."

"Not here," said Yevgeny. "We know how Western local governments issue bonded debt on capital markets. We can't issue bonds here without Provincial approval, and even then it would take time to put a bond issue together, sell it, and use the funds for our capital needs."

This is something I wasn't aware of. Most former Soviet cities in Central and Eastern Europe could now issue their own bonds and did so often. So Russian cities were in a financial bind. Nevertheless, these exchanges were good; I learned a lot. The students seemed to be enjoying the discussions. Then someone from the back shouted out:

"Stray dog problem? Rabies? Attacks of dog packs in town? You are exaggerating! That's all fake news! You do know what that is, don't you?" The verbal attack came from someone in the back.

"And you, sir, what is your name?"

"Why, it's Donald Trump," he said with a smirk, looking around for support from the class. "It's fake news!"

I once read some practical training materials on dealing with the 'difficult student' in class. So I tried out my new techniques—laughing along with him or her, shifting to serious questions to get them back on track, being respectful—none of these methods worked. Looks like we had another potential Nicolai to deal with. It was shaping up to be a rough day… His Trump reference was more to me as an American, stuck with an angry demagogue for a president, who got along fine with their President Putin but relied on his loans and investments, engaging in U.S. electoral interference to denigrate better candidates, and encouraging far right extremists. It was a well-known, transparently simple and effective strategy. The term 'fake' was used by nativists who denied news critical of them and liked to pretend it was phony, while relying on a lemming-like media eager for a story to transmit this angry claptrap to their hard right supporters. So here was another "difficult student" situation that came up increasingly with training in different cultural settings.

Following "the book," I let him go on disrupting.

"Hey, did you hear the one about how they treated dogs at Solovki island prison?" he bellowed out to the class. He looked on me with a tough, cold stare, but a rather obviously insecure and tentative grin. "You might have read that it used to be a monastery," he added looking around. It was clear the others didn't know what he was getting at either.

"There they treated the prisoners like dogs and tried to intimidate them. But they could only intimidate them to a point."

"Yes, I see," I said, not knowing what this would set off.

"But if the dog has a need to growl, nothing can stop him, not even beatings. The same is true of the Russian prisoners or anyone else for that matter. You can cow them into submission, but eventually they will resist."

"Again, I take your point."

"The punch line is that even if they are all from the same breed, one should never try and break up a dog fight from the outside. Neither America nor your management gimmicks can break us up and turn Slavs against each other."

"So Don, I believe that is your name, isn't it? I believe Don is telling us three things if I can paraphrase you . . . Can I do that?" I said, moving down the aisle towards him to make better eye contact. "First, there is no real dog problem that threatens the Games. Second, maiming or killing the strays, like human prisoners, only makes the packs stronger and angrier. That approach is ultimately self-defeating. Third, if there are problems, letting the dogs multiply and roam free in the streets is preferable to trying to manage the stray problems, no?"

"What do you know about managing? All you do is kill them!"

He sat there with arms folded, staring obliquely towards me like Nicolai, the last guy who wanted to beat the shit out of me. He was throwing me a glance of sleepy cunning, which quickly would focus and guide his fists toward me. I anticipated that on the Transsib. The same feral logic of a growl and spring was shaping up here. I expected having to deal with some of this as part of the cultural turf if I returned to Russia and worked here. Well, I was right!

"We know that continued killing is a mug's game, and you are right," I said. "That's one game we can never win. Dogs breed super fast and replace those put down on the streets. The packs get larger, not smaller, because we can't mobilize the Russian army with their firepower to do animal control work, can we? Hence, we need to rethink the problem to develop new management options. Two days ago, I witnessed about one hundred strays in several packs converge on Central Stadium and begin attacking bystanders, including children, out for Sunday strolls on a nice summer day. Not a pretty sight.

"So did you kill them all?" he threw back at me.

"I tied up Leo, the dog I was walking, and got my pepper spray ready to protect him and myself if necessary. But I was interrupted by the arrival of three truckloads of Animal Control officials wearing bright green uniforms with thick gloves and high boots. They drove right into the middle of the packs, piled out in formation, and went to work with nets, dart guns, and clubs. Once they had subdued the dogs, they used tongs to toss the carcasses into several carts to be taken off to several large city pounds. The new pounds had been set up in abandoned warehouses and other buildings and are staffed with city volunteers overseen by paid staff. At the City, we want the recent strays and similar candidates to be licensed and adopted. The recent problem at the Stadium was remedied by rapid response and efficient methods. So, to answer you, no I didn't kill them nor did anyone else. And none of us wants to do that. Most of us own dogs. Like you said, you should never try to break up a dogfight from the outside. They were attacking each other as much as the bystanders and needed to be treated carefully. There are rising rabies cases in nearby Perm and other Russian cities from dog attacks. Right now, we're trying different methods of control and seeing which ones work best. Do you have any better approaches that would protect public safety?"

He moved about in his seat, unsure of what to say. At least some of this got to him. Still, he sat there looking smug and confused.

"Any other questions?" On the screen up front, I was able to show them pictures of the attack and response taken with my phone. There were several questions, all of them serious and all related to the organization and management of the operation, and how it might be replicated. I told them, it is being replicated every day with new crews and different missions. Like other city services, we had resources, but needed far more to achieve good results.

"In short, I think we are getting a handle on what is really a serious problem with measurable effects on public health and which is a threat to public safety and the Games," I said, looking over at Anna and Andrey.

"OK, that's enough for today. Tomorrow we can discuss this case in more detail and hear from you on other services that could use methods like this to improve operations," said Anna. "We want to develop a case study writing a grant program here. The idea so far is to provide financial incentives to you; you write up service problems, options for improvement, and recommendations. Then you present them in training modules like this. Sound ok? Think about how we might do that. Good! More about this tomorrow."

The three of us gathered up our materials, chatting briefly with a few students who had questions related to clarification of particular points. With quick exchanges of eye contact, it was clear that we were in a hurry to get out of there before any more flare-ups.

We had just left the classroom and moved into the hall when up came Nicolai. He looked grim, but not aggressively so. Probably no concentrated venom about to burst out again, but I could be wrong.

"I wanted to apologize for before," he stammered. I looked at him and said nothing. "I used to work for the railway before I came to the City and had an accident."

"Tell me about it."

"Years ago, I worked in a switch yard and fell off a freight car I was guiding onto a new track. I fell on my head and was out of work for several years while I recovered. I am not quite normal yet and still have wild mood swings and loss of control problems."

"Thank you for telling me. We were both at fault for using our fists when we could have talked it out. If you need anything from me, I am at your service. See you in class tomorrow, Nicolai." We shook hands, and I watched him move off down the hall.

It was about 6 p.m. when the three of us left the building, but we didn't get far. We looked at each other with instant and perfect understanding. We all needed to unwind . . . It had been a rough day of fights, difficult students, and serious intellectual challenges that had tired us out. Ivan knew of a nearby dance club called *The Cool It*, which sounded just right. We walked a few blocks together in boisterous spirits and finally found the place.

"Is this place open? Ivan, it looks like it is abandoned."

"That's how all the best ones look. They are in rundown neighborhoods, partially abandoned buildings, but with large dance floors. Come on... Let me show you what I mean.'

We entered a small doorway to be greeted by a really tough-looking guy in a torso t-shirt and tight jeans. His nose was partially squashed, which suggested he was not about to take any shit.

"Do we need tickets?"

"Not tonight. Just go in and down the stairs." We followed orders, stepping down a narrow, winding staircase that might have worked as well on a destroyer or submarine as in a dance club. Downstairs, there was a large dance floor bathed in colored lights, loud techno music, banging off the walls, and plenty of new wave mod people mostly in their twenties.

"Might just be something here for me tonight," said Ivan, flashing a grin that was new to me and looked good on him.

"Right Andrey, go for it! Anna and I will give you references if you need them."

We sat at a table and were met almost instantaneously by a large, shapely, Amazonian blonde whose perfectly proportioned, windswept head looked to me like the mascot on the hood of a fast car. She was likely wearing a wig and definitely wearing a short, black, leather skirt. I felt immediately we had come to the right place to forget and unwind. To celebrate our release from a hard day of work, we ordered six vodkas (two each) from her to get the evening going. They were the first of many.

"So Andrey, how did we do? Any suggestions for improvements?"

"Yes! We should bring the next class to a place like this for a few hours to loosen them up first. Otherwise, we probably need to work out at a boxing gym before going in there. They were a tough bunch!"

"What do you think Anna?"

Right then, the techno music in the background stopped, and a band to the side started playing. It was like an explosion of music! They blew their saxophones, pounded on drums, and played their fiddles while the lead guy wailed out rockabilly type tunes in Russian. My feet and legs suddenly couldn't stop moving under the table. They moved in uncontrollable spasms. Elvis once said he had the same problem. His feet started moving, and he said he couldn't help it—he just couldn't stand still! Long live Elvis!

"I can't control myself, Anna! Let's go!"

I grabbed her and felt a sudden change in my body. It was no longer in my control! I suddenly began to dance with her in front of me on the floor. She moved to the beat, and I watched and understood every twitch and lurch she made. We got in synch and off I went! I suddenly began to dance, if that was the word for it. It was like I had been stung—by her, by the daytime frustrations, by my new life there, and especially by the vodkas. Where had I learned these steps? Maybe in high school? But I hadn't danced for years. I flung my arms and legs out. My body was buckling and straightening out in rapid jerks. My head thrust itself back and forward like a punching ball. Where did those moves come from? I grabbed her and spun her around, and we continued to move back and forth across the floor. It was the general air of looking for a knockout on the ropes. Anna watched me, magnetized by my sudden transformation. We must have danced for an hour or more before my legs finally gave out, and I led her back to the table.

"Nicholas, you have been reborn!" she said.

"Who is this guy? Do we know him?" asked Andrey.

Meanwhile, Andrey spotted a girl that he thought he knew, and that was good enough for him. The next thing we noticed, he was on the floor with her doing a local quickstep that she knew as well.

"Well Anna," I said. "We should top off the day with a short dance to my place, don't you agree?"

She nodded hungrily, and off we went, but not before I waved goodbye to Andrey and wished him luck. The next thing I remember, besides navigating the stairs upwards and onto the street, is that we were in my bed. Without any preliminaries, we were rolling around nude on the bed, licking each other like precious candy. We were bed dancing now. I licked every crevice on her that I could think of before entering. She guided me in with both hands, and off we went. The energy we put into it must have shaken the house. I had no idea how much noise we made—the groans and swoons, perhaps she shouted out during orgasm. Who knew? Who cared; it was one of the best of our many bedtime escapades. We always said that until we met the next time and went at it again. Such is being a teenager again in love … Could Dion and the Belmonts have put it any better?

12   ENTER DR. KRASTOV

"And so, comrades, the regime works valiantly to protect Crimea from the imperialist West and the U.S. Are we to interfere with what governments in Crimea and Venezuela do? No, my friends, that is their business. How can we presume to understand their local cultures? All we can do is help them defeat their reactionary enemies with military aid and generous loans to help their economies grow. Is that not so, comrades? The West has its sphere of influence and so do we."

The radio was broadcasting the evening news and commentary to the people of Yekaterinburg from Moscow. Krastov left the radio on loud enough that anyone listening would think there were people talking in his lab late at night and that he was working hard as well. More importantly, the radio propaganda drowned out Fyodor's voice.

Fyodor was perched in a nearby chair and was concentrating hard on how to smoke cigarettes, using his newly-acquired agility. It took some doing, but he was doing it with his paws. He had taught himself through repeated failures and eventual successes. Still, no smoke rings though. And many of the ashes missed the ashtray on the desk in front of him. Also, it was damned hard to get them lit!

"Careful with that cigarette. If you torch the place, we could be set back years."

"Got it, Chief. I hear some bigwigs are coming in tomorrow. How should we prepare?"

"Standard routine with outsiders who we need to enlist in our cause. The difference is we know some of them, and the others are from the media. Watch out for the second bunch!"

The next morning, an official car drove into the animal control facility area. Three officials hopped out of a black sedan, and Krastov, decked out in a clean, white lab coat, was at the front door, waiting to greet them.

"Good morning, my kind friends!" said Krastov, in his cultured stage voice. "Welcome to our humble den. I am Dr. Ivan Krastov. My assistant, Dmitry, is out sick today, and I will introduce you to my crew later."

The three important officials— that is, Anna, Ivan, and I—introduced ourselves to the impressively tall, lanky, and solicitous doctor, who, as we knew, ran the place. It was an awkward meeting in that he already knew us. Awkward, but also necessary. It was necessary that the media think we were really VIPs and not just some of Krastov's cronies. As the media was well represented there today, we played along. Bespectacled and decked out in a white coat with a vest pocket full of pens, he looked polished, highly competent, and alert to us (as we already knew).

"Come this way, please, and we can have a short chat before I show you around. The head of the city animal control and health services called yesterday and told me you were coming. You will note the presence of several cameramen and crew from several local papers here." They nodded to us, and we nodded back to them.

"Let's sit here for a few minutes and have some coffee or tea. Or would you prefer vodka this time of day? It tends to smooth out the lumps that arise between the many surprises and crises that come up around here."

"We are all from the USU planning department faculty but work closely with the City on plans for increased services efficiency, emergency response times, and especially security for the Games. We also train their officials in best management practices. I'm sure you know the concern that the City and their superiors in Moscow have as they take all this."

"We don't want the FIFA people getting attacked during a game, right?" said Krastov, flashing a broad grin. "Unfortunately, we have to deal with the media coverage of dogs attacking people with increased regularity. Don't we, gentlemen?" Here he nodded to the cameramen.

Led by Krastov, whose face had turned red with mirth at his little joke, we felt more comfortable and a sense that he could handle the pressures coming from all directions.

"I've often thought dogs could learn to play round football as well as humans, but that's just my opinion. I'm a fan of skiing and tennis."

"More individual sports?"

"That's right, in sports as well as organizational management. I want my staff to try and prevent any more mass dog attacks. I've tried browbeating, and that didn't work. You can't just rely on slogans and demands to work harder for the city—the gulags and beatings methods didn't work in the USSR, did it? Why should they work now?"

"So how do you operate here?"

"Perhaps the City people told you of my long-term dreams for animal control. As for the dogs, just rounding them up and killing them, which is the standard method across Russia, is wrong and out-dated. As for our staff, I believe in personal incentives—financial and non-financial—to make the people and systems work together. The staff, especially our crews, have to be motivated positively, or nothing will happen."

I watched how captivated Andrey was by Krastov's words as he explained himself feverishly, punctuated with sweeping gestures for emphasis. His eyes darted around behind his spectacles, and he often stood up to get his points across to us. Using colorful, lyrical phrases in his baritone voice, he was impressive and authoritative. Ivan listened to him with one ear, but kept turning his head toward a corner of the room where, behind Krastov, there was a cage occupied by a large, fur-ry, yellowish dog, who sat quietly in his cage. Of course, the dog was Fyodor. What caught his attention, though he had missed this before, was that the dog's eyes were moving alertly from speaker to speaker. His ears were cocked. At certain points, his head was cocked, as when Krastov presented his more outlandish ideas that were far beyond the pale of Russian organization management thinking. He knew that

Krastov was working with his speech and diction, but he half thought that trainers did that with circus dogs as well. This was something entirely different; it was odd. This was animal services, so perhaps the doctor and his dogs just understood each other's body language and tonal sounds. Still, I was surprised but not completely convinced that we had a new non-human creature before us. I knew that some dogs already behaved this way, and that it just showed the depth of their loyalty and boundless trust in their masters.

"Ultimately, I want to convert this City department into a private organization, perhaps a mixed NGO charity, so that we can generate more resources, which would allow us to expand the use of the most modern methods of canine control."

"What are your methods now?" I asked. I already knew the answers, but wanted the media to disseminate them to the public.

"Up until about six months ago, we used the standard techniques of animal control departments in all Russian cities and most of those in Eastern Europe. The strategic theory was simply to wipe out the supply, thereby solving the problem of attacks, rabies, and strays. This approach has never worked anywhere because dogs always outbreed the enforcers. Sterilization sounds great, too, but only works in the medium-term. As one of our mayors told the animal rights people from France, who were justifiably shocked by our methods: 'Dogs bite with the teeth not their balls.' I liked that one. So by necessity and the welcome urgency of the World Cup Games, we had to move on to new approaches."

"What are some of them?" asked Anna.

"I think I can help there," I said. "Sorry to interrupt you, Dr. Krastov, but I witnessed first hand some of your crews in action last week."

"Oh yes? What happened?"

"It's all over the media now, so you people should know, but I saw them respond to an attack by several large packs on bystanders out for a stroll by Central Stadium."

"Ah yes, that one," said Krastov. "We had a good outing that day, and free publicity to boot. Normally, no one sees what we do, or worse, they makes up horror stories of what we do, and we can't defend our-selves in the press except to deny all of the reports. If you like, I can have some of our crew tell you more about it. Would you like that?"

"Absolutely!"

Krastov made a call on his cell, and we all waited to see what was going to happen. Fyodor 's cage appeared to be leaning against the bars, alertly following all this. In came two men wearing the signature uniform of green coveralls adorned with the logos of retro, cartoonish dog faces on the backs and shoulder. They carried their nets and long steel tongs, essential for grabbing the dogs behind the neck and flip-ping them into the open carts behind their trucks. They put all this down and stood before us.

"Let me introduce Leonid and Anton to you. They drive our trucks on the daily missions, sometimes during the day and at other times at night. Tell them what you do, boys."

"Thanks, doc. You're from USU and the City as we understand it. Welcome . . . one of my kids goes to USU. It's a fine school; he wants to be a vet like Dr. Krastov. And hopefully, he won't have to do late night missions like we do," said Anton. "Don't get me wrong, but with a few years of gymnasium education and an apprenticeship, it's all I could do. But I like the work. Never boring, eh Leonid?"

"It's not so bad," said Leonid. "Last month, I got several medals and awards. One for identifying two successful medical targets, one for the number of dogs drug-darted, and one for the number of dogs captured and killed. I'm not alone. All the crews have received various awards and even coupons for eating and shopping at places around town. Occasionally, we get extra vacation days and cash bonuses based on our performance as well as medals and awards."

"Very good," I said. "Could you tell us how your performance sys-tem works?"

"First, we have to respond quickly when called. Before Dr. Krastov's changes, it was often slow, and by the time we got there, the damage was already done," said Leonid. "Attacks keep happening, and rabies was spreading. So with our new, more reliable, and faster trucks, we now try to capture the strays, implant chips, and then release them. They rejoin their packs and when we detect any extreme readings from the chip, such as lots of running in circles and encounters with other packs, especially near athletic facilities, we move pre-emptively. We no longer just react to reports because they are delayed and often unreliable. We try to be pro-active. More importantly, we target certain dogs for further research and development. Dr. Krastov gives us a profile of what to look for in the field. The candidates are brought here, and more specialized staff here works with them. They train them to see how far they can develop their skills to do basic tasks. You've all heard about how dogs detect cancer and other diseases. That's the idea. The majority of dogs we have to shoot with drug darts and try to find space for them in pounds. As you know, there is very little pound space here or elsewhere in Russian cities. Other dogs captured are diseased or even rabid, so we kill and dispose of them."

"Sounds quite modern to me. And that was excellent coverage in your papers and media for their responses to the attacks near the stadium," said Andrey.

"Thanks! We have an excellent, and I think highly motivated crew," said Leonid. "You might tell the City people we need more pounds and a better system of licensing, vaccination, and penalties for dog-owners who fail to follow the rules. Those are the main causes of harmful strays in the first place."

"What was it like before you introduced your new performance systems?" I asked.

"I ran it like a prison," said Krastov, and we all laughed. "I admit that I used medieval, Soviet-style, if you'll pardon the expression, 'management' methods which stressed flogging people toward their often unrealistic objectives. Obedience was based on fear, and any real loyalty was non-existent. It was the way all of us managed in the USSR period and its aftermath. That was wrong; I was wrong, too. But I learned."

"How did you come to understand that change was necessary?" asked Anna.

"I read a few books and took advice from visiting experts from Europe as well as consulting the historical records of our more successful Russian animal biologists."

"Are you referring to those who tried to tame and breed foxes to make them into dog-like creatures?"

"Exactly."

Ivan noticed that Fyodor actually seemed to smile at this comment. He was wearing a self-effacing expression as if to say 'what they did was nothing at all.' Something odd was going on here . . .

"We know your thoughts on achieving financial independence so that your work can advance further. Might your idea of creating an NGO or private charity help with the scarce resource problems here?" asked Anna. Again the question sounded to me almost like a plant—which it was.

"It could, for both us and the City. We could raise funds internationally and earmark some of them to the City for pound construction and licensing, and keep the rest for ourselves to improve enforcement, including more crewmembers, trucks, and equipment. In other words, it would be standard cost sharing. All of our funds would be used to strengthen what we do here: research and public safety rule enforcement."

Andrey noticed Fyodor yawning now. Apparently, he couldn't stomach all the hyperbole anymore. He had heard enough, become bored, and was now curling up for a nap in his cage. His plans were interrupted by a window shattering near us, flinging glass all over the room. A rock landed on the floor near my feet. Then several more rocks smashed through the other windows. Suddenly, the door banged open, and we were joined by some beefy types wearing black ski masks. Then Fyodor woke up, began barking loudly, and showed his large fangs. The crew, which had just demonstrated their tools of the trade, quickly shifted into survival mode and grabbed several of the large, wooden truncheons used to club their regular targets of vicious dogs. I grabbed one of the wooden clubs and threw another one to Andrey, as the men ran towards us quickly, swinging wildly at anything around.

They smashed some lab equipment as well as a few jars and dishes. In the din, Andrey spotted Krastov heading over by the cage, guarding it with a large mallet to protect Fyodor.

The media people must have been amazed at their luck. There were about ten intruders against the five of us, if you counted Krastov. Anna tried to avoid getting in the middle of this by dropping below the desk. The crew was doing nicely since they were using their favorite tools. They seemed to have neutralized three or four of them right away. While sizing things up and thinking about my next move, I was directly hit across the chest with a club and went down. The same guy swung again and whacked my left shoulder, the blow of his club just glancing off the side of my head. My arm fizzled in agony, pricked by what seemed to be thousands of hot needles. Despite this, I was able to roll away, get up, and, being right handed, hit him back in the same place then connect with his skull. The whack made an almost musical sound, roughly like playing a coconut in a reggae band. Down he went. I then turned to strike out at one of them in the process of hitting Andrey, and the assailant went down. The odds were shifting in our favor, when the rest of the attackers re-grouped and headed out the door through which they had come. Outside, they were met with two more of our crew who had been attracted by all the sounds. They managed to shoot one with a drug dart and club the other one unconscious. With amazing dexterity, the crew then used their steel tongs to lift them up and toss them into the trailer used normally to dump dog carcasses into the river. They also tonged the guy I had knocked out and threw him in along with the others. The rest of them got away in their car, but in all we had captured three of them. This would have to look good in the media and on some kind of productivity report!

We all left the building and stood outside beside the trailer. Anna was merely shaken and dirty from rolling around the floor; Andrey suffered a few cuts to the head and some face wounds; Krastov looked okay and wore a flinty, angry expression of determination on his face; and myself with just a chest bruise and maybe a dislocated shoulder from one of their clubs. The four crew members in their green outfits looked happy and ready for another round or two. To them it was like waiting to go back for the second half of a football game!

"Looks like we have a new entry for our productivity report, doc," said Leonid, "Assailants disabled."

"Sorry you people had to see this. Not everyone supports what we do. It will be good for the public to see that we also have to deal with vicious stray humans!" said Krastov.

"I suggest we take these people to see my friend and colleague Inspector Petrovsky at the police department," said Andrey. "If we don't, they could slip out as we wouldn't know who organized the attack. That is, unless you just want to take them to the incinerator."

"Now that's a thought! I agree with you about contacting the police. It was too well planned even though the execution was amateurish and ineffective. They didn't seem to want to do anything except to disrupt operations and to destroy our facilities."

"But I noticed that they did want to bash our heads in," said Anna.

"I noticed that too," I said.

For some reason, my inane comment seemed really funny, and I started laughing, which hurt my chest. I kept laughing though, as the pain seemed to add to the humor—was it a painful joke, perhaps? I started coughing and then lost control. Several of them banged me on the back to no avail. I coughed for another several minutes, then settled down. All of them laughed along, except Krastov, who was eyeing me suspiciously.

"Nicholas, I don't like the sound of that. Have you had these kinds of coughs before?"

"I've had a few attacks this last month."

"Any fevers?"

"Sometimes . . . I have weird fever dreams, but in the morning I'm back to normal."

"Normal?" asked Anna.

That brought more laughter from me, but at least I didn't cough.

"I think we should accompany the crew and take them to police headquarters like Ivan suggested. Let's meet there in about an hour. Nick, you stay behind, and let's have a brief word."

They all left and headed for the truck and its trailer, which was chock full of bodies lying with arms flayed out and hanging over the sides, out cold and ready for delivery.

"Nick, have you had any trouble with dogs since you arrived? I know you are interested in the stray problem. Have you been bitten by any of them?"

"Once, just after I arrived over a month ago. I ran into Anna at a corner nearby while walking my landlady's dog. She was being attacked, and I got in the middle of the scrap trying to ward them off of her. One of them took a chunk out of my leg."

"Would you do me a favor and accompany me over here?"

We walked over to the cage containing Fyodor. He looked me over and sniffed a few times. He then let out a knowing cry, an almost imperceptible whimper, and then wagged his tail. He also mouthed the words: "You have a problem, Nicholas."

"I'm not a medical doctor, Nick. But that's a peculiar cough you have that I've heard before. You didn't pass the sniff test from Fyodor, our lab mascot, so I'd say it could be early rabies. If so, we don't want that virus spreading to your nervous system, or it would be all over for you. We obviously won't be able to find the dog that bit you for proper quarantine, so you either have to have it checked out by a medical doctor or come around and see me about it, ok? I've been working on something experimental in this area. And don't wait too long."

13 DEALING WITH THE HUMAN STRAYS

In a tidy, but windowless room in the basement of police headquarters, several men leaned against the walls; one stood by an iron door. A tall, but stocky man in a short-sleeved white shirt with long, curly black hair tied in a braid behind his head was interrogating a suspect standing against a wall, opposite the others. It was the pre-interrogation area for those arrested and waiting to be offered a chair in the special rooms where formalities were required, such as witnessing officers and recording machines. Some had been waiting for hours and even overnight. It was a hot, summer night, and the windows had been open all day to allow the air to blow away some of the stink of tobacco smoke and perspiration. It never lasted long—a cage is still a cage no matter how wide you leave the doors open. It still stinks of the animals that have been kept there—wife-beaters, gangsters, alcoholics, thieves, murderers, and drug addicts. Inside one of the special rooms, a sharp exchange was taking place.

"Police informant, is that what you said you were?" The man was a knuckle-dragger, broad and thickset. He wore a raffish expression as his eyes darted around evasively.

"I have that status, yes," the man said with impudent defiance.

"You seem more like a common goon to me."

The man threw back a hard stare and shrugged his shoulders but said nothing.

"But you said to my colleague here that you inform on others for us? Is that what you do? You should be a proud man then, right?" said

Inspector Simon Petrovsky, as he moved closer to the man, glancing at his nails to see if they had been trimmed properly that day. He then gave him several quick stomach jabs followed by one to the side of his beefy, pock-marked face with a conscientious thoroughness. But the jabs had little effect on the brute. It was like kicking a large dog; you hardly got its attention. To prove his point, he launched a vigorous kick into the crumpled mass sprawling on the floor. That didn't get his attention either.

The Inspector had dark hair slicked back around a shrewd but handsome face, dark eyebrows, and watery eyes full of expression and cynical idealism. He had taken his coat off as the air conditioning down there didn't work, and it was always hot and humid. The coat concealed strong, copper-type shoulders capable of delivering great violence. As he moved around quickly, his expression changed from sympathy to hardened determination underscored by the nuanced tightening of his cheek muscles. His speaking voice, which had a dark, honey-like tone, relied for emphasis on the gestures of his hairy hands, which were the kinds one might have to negotiate prices of Armenian rugs in the Yekaterinburg market. But he was not a man to be underestimated. As a former street tough himself once, he knew his own limitations. There was always someone tougher, more clever, and ruthless in the streets. Inspectors in his view were simple people who asked obvious and even stupid questions. Intellectual type Inspectors whom he'd met were complex people trapped in their own self-images and could not get away with asking stupid questions. That's why they were wrong all the time and rarely got to the truth in his view.

"Listen carefully, you! It's information time. I want you to inform us. We are the police, and you are the informant, got that? Start informing."

The tough stared back with a lazy, blank look. So Petrovsky gave him a few more jabs to the face to focus his attention. The informant's head was like a large rock, shaven to the skull to emphasize its box-like features, squashed nose, all of which was adorned with two tiny battered ears, clearly the products of numerous scraps. Petrovsky hit him a few more until his own hand bled.

"All right, shit. You take over. This is hard work. He's all yours," he said to the other officer present in the room. "Get him out of here and bring in the next one."

The two men grabbed him and dragged him out of the room. After about fifteen minutes, in came the next one from the pre-interrogation area. This one had possibilities. He had a cunning, rat-like expression that at least showed he just might have weighed a few consequences in the past to keep himself going.

"Ok, Yuri… Your name is Yuri, is it not?"

He nodded and looked hard at Petrovsky. One of the fears of local police Inspectors like Petrovsky was that they knew where he and his family lived and could pay them a visit when someone higher up in the Kremlin reprieved them after all their fine forensic work and timely physical beatings to soften them up enoughup to confess. Petrovsky had that fear.

"Do you smoke?" The man nodded, so Petrovsky lit one in his mouth and handed it to him. "Take this and sit down at that table for a moment. Let me explain this to you again. We know you were part of the group that recently busted up the City animal control lab, which is state property. That means at least 20 years in hard labor."

Still, he threw back the same look of the rat ready to pounce or run for cover in his nearby hole . . . "Do you want that?"

He shrugged. "Who would?"

"That's the idea. We want only one piece of information from you. Your colleague already confessed to the attack. He says you planned it out."

"That's a cheap trick you cops play. It's also a lie, and I can prove it."

"Oh yes? How? Your colleague could prove it too. He already gave us several names."

"But my names are the real ones: Semyon Irtenev and Dmitry Simovich. It's well known in the street that they are looking for these kinds of services and have been asking others as well. I'm sure you already know this."

"We know a few things," said Petrovsky. "Have you been paid?"

"We're not stupid. We received half already and were to receive the rest after the job."

"How will you collect that now that you are in custody and may go to prison? Those whom we haven't caught yet will get your share. Isn't that right?"

A quiver in Yuri's neck provided the answer. He said nothing but looked around the room vacantly. Petrovsky had his answer.

"Why did these people have an interest in your services?"

"We didn't care really. It was just another hit job. Something about stopping illegal experiments because they were dumping dogs in the river. It was easy work—just smash a few things and get out."

"It didn't work out that way did it?"

"Not really. The dog crews were waiting for us. They weren't supposed to be there."

"It's a risk you take, right Yuri? All right, take him and the rest of this pack back to their cells. We will be in touch with you later."

Petrovsky nodded to the two men who took him out. *Amazing,* thought Petrovsky, *how the old prisoner's dilemma kept working.* The ones we nabbed tried, but just couldn't reduce their informational uncertainty enough to avoid the predictable outcomes of a system like this. They couldn't stay mum. So Yuri would get probation, if that; the other guy would fry.

"I have to get back to the lab. I'll finish with these people later today," Petrovsky told the officer in charge on his way upstairs to join the others.

Meanwhile, upstairs back in the police station, I sat with the other visitors from USU, animal control, and the local media, who were still waiting for Petrovsky to re-appear. He had cleaned off and washed his face in the bathroom. Some blood stains covered his white shirt, but that was par for the course. He had often thought that the supply staff should issue dark red shirts for this kind of work. It would also save on laundry bills. Petrovsky entered his office where we were seated in front of his desk with coffee already served by his trusty assistant.

"Andrey, greetings! Sorry we were interrupted, but as you saw we all were engaged in a conflict resolution problem and couldn't get finished with our discussion," he said, with his signature wry grin. "Now let's start over again with our meeting."

Andrey and he hugged and exchanged a few kisses in the fashion, after which he again introduced himself to all of us.

"Welcome to our little den of justice and iniquity," said Petrovsky. "Here we obtain justice through iniquity," he said, chuckling at his own joke. "It's just how we behave when no one is looking. Someone calls that 'culture,' I am told. I am Simon Petrovsky, family friend and colleague of Ivan here. And you are, I believe, all doctors: Ivan Krastov, head veterinarian at the animal control department, Anna Irtenev of USU, and Nicholas Krylov, a Russian-American also at USU, no? Ivan will be a doctor someday and then everyone will be too smart to talk with me." The cameramen from the media got all this on film as he spoke. It was going to be a banner day for their work—a brawl at the City animal control lab with thugs and probable eco-animal terrorists.

"Indeed that is who we are," I said. "Thank you for taking an interest in what happened at the lab."

Petrovsky looked at us quietly from behind his desk. His eyes were bright and focused. His kindly smile invited them to speak, but I could tell he had a very sleepy and dangerous cunning about him. That had to be useful in ferreting out confessions, something like Inspector Porfiry in Dostoyevsky, who was perhaps his model. He was not the stereotypical thug cop but clearly knew how to apply muscle if necessary as evidenced from his demeanor when he entered the room just now from doing his interrogations. He appeared to have come from the gym, but it was clearly sweat from more professional exercise, probably a regular event in the life of a criminal police inspector.

Breaking the silence, Krastov asked, "Do you have any idea who carried this out, Inspector?"

"Well, yes we do. But I can't divulge the names now for reasons of state security. You know that term. It covers anything we don't want to talk about yet. But you will know soon when we finish our own investigations. More importantly, we want them to stop. We are putting a guard near the animal facility with your permission."

"Please do, and tell whoever they are to introduce themselves to me, if you would. We don't want our crews throwing them in cages, do we?" said Krastov.

With that, Petrovsky leapt out of his chair and poured us all more tea and coffee. As he hopped around between us, he chatted casually and softly. "Let me explain to you who I am and my interest in all this."

Petrovsky was a taller man and had a nice, absurdist bureaucratic sense of humor. He reminded me of a Zoschenko, Gogol, or Pasternak character with his flowery but precise language. He was about mid to late 40s, liked outrageous jokes and subversive puns just like we did. But I could really sense a whiff of Dostoyevsky in his manner, which meant darker days ahead for anyone who crossed him.

"I know my friend Ivan carries a derringer to protect himself from street thugs. I keep telling him to upgrade his weapon, but he has his own tastes. Around here, though, we have to protect ourselves from all kinds of assailants," said Petrovsky.

"I take it you don't mean dog attacks," said Krastov.

"I wish it were so easy. Then I could just call you at animal control and get you to fix our problems. No, we face bigger fish, I'm afraid, or dogs if you want to continue with that metaphor."

"But can you fix our problem here?" asked Krastov.

"So far, I just see the vandalism of public property and a bit of rough stuff, which amounts to multiple assaults and batteries."

"But you think there's more to it?"

"Of course, this is Russia, isn't it?" Petrovsky laughed. "More coffee or tea?"

"Did any of the suspects tell you something you can share with us?" asked Anna.

"Not at present. But we have to be careful here of being drawn into something much bigger than a bit of vandalism. That deeper world, as you well know, leads into the feuding factions within governments and their predatory bureaucrats. It's the deeper, darker context of this oddball crime of attacking an animal control center and lab seemingly out of the blue."

"What do you think it is? I asked.

"I am just a policeman so I don't think. I simply react to promising leads and hunches, lemming-like. I am a local official in the ambiguous no man's land between old-fashioned Soviet *nomenlatura* and a special subject category exempt from the laws. I am stuck in the barb-wired fence between the old guard and the new. The first category are those officials that got material benefits from the old system and still get them despite being, in theory, subject to the laws. That's hardly me! The second category includes mayors, judges, and prosecutors who have been granted exemption from the laws by the Criminal Procedure Code Article 447. It's simply a fact that I am a civil servant but not significant enough for any exemption. So anything I do after thinking about it puts me in a precarious position. I think you see what I mean."

"I think you know that my husband is in the second category, Inspector," said Anna.

"Indeed I do, madam. I know who he is and have met him on occasion though I'm certain he would not recognize my face or my name."

"He might."

"Possibly . . . I have made my views known publicly that I am an old-fashioned cop. That means, I am independent and don't like the police being used by official thugs, especially those in higher up positions. I'm not alone in this opinion. All we want is to be neutral and enforce the law without prejudice."

"I think Inspector Simon is saying that his position is something like being in the Berlin Kripo in the Weimar Regime as the fascists and communists vied for power to take control of the country, if my memory of history serves me," I said. "He just wants to do his job effectively."

He nodded at me with a gleam in his eye. "Exactly!"

"So, Dr. Krastov, what is it you and your crews do at your lab that interests not only the media but thugs like the ones we have collared downstairs? Are you doing something subversive?" he laughed loudly again. "If so, what could that mean for dogcatchers, a vet, and a lab?

Have you trained your dogs to run drugs or roam around robbing stores? All this would make an excellent dystopian science fiction puzzle, wouldn't it?" he said, flashing another of his cunning grins at us.

"We are doing something new, but it is hardly subversive anymore, though it once was in Russia."

"Tell me more! I love Gothic horror stories! Believe it or not, I love fiction—especially crime thrillers. My favorites now are the Boris Akunin novels."

"I read him too. Nothing we do is as exciting, I'm afraid," said Krastov. "We certainly have no supernatural hero working for us like Erast Fandorin. But if you have a few minutes, I can summarize for you what we've already told the City and Kremlin officials. Assisted by the media people who accompanied us today, we even did a short video that explains our work."

"I believe you have a staff assistant called Dmitry Simonvich. Has he been part of your activities?"

"He has assisted me, yes."

"And is he trustworthy, in your opinion? Just a routine question . . . We know nothing about him."

Krastov grimaced and looked down at his lap as he tried to come up with a diplomatic response. "I can only hope he is as loyal as the rest of my crews are."

Anna and I gave each other an ironic, knowing glance. We both suspected that Petrovsky did know something more about him.

"Continue, I am sorry to interrupt."

"I have a better idea. Let me invite all of you again to my research lab and our animal control complex outside of town. There I can give you a further hands-on tour and demonstration of what we do. How would that be?"

"Should I bring anything?" asked Petrovsky.

"Bring some treats, or you might be eaten by some of our rambunctious creatures that didn't turn out properly. It's hard to make a perfect monster. It's also too bad that the three goons got away from us earlier. You might never have known they were missing!"

Petrovsky rolled his eyes, cracked his face ever so slightly into a smile, and said, "Thank you; my secretary will set up a visit with you. In the meantime, I would like to invite Nicholas here to dinner as the relative newcomer to town. Are you a vegan like all the other Americans?"

"Anything but human or dog meat is fine with me. On principle, I would eat cat meat, but I've never had one cooked properly. Anyway, I'd be honored."

I had to think about this. When I was a wild youth, I sometimes ate in jail cells or had coffee in interrogation rooms where they tried to get me to reveal the names of my delinquent friends around the Bronx precinct. I could relate obliquely to what had been going on here.

"Don't think I've ever had a friendly dinner with a policeman before."

"It's never too late," he replied, and abruptly jumped out of the chair. Coming around to the front of his desk, he pumped all of our hands vigorously and said: "Now ladies and gentlemen, I do have to get back to work. It was a pleasure, and if there's anything more from this end, I will be in touch."

The following week, several more of us drove over to Krastov's facility on the edge of town in the USU departmental vehicle. We had picked up a colleague, Yengeny Risanovsky, from the city health department and a medical doctor named Andrey Lubyantsev. Andrey Kostov drove, and Anna told him where to go and how to drive as usual. As before, I enjoyed listening to them banter back and forth about his driving. She didn't want to drive but preferred being navigator and first captain of the ship. I always like having someone like that in the car to relieve the boredom of driving and having to blame myself for getting lost and engaging in near misses with pedestrian and cars along the way. When we arrived about a half hour later, from the window of the car in the back seat, I noticed Krastov standing in the parking lot waiting to greet us as always in his white lab coat beaming with congratulatory smiles. His head glowed like a light bulb, perhaps heating up the metal rims of his spectacles. As we emerged, Krastov shook all of our hands vigorously in a solid display of energetic bonhomie.

"Welcome! Welcome to you all!" he trumpeted in the parking lot. Gesturing us along like a herd of sheep, flashing a broad, confident smile, he announced: "To begin an explanation of our activities here, let me introduce you to my assistant, Dmitry, and to Leonid, our chief of field enforcement. Let's start with a walk-through, at the entry point where we have to sort out what to do with our captured dogs. This way please," he said, as he herded us toward a large windowless white structure with a sign in front reading: 'Today we shall behave as if this is the day we will be remembered,' – Dr. Seuss"

"I like your quote," said Anna. "Didn't Dr. Seuss say 'I' rather than 'we'?"

"Right you are," said Krastov. "Only a professor would know that, and we don't get many professors out this way. Dr. Seuss was referring to himself and never anticipated that an animal control team would use it. So we edited this line a bit."

Entering the building where an excruciating din could be heard from a distance, it seemed like a madhouse full of dogs barking, crying, shrieking, baying, and moaning. He said to us, "Put on this headgear. It can block their sound, but I can still talk to you."

Inside were rows of cages filled with stray dogs of all sizes and colors. Some attacked the bars of their cages when they saw us; others stayed curled up and looked up at us sadly with forlorn expressions, or lay there limp as if either dead or drugged.

"This is the receiving station where the dogs are sorted. They were spot sorted in the field by the crews, of course, but that method used in the chaos of operations has to be pretty subjective. The limp ones have been drugged, tagged, and vaccinated for rabies. The confused ones will be examined further to see what their story is. Too bad they can't talk. Most will then be released to anyone who wants to adopt them."

"What happens if no one adopts them?" I asked.

"We are always asked that. The same will happen here as anywhere else in the world. They have a statutory period or reprieve of thirty days in this place. You see, we have some space but hardly enough for the whole city. And we also have new guests arriving every day, thanks to the efficiency of Leonid and his crews."

"That's correct, Doctor," said Leonid. "We keep them here. If no one adopts the ones vaccinated, they are taken to the next building to be killed and disposed of. I'll explain how that works as you may find that unique. At least, others have told us that."

"Why don't you place them with foster families temporarily?" I asked.

"Of course, we've tried and still try to do that. But as yet, there are very few real foster families in Yekaterinburg or elsewhere in Russia. Fostering requires staff to follow up and make certain the 'families' don't get frustrated and simply release what are mixed up, distrustful, highly energetic, and wild dogs that are hard to control. Neither we nor any other city department has the staff for that and can't bring them back here to any kind of cages reserved for rejected adoptees. We have a website, 'Catydog,' for Catherine the Great and our needy dogs. We post pictures of different dogs up for adoption, like this one." He pointed to a poster on the wall behind him with a snapshot from the website and a hangdog, deprived-looking mutt that needed to be adopted right away. "But few visit this site for referrals and we need to work on that. The place, as you can see, is not a welcome draw for foster families, those who might adopt dogs, or for tourists. It would be about as fun for most people as visiting a prison. As in other areas, we have plans to transform the entire cycle of dog control for this city," said Krastov.

"You said you kill them in unique ways," asked Petrovsky.

"We kill them by injection . . . standard procedure anywhere," said Leonid.

Dmitry stood next to them with a broad smirk on his face and finally said, "Then again, some of them simply disappear." The smirk told us that there was really a nasty end to the captured mutts.

"We don't do this work just to kill dogs. All of us are dog owners ourselves, but we also have families and loved ones whom we don't want to contract rabies," said Krastov, as if Dmitry hadn't said anything. "Explain what happens after they are put down, Leonid."

"The ones not adopted are taken to a nearby *abattoir* run by a Chechen. He processes sheep carcasses and sells *halal* lamb locally and for export. He does the same things for our dogs."

"What!" said Petrovsky. "You mean *halal* dogmeat?"

"That's right. He says a prayer, then slices them up. Dog-eating countries like China and Thailand buy either the whole carcasses or special meats cut to order by our man here and his staff. Even anti-Muslim Hungarians like the meat better than Romanian imports. As you know, Romania has more stray dogs in absolute numbers than anyplace on earth. We're also looking into dog-brain tacos for Mexico. We've heard that Macedonian Slavs are into eating brains. Why not dogs instead of pigs or boar?"

"Tacos?" I asked.

"That's right. The Mexicans like cow-brain tacos. Why not dog-brained ones?"

"An *abattoir* . . . I didn't know we had any sheep around here," said Andrey.

"With your diet of cheap beef burgers, you probably wouldn't," said Anna.

"All this makes us hungry for more, does it not? Now for the main course," thundered Krastov, in his booming baritone with a sweep of the arm in the direction of the lab. "We use every bit of the carcass. The stomach contents become manure for fertilizer; the bones are ground up for cat food; and the blood is turned into biofuel. We are working on markets for the teeth and fangs but nothing yet. The city keeps all the revenues and divides it between the's health department and ourselves. We sell about 1000 carcasses per week to the butcher. The more strays we catch, the more sales we make. It's sad but true."

"It all sounds innovative. It's all right up there with modern metric-driven productivity approaches to improve public services performance. How did you get anyone here to approve all this?" I asked.

"Now that was a bit of a problem."

Here Krastov looked around. His face shifted gears from his loose public expression, which accompanied his theatrics and marketing puffery to sterner features, with tightened jaw muscles and hardened eyes, allowing a cold intellect taking us each in. Then his whole face cracked into a wry grin.

"Not long ago, the Deputy Regional Governor showed up here for a surprise inspection. She told us to wash the floors and hang cleaner curtains. To our amazement, she then recounted the old fairy tale of the golden fish granting its captor's wishes. She explained that in the government, we were not golden fish and couldn't magically solve all our problems. Taken aback, we told her we don't do Russian fairy tales here—we're not children. We explained to her, I think patiently and clearly, that we were trying to solve public safety and health problems here that curtains and soap couldn't fix. Whether from mindless officiousness, stupidity, or just jealousy at civil servants using science to strike out into new areas of research and knowledge, she couldn't or wouldn't understand our concerns. So what to do? Thanks to the upcoming Games, we first got the attention of our mayor, who gave us access to his office through Anna's husband to someone higher up in Moscow. Yes, that's right—one of the many higher-up operatives on call.

"The Kremlin actually sent someone to us who understood the bigger picture of not only World Cup Games but the need for maintaining Putin's political popularity. He also understood the inability of governments to respond despite the usual empty words and assurances from the authorities. He understood that public sector workers were being mistreated and wasted at the local levels and that had to be stopped. It no doubt helped that his mother was a school teacher in a rural Russian town. Many of those out in the public protesting bad services were actually public sector workers themselves who felt betrayed by a distant, almost colonial regime. He told us what we already knew that activists like animal and health rights group leaders were focusing on these broken promises and that people were getting very angry out here. In fact, he came to us seeking solutions (imagine!) and we gave them. The regime had to do something fast. We explained to him that we were all Putin supporters here—I noted the portraits of him next to my collection of religious icons at home (luckily, he didn't offer to come over and have a look as it was nothing more than a tall tale). We both lamented that the euphoria of the 'Crimean Consensus' was over and that all have sobered up. I believe I even was able to produce a few timely tears that rolled nicely down my cheeks at the appropriate time."

Then Doctor Andrey Lubyantsev spoke up.

"At the City, we have been fully supportive of Dr. Krastov's plans to transform the animal control department into what is called in management circles an efficient 'revenue center.' We support them because health services funding has been drastically cut around here, and activists have justifiably used that as a catalyst for discontent. Moscow wants all this stopped, and so does the mayor. Without action, we could all lose here. Dr. Krastov's plan gives the city a new focus and an operational vehicle for getting the results we could boast about and even to serve as a mechanism for accountability to focus blame on us if we failed. The public needs this. It was a risk, but one that we had to take. The obvious benefits were that we could: eliminate threats to the Games from packs of stray dogs, make money for the city budget, and generate good publicity for both the city and the regime. As you know, reliable government surveys show Putin's popularity ratings have plummeted to 64 percent from 80 percent since 2014. Right now 45 percent of the people think the country is headed in the wrong direction. That's more than at any time in the last ten years. Both the public and public sector workers are angry and are being mobilized by advocates. It's all very dangerous and could explode in street rioting. "

"But weren't there problems with that plan itself? Weren't they a bit flawed?" asked Dmitry. "Some of the activists opposing Putin are right here in town and are members of animal rights groups. They opposed what we were doing here—'killing for profit' is how they put it and what we plan to do. They also got wind of some of the research we are doing here and our plans to use dogs as family nannies. They are calling it 'species transgression and appropriation'."

Krastov's jaws tightened visibly. He shifted around in his chair impatiently and stood up, pointing toward an exit in the back of the room.

"Dmitry is getting ahead of schedule. The research program is next on the agenda so let's go into the next building."

"So where do you stand on the animal rights positions, Dmitry?" asked Petrovsky.

Krastov looked nervously at Anna and me.

"They have some valid points, but they must not be allowed to interfere with our work here," he answered with minimal enthusiasm. The words reminded me of flat beer—rote and without gusto, which I found odd on a team of go-getting dogcatchers. Petrovsky looked him over with that scary, penetrating, forensic quality that I had sensed from my high school delinquent days and frequent run-ins with the police. Watch out . . . He smelled lies from this one, and his bullshit antennae were up.

We then were herded into another building with windows and a more livable atmosphere. Again, Andrey spotted Fyodor over in his corner cage, carefully checking us all out as we came in. He looked like he had just put down a book for the occasion and was concerned about the intrusion. He had almost been caught reading. Weird, Ivan thought, and Petrovsky noticed it too. Krastov's dog would check people out patiently by gazing at them with his wet eyes, which were like enormous marbles. Fyodor betrayed an active intelligence that was eager to grill newcomers and find out more about them. Anyway, despite its obvious and lively intelligence, Fyodor looked harmless. To Andrey and the rest of us, he just didn't seem like a normal dog.

The large room we were all in featured easy chairs and an electric samovar. Leonid poured tea for everyone, and Krastov began.

"I think Dr. Krylov saw us in action first hand a week ago by the Stadium. Could you summarize?"

I told them about the crew's quick responses to the attacking packs of dogs in their brightly colored, green uniforms with departmental logos, their antics with songs, and a fiery hop dance or two before leaving with the booty of captured and drugged strays. All this made Dmitry's wooden words more incongruous with the spirit of the group.

"I hope I got all that right, Leonid," I said.

"Quite accurate."

"By their own wishes, the crews now have some after work gigs," said Krastov, "creating new limericks that they turn into songs. The songs typically relate to canine themes such as our work routines, long-deceased dogs we have owned or adopted, and dogs that we remember from our youth that we still miss. This has given us all notoriety and has induced support from sponsorship funds. International dog rescue and research groups are donating funds, which the city keeps for us in a special fund. With these new funds, we have purchased new equipment, trucks, stun guns, and even video equipment to convert our operations into YouTube type snippets. We have also purchased modern new training equipment for the dogs and spent funds upgrading the cages and laboratory facilities."

"So the funds are already coming in? You are getting more funding for your work?" Anna asked.

"They are, and both the City and we are grateful," said Krastov.

Leonid then left the room and went back to join his teams in the next building and truck shed.

"That's one of our best men there," Krastov said, nodding towards the door. "We want them all to care about the jobs they do, so I try to recognize them when they perform well and encourage them to improve on methods we use here."

"From what I witnessed last Sunday, morale is extremely high here. I've never seen dogcatchers anywhere work with such zeal and enthusiasm," I said. "I thought the whole thing was a put on, a hearty caricature of dog catchers. So did the public around me, and they loved it!"

"I think so too, but of course I'm biased. And I think we need better job titles for our people, don't you? Like 'canine attendants'?" said Krastov. "I try to reward group initiatives, such as the ideas for uniforms, logos, songs with performance bonuses for meeting our standard metrics that we use to deal with strays. The crews created the logos and the songs themselves under their own initiative. The crews also care about safety on the job, and I've had few requests in the last five years for transfer. Few of our employees have left, meaning our retention rate is high. On the other hand, we've had requests from 'canine attendants' in other Russian cities who want to work here. Our crews receive commendations each month for their work. But you can only tell about real morale when individual divisions occur, which they inevitably must in any intense working context with high daily risks involved. We try to keep it loose, with lots of chirping and clowning around among the crews. That's essential for group solidarity and what the anthropologists call 'joking behavior.' All unhappy families are unhappy in their own ways, to paraphrase Tolstoy. By the way, I've been around here for fifteen years and didn't know anything about motivating personnel with rewards and encouragement. I did what other managers did out of fear of retribution from above or from staff betrayals to Party officials. The Soviet system used fear and control as management tools, and it never worked. Nobody trusted anyone. I was a terrible manager and had to learn lots of new tricks too!"

"Very impressive ... I understand you met with Greg Gold of FIFA," said Anna.

"Indeed we did. He also gave us the green light and even wants to donate funds from FIFA to continue our work here. He rightly figures we can use the FIFA seed money to generate more funds. For instance, we've been talking to the Austrian Four Paws Foundation, which funded the Bulgarian bear park to rehab former gypsy dancing bears. They have programs in neighboring countries such as Ukraine, for instance, to castrate stray dogs. We might be able to join forces and share costs with them in the future."

"First, we have to put up with Gold's hyped PR and now its rehabilitation of dancing bear. I can see the two in a vaudeville act someplace!" said Anna.

"I know! I know! That sounds like a long way from stray dogs, but the City needs pounds and licensing regimes and more dog-catching crews like ours. Four Paws type foundations could help us out. Gold views this as a potential cost-sharing model for all World Cup cities with stray dog problems—which turns out to be most of them."

At that moment, a high-pitched whine flooded the room, and a screen was suddenly lowered as the ceiling projector lit up, ready for action. It was time for the main feature. I had a few gulps of tea and grabbed some pistachio nuts from a nearby bowl.

"So, I think you've heard enough and observed how we think our operations have been made much more efficient. We report on the metrics: faster response times, more catch and releases, and quicker sorting of adoptees from others in the kill pound. We have indicated that with the City's support, we are getting a separate official status for funding, to either become a charity, a foundation, a private enterprise, or simply by becoming a special fund in the city budget. Whatever happens, our operations are now on a solid footing."

"You can also receive external funding from such sources as FIFA and international dog rescue leagues," said Andrey.

"We already have. More of those funds will help build more dog pounds and fund better regulation, licensing, and vaccination controls that all require many more trained personnel. Now let me show you what else we have been doing."

On the screen we could see a dog staring at us as if expecting a treat. In the next scene, the same dog's jaws were moving in response to questions being asked by a trainer. He was forming vowels in a kind of low growl or gruff voice.

"Have you been a good boy today, Fyodor?"

"Of course, treat please!" he said, slowly.

The scene changed, and the same scene was repeated with the caption "one month later."

"Have you been a good boy, Fyodor?" asked a voiceover.

The dog's expression changed, and his mouth contorted into words. "Define 'good', please."

We all laughed at that one.

"Christ, you are creating a new race of dog sophists! Philosopher dogs!" I said.

In the next scene, we watched Fyodor a few months later grasping a pair of pliers in his paws and working with them to turn a bolt head protruding from a board. He did it slowly and deliberately until it came out. He then put the pliers down, sat down, and looked proudly at the trainer filming him, no doubt expecting a major treat.

"Amazing!" I said.

But the next scene became even more surreal. Fyodor was now sitting in an easy chair wearing a plaid vest and sporting a watch and chain from its pocket. He was wearing tiny spectacles, no doubt to assist him with the reading.

"Come, Fyodor," came the command from somewhere. The dog got off the chair, stood upright, and walked on his hind legs toward the camera.

Petrovsky interjected: "I could use people with such skills on the police force. Most of our people still walk on all fours!"

We all got a good gut laugh from that one!

"Indeed, we see a larger use for such creatures, and we do hope to create a new category of 'non-human creature,' through which the law could protect them. Other countries have worked to do this, and there's a strong international movement to do so."

"Aren't you getting into an ethical gray area here? It looks like you are trying to change nature," asked Anna.

"Dr. Anna's question points to the long and turbulent history of this kind of work in Russia. She is right, and we could be treading on thin scientific and moral ice here. The animal rights people would like our work stopped on the quite misinformed grounds that we are creating a new form of humanity. Not so! Others would like to stop us on the grounds that we are creating a new Frankenstein's monster. A more popular charge out there we've heard is that our lab is like that of Dr. Persikov's in his Red Ray State Farm whom you might recall created a mysterious ray that accelerated vital reproductive processes. If you've read Bulgakov's *Fatal Eggs,* you know that processes like that get out of control and usually destroy humanity. We are not so arrogant as to think we can change nature here. We are no longer required to follow

Trotsky's line that 'man is free to adapt nature to his wishes.' We know what we can't do and make no claims to the contrary. We are humbled by nature and its processes and know our limits. Bulgakov, Shelley, and Wells wrote good dystopian sci-fi stories, but all we here do is old-fashioned veterinary trial and error, supplemented by some organ modifications and transplants that are commonly performed today by vets everywhere. Plus, we have ended up with superior dog training techniques to fine tune our canine candidates. But let's talk further about both of those important charges later. But before we continue, let's walk into the next room. I would like to introduce you to someone."

We entered, and Dmitry locked the door behind us. There was Fyodor, sitting in his favorite chair eyeing us closely. "Come in, ladies and gentlemen," he said in his low growl that we had just heard on the film. "I expect you have some questions for me; please be seated."

His frank and unusually bold stare was at first unnerving. I think we were expecting some dogs playing and cavorting that were still rascals at heart. I'm not sure what we expected. But this was still a shock.

"Fyodor wanted to meet with you and entertain your questions," said Krastov. "Fire away!"

"I am Dr. Andrey Lubyantsev from the city health department. I would like to know if you have any human organs inside you? Since you are so close to being human, are there human organs inside of you?"

Fyodor's laugh was a quiet whinny, a rapid sequence of squeaks. Accompanied by his endearing grin and movements of his large pink tongue, it was a rebuke to another foolish question by the untutored.

"My good sir, there are very few dogs in Russia that could not read and understand the word 'sausage' without having human brains. Even Bulgakov's Sharik learned to read on his own from colors. No, our Dr. Krastov is no Dr. Bormenthal or Philip Philpovich from *Heart of a Dog*, replacing testicles and switching human for dog brains. As for whether I have any human organs inside me, how would I know that? Ask Dr. Krastov."

We all chortled at that one!

"Thank you, Fyodor, for your literary explanation," said Krastov. "Fyodor, like all of our 'new dogs' is custom made from upgraded organs of his own. A necessary part of our operations is the proper identification of dogs that are suitable for elite treatment and might 'evolve' to a higher, next stage of canine consciousness and behavior. The crews respond to our incentive system for spotting the finer animals and get cash bonuses if we use them. Tsar, one of our prime candidates that, as some of you know, just died from cancer, was one of those. The crew member who spotted Fyodor a few years ago got a trip to the Crimean coast with his family. No, Fyodor didn't go along. We have other specimens who have undergone several upgrading treatments and that receive regular special training in the adjoining room. For example, some of our visitors at a vigil for Tsar brought a 'walk-on,' whom we call Tsar II; he is now a candidate. As for the other ones, we can visit them later."

"But they have a long way to go. I have to listen to them at night," said Fyodor.

"What happens to the dogs that you are not able to upgrade, as you say, after repeated attempts?" asked Petrovsky.

"I still have my sense of smell. I bet you're a cop," said Fyodor.

"Didn't I take a shower this morning?"

"It's the way you move, your razor sharp gaze, and the forensic precision of what you want to know that gives you away. You are too switched-on. Also, your too-shiny, flatfoot shoes."

"Thank you!"

"The frank answer is that they are simply disposed of. Remember that doctors used to use stray dogs acquired from pounds for heart transplant research 60 years ago. Most operations involving those failed, and the dogs died. Later, the doctors succeeded, and the dogs were no longer needed," said Krastov.

"I'm not indispensable. I know I am the lucky one, thanks to Dr. Krastov and his team."

We were mesmerized by Fyodor. We sat there stunned, admiring, curious, and still a bit nervous that he might do something else astonishing like read our minds or fly! It was like watching a living sci-fi movie. I saw that he was sharp; he was driven by a keen intellect and penetrating insights. But, I wondered what he had lost as a dog. Owned dogs like Leo are endearingly shy, empathetic, and look at you warmly and sympathetically. This one seemed to have lost those qualities, and, even though he did have a wry humor at times, he was blunt and coldly calculating. But what were we expecting, a live version of Disney's animated dog Pluto?

"I have a question, Dr. Krastov, and I don't know quite how to put this."

"Fire away; that's why you're here!"

"You're trying to teach dogs to become almost human. When Communism fell in the late 1990s, the dancing bears owned by gypsies were put in a Bulgarian park in a place called Belitsa. The plan was to have them unlearn captive behavior, which proved impossible. The bears had been beaten and treated cruelly since they were cubs and learned to depend on alcohol. Then they were taken from their owners and set free to fend for themselves. But, of course, all they could do was dance for coins and yearn for keepers to take responsibility for their lives again. You have captured stray dogs that were mistreated and have trained them for special roles. I wonder if this is some kind of 'freedom research lab' producing similar kinds of animals, those that simply want new masters to avoid taking responsibility for themselves?"

"Wow! What a thoughtful question, Dr. Krylov. It's one I want to reflect on a lot more, and maybe you can help me. But for now, an answer is that we don't want them out there 'free' again to fight, bite, get killed, and become diseased at all. We want to build up their trust to be cared for and well-treated. For some of them, that is a distant memory at best. Many never knew this experience at all. We want most of the dogs to be rehabilitated into healthy, normal dogs to return to human ownership. For a select few like Fyodor and maybe Tsar II, we can hope that something new has been developed here. Something precious that has to be protected from anyone who could misuse them or any of our techniques. All new 'technology' and scientific methods have to guard against this possibility—and we do too."

"In short, you don't view this as captivity or encouraging animal freedom at all?"

"Absolutely not. The dogs are captured as a necessary measure for city health control, and we want them to leave here alive and well. Unlike some of the animal rights people, we have no intention of turning them loose as part of some naïve freedom lesson. Most of them wouldn't last a minute out there fending for themselves in the wilds of city life or in the countryside."

"Thank you, Doctor! Very candid . . . "

"As for those mentioned by Anna who would stop our work from a fear of what we could discover and create, as in the 1930s. Remember this: Russia was in the forefront of research on animal behavior, genetic work, and organ transplant. We should carefully recall what happened then and resist caving in to popular protests. Vladimir Putin, at least, wants to ensure that the hit to science here never happens again," said Krastov.

"Dr. Krastov is referring to the Stalin-Lysenko fraud where a few egotistical, power-hungry bureaucrats with no scientific education or training turfed-out legitimate scientific work. They accused serious scientists of trying to change nature, which, of course, terrified the public. Legitimate scientific professionals with a practical bent like Dr. Krastov, instead are trying to use nature and natural selection to create canine hybrids with human-like qualities. This research lab and many more like it around Russia are doing more than what is commonly known as selective breeding and instead using multiple techniques to try and develop new creatures," said Dr. Lubyantsev. "The Chinese have already just discovered that cloning or breeding Kummin wolf dogs leads to stronger and smarter offspring for police and border security work. We've known that for years. But only now, perhaps from the urgency of security for the World Cup Games, have we started planning to build a repository of top breeds for other uses besides security. Dogs are already good watch-dogs so the leap to a better one is hardly a great scientific leap forward. But some are scared and shriek about Dr. Frankenstein or H.G. Wells creatures being let loose on the planet. "

"That's right. What Dr. Lubyantsev is telling you is that if your productivity falls off no matter what the job, you could be replaced by a dog. No reason why they couldn't be driving metros or buses, is there?" said Krastov.

"Hey, they couldn't do any worse than the drivers on my bus route," said Petrovsky. "Means we could bribe them with treats and avoid paying fares, doesn't it, Dr. Krastov?"

I laughed along and joined all the banter. But then I said: "I get your jokes as they nicely capture the ignorance out there among the public. But maybe the joke is on us for laughing at the Chinese."

"What are you getting at Nicholas?" Krastov asked.

"Just that the Chinese are obsessed with replacing labor by artificial intelligence and robotics that can do machine learning, aren't they? But Dr., as Lubyantsev noted, the Chinese also cloned Kummin wolf dogs to perform border security tasks. They could easily use electronic surveillance systems and AI to handle them. I'm just saying that some tasks might be better performed by improved dogs than AI or machines. Let dogs keep doing them. But improve their productivity, and that's where your work becomes critical, Dr. Krastov and Dr. Lubyantsev. Take the skills required to teach a dog or a machine how to catch a Frisbee in mid-air. Some dogs do it instinctively without being taught how to calculate wind speed and air resistance. Why not let them specialize in this? So yes, let the dogs drive metros and buses if they can do it easily. I'm sure Fyodor could handle it without a lot of trouble, couldn't you, Fyodor?"

"I'd rather read books and give university lectures like you than do manual labor. I've read about hard work, and it sounds bad. Don't forget, I can still recall my life in the mean streets, and I don't intend to voluntarily go back there!"

Up on the screen, a team of doctors operating on a dog could be viewed from above. "Here we are working on an elite dog candidate," said an authoritative voiceover.

The dog was stretched out on a table with his organs clearly visible. Its flesh and fur were pinned back on both sides of his body, revealing his insides. I realized that all that dog could hope for was that he would be one of the few successful mutants that came up against Dr. Krastov's scalpel.

"The rationale for Dr. Krastov's work in Yekaterinburg is at two levels," continued the voiceover. "You've heard the first or popular level already. We are doing regime-friendly work, of benefit for the upcoming Games, President Putin's image, and the critical applied knowledge of how best to deal with strays in the future. Recall that Stalin came up with the idea of a 'New Soviet Man,' meaning some kind of robust new genes forged from the Marxian class struggle. That was simply old-fashioned eugenics and biological nonsense right down there with Lysenko's pseudo-scientific crap trap. So we added a twist of our own. The "New Putinian Dog" can be created now with the application of genetic research, and others like him can be created right here from work by scientists working for the City of Yekaterinburg."

"Hear! Hear!" shouted Dmitry.

What kind of shit propaganda was this? I wondered. Had the bootlicking gone too far? On the screen we were then treated to a video of the animal control crews doing musical numbers, *hopak* dancing in the streets in Cossack style, and then driving away in their newly painted vans and trucks with large smiling dogface logos on the sides. They had turned a grim, serious business into valuable public activities to garner public respect for both their work and the dogs they were catching. Gone were the old buccaneering days of machine-gunning packs of dogs, which the public had seen around Russia, as well as nearby Romania, Armenia, and Ukraine. Other than the occasional health necessity of gunning down rabid dogs or packs of them, such crudity was no longer practiced. Canine machine-gunning was legendary, and the Former Soviet Union had become world famous for its animal control brutality. So, it appeared to me that the work of Krastov's crew had at least softened the image and generated revenue for the City.

"We should point out that no human organs have been used on any dog here. Any modified dog organs such as speech chords and brain tissues are meshed using common biochemical techniques for key hormones. What we have achieved here has all come together after many failures. All of our work relies on the best medical technology available, including mechanical skin grafting," continued the voiceover.

"This is all done on a trial and error, case by case basis with lessons learned to be applied to our planned breeding project at later stages. Ultimately, we would like to see a new non-human creature or dog species constructed to fit into the organizational and industrial structures of Russia. Dr. Krastov's guiding theory has been "forced evolution" from dog to a new, non-human creature via destabilizing medical and chemical interventions. What this has meant in practice so far is trial and error with intense data collection and documentation to refine our methods for replication. We have shared our data with scientists working on similar projects in other countries, such as Hungary and Poland. Comparing what we have done with the 60-year experimental work of Dmitri Belyaev, there has been a slow evolution of the domestic dog from the wild fox via natural selection and genetics. His use of environment and genetic science relied, as we do, on natural processes and laws. What we are doing here is completely unlike Stalin and Lysenko, who planned to change nature and natural laws somehow with pseudo-science. Rather, we are following in the line of such Russian masters as Pavlov, who examined the effects of environment and instincts on subsequent behavior, and American behaviorists like B.F. Skinner, who worked with rats. We are also following in line with the work of the Russian Krushinsky, who found that other non-human creatures such as woodpeckers had complex social lives and examined the question of whether dogs could think and extrapolate," continued the voiceover in serious but soothing tones. Thankfully, there were no background violins to underscore the seriousness of what we were seeing.

Ivan suddenly added some background to what had been said about Lysenko and Stalin.

"If I might add a footnote on the bigger picture, the Putin regime is also quite different in its approach than Stalin, who isolated scientists in closed cities. Lysenko was a scientific charlatan who was motivated strictly by power. Stalin was worried about the public asking a lot of questions and being able to think. He feared that scientific critical thinking patterns, skepticism, and demand for more critical information might spread and contaminate the rest of the closed USSR society. It was a closed society and a closed economy. The USSR tried to prevent interpersonal collaboration. Only later did animal genetics and behavior become the exception. Now Russian scientists want to be cutting edge again. The Kremlin wants that too despite the threat to an authoritarian regime, but one that is not exactly a closed society anymore. All this bodes well for continued, top-level regime support for Dr. Krastov's work here."

"Putin also knows that the Chinese are doing serious genetic enhancement work and succeeding. The risk of trying to impede or silo animal genetics is far too great for a Russia now faced with such competition from the rest of the world and especially China," said Anna.

"All true . . . and thank you for rounding out the picture. Let me try and explain more of this as we are being deliberately misunderstood by the gutter press and by hysterical animal rights groups who frequently state that we are running a Dr. Frankenstein operation here."

"But it does seem you are modifying dog organs in your trial and error processes. You did mentioned modifications in brain tissue and speech chords, did you not?" asked Anna.

"Yes, I did, and we have to—all vets do this for complex operations. Here we upgrade them in the same way you would have your bones fortified with a partial knee replacement to allow you to walk better or have your eyes enhanced by cataract surgery and insertion of multifocal lenses. The difference is that your behavior doesn't change. Our working hypothesis, consistent with Belyaev's past animal behavior work, is that environmental change measured by the selection of tamer, recently-owned strays can trigger already extant genes in canine genomes that can produce dramatic behavioral changes. And why wouldn't they? Such dogs are already easier to work with because they were beneficiaries of stable homes and families, at least for a time." said Krastov, his face beaming.

"We use a medley of techniques that drive incremental but logical steps toward positive canine behavioral changes," he continued. "We started with operant conditioning via training consistent again with researchers like Pavlov and Skinner; moved to medical interventions to upgrade organs such as vocal chords and paws; and supplemented all this with additional chemical work to increase and change hormone production such as cortisone, testosterone, and melatonin. Behavioral changes were then being triggered by genetic activation of already extant canine genes. These changes tied back to changes in the environment, which interrupted natural selection. So once again, all we are doing is trial and error stuff to create a non-human dog person. The results have always been right in front of every scientist, but we have never been smart enough to see them."

"And you think you can establish this causal link?" asked Andrey.

"We already have. Researchers had always thought dogs were nothing more than stimulus-responses machines with barren inner lives. Ring bell—dog salivates! But we see from the most common house dog to Fyodor over there that they express hope, disappointment, remorse, jealousy, guilt, and disgust, just like we do. I see a dishonest look on Fyodor's face sometimes as he looks around pretending not to hear me when I tell him to do something. No matter how smart or near-humanlike he is, he is still a basic dog. All dogs behave the same way and even have the same expressions-—they have heard you, they are ignoring you, and they even feel some guilt at their own shifty behavior. Konrad Lorenz figured all this out a century ago. Despite all the hysterics and inflammatory statements in the media, we are not really doing much new here. Dogs were always ready to go; their systems just needed to be activated. The stray dog problem coupled with the urgency of the Games gave us the opportunity. Through the use of a number of known medical, genetic, and psychological techniques by trial and error, we seem to have activated extant genes. I'm not suggesting we haven't had failures—dead dogs in the process as we learned by doing. But no mutants running wild in the streets!" Krastov said with a throaty laugh.

On the screen above, Krastov moved ahead to shots of structural and behavioral changes in dogs.

"Note the changes in bodily parts produced by modifications to gene expression patterns. Here is a dog walking upright, known as bipedalism. Wasn't that you, Fyodor?"

From the corner where Fyodor was sitting in a chair, watching the show, came: "Indeed it was! I don't think you've developed any others yet, have you, Doctor?"

"As I said, besides Tsar, not that we know of."

"It was thought that evolution of new brain patterns to produce such behavior would take 200 years," said Dr. Lubyantsev. "We don't have 200 years. We have the notes and publications of earlier researchers who studied the multi-genetic determination of anatomical and physiological structures, such as hand movements and changes in larynx, vocal chords and tongues. Here, Dr. Krastov and I just took some short cuts."

"We found like earlier medical researchers that there was interplay between the human body and the brain. The growth of the brain created corresponding developments in the body and mind. Conversely, we found that the brain was also influenced by the bodily functions. The feedback loop accelerated the rate of change in humans. We found that to be the case with dogs as well," continued Dr. Lubyantsev.

"I still don't understand how you select the dogs for special training and development," said Petrovsky. "In police work we do profiling to catch our culprits."

"We would like to be at that stage. Much of our work might be termed 'action research' because we usually have to identify the right dogs during our stray eradication work. As you might expect, the chaos affects our concentration. So our method is more random," said Dmitry, looking around with an oddly ingratiating but fierce little smile.

"Actually, our method isn't so random, Dmitry. We try to use the same method here, Inspector," said Krastov. "We profile and select. We look for recently-owned, tamer dogs. We are dog people here and can spot the right ones even in packs. We mentioned that Andrey, Nick, and Anna brought a walk-on called Tsar II in today because he followed them from the metro and protected them from attacking dogs. Some aren't obvious until you can sense that like human delinquents running with bad crowds, they don't belong there and would like to get away."

"And that often happens?"

"To date, we have identified and are working with six candidates, isn't that so, Fyodor?"

"And I can say they are progressing nicely. Not as well as I did, but on the right path forward."

Petrovsky got a laugh at that one. "At least you've trained Fyodor well, Dr. Krastov. I can see that!"

"What Dr. Krastov is saying is that there seems to be an arc to their behavioral changes, and evolution and development. We all know that dogs wag tails in different ways to demonstrate loyalty to humans and their readiness for service. With this unique receptivity to human cues, they can easily learn to walk on two legs, read, write, talk, and then even manage other dogs and different groups of people," added Dr. Lubyantsev. "And why not?"

Suddenly Fyodor started rattling the bars of his cage. He turned to us with a dumb grin on his snout.

"Look, what you see and hear is all true. But I'm usually not in the mood to be receptive to anyone. And I certainly don't feel like learning new things all the time!" said Fyodor.

"That's right, Fyodor. We need to recall that dogs really do have moods. They can be depressed, bored, excited, or happy on any given day," said Dr. Lubyantsev.

"They certainly do. And I would note in our defense of being a normal vet hospital and research activity that we have no breeding farms for fur research as in old Soviet days," continued Dr. Krastov. "We have no need for them. The stimulus for regime support then was fur exports; now it is to ensure that the Games happen smoothly. This is a City project in need of scaling up to the national and international levels. We have been trying to make the qualitative leap into the area of creating a new, non-human creature without genetics. And I think Fyodor's behavior speaks for itself. This is successful applied research in the extreme. We are performing case by case tailoring; we make no pretense of creating a new species. The media and animal rights people still have it all wrong. They don't know or care about accepted history. Or they have their own versions. In fact, it took Trut and Belyaev seven generations of fox pups to breed in doglike traits. To return to Inspector Petrovsky's question, only 10 percent had 1E or elite traits in the seventh. But only 2 percent had them in the sixth. By that point, they could claim success. But things had to be scaled up so they were able to obtain land and resources for a fox farm and off went the study of Soviet animal genetics. They found that artificial selection for tameness catalyzed changes in animal (fox) behavior. Working along similar lines with more modern medical techniques now, we have sped up changes in canine behavior."

"And you came up with all these new activities just because of the Games?" asked Petrovsky.

"Actually not … We had been doing applied research and working hard on the prototype, which is Fyodor here. But the Games just gave us the political cover from higher ups. We were able to keep going without having pesky 'inspectors' demanding approval documents and bribes all the time. I'm sure you must know how that works in the police. Some of your best forensics and leads might get you into trouble with the political power people. You needed cover to continue, right?"

"All the time!" said Petrovsky, flashing his quick little grin.

"So, we are working along several fronts to demonstrate that tailored medical and chemical interventions allow us to construct the next phase of development, the dog-man," continued Krastov. "We are developing a dog-man creature with functional uses—walking, talking, reasoning, problem-solving, plus smelling with a nose that can sense terrorist bombs and weapons."

"Come on, Doctor; I don't like being called a dog-man. It sounds worse than son of a bitch!" said Fyodor.

"Then think up a better name for me! Something to describe a dog that like you, does most of these things already."

"How about just smart dog?"

That brought us all to relieve the tension with some hearty laughter.

"Ok, Fyodor, you win. We'll stop using dog-man. It does sound creepy, like something out of Dr. Moreau's island lab. It's actually worse than non-human creature. But let me continue on what we have planned for smart dog 'persons' like you. Eventually, you will be able to do the work of five human soldiers and specialists—only better. Dogs like you have always been human guards, hunter assistants, airport sniffers, purveyors of medical miracles—all functional necessities. Dogs have always been connected to humans, learned their cues, and looked carefully into their eyes. You did before your training here began—that's part of why you, Fyodor, were selected, luckily, off the street. All dogs have an endearing shyness that humans love. And it has been clear for thirty thousand years or so that dogs like humans too. No one has ever done real published research on these ideas with control and measurement groups. We hope that with USU staff and city help we can do that here," said Krastov.

Krastov paused here and, it seemed, a bit theatrically smiled at all of us. He looked at his watch and thanked us for our questions and said that he hoped we could all get together for future working sessions to assist them with their work.

As we engaged in good-bye pleasantries and light chatter, I noticed that Petrovsky spotted Dmitry standing to the side. As we prepared to leave, Petrovsky approached him before they got to their car and asked:

"Dmitry, tell me. What really happens to the dogs that don't make the cut for further research?"

"Quite simple. We kill them with clubs or death darts and dump them into the river by the weir to let them float south."

"Is that what you would do if you were in charge?"

"It's too much trouble in my view. I would simply incinerate them here in one of our ovens."

Here Dmitry seemed to choke on his emotions and fell into a fit of convulsive giggles. Honking like a silly old woman, his shoulders fluttered about in a peculiar dance of laughter. Seeing nothing amusing about any of this, Petrovsky didn't know what to make of it and thought only of doing a Heimlich maneuver if the guy started to lose consciousness.

"And what of the ones with potential for training and evolution?"

"I think that is mostly nonsense. If you look closely at our prime specimen over there, Fyodor, you have to notice there is something strange about him."

"How do you mean?"

"I mean he gives off insane vibrations, doesn't he? Note how often he wags his head back and forth. No normal dog does that. Combined with his off-focused eyes rolling around in their sockets, he seems to be a regular nutcase. We have created a potential lunatic here that is half human. Underneath, he is still an untamed and wild animal. Who knows what he will do?"

"Is he supposed to be normal, Dmitry? I mean is he mad or simply exuberant from all the attention he gets all day long? My dog occasionally has fits of excitement like that when he wants to go for a walk. But I would hardly label him as insane. Dmitry, you're not worried that he could take your position here, are you?"

"Of course not. I have seniority here and even if something like a Fyodor were hired—there would have to be a position to fit him, a new one, which is unlikely."

Petrovsky heard all this but watched Dmitry carefully. Dmitry had explained himself with the resentful look of an underfed dog hunched over his bowl. He looked like a dog that feared the bowl would be suddenly stolen from him. To him, Dmitry was trying to play doctor—he was not a doctor but had picked up the jargon and concepts from years of being around Krastov and now thought he was his equal. Dmitry was obviously jealous, an insecure skulking menial who wormed his way up the ladder to power. To Petrovsky, he was following the path of science to villainy, not toward the truth. He had seen plenty of people like this in the police and security services at all levels of the state. He had put them in their places more than once, and he had also been burned by such people in the past. He was sensitive to the damage they could cause to an office that needed to get things done and work together as a team. Still, though emotionally clumsy and intellectually pretty dim, Dmitry was probably one step above a Lysenko in the huckster league.

"You're not insecure around the clever dogs like Fyodor, are you?" asked Anna, who was listening to their conversation with one ear. She flashed him her playful smile, which should have put anyone on guard. "Don't you get enough attention here?" she said with her sly giggle.

Dmitry sneered back at her menacingly thinking, *Who is this bitch?* "I don't like it when we try to make dogs something other than what they naturally are." he announced.

"And what are they supposed to be? Man's best servants?"

"They are the servants of man and need to be told what to do and nothing more. Anyone who denies that denies nature and the natural order of things," he insisted.

Just then one of the dogs that hung around the lab all day, probably one of the crew's favorites, wandered by them. It was a smallish terrier dog, black and white with a large black spot on his left eye. Dmitry raised his voice to speak above the din of all the other barking dogs in cages nearby. At the same time, he threw his leg back and vigorously kicked the terrier out of his way. Then he continued talking.

"What are you looking at? He is nothing but a stray and shouldn't be in here." He glared at them with the mocking self-assurance of a tough peasant. Petrovsky mused that if he had ever encountered an evasive, lying cheat, this guy was it.

Over in the corner, Fyodor was quietly taking this all in. He had heard Dmitry talk like this before from other visitors to the lab. He had also witnessed his gratuitous cruelty before. It was nice to reconfirm his earlier conclusions that if had to bite any more human hands, Dmitry's would be the first one.

Petrovsky gave Anna the "we've heard enough from this asshole" stare and said, "I think we ought to leave now. Thank you, Dmitry, for filling us in. Let's keep in touch."

I sat together with the two of them in the back seat of the car on the way home. "That guy is a piece of work," Petrovsky said.

"From years of watching petty faculty types go at each other in their power games, I would keep an eye on that one," said Anna.

"Could be a jealous saboteur. But isn't he a bit obvious?" I asked. "His type is why university departments, organizations, and scientific endeavors often fail to accomplish what they could. Look what Lysenko using his connections to Stalin did to Russian animal science . . . The roles don't change, just the people in them!"

We rode home in silence mulling over these thoughts, and I marveled that something bigger was happening right before my eyes that I couldn't quite grasp.

14   KICKOFF!

The World Cup games had just started a few weeks ago in Moscow to great fanfare. Now the only games to be played in the Asian part of Russia, as the Yekaterinburg area was known, were underway. It was a bright, sunny Sunday, and Mexico was playing Sweden in the Yekaterinburg Arena. This was a Soviet neoclassical style stadium with the usual bas-relief columns to give it gravitas and a sense of fitting in somewhere in Russian history. As the stadium could only hold 23, 000 people, which was under the minimum 35,000 required by FIFA, local officials tacked on a temporary structure of 12,000 bleacher seats outside the original 1957 facility. It wasn't perfect, but it was mostly out in the sun or rain and no one in the stands complained. Since this was Russia, they had plenty of liquid fuel and food to keep them happy. If there was a break in the drinking and eating, they could always try to focus on who might have done something exciting on the field like passing the ball, faking a foul, or even scoring a goal. We had been there almost an hour, and there was still no score. I'd been to games like this before. Once in Quito, where I had lived for six months while teaching there at the university on a Fulbright grant, the game I attended puttered along for several hours. Seemingly nothing was happening but lots of penalties and impressive displays of individual dribbling. But that was Latin America, and to relieve the boredom, the fans started fighting in different spots of the stands. That produced lots of shouts, screams, blood, and broken bottles ... Not bad! At least we could watch the fights! But here, the game was quite irrelevant to both of us. That's not why Anna and I had come.

Entering the stadium, we saw people we both recognized from the USU faculty. I even saw Sveta, my landlady, who flashed me a restrained smile. I wondered what she was thinking about Anna . . . Was that a glint of jealousy in her eye? I dismissed the thought. When was the last time anyone was jealous of me? I was more worried about Leo, who must have been left at home with a bone by himself. We saw Andrey with a few guys about his age, presumably grad student pals. Later, we ran into Risanovsky, and he gave us a big wave from afar in the stands. The main attraction for us was being with each other. We had received the tickets from Semyon, who claimed "other business" as an excuse and sent her on to spend Sunday with me. Generous, but odd by any standard. Superficially, I was just a visiting professor getting a local tour. He knew there was more to it, and, unfortunately, I knew that he knew. The seas were probably going to get choppy later, but I only wanted to enjoy as much time with her as I could.

A few times that day between giggles and licks of her ice creams or bites of her grilled sausages, her eyes suddenly changed expression and became serious. She motioned with an eyebrow or flick of her eyes to the left or right. Following her cues, I noticed some characters that were definitely not there for the games or as groupie tourist fans from Mexico or Sweden. As it was said, the Russian police and security services had their funny ways, but you didn't have to be told twice by them to obey. The voyeurs we noticed were definitely not hooligans. Since this was Russia, hooligans knew that if stray dogs could be disposed of without public notice, they were at much greater risk of at least a good flogging. Nor were they simply romantic voyeurs—in the summer, displays of romance were everywhere. There were too many couples to observe other than us with more tasty displays of flesh and passionate swoons. The surprising thing to me was that the state security people didn't even try to look legitimate. That meant they were probably just what we thought they were: some of Semyon's goons out gathering evidence with their iPhone cameras. I could not have cared less; she apparently didn't either. And good for them . . . We were emboldened—even did exaggerated poses for them kissing or hugging out of mockery!

At halftime, with the score an exciting 0-0, the fans pulled out all the cultural stops. A large group of *hopak* squat dancers in colorful Ukrainian garb bounded onto the field and hopped around in perfect unison. Another musical group accompanied them, whistling and shouting encouragement. They clapped, bounded up and down like frogs, sang, and whistled. The crowd sat effaced and humbled by the raw beauty and gravity of the music. If they listened carefully, what they heard were sonatas and songs on dog-catching, modernized from the ballads and songs of their forefathers. Every Russian knew this was their heritage. The Mexicans and Swedes would have their shows later, but nothing could match this. Now the squat dancers ran off to be replaced by another fired-up crew of dancers in bright green uniforms sporting dog logos on their backs. And there they were! It was Krastov's crew in person! They gathered round the mike and sang one of his limericks gruffly pounded out as an Orthodox *missa*. It was full of sad gusto and brought the crowd to its feet. Some in the stands understood that the lyrics referred to a lost dog someplace that had been killed by an ancient dog-catching crew that knew no better. As a heart-rending interlude done by some musical amateurs full of energy and innocent mistakes, the fans loved it. Anna broke into giggles and bubbled along with the music like a carefree kid. Some people in the crowd began to sing in a high-spirited and uninhibited way. As more shouts of 'hurrah!' resounded, I was in an ecstasy of bliss, and, like the crowd, joined in singing along with the music.

"Did you know that Krastov had quite a history around here before he became a successful scientific entrepreneur?'

"Oh, yes?"

She spoke as they watched the doctor down on the field in his white coat, emblazoned with the dog logo shouting out and joining in the *hopak* squat dancing.

"He is known as a delightful character, mentally unbalanced but always endearing. People have always been intrigued by him. They call him the 'mad vet,' and he used to do rage dancing at his lab way before its time. I learned this from some of his crew."

"Sounds like a breath of fresh air! Was he always a city dog vet or did he work on farm animals before?"

"He worked in small villages on farm animals. He was known as a free spirit and preferred the fresher air of villages. He apparently got his hair cut annually and just threw the extra hair back into a long pony-tail. The rest he had cut by shepherds with wool sheers. A real earthy type, but a mad professor at heart. Driven wild by brainwaves he called them."

"Brainwaves?"

"When he got stumped and didn't know how to proceed, some-times he would throw his head back at his desk and go into a trance for hours on end. Several times his crew thought of calling in the medics because they were worried about him," said Anna.

"What kind of problems stumped him?"

"Professional ones, like how to fix canine vocal chords so their voic-es wouldn't be just more nuanced growls and barks; or how to get dogs to walk upright without losing balance."

"I don't get it. Smart dogs can already do these things. I've seen trained poodles and circus dogs walk upright. And I've had many housedog pets that contorted their vocal chords into different tones to get the point across that they were hungry. Some can even sing along accompanying groups playing pianos and strumming on banjos. So these challenges weren't totally new."

"They were new if you had grander objectives, like producing a new race of talking and walking dogs that could someday join the work-force. It meant that he had been thinking about creating a non-human form of dog for a long time."

"How did he end up here?" I asked her. "Got tired of talking with shepherds and exchanging village gossip about cows, did he?"

"Rumor has it that his wife of ten years ran off with a local. That soured him on rural life, and he came to Yekaterinburg, got a job with city animal services, and has been here ever since."

As they were chatting in the stands, she noticed someone approach them from the stairway aisle. Not selling beer or food, the man aimed his oversized iPhone and began openly snapping pictures of them. Both of us watched this clown trying to do surveillance.

"Is that the best they can do? What an amateur!" I said.

"He has to be one of Semyon's people. No one else could be that stupid!'

"Ok, but I'm worried about you. We need to be more discreet."

"Aren't we already? Semyon got us the tickets, and we're sitting together."

"But at other times, we are at my place, and they certainly know where I live. We need to be careful."

"Come on, Nicholas. You sound like a timid, old peasant woman."

"Well, maybe I am. I don't want anything to happen to you."

We kissed long and passionately, oblivious of the photo-op we were creating. On the field, the half-time spectacle was about over, and the game on the field would resume shortly.

I looked at her and thought how she scrambled out of bed at my place sometimes in a rush to get home or to the office. I liked watching her dress: the subtle rippling of her nut-brown leg muscles as she walked around like a stripper. Her ripe little breasts were just inviting enough to be licked into the shape of hardened cones. Unconsciously, she seemed to be playing a game of arousal. At times like that, I lost control and bounded out of the covers, pinning her back onto the mattress. She squealed and giggled in inviting protests. Those were the times when we had the best sex, working ourselves into several mutual orgasms in succession. I had never been this aroused by anyone and was not about to give her up.

"What is it? I can tell your mind is calculating something."

"You," I said. "We've gotten this far, and I hardly know who you are besides your professional self."

"Intriguing, aren't I? But there's nothing much to report: born after most of the Soviet Union had already collapsed. My father was a railway engineer and drove freight trains before he retired. My mother teaches elementary and primary school and is about to get her pension. I have a younger brother and sister who met and married Brits studying here and moved to England. I studied engineering and biology and got a job at USU a few years ago. See? Nothing exciting. No boyfriends really and a rather dull life until you came along."

"Let's see if I can liven things up for you then."

"I think I know what you mean!" she said. For emphasis, she put out her tongue and licked my face before sliding it into my mouth.

I glanced behind her, only to catch sight of the same amateur sleuth moving up the stadium stairs then returning a few minutes later for more shots of us.

"That guy Dmitry is another piece of work, don't you think? How did the conflict between them begin?"

The sudden blare of mariachi trumpets shouted out as a band erupted somewhere in the stands when the Mexicans scored a goal. We weren't watching the game very closely, but now saw Mexican flags waving here and there from different parts of the stadium. I knew that flag. I didn't know the Swedish flag and still hadn't seen one, since they hadn't scored yet, and no one was waving it. In most games the action takes place somewhere else far away from where you are sitting. so you end up being perpetually surprised. There were large video screens showing the action, but that means you could probably have stayed home and watched it on TV. You were wasting money for the experience of going to a game merely to look at the scoreboards. The real dramatic action here was off field, such as hearing the excellent mariachis and watching the idiot cameraman wandering around trying to blend in as a fan.

"Petrovsky told me that their rivalry began over a petty humiliation several years ago," said Anna.

"Not surprised. He seems like the type that would store up slights to get even later."

"But with the additional feature of being an effeminate bully who takes out his insecurities on dogs. Did you watch him go into convulsions and catch the creepy laughter earlier?"

"I noticed. Weird guy! So how did it all happen?"

"About three years ago, they were all out in a rural village searching for elite dog candidates to experiment on. Krastov organized missions like this in their off time, frequently turning them into picnics and socializing events to get to know his crew better. After a while, they stopped by a rural bakery for a bite to eat. There they served up only beer and hard, black bread. The bread was made in bricks, hard as rocks, and impossible to chew. I've seen them around here. You have to use a screwdriver to chip off pieces of bread! All of them realized that they couldn't eat that crap. It would take all day! To relieve the growing boredom, Krastov told Dmitry to run out for a pass, American football style. He ran a quick slant play to the left. Krastov nailed him in the stomach with one of the bread bricks, knocking him off balance. He then fell backwards into a mud puddle. That gave all of them a real laugh, but Dmitry was deeply humiliated by Krastov's antics. Krastov gave him his hand to help him up, but Dmitry refused."

"So if he had made a good catch, there would have been no bad blood between them."

She always saw the lighter side of things. "Maybe so, but he probably would have found something else to grind his teeth about, if I read him correctly."

After a few hours of staring at the players dancing around the field, dribbling the ball in ever fancier ways, they began to feel claustrophobic. They felt eyes watching them from busybody scolds and paid snoops. Even though most were only fans engaged in their own amorous doings (after all it was a hot day), Anna felt especially vulnerable. They were having their little holiday, disappearing from view right in plain sight. And they were only holding hands and touching. But she kept noticing a few people looking at them with different motives than the usual scolds and voyeurs who often watched lovers cavorting. No, these people were taking shots seriously for the record. It was another guilt-free liaison, but now they were both feeling guilty. The liaisons released her from being trapped in a marriage that long ago had soured. More than once she had laughed at Semyon's uncontrollable fetish for power when for her, life meant so much more—even in Yekaterinburg. They held each other's stare for an instant and began to gather up their things to leave. They could feel the pictures being taken as they left. Ok, so be it ...

As we bounced along on the tram from the stadium to their neighborhood, it happened. I burst out laughing; I just couldn't control it.

"What's the matter?" she asked, now infected by my mood and laughing.

"So bad! Guys running around passing the ball back and forth, hoping to hit one between the goal posts. But they hoped even more for a foul call from the refs. It all reminded me of the Simpsons episode where they passed back and forth until the crowd chanted 'boring!' and started a riot to relieve the boredom because no one scored. Do we even know the score when we left?"

"Not really. Believe it or not, I saw that Simpsons episode in Russian and thought it was good. What are your sports?"

"I like tennis because at least I can play it. I don't like American football, but it perfectly fits my adopted culture: strategic planning and violence. But I can't really play it either. I like baseball because I have the build of an infielder and can throw. I played that when growing up. Mind you, I have respect for round footballers. I watched some of them play matches barefoot and play shirtless in alleys, squares, and parks. They grew up in poor countries in all this, hoping for the big breaks; many of these guys we saw on the field today got the breaks. "

"It's true that soccer is the people's game, and a lot of players were mostly dirt poor. It's like the baseball kids in Central American and the Caribbean islands that I often read about, who play with sticks and rocks without gloves. When they get discovered, they're the toughest ones. Me, I just play tennis sometimes so let's play," said Anna.

"How do you think Fyodor handles exercise and normal bodily functions?"

"You mean going to the bathroom and keeping fit?" I asked.

"Right. He can't just lie around, and there's no obvious place for him to run."

"I saw a soccer ball in his cage that looked pretty chewed up. I thought it was a toy, but now I think he may kick it around either in the lab when everyone is gone or maybe even with the crew. As for bodily functions, he probably uses the WC just like the crew."

"Oh look! What a surprise! Speaking of exercise and bodily functions, here we are at my tram stop," I said. "Let's go in a volley a bit!" We entered my apartment seemingly unnoticed at least by Sveta and Leo. They probably did notice, but by now they weren't surprised at my erratic returns at all hours. My imagination had been drinking her in for hours, and I was really thirsty. We moved quickly into our newly-adopted routine to undress, then head for the shower. Why delay? We were tired from sitting in the stadium and enduring a boring game varied chiefly by fights between imported nationalist hooligans and on field penalty disputes, which erupted into opportunities for catcalls, shouts, and airing of personal grievances. Looked at in this wider, big picture way, the shower offered us unlimited freedom of movement, which the bed did not. By now, I knew that we could easily get swept away in our ecstatic gymnastics and pull a back or neck muscle in bed. So we took turns lathering each other up in the shower while probing every orifice with our tongues and fingers in slow rhythms. Not surprisingly, we found that there was always something newly erotic about soapy, brown flesh that turned us both on. Then for the first climax, I held her thighs and lifted her into place around me in front as I entered and thrust into her standing up. This was a dangerous move as we had fallen more than once in there. Exhausted and intoxicated after the successful completion of this, we both fell into my bed without even drying off and fell instantly to sleep.

I woke up sometime later and saw her sleeping quietly nearby, feeling the warmth of her arm lying across my forehead. Through the shades I could see it was getting dark outside, so it had to be around 8 p.m. or so. Full of that wonderful sense of bliss from the experience of love with someone I cared about, I was delightfully and naively certain that everything would turn out all right in the end. What did that mean, and what was the end? Sure, it was a cliché but also a strong definite feeling to reinforce my conclusion. Now I saw the world and the future in a thousand different colors. My spirit was energized, and I had recaptured the innocence and optimism of my youth. It was like my first love where I imagined the possibilities were infinite and new.

That attitude affected my subsequent loves and now this one. Lying in bed, we both imagined that the world had been reset for us. It was all impractical but full of playful rapture and sexual intensity.

I saw that she was staring at me as I wallowed around in this enraptured world. "And what about your wife? How does all this fit?"

"Ah yes, that. It's probably like the same complicated mess here you're trying to make sense of."

"Mine follows the thematic logic of a simple Russian fable: we each get our wish, but it leads to tragedy."

"My mother used to read Alexander Afanaseyev fairy tales to me when I was young," I said. "My favorite was *Teremok,* maybe because we lived in a crowded rat-hole of an apartment in the Bronx. You probably know it as well: a mouse moves into an empty wooden house in the forest. Other animals ask permission to move in, and he invites them. Then a bear wants to move in, but has to stay on the roof because he is too large. He ends up crushing the house."

"I know that one well," she said. "I feel like I'm being squeezed by Semyon's invitees who come in to oogle me and get wined and dined. They are like the fairy tale bear, crushing the place.

"Careful, I was *one* of those invitees … And I did a bit of oogling myself."

"So did I when you came. But unlike the other forest animals, I'm not staying around to rebuild the house."

"Glad to hear it!"

"So I'm the trophy wife Semyon shows off to his associates, and he has been good to me in the sense that he lets me do what I want. His associates that he invited from the Kremlin forest are not the problem. Since this is the twenty-first century he reminded me, he would maintain several mistresses that I was supposed to tolerate. He imagined we had an 'arrangement.' But he did; I didn't. I'm not into kinky promiscuity."

Looking at me squarely in the eye as she spat out these words, I noticed that she had a definite hint of an underbite, a slight jut to the jaw that gave a pugnacious edge to her beauty.

"You sound guilty. Is this our Russian soul struggling with guilt and the craving for freedom? You think it's wrong to tolerate his peccadillos?"

"It has nothing to do with religion and the soul. I'm a woman who once loved and paid for it with humiliation and even fear of men that I cannot trust."

"Fair point..."

"But as a believer, I believe that I am protected by a divine tractor beam. That gives me all the freedom I need."

"You'll have to explain that one."

"It's my simple way of making sense of things. If you try to distinguish right from wrong, tolerate others as best you can and forgive them most of the time, you fall within the heavenly glide path and have freedom of will and can make your own choices. Don't you think?"

"And your choices might be . . . ?"

"To be here with you. And to bolt from him if I feel justified."

"Makes sense to me."

"How can you rationalize being here then? You're married, aren't you?"

"I can't. You've thought it all out, but I have no deep philosophical or religious justifications. That's why I can only teach planning. Spiritually pretty shallow . . . I just want to be with you and no one else—and damn the consequences."

"You will be going home to your wife soon. You will forget me as if I never existed."

"Home is where your dreams are to paraphrase an old saw. Mine are here with you."

"If I tried to leave, he or they could kill us both."

I took her in both arms and held her close to me on my bed. "That's why I have to leave then. I don't want you to get hurt."

"This isn't a romantic soap opera or an amateur script being read. This is life right now! Let's stop the theatrics. We were talking about your family. What about your wife?"

"That's another B movie. My life there was bad soap drama. Laurie and I were married for 15 years in a tidy, efficient, and humorless relationship. She had her life, I had mine, and we rarely crossed into each other's space. So I was surprised one day to find her gone, revealed starkly by the sudden absence of all her jewelry and clothes. Empty drawers—empty life. That happened over a year ago and left me taking care of our two kids, who are now in college and beyond my care except for an occasional cash subsidy."

"That must have been a shock even though you are making light of it."

"Well, it was. It certainly was a surprise, though in retrospect, it shouldn't have been. We hardly talked at all for years. So I didn't plan this. But with a flexible teaching schedule at a small college and few obligations otherwise, I made it work."

"Why did she leave you?"

"Usual American-style story, now for bored suburban couples who never talked to each other except via email or FaceTime. Laurie abruptly moved in with a corporate vulture she had met someplace and had gotten her pregnant. Could have fooled me! I knew she met men but assumed that they were mostly for her work in finance. Piecing things together later, I think she even invited him to the house several times when I was there. I thought he was there for a business meeting that spilled over into dinner. I hardly suspected anything probably because he looked and sounded like a real loser, a flake. Perhaps I was thinking that if she ever did look around for male companionship beyond me, she would do much better than that. Apparently not... She was like the athlete trading up from the minor leagues and their low subsistence salaries to the big leagues with fame and much more money. We may have full-time jobs in the U.S., but most are dead-end, without much status or salary. Most university faculty are like me, rather obscure people who just get by on their salary. It's not a complaint. It's just how life really is."

"At USU and Russian universities, we have status, but no salary or full-time jobs."

"No place is perfect, is it? So, 'vulture Victor' as I called him had a horse ranch outside of Elmira, and he needed a trophy wife to hang up with the saddles and bridles to produce an instant family. He needed these trappings, I gather, to be the big cheese in his superficial money hustling world. You might think that academics are envious of the overpaid hucksters in the financial world. No, we just could use some of their money."

"So what did you do? Surely you fought to get her back? That's what a Russian man would do. It's what Semyon would do. Not get mad—just get even."

"I saw no need for heroics. I didn't challenge him to a duel or bother with the preferred feral approach of a growl and a spring. No, I was actually both surprised and relieved. The suddenness of her departure fooled me. She was of homely stock, a nice, orderly, methodical little housewife when I married her. Apparently, she had another side that I missed."

"Men are all so blind."

"At least I was. So I went to the associate dean and my longtime confident and explained things. Bob Sofen was just the man I needed. He told me to whip up a grant proposal to get out of the country for a few months the next summer and get my head straight. He would even combine it with a medical leave for emotional renewal, and here I am in bed with you being renewed!"

Anna giggled. "A happy chain of circumstance so far then."

"Seems that way to me... And you have contributed. I spent the year after it happened around Bonaduz in a dazed state. Curiously, my sex drive, which had been repressed for years, suddenly came alive like a volcano erupting through rock, pouring hot molten semen in magnificent streams in all directions. I chased every skirt on campus and often limped back to my home bent with pulled muscles. But then followed emptiness. Mostly, I came back frustrated and humiliated. That's the way it has been the last six months. And then you crossed my path!"

"Odd. You seemed slow and uninterested at first. I never would have guessed all this happened to you, except perhaps that fine day on the mountain in the Oleny forest."

"Being with you then, watching you climb around the rocks, it all rekindled my physical and emotional being. But enough of this talk… "

I looked at her like a hungry animal. I abruptly clutched her shoulders, and down we went back onto the bed. We were back at it again, she panting and groaning, me gasping for breath with the strength of a drowning man seeking oxygen to continue living for a few more moments. She often grabbed me so tightly that when I checked myself over in the mirror, I noticed that I was bruised up. In contrast, her lithe body absorbed my tight little clutches without visible damage. It was an afternoon lovemaking sequence we would often repeat, ending up in the shower again to continue our soaring sexual explorations through intense physical cavorting. We rolled back into bed without even drying off. But our wet bodies became even more erotic to us, and we would soon return to more exertions. In the aftermath of these periods of sexual amuck time, we released our thoughts and feelings in unending streams. I had never had such delirious, sexual psychological releases with anyone. I had once done something with a girl in college after we both had smoked some superb quality pot, but I could barely remember any of it afterwards. The times with Anna, embedded in my mental and physical being, stayed with me, and I fell back into vivid recollections weeks later. I reflected that this was all quite odd in that despite these bouts of aggressiveness, I had always been shy with strong, open, beautiful women, fearing I would say the wrong thing, and they would simply flee. These doubts never appeared with Anna, and she proceeded to draw me out and beyond myself. With her, I no longer thought—I just reacted and was swept along in the churn of the powerful wake of her feelings and ideas. If love meant one could talk freely about almost anything with your partner, I was experiencing just that kind of character revolution. I felt I could talk with her effortlessly without hiding anything or remain silent and say absolutely nothing. Since the beginning, which was only a month earlier, I felt I had known her once before, maybe in my childhood days though that had to be impossible. Perhaps she had awakened my dormant Russian soul from its now fossilized existence in America.

Now she stared right through me with her richly furrowed brow. Her mood changed to dead serious. "I'm worried about Dmitry and also angry at what he is obviously up to."

"Not now... I am too. And why should we care?"

"Because the two of us are alone now ... I can't really complain to my faculty, can I? And Semyon has too many thuggish allies that he can call upon in a moment's notice to do his bidding. Many people owe him favors for pulling power levers in their favor. You know, for getting them official positions, city contracts, and the like."

"It always comes back to this. We are quite powerless, and the only question is how much risk are we willing to take?"

"Haven't we moved beyond all that?"

They both sat in silence for a few moments, brooding.

"I want you to meet someone that could become an important ally if we approach him properly."

"Who would that be?"

"He's just a wild and crazy guy, known about town as an oddball. Wears loud, multicolored clothes and sports tons of hair. May even be a relative of yours: Boris Illich Krylovsky. He is also an important leader of the animal rights groups around here, and he does have a kind of back channel power."

"How do you know him?"

"It is hard not to if you happen to like dogs, live here, and have a social conscience. I've always liked animals and wanted to protect them. My animal rights leanings are just one more dimension of me that you don't know much about."

"What a cornucopia of surprises you are, a more intoxicating mystery each day! The next thing you will tell me is that Krastov also works with him!"

"You've forgotten: this is Russia, the novel as well as reality. We are all characters in a grand novel here. In fact Krylovsky often does work with him. And Krastov may be the cleverest politician in Russia and will probably out survive us all. Not bad for someone who has never held office."

15 NEIGHBORHOOD STRAYS

The next day, I spent time at USU reworking modules for an up-coming training class in planning with Ivan. He was a hard-work-er, and I found that he learned fast. With projects like this, I hoped I could help his career a bit here or after I returned to Bonaduz. Personal working relationships like this are often an indirect benefit of over-seas research grants, university campuses, and established research in-stitutes. If anyone asked what I accomplished here, I would be hard pressed to come up with anything tangible, other than helping a few host institution careers, such as his.

After a few hours of work that morning, I was tired and went back to my flat where I read for a more hours to relax. I had been reading Plutarch's Lives, focusing on the part where he described a law made by Solon, a founder of Athens, which stuck in my mind. By law, the mas-ter of any dog that bit someone had to deliver the dog up to authori-ties with a 4½ foot log around his neck. That was a crude method to prevent the dog from biting anyone else. So the Athenian biters would be walking around the streets crashing into things with large logs tied around their necks. In my mind, it begged the question of: what if there were no owners? I assumed strays then would be taken care of with advice from either the Oracle of Delphi or by sending soldiers to massacre them, just like any enemies of order and peace at the time. The law was absurd on its face. As with many of his strange laws, Solon avoided having to explain any of the obvious contradictions with real world behavior by frequently leaving town. His other laws were often equally odd and rigid. He was an early example of the demagogue who had power but avoided real responsibility, which seemed to me like a plague—Russia was full of those types now at the top of the Kremlin. And the people were left to deal with this tyranny as best they could.

As I was brooding over all this, there was a knock on the door and as usual this time of day, Sveta appeared and handed me Leo's leash. Off I went for our evening walk. It was a good way of relaxing, and I enjoyed the fresh evening air and the chance to watch the neighbors coming and going from shopping and work—a nice slice of normality for me. Overhanging trees in our neighborhood muted the streetlights. A fog had rolled in as it sometimes did in summer near the Urals. It was chilly that night, and I had difficulty seeing very far ahead down the sidewalks. Several times, I actually stumbled in the dark over roots that had flipped up slabs of the concrete. Nothing unusual here; I had the same problem in Elmira. Cursing out loud several times, it really meant my mind had slowed down, and I had a flat learning curve. Fluttering his ears, Leo looked up at me in curiosity several times, and I felt like an idiot. A few streets later (since he hadn't yet taken his evening dump), I saw some large dogs that abruptly crossed the street and headed towards us. In the fog I could make out that they were either: large dogs, wolves, or coyotes. Either way, a problem. On guard now, Leo gave a low growl, which added to the predictable drama of what was about to occur. They weren't wearing 4½ foot logs so we were in trouble.

At the next corner, I dropped his leash and yelled, "Stay there. Get ready: here they come, Leo!"

As usual, when I could have used a few bystanders, no one else was around. Odd that I never saw any other dog-walkers around here. I noticed a large dog bounding along on the other side of the street. He paused occasionally to sniff at some exotic piss smell or a fish bone from someone's lunch discarded in the street. He started off again, noticed me, and changed course. He came at me with an ears-back gallop. When he got to me, I was ready with the spray canister before I sized him up as a wry clown. He jumped up and down in front of me, tongue hanging out of his mouth, darting back and forth. Then he gave himself away when he crouched down like a pseudo-beast of prey, like dogs do when they want to have some fun. I reached in my pocket for one of the small treats I fed Leo and let the dog smell it.

"Beat it!" I shouted, hoping I could get rid of him.

He stopped his cavorting for a second and looked at me. He was just clowning around. It seemed the attention I gave him worked in reverse—my indifference and attempted fierceness worked as a goad. For a second, he sized me up as a new potential master, someone with lots of good meals and a cozy shelter for him. Could this be another 'walk-on' for Krastov's animal work?

"Come on, you bastard! Move off!" I shouted again. To back up my command, I tossed the treat as far as I could, and he obligingly ran off to get it. After chasing a few of these down, he became more interested in smelling things someplace down the street and forgot about me.

Even strays retain some of their clownishness and should be rewarded; they certainly should not be gassed and incarcerated in kill pounds. With this relaxing and magnanimous thought churning around in my head, I noticed just then that a different collection of dogs had gathered, and they were about to dart at us from across the street. There were about a half-dozen of them, trotting together. Then they skillfully veered apart into an attack formation and came at us from two sides. Impressive! The reality hit me that despite all his boastings, Krastov hadn't really gotten rid of most of the city's strays at all. And these were big ones. They moved like sharks and swam towards us, zigging and zagging, but staying together and focusing on the objective, which was—us—until they suddenly separated for the kill. Droplets of water from the fog glistened on their fur, revealing they had curly hair and weighed in around 80 pounds each. Their eyes shown like menacing beacons aimed directly at us. I took out my pepper spray canister and tightly secured it by the wristband in preparation for some powerful lunges. It was not a good time to be fumbling around with a canister. Then I got an idea. When they got within close range, I bellowed an order at them:

"Sit!"

All dogs have been taught to 'sit' at sometime in their lives and in all languages. Owned dogs from the beginning sat in order to get treats. Strays have probably been disciplined by human overlords at some time in their lives. So why not these? Still, I was surprised to see the two of them sit down obediently, open their jaws in deadly smiles, and pant obediently in expectation of treats. It worked! But instead of a treat, I approached them and gave them a few quick blasts from my pepper spray canister. It was a cheap trick on my part, but the distraction should give us at least a minute before they remembered their mission.

"Come on, Leo, move it!" I yelled at him as we ran for it in the opposite direction. I didn't even look back until we had sprinted at least five blocks. I stopped and wheeled around with my pepper spray, ready to fire. The strays were nowhere to be found. We got a break. Apparently, they were not the vengeful sorts and had scampered off somewhere else. Through shifting rents in the fog, I could see that we had wandered into a more upscale neighborhood of larger homes. It was likely the area Anna had described where she and Semyon had their in-town residence. Though it was a few blocks from the tram stop near where I had first met her, there was still no one around. No dog walkers here either. The tangerine glare of the streetlights was as weak as it was in my neighborhood. The large tree canopies blocked much of the light anyway while the rest was probably dim from the weak light bulbs. Trying to get my bearing so we could head home, I saw several dark figures on the other side of the street. Not dogs this time—humans. And they seemed like stray types to me. They just stood there observing us like they had known we were coming. Maybe they had followed us all along. Maybe I just hadn't noticed them. I saw one of them throw down a lit cigarette, and then two of them started moving in our direction. They lunged across the street taking large, athletic strides, appearing to drag their arms behind them. I had my spray canister tied to my wrist so I still felt somewhat secure. I watched these guys lumber towards us—walking on the balls of their feet like muscular jocks in training. They weren't actually walking on all fours, but they definitely did not have the casual moves of summer tourists. They came right up to us. Leo was growling and knew these were bad types, which dogs can always sense earlier than humans. "They definitely aren't here to bring me treats," he was probably thinking.

I could see their faces now as the streetlights revealed them to be none other than my two associates from the Transsib. They certainly got around. The taller, beefy one still had his pock-marked pineapple and distinctive third eye forehead wart that reminded me of the Cyclops character in a bad film. Still flashing that cocky, conquering grin, I could see the reflections of his teeth from a hundred feet away. His burly side-kick was still shorter and stockier. I thought he might have grown up a bit. He still had his angry forehead above the long but slightly broken nose and receding chin. Combined with his nicely sloped brow, he had the perfect little rat face. It reconfirmed the accepted anthropomorphic principle that features like that really do reveal character. I always thought that was true, but was never sure of the direction of causation. In any case, neither of these people was to be trusted, before on the train or now.

"Well, well, just look who we just found Sergi! It's our tourist from the Transsib. I thought people like him hung out permanently in the Sheraton lobby with the rest of the plastic whores."

"Let's see some ID this time. No funny business, or you're dead!" Cyclops said to me.

The familiar odor of his onion and tobacco-infused breath came back. I was surprised that he was wearing an open coat with pants up almost to his ribs. It made him look even more like the cheap pimp that he was. And the guy looked even stranger than the normal one-eyed monster. Here he was again, flashing his official police ID, if that's what it was. I had one like that when I was a teenager to impress people, mainly neighborhood toughs. I mean several of us had phony IDs like that, which looked pretty good for a $2 print job. They moved in closer, eyeing me now with clenched teeth grins, just waiting for me to make a wrong move like last time.

"Still in the ID business, are you? What brings you here? I thought people like you lived on trains?" I said as I casually reached inside the jacket for my papers. Their beady little eyes followed my right arm hand closely, perhaps expecting a gun.

Rat face twitched his nose and was about to say something snide when I flipped my other wrist over quickly and sprayed them with the canister, which I still wore, nailing both of them with clean shots to the eyes. His forehead, an angry knot of muscles, merged with the rest of his mug, and he banged at his head in a vain attempt to stop the pain. I was glad the thing worked both times tonight, or I would have been in deep shit. Down they went, cursing and screaming, holding their faces and wiping their eyes. With all the noise sure to attract someone, we turned around and sprinted as fast as we could back towards our neighborhood.

———

The waiting room at police HQ was similar to those I had been in as a young delinquent in the Bronx. The room was windowless and shadowy despite the clear, bright sunlight outside that day. The usual range of disreputable characters, sitting around, waiting to be questioned, rounded out the somber atmosphere. They had likely been rounded up the night before by an inspector: some looked like informants or witnesses. Their hangdog faces looking up at anyone who passed by indicated they had been waiting for many hours. There was one older man with a very long beard that actually hung down between his legs and incredibly continued down the chair. A Kafkaesque-looking character, he might have been there for years only to find out he was in the wrong room. Then there were the high-society contingent: men and women who remained standing as if they would be summoned at any minute now. By the time I left an hour or so later, I noticed that they were still there but sitting in dejection, having lost all sense of their class privilege.

It was the day after our neighborhood run in with Ratface and Cyclops. I was reading my notes for my new teaching module, which I was designing at USU when I heard:

"Nicholas, what brings you to this end of town?" said Petrovsky, who suddenly appeared and was now waving me into his office with a sweep of his hands. He was in his usual high spirits, which had to be admired in any policeman given the types of characters inside the force and from the streets he had to pound on a constant basis.

"In the future, when you want to get together, here is my private number. And while I'm at it, can you come for dinner tonight at our place? The address is on the back of the card."

Without a second's hesitation, knowing that Anna would be at her office tonight and I would have to try and cook something for myself, I said, "I'd be honored."

"Now what important matters can we dispose of here so I can get back to the work of preserving order and serving the right people?"

The window of his office overlooked a large courtyard that was tastefully planted in trees and shrubs. In the middle of it was a large linden tree. An old tree, one expected to see it in a forest or large city park. Yet there it was. It often amazed me how perfectly dreary flats in European neighborhoods would open up to miniature forests inside. It seemed contradictory and not quite right, like something out of a dream, which you tried to piece together in the morning but couldn't.

"I need your insight and advice. Political life here is kaleidoscopic and multi-dimensional to put it as delicately as I can. I know all that and have been updated by several reliable sources."

"Like Anna, I bet."

"She's certainly my number one advisor in all this. I haven't told you, but several toughs tried to mug me on the Transsib before I got to Perm about five weeks ago."

"I hope you didn't interrupt them. They might have been current or former MPs. What did you do?"

"They followed me from the dining car, cornered me in front of the WC, and showed me police ID cards and badges. But, being a veteran of phony IDs when I was underage and needed booze, I figured they were phony. I made better ones myself in my days of wild youth."

"So I imagine you tried to reason with them."

"Naturally... we tried to 'get to yes' and work things out reasonably. Since they didn't seem amenable to the usual conflict resolution techniques, I placed them inside the WC for the rest of the evening."

"Nothing reported here as far as I know. Of course, the Transsib is a federal railway and would probably report incidents to the Kremlin, not to local police. Did they see you get off at Perm?"

"That's what I don't know. More importantly, they tried to do it again last night near my neighborhood as I was out walking the landlady's dog."

"The same people?"

I nodded. "And how did that end?"

"Pepper spray. Zveta's dog Leo and I had just been attacked by some strays, and I was feeling like a real sharpshooter with my canister. So I used it again on them. It worked quite well, well enough for us to escape from them by scampering off."

"So you want to know what's going on and will they keep trying, maybe with more serious tactics?"

"Any thoughts?"

"Nothing definite. They could be irregular militia members. There are lots of them as you know, and they are shadowy figures. Some of them are right out there in the waiting room. I imagine you noticed that crowd while waiting outside this morning."

"These people were in shape and seemed like professionals. The waiting room outside seems full of defeated types, probably retired or looking for their next petty crime jobs."

"You say you were near your neighborhood. That could be bad, and they could be scoping you out for a bigger job. Or, I know that Semyon and Anna live near you. They might just be guards for Semyon, and you ran into them the second time by accident."

"So where does this leave me?"

"You could be in more serious danger. But my hunch is if they are connected to Semyon, you are probably protected from more serious bodily injury by his wife Anna. Am I wrong?"

I nodded. "Could well be. And if they are not connected to them?"

"Then we have the usual uncontrolled militia problem. People disappear all the time in Russia, and no one can be certain who did it. They turn up in rivers or under bridges, and we haven't a clue who was responsible. Certainly no prosecutor or court would want that kind of case. I can only suggest that you tell Anna what happened and also tell your colleagues at USU about it in case you suddenly disappear. They should know what you are going through at least, and that could help later."

"Thanks! I won't take up any more of your time. So around 8 tonight at your place then?"

"Watch your back and keep safe."

———

Living in the cloistered world of academe for the past 15 years, I have been surrounded by colleagues with delicate egos, with the thin skins of people who were over-read and under-experienced. I had to get a grip at faculty gatherings, especially dinners, making sure I didn't let a chance quip or comment out that would create another enemy. Enemies could be troublesome on promotion committees, most of which operated by secret vote; they could even be worse on those with open votes. The public image of college faculty was cheerful serenity with lots of smiling, cultured brains displaying a wonderfully blissful collegiality. A brochure for student recruitment and to hustle funds ... It was the ideal world on the surface. Almost any outsider wanted to be a part of this heavenly, intoxicating world as I once did before spending years there and getting trapped inside. But now I am back in Russia. It was like winning a backgammon game. I had made it home partly by strategy and mostly by luck. There was no need for any subtlety here, just animal instinct. Surrounded by stray dogs that either attacked me or wanted to move into my flat, I felt right at home trying to figure it all out and survive.

I headed out to Petrovsky's place with a sense of freedom and release. I even brought along a few bottles of Armenian red to guard against the risk of being poured cheap vodka and Russian rot-gut wine throughout the evening. Since being decimated by farm collectiviza-tion in the Soviet days, the Armenians had made a spectacular wine comeback, almost as much as the Georgians and Hungarians. After all, they kept on making their excellent cognac through the darkest days of Stalin and Brezhnev. Suppressed below the surface, they, like most people in the former Soviet republics and satellite nations, had their world-class skills. Now they were at it again.

Traveling out through Kirovsky Rayon, as per the guidebook in-structions, I found his place on the outskirts of the city by tram. The tram trundled through areas with older apartment blocks and some newer flats or one-story duplexes with little gardens, all in rows. They were smaller but tasteful structures designed for working profession-als in the civil service or state and private firms. They were tastefully painted in muted pastels to give the buildings life, directly contrasting with the oppressive brutalism of Soviet cement gray still found all over Russia for those less fortunate, who could not buy their flats or pay higher rents and move to better places. I noticed a few small lakes that appeared to be used for summer bathing by the locals. Then to my em-barrassment I saw The Church on the Blood from the tram window. It was a beautiful white structure with golden domes. I had forgotten to visit Father Pavel Petrovich as I had promised. I felt like an idiot, but at least I knew where it was now.

"Come in, my friend! I hope you didn't get lost or bang on a neigh-bor's door. All these places look alike." Inspector Petrovsky greeted me like an old friend at the door, even though I had known him less than three weeks.

"Not at all ... Very tasteful and your directions were perfect. Thank you for inviting me; I brought you a small package of libations in case you run short."

"Come in, and let's sit on the patio here while I prepare dinner. I'm going to grill sausages and chicken if that's ok with you. We'll have some salad and wash it all down with what I saw was your excellent Armenian red. Ours is still not so good since the Soviets collectivized the vineyards, even in some of our unfortunate suppliers like Hungary. Their Bulls' Blood or *bikaver* was the joke in those days, 'red piss' we called it. Now it's superb if you can pay their prices."

A large, curly-haired reddish dog wandered in, wagging its tail. It came over to me and jumped up, putting both paws on my chest.

"Get down, Romanov. How many times have I told you not to scare the guests?"

"It's ok. I know how they behave and have almost always had a dog like this. They think everyone likes them. And they're right, everyone should!"

"I've trained him to eat everything but the guest's wallets, but he just doesn't learn. Terrible watchdog since he's overly friendly. But as a cop, I admire how he steals food from us with such wily skill."

"Is your family here as well?"

"Just my daughter, Vesselka, who might drop in later...My wife, Irina, died a few years ago, so it's just me raising her now and trying to keep the dog fed and walked."

"I'm sorry."

"Yes, cancer will get us all they say. Married her out of gymnasium, and we had one daughter in our twenty years together. Since Vesselka is out mostly, and I work odd hours, Romanov takes care of himself. When I get home, I admire how he snores and shakes in the ecstasy of his dreams. I often unwind and relax by entering his fantasy world there on the floor. Maybe he chases rabbits like I chase criminals, but at least I don't dream about them. At the same time, Romanov is often in a dream-like state and only partially comes into my world. That's when he sharpens up to steal morsels in the kitchen. He won't steal off the grill because he's finally learned what burning meat does to his mouth. He's got the basic cause and effect down now."

"Good for him!"

"What about you? Married? Kids?"

"Wife ran off a few years ago with someone who had lots of money looking for a peppier wife. I fell for her originally because she was enticing, seductive, and had that mischievous look in her eyes. She seemed to burn inside with sexual energy. All that was true, but it didn't occur to me that the qualities were transferable onto someone else. She probably ramped up those qualities around someone with money. So, even professors can learn.

"So what did you learn?"

"Always buy a used sailboat rather than a new one. New ones often sink with you in them."

"One that is already broken in to match your stage of life? I get it. Find someone who will steer you on the right course this time."

"That's the idea. We also had two boys, who are now both at university, so I don't see much of them. Elmira is too small for their tastes. By the way, your menu sounds good. Nothing too heavy. Maybe you must outgrow that kind of taste as you move further away from the Russian republics, no? Or maybe it's your stomach that outgrows it."

"At least you try to outgrow the effects of the Soviet system ... I can't believe people ate that greasy shit under the tsars and dictators. Did they eat like that, Romanov? He doesn't care about his health. He eats anything."

"Refined tastes that perhaps disappears when tempted by junk food?"

"You may have something there. Here, let's start with a glass of red, and you can tell me the rest of your story. I was interrupted this morning by the flow of normal crimes we have around here that I investigate and try to solve. I often get my culprits and have a pretty good success rate, even with the courts. But the drama of your case seems more intriguing to me."

"My case already? I know you are a cop and can put me in jail. That's ok; I wouldn't have to go back to my claustrophobic little world and empty house. My kids can always come here and visit me in jail."

"Don't worry about jail. You would be lucky to end up there rather than dead or missing. Anyway, my invitation was in part social to get to know you better and in part work. I wanted to tell you what I have learned."

It reminded me of the rush of suspense I would get when about to hear of the latest faculty betrayal or petty conspiracy to do someone in.

I got the same emotional chills and thrills from this type of dirt that normal people got when listening to their special music.

"What appears to be going on is that Semyon is now plotting away with none other than Dmitry. Dmitry wants to push Krastov aside, and Semyon wants a piece of Krastov's activities, which are popular with the Kremlin."

"The best of enemies ... Does he plan to rely on Dmitry's thugs or use some of his own? Will Semyon also do away with me?"

"We don't know that much. Only what seems to be shaping up locally. As for your safety, at least Semyon seems to have no intent on rubbing you out. And Dmitry doesn't know you. But some of Semyon's thugs obviously do. We have to remember that Semyon is a Russian civil servant, and they, like we, no longer specialize in duels. Rather, the modern way is dirty tricks. But amateurs like Semyon and Dmitry sometimes do both. No, in Russian society the pleasant social demeanor must be maintained at all costs. The dirty tricks are used behind the scenes. The rub is that at least in olden times, the dirty tricks could be more distressing than any duel."

"Like getting roughed up and harassed by Cyclops and Ratface?"

"Something like that. But one cannot always predict what will happen because your case is somewhat special."

"How so?"

"He knows that Anna and you are lovers. Also, she loves you, and others in her wide-ranging social network know that. He would put himself in danger by doing you harm."

"How does Semyon's operational brigade work?"

"One theory is that Semyon has enough power to protect you from any rash actions by Dmitry, who as we have seen is overwhelmed by petty jealousy of Krastov's successes. Dmitry is a simple character in this play. Semyon set all this in motion and probably would not be able to control his own goons even if he wanted to. That you had a run in with two of them on the Transsib before you met any of them adds complexity and an additional dimension of unpredictability. They want to get you on their own steam. Otherwise, regular toughs here are fragmented into thuggish cliques that may go rogue after receiving side payments from rival groups of toughs. And Semyon has been known to recruit and use his thugs from the *siloviki,* which are FSB or Russian Security Council factions. These nasties use illicit tactics and are often in cahoots with crooked state authorities working for the Putin regime."

"You could write a gripping book on all this!"

"It gets even better. Often mid-level Party officials like Semyon can command small tribes of goons to do their dirty work but still appear to be acting with the color of authority from the Putin regime. That preserves the fear and loyalty up the chain of command to keep a rough kind of accountability in all this. Meanwhile, it appears Dmitry has accused Krastov of being demented and says he often fears he is going insane with dementophobia. As far as who the higher ups are in the chain of command above Semyon, it's all like trying to see through shifting rents in a fog of darkening rumor and speculation about short-term alliances and conspiracies. My guess is that Semyon is in over his head. He thinks he is a bigger man than he is because he has the right mindset."

"Mindset?"

"KGB and now FSB people have a particular mindset. I'm not very original here, and you can read this in any book on modern Russian political intrigues. Like FSB people, he thinks anybody can be turned; that advantage can be sought in any situation including anarchy and that he can collaborate with any partner from organized crime to the Christian clergy on ever shifting terms. That is, he is really untrustworthy."

"Not a surprising conclusion, given all I've gathered from watching him and from hearing about him from reliable sources. It does underscore why Russian state institutions are so weak: they are the lengthened shadows of certain individuals, to paraphrase Emerson. "

"This is all for your information; you've probably read about this kind of thing going on here before. As I've said, many novels and books have been written about Kremlin plots and Russian urban and regional warlords in action. They are all best sellers," said Petrovsky, "but not very original from my perspective."

"I learned about the tangled branches of the tree of the Russian state from reading books and doing some field research."

"No, this isn't the formal state you see on the organization charts. Bureaucratic infighting is an old theme dating back to the tsars. What I'm talking about are officials with quasi-state authority all acting as if they were really officials. They are highly dubious individuals or riff-raff. They are slimy informants who, unfortunately, we often have to use for our investigative work. So in that sense, we in the police nurture them and are complicit in all this.

"But it gets worse. What bothers me, as a lowly city cop trying to do a decent job, is the many militias or paramilitaries of retired or fired cops who are in league with official cops on my own force. That discredits us all and diminishes trust in the official police. There are mafia-type organizations that control turf right here in Yekaterinburg and other cities. The public is more afraid of them than drug gangs. They even wear ersatz uniforms and regularly extract money from residents with threats of violence to them and their families. And we can't do much about it."

"I've read about gang activity in Brazil, especially before the World Cup football Games there in 2014. The state of Rio cracked down on revenge killing by police in the favelas or slums before the games, and it worked—the death toll went way down. They also tried community policing, which worked to increase trust between residents and police, and that was also successful. Do you think Cyclops and Ratface might be militia members?"

"I would almost bet on it. Which militia is anyone's guess . . . The Brazilian police ideas were good, and we knew about them here. They worked. In a federal system like Brazil, the locals have much more authority and financing authority than we do here. In Russia, the orders from the top are more concerned about getting the strays before they damage Russia's image—packs of rabid hounds with foaming mouths attacking children etc., etc. That won't do. They think strays are a social abnormality. Only Third World countries have stray problems, not civilized places like Russia! Russians can live with corruption and crime, and our institutions can at least control them to a degree. But the Kremlin won't allow anything that would threaten the Games! That's why Krastov and his people suddenly have become the top dogs."

"Well, that's a lot to think about. Reminds me of my days as a part-time delinquent in the Bronx. We were tough, but somehow there were always tougher thugs around. A losing proposition for long-term survival."

"Funny how people like us end up as criminals or cops. But usually not professors …"

"People with our backgrounds also become criminal lawyers or criminal justice professors—potentially they know the most about criminals and can be the most effective, unless of course they get tired of classrooms and paperwork and go back and join their mates in their crooked schemes. Me? I found it easier to write papers and talk without being beaten up in the safety of graduate classes. It was a real luxury so I kept at it."

"Like many of us, I was an incorrigible tough as well. Vesselka doesn't know about much of this, and I prefer to keep it from her. I ran with a bad crowd. I had a defense lawyer after one escapade who made an impression on me. It turned out he was a hardened delinquent when he was my age and now had a son whom he wanted to go straight: surprise! It was Ivan, who as it turns out, now works for you!"

"Small world!"

"Lots of small worlds. The key is to put them all together coherently. Then you would solve crime as well as the world's other big problems."

On that note, they clinked glasses: "Nazdrava!"

"So I decided to put my street knowledge to some use in bringing down thugs who would corrupt people like Ivan and other kids with lots of smarts, but were surrounded by bad crowds."

I could see that Petrovsky was a tough, seasoned cop but also a sensitive person who I could talk with. Despite my lawless impulses, I always looked up to neighborhood cops like that, and they often served as sources of trustworthy advice as I was growing up. Some kids had their fathers; others had priests and teachers. I had a few cops I liked—they accepted my delinquent tendencies to a point, and I grudgingly accepted their authority. It was a crude, imperfect bargain, but it worked for me.

"I spent a lot of time running from police in my youth. In the Bronx and New York City, we lived in an old brick high-rise with a fire escape outside and pigeon coups on the rooftops. Don't laugh . . . we actually bred them for solace and companionship. No one touched each other's pigeons; it was a matter of honor among all of us, an unwritten norm. But otherwise, we fought among ourselves and ran from the police across rooftops, often jumping across buildings six stories up. Some of us fell and even died; some were caught several times and ended up in prison. All good people, and I still respect them and what they were going through. Throughout those experiences, I somehow kept that golden, childish innocence, optimism, and reckless disregard of consequences. Then one day, someone saw me running and jumping and found out my name. He came to me, and I thought he was a cop. But instead he introduced me to a college track recruiter from USC in Los Angeles. They apparently had several on their track team with dodgy backgrounds like mine who came from different urban crime zones. The "Torrance Tornado," Louis Zamperini, who won gold medals at the 1936 Berlin Olympics came directly from the streets as a fast-running LA delinquent and was recruited the same way I was. So it was either jail or a gold medal, you had your choice. In my case, either jail or a Ph.D. I was nicknamed the 'Russian Locomotive.' That's how I went from the mean streets to college and then to a teaching career. Not bad for someone who had never thought about college at all!"

"Only in America!"

"I can tell you all this, but I have to try and maintain that appropriate air of intellectual and moral responsibility among the colleagues. I still don't want them thinking they've been around a dumb thug for all these years."

"But of course, that assumes your colleagues are respectable, doesn't it?"

"I can see why you are an effective cop. And the assumption about university faculties is usually naïve, gleaned from some Victorian novel about academic collegiality. Several years ago, the chair of my department went to federal prison for arson. He tried to burn down the hotel where the annual City Planning conference was being held in New York."

"Why?"

"No one got a straight answer. It seems that he had a grudge against someone from a faculty who had laughed at one of his paper presentations before, mocked him for shoddy work with even a whiff of plagiarism."

"We don't burn things down here. We just kill our enemies who mock us."

"Much more efficient. His alibi when the police caught him being warmed by his little fire on a nearby sidewalk was quite original though. He said he was testing police response times to apparent emergencies. The cops remembered that one with laughter and often cite it as unique among faculty follies and criminal missteps around there."

"Didn't work though, did it?"

I heard a door slam in the next room as someone arrived with a noisy flourish, tossing packages and boxes around in the kitchen. Petrovsky's face made a slight ironic movement. "It's Vesselka arriving from somewhere."

In she came. A tall, blondish girl with curly hair, dressed in old jeans and a worn-out sweater—she came over, stood in front of us, sized us up quickly and sat down.

"What's for dinner? Anything special?" she asked.

"Vesselka, this is my friend Nicholas who teaches at USU. He is a colleague of Anna Irtenev in the planning department. Vesselka is studying biology there and hopes to be a doctor or vet someday, right Vessie?

"If you say so," she said with a slight pout on a face of straight-forward beauty, unblemished by any creams or lotions. "I hear about what I'm going to do all the time," she said in my direction. "It was engineering last week, wasn't it?"

"Nick teaches at Bonaduz College in New York and is visiting for the summer."

"New York!" she said dreamily. "I'd like to go there someday and be a famous fashion model or heiress to a fortune, so I could spend a lot of money and go to expensive clubs every night."

"That's good. Join the queue," I said with a laugh. That also brought a giggle from her, subtle recognition that she knew they were all bullshit ideas.

"Sit with us, Vessie. We're just having some wine and are about to grill something."

"Just for awhile. I meet my study group later. We're in summer classes, and finals are next week," she said to me.

"So what brings you to Yekaterinaburg?" she asked, giving me a quick glance of recognition. "You sound like you know some Russian. Or are you here to teach us English? I like New York English. I learned it watching *The Sopranos* a few years ago."

"I am Russian-American; my parents left Russia years ago. I'm just here to do some research on city services planning. Wasn't *The Sopranos* dubbed?"

"We got a pirated version in English with Russian subtitles."

"Vessie, he's gotten mixed up in a rather large problem that may interest you."

"What kind of malls do you have in New York? Are they fun?"

"So your TV Englishease is really impressive. Simon, I'd have placed her from someplace like Boston or New Jersey. But, no Vessie, I work and live in a small town in upstate New York. There is one smallish mall with the standard chains selling the usual boring stuff there, but as you probably know most people shop online now."

"But we are what you call Gen Z, aren't we?"

"I bet you are! What does that mean for malls?"

"We go to these places for fun. To be entertained . . . We don't buy much because we don't have any money, but it's a rush or a thrill as you say. We like to play with bright new toys and do the games."

"Whenever you get money, how do you shop then?"

"She's inherited my forensic skills there. Can spot a deal at 50 yards . . . "

Here I should point out my dilemma. I've looked at myself in the mirror and know I have a shifty face and furtive manner. I would be put off by me. But most women, at least, are not. Anna, for instance, seems to like my looks and manner. Now here we have a mouth-watering little teen-ager chatting me up. Actually, we are chatting each other up. I seem to be reverting to my teen-aged wild years, which I quite liked. I feel alive again. But it can't go anywhere rationally and is just my uncontrolled id in action. The superego constraint of guilt and societal mores, which also prevents people like me from being jailed, not the least by her father who is a cop, is the harsh reality kicking in; I have to settle down. My urges have unfortunately been shattered by modern society. I'm not a modern Flashman . . . I'm really not.

"You use lotion and skin cream. How do you buy it here?"

"You noticed! How surprising for a middle-aged professor."

"Here . . . I'm pre-middle aged really, if you must know."

"We buy on social media sites and user bloggers to help us filter the best options. They tell us the best creams and also where to get the best recycled clothing which we all like to wear."

"Very tasteful, I should say!"

"Why don't you ever complement me, Father? You don't even notice me!"

"Of course I do. I just don't want your beauty to become your identity. So I lay off."

"He has a point. But I'll say it anyway as an outsider."

"Thank you. Very kind . . . You must notice that I buy with a social conscience with ideas from You Tube commercials. I have my wishes, but Daddy here is a civil servant and hasn't much money."

"Very mature and responsible. My kids always reminded me what a financial deadbeat I was and told me to get a real job."

"Like a police inspector?" said Petrovsky, twisting his mouth up like he'd swallowed a dead rat.

"Nicholas was just telling me about his wild youth. He raised pigeons and was recruited running from the police between apartment building rooftops by a university that wanted to give scholarships to potential sprinters. Sounds like the criteria was not falling between buildings and getting away from them."

"Indeed!"

"Is that how you got your first real job then?" she asked.

"No actually, what your father says is the glamor part. Before that, I needed money for daily expenses. My family was quite poor, as were most of the families in the Bronx, my borough or section of the city. So, I got into some serious gambling."

"Gambling?"

"That's right. In my early teens, I learned to play backgammon from watching masters in the parks and getting tips on the moves from them. I got quite good at it and used to beat the tourists and the 'fish'—'pigeons' and 'marks' as we called them, that happened to wander by and were curious. I won quite a bit of money."

"Why backgammon? Odd for an American, no?" said Petrovsky.

"I'm only half American, don't forget."

"I like chess," she said.

"As do most Russians, and they are the best in the world at it. But I like the chance part of backgammon. It's all about strategy like chess, but it also depends on throws of the dice—so it's both skill and luck. It mirrored my life at the time—sometimes safe, sometimes back on the street. I could size things up pretty fast, was good at math, and so I used these to gain little advantages over my opponents. I also liked the objective of trying to get home. I wanted to have a secure, safe home and that was the point of the game—to get home."

"Wow, never had a clue about the deeper parts of backgammon. And to think that you could earn a living with a board game! I always think of casinos and glitz when I think of gamblers."

"Not me. I hate those places. They are so depressing," I said.

"So I can always become a gambler if I flunk out of USU. Now what's this project you two know about that might interest me?"

"My assistant, Ivan, whom you know, is pretty good at backgammon he tells me. Talk to him about the moves and maybe you can start a second career!"

Petrovsky leaned forward, took a few more gulps of wine, then filled up our glasses for at least the third time.

"Recently, Dr. Krylov and I visited the city animal control department with several others, including the head of health services, who is a physician. Before the World Cup Games, you know that a lot of stray dogs had been running around attacking people and increasing the number of rabies cases. You've told me how you had some narrow escapes yourself. For the city, all this was a health crisis and public relations disaster in the making. A Dr. Krastov was there and explained to us his rather bizarre new control methods, which have diminished the number of strays. They are using street theatre techniques to wow the crowds with flashy colored uniforms, dancing and singing, all the while engaging in animal control."

"They should be on YouTube."

"I think they already are. Check it out. Anyway, they practice instant street-level profiling: drug darting some strays and killing the bad ones outright. Some of the drugged ones and others selected rather subjectively are either sent to pounds for adoption like they do in Europe or treated with some genetic operations he uses to develop them into what he terms higher forms of dog."

"And get this. They had one there called Fyodor, who can talk! He even reads books! Smarter than most people . . . He could be a candidate for a job on my faculty," I said.

"What he's doing is a bit wild, but apparently has the green light all the way up to Putin because it is saving the Games and putting Russian animal biology back on the map from the days of the experiments of Dugatkin and Trut."

Vesselka's eyes were like torches piercing us, taking it all in, but calculating before she spoke.

"We thought we might see if you could apprentice at his facility since something quite new is going on in your field right here in town. It might also appeal to your social conscience as it looks like Putin, out of necessity at least, wants to solve this serious health problem."

"It sounds cool! Not sure if I want to get mixed up with Kremlin types. They give me the creeps."

"Can't blame you," I said.

"And you two do know what Putin is not doing to solve the health crisis in Russia, don't you?"

"I don't. Tell me about it," I said.

"I need a drink first," said Petrovsky, rolling his eyes. "I've heard all this before. Another round of wine or something stronger?"

He poured us all more glasses of the robust red wine. It was from Georgia and as good as any $20 Napa cabernet I'd ever had.

"It's really quite simple and everyone knows about it," she said to me. "We get our news from independent bloggers and news sources. Of course, some are banned and others taken off the web due to censorship. But the officials are ham-fisted and flat-footed (no offense to you, Dad!), and we simply work around them to learn what's going on around here."

"So what is going on?"

"Nothing much here. People like us, my father, and university students and faculty are all covered by health services. We can go to elite hospitals and clinics. But most of Russia can't. We have a hundred billionaires in Russia, yet 13 percent are poor and more lack basic services. Discontent in regions like Novgorod is getting so vocal that Putin has dispatched his loyal technocrats to blunt public criticism. We only spend 3 percent of our GDP on health whereas the minimum for any European country is 9 percent. In inflation adjusted terms, it is even less than 3 percent."

"Well, you certainly know your figures. But is the quality of care also falling? I visited a few hospitals in Ukraine once and found the top hospitals were as good as any in the U.S."

"That's right, Dr. Krylov."

"Please, you can call me Nick."

"Well then, Nick. That's right. But you can only find the top hospitals in a few big cities like Moscow and St. Petersburg or in areas where there are Putin allies. What's going on, to answer your question, is that, despite Putin's unfulfilled promises to increase pay for health care personnel, he has been actually cutting services at clinics and hospitals and cutting pay for medical staff and health care personnel."

"How do you know all this?" asked her father. "You know his popularity rating is still strong at 60 percent."

"That's right, too, but voter support for him has dropped to 45 percent from a high of 75 percent a few years ago. He is losing support fast, and mainly over the health care issue. How do we know? Anecdotally—health sciences students talk. They come from all over Russia and are studying at USU. We also talk with the Alliance of Doctors trade union which has over 20 regional branches and a website on which over 20,000 people have voiced support for them."

"Aren't they afraid of being fired or worse?" I asked.

"Yes. They were initially afraid because they were being fired and harassed. Then they grew more confidant and righteous—strength in numbers. Now there are too many discontented people angry at bad health care, and the numbers are growing all the time."

"And yet, Putin's popularity rating across Russia and even in Novgorod is above 60 percent," said Petrovsky. "His base loves him."

"He can do no wrong; something like your President Trump and his provincial hard right base in the U.S. as he also cuts health care services for everyone, especially the poor. They still love him and can be counted to vote against their own interests."

"Not my President! I voted Democratic and always have."

From the shock of being reminded of the tragic coincidence of being misled by two ruthless populist but popular leaders, I started coughing. At first, I thought it was the rush of troubling thoughts, then maybe the wine, then maybe the grilled meat we had been nibbling on as we talked. But it got worse and shifted into a harsh, body-wracking set of fits. I had to spit some revolting phlegm into my handkerchief. Both of them proceeded to hammer me on the back. At some juncture, the chest spasms and coughing fits eased off. They were both concerned and gave me some water to calm things down for a few moments. I sat there in embarrassed silence, feeling humiliated.

"You've had this cough for awhile, right?" said Petrovsky. "I noticed you coughing several times when were in meetings."

"Indeed I have. I'm sure it's just living in a new place."

"Don't think so," said Vessie.

"Nick, I want you to contact Dr. Krastov tomorrow. He tells me you have already spoken about this. You really have to contact him now. Ok?"

"Alright."

As I gathered up my things to depart, I said to Vessie, "That reminds me; there's a meeting tomorrow night downtown where Dr. Krastov will present his work and its purpose. It promises to be lively as the media and local groups including animal rights supporters will be there."

"I already knew about it. So, I'll be there with some friends," she said. "It was nice meeting you, and get better, ok?"

"And Simon, thank you for the excellent grill, wine, lessons in Russian politics, and for your friendship."

"And now you need to get home to bed, then in to see about your cough tomorrow without delay. Otherwise, I'll have you arrested and taken to Dr. Krastov's facility for incarceration in his lab!"

16   SEMYON AND DMITRY AT THE OFFICE

The large corner office was quite drab with pale blue walls and oilcloth-upholstered doors. Since it was on the second floor and windows opened into the small stone courtyard, it was dark inside most of the time. Semyon looked around and mused that he really ought to have leather-upholstered doors like his superiors in the same building. He knew that even though he was not in the Department of Security and therefore one of the chosen ones, he was still an important provincial official. Perhaps he was lucky to at least have some tasteful prints on his walls of old Yekaterinburg. But shit! Cheap oil-cloth doors? Hardly befitting his stature.

Semyon checked his Rolex to see if its time matched the large wall clock in his office. It was hard to see the clock from his capacious dark wood desk as it was on the opposite wall surrounded by blown up photographs of industry in Sverdlovsk oblast. He reminded himself often that he was an important official of Sverdlovsk oblast (or province), the administrative center of which is located right here in Yekaterinburg. It was the last oblast in real Russia, he often boasted. East of the Urals were the sticks or steppes, then Siberia. People who worked there or were sent as punishment were not only physically deprived, but out of Russia, in his view. They were nothing but provincial shit kickers. By contrast, his oblast was in charge of the World Cup games and had a grand total of 29 districts. Surrounding him on deeply varnished, but oppressive hardwood walls between the old city prints were photos of early twentieth century, heavy industrial factories in the area—machinery, metal processing, military equipment—many of which were still operated by the state. These factories employed most workers and belched grey-ish-black fumes into skies from the very tall stacks that climbed into the skies like beanstalks. Squinting a bit, as some people in their fifties have to do, he could see that the times exactly matched. Efficiency and time management, precepts he had learned about writers like F. W. Taylor and Peter Drucker, even if they were capitalist stooges. He didn't want to be surprised by someone showing up early for a meeting he had forgotten about or failed to anticipate. Not him: he moved fast, gliding here and there in cadence and impeccably on time.

He sat back in his immense chair and reflected for a few more moments. It had been twenty years now that he had been an official there, rising from minor party minion to his present status as deputy governor, which also included membership on the Yekaterinburg city council. After all, he was a powerful man and had made friends and broken many enemies over the years. His power was demonstrable in the multiple colored phones adorning his desk. The green one went to his secretary, Irina, outside. He also was linked to his receptionist, Anastasia, by the yellow phone and to his permanent lackey, who sat in his grey suit and white shirt outside all year, long awaiting further orders, usually deliveries to other government offices. The red phone allowed him access upwards into the regime to his Putin contact, Yevgeny, in Moscow. For calls to and from Anna he used his cell. All in all, this collection of colored phones was very impressive to the local outsider. Visiting foreigners only scratched their heads at why all this couldn't be done away with now in the age of emails, FaceTime, and text messages. But such systems weren't mentioned by management gurus in the 1930s, were they. His inner office was also separated from the waiting room by two sets of wooden doors padded by thick leather. Not everyone could enter in the inner sanctum of the powerful, and it was important to remind the public of that core fact with clear symbols and trappings as well as an occasional display of the iron fist.

Suddenly the yellow phone rang out. How could he tell? Fortunately it had a blinking light on its face to distinguish it from the other phones.

Otherwise, how would that look to the deferential visitor seeing him pick up each phone only to discover it must be one of the others? Efficiency, that's what it was all about.

"Your 10 a.m. appointment is here, Mr. Semyon," said Anastasia.

Ah yes, here it was on his book. Must have forgotten his morning duties and been distracted...

"Who is he?"

"His card says he is from the city Animal Control division."

"Didn't you try to get rid of him before this?"

"Of course, sir. But he said it was urgent and could affect provincial relations with Moscow so I put him on the calendar last week for today."

"Ok, but call me in 15 minutes with the usual interruption to get rid of him if he is one of the unwanted. Got it? Can't have my time being wasted by lower bureaucrats. Besides weren't we going to have coffee outside around eleven?"

His thoughts drifted to the nearby flat he kept for lunchtime trysts with Anastasia. God, what shapely legs and nicely rounded tits! His back still hurt from the previous meeting there when he pounded away from her backside for about thirty minutes. At this rate, he would have to start using a cane.

"Of course. That's right! Is your back up to it?"

"Of course it is. It only gets stronger with the proper exercise! Ok. Send him in then."

Dmitry entered with Anastasia and stood at the doorway entrance as Semyon, still seated behind his desk, finished checking a few boxes on an important form. He slowly looked up, saw them, pondered at length for effect, then reacted in surprise.

"Yes, yes, come in and sit down. Will you have a coffee, sir?" His desktop was just above the level the average six-footer would perch, meaning that most supplicants would be staring slightly upwards. He had carefully worked out these nuances, which were important in his official interactions. It was not expected, for instance, that a provincial official would get out of his chair and genuflect for a mere local official.

But he did anyway, coming around to shake hands. Semyon sometimes did this just to size up people whom he needed to get a bead on. Dmitry's handshake was cold and flabby, like holding onto a slippery fish. Semyon did his usual show of strength with the muscular handshake in which his hand would quickly rotate over the others, signaling that he meant to have the upper hand during the meeting.

"No thank you, kind sir. And let me say I am honored that you granted me this brief interview," said he, with an ingratiating glance transmitting the message that he knew the game and was ready to join in it, officially or unofficially. "I know your time is precious." Semyon picked this up quickly and stared down at him from his oversized desk full of colored phones and stacks of paper.

"What brings you in today Dmitry Simovich?"

First impressions were always important to Semyon Irtenev. What he observed here was a slightly overweight man in his late forties wearing an oatmeal-colored plaid sport coat with gaudy, mismatched stripes and patterns. People wore coats in July and August here as the summers were usually only about two months long and not that hot. But the rest of him was irritating. He had shaggy whiskers that needed a trim, and he seemed to smell of a zoo. But that could be how people looked and smelled who work with animals, especially chimps and dogs. They started to behave and even look like them after a while. If all this wasn't enough, his visitor reeked of tobacco more than the average person around here. With his pasty white hands, Dmitry reached into his coat for a pack of 'nails' and lit one up to collect his thoughts. He then plumed smoke at the ceiling that drifted annoyingly towards Semyon. His face wrenched into a tough, determined grimace, giving Semyon a quick stare through the clouds just like he must have imagined a '40s film noir hero. He puffed after each comment, waving the clouds around, staring shrewdly at Semyon, and then hung another nail on his lower lip like a clothespin.

"I'm here in my duty as a private citizen. I have evidence to support the conclusion that there is a serious threat to the regime and that it comes from right here in town."

"Of course, Simovich. And you suppose I receive threats to the regime here as part of my job? In fact, I do receive them—dozens every day from all kinds of cranks that get through this door."

"Yes sir, I would imagine … "

"You imagine right. Are you another crank, Simovich? Because if you are, I'm not in a good mood this morning, and I'll have you detained for making spurious allegations."

"No sir, I am not a crank, and please hear me out for just a few moments. If after that you doubt me, I will leave."

"Very well, continue, but be brief," he said with a royal wave of his hand.

"I work for the Animal Control Department as I think you know. The department is in the news daily for its efforts to eliminate stray dogs and to preserve the reputation of the Games."

"Yes, we all know that and are pleased all of you are doing so well."

"But there is a flaw—a risk in all this that could threaten both the efforts of the City and President Putin to protect the Games."

"And what might that be Dmitry Simovich?"

Here Dmitry stubbed out his latest ciggy in the ashtray on Semyon's desk and proceeded to place a map of the city in front of him. He grimaced and shook his head irritably.

"This is where we have been dumping the carcasses of hundreds of dead dogs in preparation for their incineration." He gave Semyon a weak, beseeching glance like it was critical that he understand that vital point.

He indicated to two spots on the map, one near the river outside of town and another near the Animal Control facility. As Dmitry bent over the map, Semyon got a surprising view of what appeared to be a 9 mm Markarov pistol inside his jacket stuffed in a leather shoulder holster under his left arm. Now why would someone from Animal Control need an automatic? Probably to kill strays he imagined. He hoped that's all they killed.

Semyon looked over at him. Dmitry now wore a self-satisfied grin. Semyon looked confused.

"Tell me, Dmitry, isn't that what you do there? Kill strays? I mean I've read that some are captured, released, singled out for experiments and even put up for adoption. Don't some of the targeted cohorts, the sick, rabid, and vicious ones, have to be killed, dumped, and incinerated as a matter of policy and statistical reporting for different metrics?"

"You don't quite understand," he said, shifting around in his seat with more shakes of the head and grimaces. "This isn't a research project. We are charged with protecting the public now, and especially the Games, with all means available. And I have videos," he said with a wink.

"Oh yes?" Semyon said, glancing at his watch now. "Could you be more specific Simovich?"

Dmitry removed a laptop from his briefcase that was already loaded with videos he proudly wanted to display to Semyon. He placed it on Semyon's desk and came around to show him. Pointing out on the screen shots of Krastov's crews shooting dogs, then heading for the incinerators with truckloads of their carcasses, Semyon now saw clearly that it was indeed an automatic pistol that he was carrying.

"Sorry. I'm a bit pressed for time. What's going on here, Simovich?"

"Here we all are shooting strays and loading them into the wagons to be towed out to the dam area outside of town."

"Simovich, did you really come here to inform me that Animal Control dumps dead dogs into the river? Everyone dumps shit into the Iset River! Really . . . "

"No! No! Let me explain. It's much worse, sir. Let me show you the rest." He continued pointing to the screenshots. "We are dumping most of them into the river to be carried south of town. The overflow of carcasses we take to the incinerator to finish the job."

"So why not dump them all into the river?"

"Because someone might notice the change in the color of the water or even the carcasses floating by. The main threat to these operations is the animal rights and environmental groups. So far, we have kept under their radar."

"Come on . . . You're just trying to avoid fines? Who really cares? It's all very interesting, but I've heard these stories before. And why are you telling me all this now?"

Semyon had his hand on the button to summon Anastasia to get rid of this clown before he wasted any more of his precious time. He might even coax her to head for the hotel early. His fingers drummed loud rhythms on his desk in hopes that the guy would take the hint.

"The animal rights people don't have documentation of this. Videos like this could bring them into disrepute, and you could take credit for eliminating them as a thorn in the Kremlin's side."

"Yes, it's all possible. But look, Simovich, why not go home and think up something bigger if you want to be of service?"

"The bigger picture is that we are not killing enough of them."

"Who are you talking about? The animal rights people?"

"No! The stray dogs. "

"Looks pretty thorough to me. But I'm not an expert on dog-killing."

"Stray dogs are like coyotes. You kill 500 million this year, and you get 500 million new ones next year for a net change of zero. To get a reduction in the overall population of strays, you have to kill 90 percent of them. And without constant removal of 90 percent, the population can recover in less than 5 years."

"All true, Simovich, I'm sure." Semyon thought maybe someone could make a good B movie out of all this: *The Invasion of the Urban Strays.*

Semyon started folding papers on his desk and stood up, hoping Simovich would get the hint.

"Ok, so what do you suggest?"

"The only good stray is a dead one," said Dmitry. "We need to get beyond the traditional trapping, hunting contests, bounties, and so on. They don't work and often end up catching the pets of powerful officials and their families, provoking a backlash. No, I suggest we employ guided drones to bomb them."

"What?"

The guy's a real nut job! Probably one of the many pseudo-scientific crackpots around here—you know, makes useless inventions in his garage like 500-pound nails that self-destruct. This city is full of them—the type that invents mostly useless gizmos and computerized junk that gets them a bit of notoriety.

"I have associates who use drones for commercial farmers to survey crops and real estate developers to plot out building sites. They even use them, I am told, for better security and occasional weapons delivery. Is that the idea?" said Semyon.

"Exactly! So why not use them for elimination of strays?" said he, with obsequious nods and chuckles accompanying each comment.

"So why don't you talk with him? I can give you his number. But I've also learned that drones can easily be defeated with counter-technology. After all, they are just fancy model planes. Someone always has a more advanced model." Semyon said this knowing little about technology and caring less. But he wanted to see how this guy would react.

"Yes, that's true. We know about the signal jammers that crews can carry in trucks along with special cartridge-sized shotguns for drone-shooting. It would make for good sport and also serve as a defense in case they arm their drones with weapons."

"But isn't that the problem? They could wipe out the drones and turn them against us."

"Well, yes. But then we can find a more advanced guidance system to counter their counter-technology."

"And who will pay for all these gizmos?"

"Easily done. Krastov is planning to set up a charitable organization for his animal research projects. And that requires provincial approval. With your approval conditioned on drone funding, we could use the charity for this and other uses as we see fit. We might even share some of the contributions."

Semyon was really bored by Simovich's transparent attempts to ingratiate himself. Along with his breathless assertions, you could almost see his tongue hanging out. More importantly, he was getting impatient for Anastasia. It was obvious from his quips, punctuated by the strange gleam in his eyes that he simply wanted to upstage his boss, Krastov. Semyon had met him and seen him on TV. He didn't strike him as a particularly bad guy. No real ego, and he seemed to know what he was doing. It was also obvious Dmitry was going to betray his own crews at the Animal Control department. What a sleazebag! I should know. But could Simovich's game be as obvious as it seemed? His shifty little eyes expressed a kind of animal distrust. So, it looked to be just that simple. Semyon sized him up as a walking personality disorder that likely forced Dmitry into constant social conflicts as expressions of his obsessive need to maximize power. Semyon knew all about such problems—after all he recognized that he was a power-hungry thug himself. But he did have a thin responsibility as a higher up official and therefore could be judged on a moral scale. He also had a responsibility to be careful. Ruthlessly careful . . . After all, to him ethics meant having at least the right objectives, regardless of the means necessary to attain them. For pursuing the 'national interest' that meant doing really well by doing at least some personal good.

Semyon also knew that Krastov had high-level regime support making it imperative that he be viewed as a supporter and one who threw his weight behind him. He knew that Krastov wanted funding for a new animal control research facility. He could divert provincial funds appropriately—merely transfer them between line items and approve them himself. The catch was that this is Russia. With overall public support waning, the Putin regime needed more revenue and legitimacy. If framed properly, Krastov's operation could provide that. Another reason to tread carefully here. Semyon knew that regime support for people like himself and Krastov was ephemeral and could change tomorrow. Putin and his people operated a "soft" authoritarian regime now that was morphing into hard-line tactics against even insiders that might threaten or challenge him. After all, he did know how Stalin once treated his close "friends."

"You have some good ideas that we need to explore further. You would be available for a confirmation tour of your video for us, wouldn't you? We can also provide more details for you on the drone idea."

"I think that could be arranged," he said, after a thoughtful blow of a smoke ring and followed by another wily glance at Semyon.

"Give your contact details to the receptionist on your way out, and we will be in touch."

"Thank you for seeing me, sir. It has been a true honor," he said with his weak, decayed grin as he stubbed out his butt in the ashtray on Semyon's desk.

As it is said: the decayed grin reveals the rotten soul. I never did liked boot-lickers. But let's see what this moron can do for us, thought Semyon.

Against his instincts, Anastasia convinced him to meet Dmitry and see what he had to offer. She was better than he in foreseeing trouble but also in spotting opportunities. All he had to do was give up an evening with her and follow this clown down to the river. What could go wrong?

———

A few nights later, two figures could just be made out in a patch of forest by the Iset River. The moon was half power, allowing a distinct view of the surrounding forest and clearing nearby. There were few sounds except the rushing water carrying tree branches and rubbish by accompanied by the doleful sound of an occasional bird chirping away gently in hopes that summer would last for at least another month. Sometimes the light fell at a certain angle on the trees, and they assumed human, even monstrous, shapes that Ivan recalled from his childhood. They didn't appear menacing or friendly, just oddly lifelike. They could be one of the sets from his favorite opera: *The Nutcracker.* There were no barking dogs around as the strays had transmitted to their canine colleagues through their special, coded, sensory emissions that this was the wrong place to be. Two figures lay hidden in some thick bushes with their video and sound equipment ready to go. They were hidden between a clearing and the banks of the river, and thus had a clear shot of anything unusual. But the waiting part was getting on their nerves.

Even the loud chirping was getting annoying. They had been there for three hours and nothing had happened.

"Damn mosquitoes! I'm getting eaten alive. Where the hell are these people?" asked Ivan.

"They're coming. I thought you were the outdoor type," said Boris Krylovsky.

"I am, but sitting around in the bushes by a river dump is not my idea of the outdoors."

"Quiet, I hear something."

Then the sounds of approaching heavy equipment rumbling towards them grew louder. It sounded like a whole convoy of trucks headed their way. Right on cue, two large dump trucks roared into the clearing in front of them and parkedparked near the bank of the river. If it were a larger bevy of cars, possibly police or assorted officials, they might have been more concerned. The loud ricocheting of explosions, usually the backfiring of trucks without mufflers, the shouts of groups and gangs of men working together, all these sounds seemingly attracted no one's attention anymore. After all, these were just typical noises from any episode of commonplace action flicks or TV shows. Nothing authentic to be concerned about here. But of course, there were no people around here either—no river walks or tourists to lighten up the images.

Most people knew about the dumping and had heard from downstream city officials about the really strange refuse floating their way. Here would be documented proof. They had been coming here to film the industrial waste dumping that had been damaging the environment for years. Sure enough, one of the arriving vehicles was a large truck with visible license tags and a two-man crew that proceeded to quickly get into their routine. Without any need for orders or managerial direction, they removed large pieces of industrial junk from the truck with their crane onto an attached flatbed wagon. It appeared from their spot in the bushes that the crew then proceeded to roll all the junk from the truck into river. Some of it sank in the river while the rest managed to float downstream. They did all this work by hand, including emptying tanks of chemicals into the water to prevent leaving evidence. All this took no more than ten minutes, and off they went.

But what's this? Just as one drama ended, was another about to begin? Two more loud off-road vehicles, probably SUVs or military trucks, roared up and skidded to a stop in the clearing near the river. Out piled three men, two wearing military camouflage or police type uniforms and one in a lab coat. In Russia, since multiple security services exist, one cannot really distinguish what police or military unit they represent, if any. That kind of open stealth works out great if the aim is to avoid accountability, and it clearly was here. The setting was almost perfect as the lack of background noise allowed Andrey Kostov and Boris Krylovsky to hear their entire conversation.

"So, what have you got to show us?" said one of them as they emerged from their cars and stood together.

"Plenty," said the other, as the bluish light of his iPad illuminated their faces. "Watch this. Here we are doing a dog dump. These are the dogs we kill around town and stuff in wagons to be brought here."

The others thought that was rich and laughed. "I dump junk here all the time. Are dead dogs really that odd?" said one of them.

"Yes, it is, you dumb shit," said another. "The bodies of often rabid dogs pollute the water. They then float down the river with their diseases, polluting the water along the way to other cities. Sound good to you? Want to have a drink of this water?"

More laughter. "Maybe not …"

"My point to this little demonstration is that we've been doing this for years," said Dmitry. "And here is all the evidence. I can sell this tape to the media or to you, as we agreed. I think you have a real need for documentation. Which will it be, gentlemen?"

Look at these two cretins, thought Dmitry. The police, if that's what they are, get uglier and more stupid-looking every day. The one guy belongs in a freak museum. The other one looks like a small time vaudeville stage crook. All the anthropomorphic qualities of one born to crime . . . Maybe we could use their brains to create special platoons of dogs to steal things. But that's a bad idea. Dogs and foxes already know far more than humans about real theft, especially than these two!

Right then, one of the figures raised his arm, apparently with plans to knock down or club one of the others. Another one of them wheeled around quickly and with what sounded like an air gun fired several shots. Several pops and whooshing sounds from the air gun could be heard. Down went two of them. As one of them staggered to get up, he was kicked and given another blast from what appeared to be a dart gun. The man fell back and lay there in a heap. As this happened, the other figure ran forward, hopped into one of the cars and drove off quickly. The man in the white coat, who was clearly Dmitry to them, could be seen clearly rolling the other man into the trunk of his car. He then drove off in a rush.

"Shit! This could all be a B-film! The media should give us an Oscar for this!" said Krylovsky.

"I think we got the bastards!" said Andrey.

"Looks like we got more of them than expected and a new caseload of bastards. I think we've only filmed the first act here."

Andrey and Boris jumped into their car and tailed Dmitry across town to a waste facility. He had clearly been there before as he drove up to a brick structure adorned by a tall stack, which reeked of spewing ashes and fumes. Here he threw open his trunk and, grabbing the incinerator's metal door with one hand, opened it and rolled the body inside. In another deft move, he closed the door and drove quickly off, noticed by no one except the eye of their video camera.

Dmitry then drove off, and the two of them sat still in the car. They each lit fags to calm their nerves. Neither of them smoked much except in times of emotional stress. This was one of them.

"What a character! He must have incinerated a lot of dogs in there, don't you think?" said Krylovsky.

"I'm sure he has. But think about the effect on people like Dmitry who put down abandoned dogs for a living. They work in animal shelters and inject dogs to get rid of them and make space for more stray dogs."

"Hard to feel any empathy for that goon. I'm sure doing that kind of miserable task day after day led to desiccation of his soul. In a normal person, it would lead to erasure of any moral self. But this guy is clearly not normal, and I doubt if he had one to begin with."

"Most of them probably had souls and moral compasses sometime in their lives. I had a neighbor in my block of flats named Timofei, who was a member of the animal control crew here years ago. He did it for the rush of chasing strays around and shooting them down with dart guns. In the beginning, he would tell me wild tales of their escapades around town. He drank heavily, laughed and sang as he spun out wild anecdotes to me almost daily. He loved his work. But then he was promoted and had to do the job of injections and incinerations after he did his job of killing strays. He ended up with two bad jobs."

"What happened to him?"

"He started to deteriorate spiritually and physically. He came home late at night sometimes with a hollow look about him. I was worried about him. He often knocked on my door and wanted to talk."

"What did he say?"

"Often incoherent statements. He would suddenly show at my flat, moaning and even crying. I got real worried about him. I tried to calm him with the usual sublimation devices, lots of vodka and beer, but they had no effect. He would go on about the live dogs encountered every day, ones with broken limbs, mange, neglect benign or malign, old age, malnutrition, and intestinal parasites. After telling me about a few of them, he would shift to how he had to put them down."

"And you had to listen to this?"

"Timofei was my neighbor, and I felt it my duty to listen to him. I was also worried that he might kill himself. He looked and sounded bad. Of course, he couldn't tell anyone at work, least of all his superiors in management, for fear of sounding weak. You know: 'not a team player, Not one of us!' Shit like that! After all this is Russia."

"What did he say about putting them down?"

"That is where it got really bad. I even thought of moving. He had to 'take care' of the dead dogs by putting them in bags and taking them to an incinerator just like this guy here is doing. But before that, he was sure that the doomed dogs could smell his shame, his disgrace. He would hold the sick and dying dogs still and guide the needle into their veins. When the drug hit their hearts, their legs would buckle and their eyes would dim. He couldn't get used to doing this. Driving home he felt morally compromised and often had to stop the car and double over crying in uncontrollable heaves. If he took a tram home, others would watch as tears flowed down his face and his hands shook. He tried to avoid them by peering out the window at the tapestry of concrete nothingness. He was numb and desensitized. He told me he felt helpless that he was responsible for their humiliating passages from life to death. Later on, he held their paws and talked to them, even sang to them at times out of guilt before he gave the injections. He tried to give them love. But trying to escort them and help them through the death procedure only made it worse for him. He later tried to focus on the job and blot out of his mind what he was doing. But that didn't work either. His crying became an almost nightly ritual at my place. I was really scared!"

"But you can't blame yourself. You did the best you could by listening to him."

"No, of course not. But I started having bad dreams of killing dogs myself and having to explain it to people. I wish I could have recommended someone for him to see and get therapy at USU. But I didn't know anyone."

"What happened to him?"

"He came over one evening and told me he had quit work and was leaving town. I asked him if he had another job, and he just shrugged. He said he was going away and had relatives in another distant part of Russia. I didn't ask where and never saw him again."

"Listen, that guy we just witnessed shoveling the human body into the incinerator, this Dmitry, is in a class all his own. He's both a dog killer and human murderer. We should not feel sorry for him or listen to his tales of woe if it comes to that."

"Agreed ... Krastov's crew have performed a kind of triage every mission. They kill some of the almost gone and diseased ones; separate out others as candidates for possible adoption and new lives; and also select still others for training and potential development of a non-human species of 'dogmen' as he puts it."

"So they get a rush from the chase and kill. They get to use their heads and better judgment to save others. At least that should be less of a moral burden than what my neighbor went through."

"Working with stray dogs in the streets gives you a better appreciation of how hard it is in those extreme circumstances to take care of one another, does it not?" asked Krylovsky.

"Indeed it does," said Andrey. "How about I take care of you for a few stiff drinks? I need something! After a shot or two, I'd like a couple of strong coffees after all this. I have to get back to USU and do some writing."

"I can sense that. All the killing and waste-dumping got your creative juices flowing, no? But make certain you don't write or talk about any of this just yet, understood?"

Andrey looked over and nodded to him as he drove. They parked the car near campus and walked over to the Hungry Wolf. The familiar place was an institution in this part of Yekaterinburg and always provided a good alibi for those having trysts and alcoholic professors tanking up during the day since no one could tell exactly when people came or left. That was almost the point of places like this. Scanning the tables of the large and dark wood-paneled interior, one could see that the patrons were mostly into their own conversations. It was a student pub, restaurant serving three meals a day, and also a tea room in the classic Russian style—a few tables with simple tablecloths, a counter with a samovar, and brightly patterned wooden trays filled with heaps of spice cakes, apples, and bread rings. Students threw down shots of vodka in parts of the place. In the others, men sat drinking tea, quietly smoking, and reading newspapers. The place was always lively with some arguing and laughing while others tried to sing in chorus. The student bartenders changed all the time and typically got into conversations with their professors, student pals, or just passersby. Regulars even had their *stammtischs* or special tables reserved for their groups.

Every university town had two or three of these old places, and they were always popular places to gather.

They sat down in the corner at a well carved-up wooden table. "Think Gorky's initials are here somewhere?" said Andrey.

"I'm sure he'd like this evening's irony. He could write a sensational short story: a militia extermination squad itself exterminated in an attempt to kill a member of the dog extermination squad. Even as fiction, no one would believe it."

"Or care!" said Andrey.

They both laughed and toasted to what ultimately was a good evening's work.

"Don't forget, Andrey. Two of these shits are still out there. The one with the white coat is probably neutralized because we know who he is. But the other one could be trouble."

"The animal control meeting is coming up in a few days, and we might see him and his colleagues there."

"Who are these people, Andrey? What makes them tick? I'm used to dealing with unruly animal rights factions and trying above all this to protect animals, mainly urban dogs since we live here. But these people don't fit the pattern."

"No, they don't. Dmitry works for Krastov as a minor sidekick in limited capacity. He is not really a scientist, but wears a white coat and drops as much of the jargon as he can pronounce to impress non-scientists. Krastov is a serious man who has assembled a team of enthusiastic dogcatchers that have learned from him how to sort dogs: for killing if they have rabies or bite people, for boarding and adoption if they seem healthy, and for research if they show special talents. The latter has gotten Krastov attention from Putin's regime and the Kremlin."

"And, of course, Dmitry is jealous."

"Exactly. He is a simple con-man, using Krastov's reputation with higher-ups such as Semyon at the provincial level. But at the core he detests dogs and would like to kill them all. He would even like to use drones to kills stray dogs. Think of all the PR disasters that you can—that one would have to be at the top. At the same time, he wants to discredit Krastov with videos such as those we saw him showing to the hit squad at the river tonight. He imagines that somehow then he could take over the lab and crews and bask in all the glory."

"Does he have any credibility with the scientific people on this?"

"Of course not. But with unlimited confidence and a vast ego to gloss over his scientific ignorance, he intends to snow them all. Not easily done in Russia."

"Lot of that hubris going around here, isn't there? Look at Putin. He hasn't done badly for a minor St. Petersburg official. He fooled most of the people with his pomp and look where he is now," said Krylovsky. Ivan noticed a gleam of real mischief in his eyes that hinted of a wild and rebellious life.

"So I know most of these players from casual meetings and discussions," said Andrey. "Krastov is straight-forward—exactly what he seems, a good medical professional with surreal plans. Semyon is a mystery because his wife, Anna, teaches at USU, and she is also having an affair with a visiting professor there, and she loves him. Dmitry is a small-time striver who will get caught eventually. He even plans to ally himself with animal rights people against Krastov. Did you know that?"

"News to me, and I thought that group of activists was my specialty."

Ivan went to the bar and got two more large shots of vodka. They both needed them. Ivan had planned to get a local draft beer, but that plan was changed immediately when he got to the bar and saw all the different kinds of his favorite beverage.

"Krastov treats his crews well, and they support him," said Ivan after returning to the table with their drinks. "Any attempt to garner their support and stage a coup by Dmitry would be a big mistake. As you've seen, he has made them into a popular musical group, and they've all been on TV doing ditties about their dog work. The public loves them. The Kremlin loves them. Crew morale is high. And, as for the animal rights factions, that's your department."

"I don't think that's going to happen," said Krylovsky. "No animal rights group around here or any faction would support this guy Dmitry.

We don't want to get mixed up with some charlatan who allows himself to be filmed in the act of clubbing and killing someone, then shoveling him into an incinerator, do we? What about this Semyon? I hear he's quite powerful."

"Of course he's powerful," said Andrey. "But so are the many other higher up officials across Russia that operate their cozy little fiefdoms. They're all tough, but once you get in that competition of scoundrels, there is always someone meaner and tougher. Those on the make at the provincial level like to show off their supreme power and do so locally all the time. They constantly remind us down at this level how weak and dependent we are in their system. The hit squad that confronted Dmitry tonight probably worked for Semyon. But this is not Stalin's 1930s Russia where he knew what was going on and signed off on execution lists regularly. This is more like Tsar Nicholas I's Russia in the early nineteenth century where he nominally presided over vast, corrupt military and civilian bureaucracies. Whereas Nicholas complained about his power being diffused among 30,000 clerks, today it is 15 million! This benefits FSB, which Putin has given free rein and which runs lots of mafia-type operations and rackets. If there's an organization chart, Putin probably drew it up and guards it. Still, Putin's regime is not a standard dictatorship; it's more like decentralized authoritarianism. So he might say something supportive, like planning to spend more for health care or local services, but then takes no action at all, leaving us to our own devices here. Or the reverse: he might condemn particular official actions and do nothing. The result of split authority and diffuse power is that his minions like Semyon can make and enforce their own rules. That gives them free rein to hire thugs and take care of their own personal power problems.

"So as long as he acts without embarrassing anyone above him, he is ok?"

"Right ... But the Kremlin would still want to avoid supporting a murderer who ends up with his pictures in the media incinerating his enemies, don't you think?"

"Very sensible. You must be a USU intellectual."

Krylovsky's eyes didn't lie. He was a wily rogue just under the surface. Ivan admired and supported Krylovsky just as one in the IRA would latch onto a Gerry Adams. Adams has always been a slippery, diplomatic, smooth-talking man of mystery. Ivan has been a full-throated apologist for canine rights and freedoms. Those who know him at USU are aware of his leanings. But most students there already had some radical or socially activist connections and activities. It was simply part of being the modern student. Now Krylovsky, as a veteran of animal rights violence campaigns, such as freeing dogs after torching pounds or even attacking dogcatcher crews, had to sound like he supported law and order and offer gentle reproaches to the many violent zealots in the animal rights factions. It was the same delicate dance performed by Gerry Adams over the years. Publicly, Krylovsky sounded moderately tame and tried to appeal to the broad base that included dog lovers of all stripes. But that was proving complicated.

Boris Krylovsky was a square-jawed man of imposing height with strong shoulders, and, as Ivan noticed, he had that twinkly, mischievous glint in his eyes. With his long, dark hair thrown back in a tight ponytail, it could be said, more accurately, a feverish glitter lit up his eyes. The Putin regime had a use for Krylovsky types. Like many standouts, he had been arrested a few times and put behind bars in several provincial cans. But prosecutors could never make charges of violence and terror stick. They knew he was up to something with his animal rights weirdos. At the same time, they viewed him as useful in keeping the hotheads in line. And that kept any embarrassing public encounters from tarnishing the regime, especially at a time of international attention during the World Cup games. As with any diffuse movement, especially for environmental and social causes, the trouble was the hotheads. They rarely had any brains in his view and joined "animal rights" for many of their own reasons. Their major asset was advocacy, though without facts, analysis, or tact. In other words, most simply complained. Many were anarchists that wanted to disrupt and tear down the fabric of society so their imagined utopias would emerge. What was that utopia? Most couldn't articulate anything coherent but babbled along the safety of retread ideas like "freedom from capitalist exploitation," which he found intensely ironic in the post-Soviet collectivist era. Their utopias were composed of old-fashioned slogans that had never persuaded anyone except intellectual cretins. Anyway, he found after an exchange with Petrovsky after he was arrested once almost ten years ago, that he had more in common with the police than with most of his followers. He found he could talk impassioned ideology and politics intelligently with Petrovsky and several of the others. Even in his jail stints, he found senior police officials interesting to chat with sometimes all night, as part of the interrogations. He learned as much about them as they did about him.

"There's something else you may not know about. Anna's lover . . . .he may be a long lost relative of yours."

"I've heard about this guy—Krylov, isn't that his name? What's his story?"

"He came here for the summer apparently to get away from his humdrum university faculty life and from a bad marital break-up in the U.S. Now he's in the middle of all this. Generally, although not a scientist or medical professional, he's behind Krastov and his work. Since he has all their support plus that of Anna, he has cover for now. Anyway, you two should meet."

"Great! Let's plan on it."

———

Semyon sat in his office the next day staring out the window at a tree where a pair of birds was fighting over something. Just as it was getting interesting, Anastasia came in with a package. His eyes shifted from the bird action to her lithe little body, which he followed around the room as she tidied up his desk and brought him a coffee. He had always been attracted by her petite but curvaceous lines, the seductive come-hither look in her eyes and her suggestive pouts. Suggesting what? To him, they meant "let's get out of here and press the flesh someplace this afternoon on a nice hard bed!" She smelled so fresh and eager.

"Why do I really have to work?" he muttered to her. "There must be an easier way."

"Can I guess why you work?" she said, sitting on the edge of his desk, carelessly letting her ample brown legs emerge from her short skirt. Semyon's throat was getting dry now, and he looked around for a glass of water. His throat was now completely dried out and beads of sweat covered his face and chest as he tried not to look at her dimpled thighs. His efforts failed.

"The President is looking around for new replacements for his aging Protection Service or FSO loyalists, isn't he?" she asked. "Remember the old Party and Komsomol that served as elevating mechanisms for talented officials? Well they're gone. So what are we left with? The FSO instead . . . I've heard that President Putin has already appointed some of his favorite guards to regional governorships and found some be-spectacled engineers to run a few of the ministries. All of them are pretty lackluster in my humble opinion. But you aren't. I've always believed that with proper timing and support for your moves, you can move up. The FSO appointment practice goes back to an event around here. Do you know what that event might be?"

"The opening of a new railway station back in the 1930s?" he guessed.

"You can be so dense sometimes, can't you?" she said. "After Tsar Alexander III's father was murdered not far from here, he created a spe-cial guard to protect him from the people. As you might recall, later one of USU graduates and Boris Yeltsin's bodyguards and drinking mates built up the new FSO. Is all this coming back now, Semyon? Pay atten-tion. And you remember Boris, don't you? He gave the town its name back honoring Catherine. Now the FSO does more important things than guarding tsars from assassinations. It does persuasive public opinion polling to show how popular Putin is. Sure they're rigged, but that's not the point; it takes skill to rig them properly. They also do intelligence reports and the usual hum-drum, but cleverly slanted political analyses that magically demonstrate his popularity in all things. You can do that, can't you? If you can't, I certainly can show you how to do it in an hour or less," she said with a grin while staring at him hard and licking her lips.

"How you read my mind sometimes, you delicious snake!"

"If I was a poisonous one, you'd have been dead a long time ago!"

Anastasia slipped out, giving him a quick glance back and that signature smile of enticement hinting always of future carnal possibilities. The front of his pants had bulged so grandly now that he could barely get out of his chair. Just one more risk of having a high-powered job in service of the Russian state.

But he had to get a grip on himself to perform a few more important duties of his day. Semyon began opening his parcels and letters hoping, as always, to see what the mail would bring him this fine morning. Maybe a distraction would settle him down, and he could focus again on his real jobs of box-checking and report-writing. What Semyon didn't need right now was a meeting. He only went to them out of an obsessive fear of missing out (known in the West as FOMO). It was a real fear for many officials at his level. Especially in his position, he had to be wary of any destabilizing personnel changes above him, which seemed to happen all the time. In each case, he had to re-calculate his crude friend-enemy lists and those currently friendly whom he would have to watch out for. It was like drawing a power map with himself in the center of it. He liked the permanence of the state bureaucracy, of course, which gave him time for recreational activities. But often he was cut short and had to tread carefully.

"*And look here,*" thought Semyon, as he opened a large envelope. "*It's a CD. Odd to get one of these in the mail . . . Smells like trouble,*" he thought as he tiptoed over and locked the office door, then inserted the disc into his computer. So here on the CD were some guys dumping industrial waste into the river. Ho-hum. He fast-forwarded it a bit to some more guys huddled around an iPad. Looked to him like the same place. The setting was a clearing in the woods at night. The characters, which he could barely make out, spoke clearly of dumping dead, stray dogs into the river as well. Interesting, but not really news around here. And what's this? Looks like a scuffle. One of them could be clearly seen trying to club the other, but was apparently shot, along with his mate, by what sounded like an air-gun. Probably a tool of the dog-catching trade. Down went one of them. The other one got up and drove quickly away. The downed man was then picked up and rolled into the trunk of a car by someone else in a white coat. He fast-forwarded to the next scene, where the white-coated man with some difficulty could be seen rolling the unconscious body into the open door of a flaming incinerator. The fire helpfully illuminated his face—it was none other than his earlier office guest, Dmitry!

Shit! Thinking feverishly, what a bullet he just dodged! Dmitry had just demonstrated on camera what an untrustworthy slimewad he was—a small-time murderer in addition to being an obsequious liar and vicious con-man. And here was proof in case he needed it. As the sweat dotted his forehead, he recognized that he had been about to make a triple mistake. Dmitry was obviously untrustworthy; Krastov was clearly popular with higher-ups in the Putin regime; and going after Krylov for revenge would only alienate Anna further from him. He also knew that Anna already expected that he would do something precipitate against her and Krylov out of jealousy. He had thought of ways to get even with him. But why would he be stupid enough to do any of them and end up jeopardizing a dog research program that could benefit Putin, the city, and most importantly—me? Still, a bit of revenge was good for the self-esteem sometimes. But now he need to reverse course and get Putin to bend any laws or regulations in order to support Krastov, making sure that he got the green light to showcase his innovations and bring even more respect for the regime, Russian animal genetic science, and Russia. Most important, Putin needs to know that unconditonally he supported Krastov in all his scientific endeavors. Well, that's enough work and clever thinking for today. Thinking things through in such strategic detail, for him, was rare and exhausting work.

He picked up the phone. "Anastasia, I think we should step out for a moment and review the FSO appointments process you spoke about earlier in a bit more detail. As always, you get to the crux of the issues when we need it done."

17 ANIMAL SPIRITS

It rained the whole day of the public meeting organized by the city animal control department. The rain fell in sheets, interrupted by long periods of gray skies and colder temperatures. It all presaged the harsh dreary with non-stop snow and ice of winter. When I was a kid, we spent the summers jumping off piers into the East River in a gritty section of the East Village. The river was full of oil and sludge, but it was wet and cool and we got used to it. When we weren't leaping into the hot grime, we took the subway to Jones Beach and joined thousands of others trying to find a few inches of sand from which to get into the waves and cool off in the ocean. It was pretty basic, but all of our friends were there and we felt good. Grubby optimists we were! In Yekaterinburg, people seemed dismayed and almost punished by the weather. The summer had been pretty dry so far, and I had nothing to complain about. After all, I was away from Elmira, my empty house, and the boredom of a small college town when school was not in session.

I hadn't seen Anna in more than a week, and that bothered me. Even Sveta at my apartment was acting weird, giving me sidelong glances and not knocking on my door and asking me occasionally to walk her dog. That was odd, but ok with me. Her enticing glances were becoming more frequent. They beckoned me, but fell flat. She was attractive but in a plastic made-up, doll-like way that lacked imagination. Anyway, she didn't appeal to me, and I could tell she was miffed. That only made it worse for both of us—I felt guilty for my genuinely spontaneous indifference. She acted like someone spurned and interpreted my inaction as calculated indifference, which was always a dangerous reaction in women, I had discovered more than once. All this added to my depressed mood, worsened by the pounding rain outside.

I arrived at the hall rented by the department from the local football team and met up with Petrovsky, his daughter Vessie, Ivan, and eventually Krastov, who asked me to help them out with some set-up logistics. Dmitry was not there, which was predictable but curious since he was supposed to be managed and directed by Krastov. Whether he had now officially gone rogue or Krastov was simply ignoring him was not my problem. None of us really trusted the bastard anyway!

"Could you help me out, Nick?" Krastov asked me. "The meeting here promises to be a gathering of local scorpions in a bottle. Anyone can come, so we can expect some din and need to be prepared for it. If you and Ivan could keep an eye on Fyodor, it would be a big help. I wouldn't want any humans biting him if you follow my drift. I'm really glad to see the inspector is here; I hope he brought some of his athletic minions along."

People of all stripes were filling up the auditorium. The noise of conversation and laughter was growing. I had been there only a short while when Ivan came over with his pal Krylovsky and introduced us. "Nick, this is Boris Krylovsky. I believe you are long lost relatives."

And what an appealing character! If I had a long lost relative like this, a scraggly looking man of about six feet five, I would be happy to see that he looked like this wily troublemaker rather than a staid banker—worse still a pseudo-intellectual, college professor type. Here was either a biker with earrings, pony tail, and black leather jacket, or a throwback to nineteenth century, bomb-throwing Russian nihilists. The other possibility was that he was none of these people and just a normal student activist at USU in his late twenties or early thirties.

"Glad to finally meet you!" I said. "I've heard about what you do locally, and it is impressive. I understand a lot of the animal rights groups that you coordinate will be here. Ivan told me you are at least one of their leaders."

"Right you are . . . one of them. We have many small groups with roughly the same objective—to protect the lives of dogs and other animals. I like to think we run the most sensible faction that could improve the lot of these dogs, and that we could get all the support we need from the city and even the Kremlin. But you heard the doctor speak of 'scorpions in a bottle,' and he is correct. The groups encompass a range of positions from reasonable response to the animal rights terrorists, which would like to blow things up in the name of dogs. Yekaterinburg has a long history of political activism dating back to the Romanovs and is once again becoming a hive of Russian local activism. You've heard about some angry groups fighting against the efforts by the city to eliminate a public park and put in an orthodox church. Nobody young goes to the Orthodox Church anymore, at least to a staid, socially antiquarian one like that, so you can see people are pissed. So expect to see different kinds of protest groups in action here on this issue."

"From my short time here, my impression is that the city wants to appear responsive to local demands and that right now animal control is the hottest topic around—a lightning rod for activism and a chance for the city to show its colors as smart and humane."

"Maybe, Dr. Krylov. Let's hope it all works out."

"Please, call me Nicholas or Nick."

He nodded to me and then moved off to sit in front of the stage with the others. They all seemed to know each other from previous encounters, meaning residues of probably good and bad blood. Then she came in. I didn't recognize her even after she took off her rain parka, and she flashed me a weak smile.

"I'm sorry I didn't join you earlier, but here I am. I had some work to catch up on at USU."

"Rain is always a good excuse to get caught up," a line I threw out to get things back to reality.

Looking her over, I noticed right off that she was wearing sunshades and seemed to have a bruise on her right cheek. She moved closer to me, and we kissed as if we hadn't seen each other in years. It was like old times. She smelled of that familiar fragrance with the natural perfume of her skin. And she cuddled and squirmed . . . I felt all these intoxicating sensations in less than a minute.

"All right, let's hear it."

"Quite predictable, really. The pot had been boiling. We had it out last night, and you see the result."

"He's known all along. I suppose he got more proof?"

"Less predictably, he's been getting it from Sveta, your landlady, who was one of his mistresses."

"What! Sveta?"

"She may have had your place bugged during one of your absences from the place. She may even be the leader of one of the animal rights splinter groups here tonight. May have even placed a microphone on Leo."

"Come on! And I took her for a quiet, attractive, but lonely woman. Certainly not the type for intrigue and betrayal."

"People fool you. She's all of that and may have a crush on you as well."

I laughed and shook my head in stupid disbelief.

"Fooled me all right! Anyway, it's you I'm worried about," I said. "Should we put you up at someplace like Ivan's until we sort this out? I don't want you getting really banged up the next time his pot boils. And we might tell Petrovsky about all this for future reference. He'll keep it quiet and can't really get involved with people in Semyon's politically untouchable category."

She looked up at me. "I'm not sure you understand. You're no better off than me, alone at her place anymore."

I could see her eyes focusing on something behind me. She urged me to observe what was taking place.

"Look at that! Semyon and his new pal, Dmitry, have just arrived and are sitting to the side a few rows back. Krastov has gone over to talk with them. This could all be interesting!"

Loud clapping and the Singing Mutts filed onto the stage in their green outfits to begin a ditty.

"This one's for you, Elvis," said one of them over the address system, and they started a barbershop quartet arrangement of "Old Shep." Leoinid took the lead, and the rest did a fetching chorus of doggie woofs, wails, and moans.

"Oh, when I was a lad
And old Shep was a pup
Over hills and meadows we'd stray
Just a boy and his dog
We were both full of fun
We grew up together that way...
Yes oh yes, I remember the time at the old swimmin' hole
When I would have drowned beyond doubt
But old Shep was right there
To the rescue he came
He jumped in and then pulled me out..."

A bit corny, but the Mutts got better all the time! By now, the room was almost full, and the crowd had quieted down as Krastov took over. He moved around the stage waving and smiling—a real showman when not throwing nets over strays and rewiring dog brains in his lab. And in came the surprise guest of the hour wearing his glasses, cardigan sweater, and walking on his hind legs over to his chair on stage. Dr. Andrey Lubyantsev of the city health department led Fyodor around. Anna and I sat with Ivan in front for a better view of them.

"Thank you for coming to our first informational meeting!" said Krastov. "We have invited all groups here to present their well-known and disparate views on control of animal health and safety in this city. We are aware that it is a contentious issue as it is everywhere in the world. We at the animal control department work for the City health department to provide ethical treatment for animals. But we live in a real world of finite resources where choices have to be made. Our ultimate goal is to preserve animals and ensure that they live in harmony with people. To that end, let me introduce you to some of our core partners. Dr. Andrey Lubyantsev is our boss. Dr. Anna Irtenev and Dr. Nicholas Krylov work with us from USU. Sitting here is also Fyodor, whom you may have seen on media. Fyodor is one of our specially selected dogs, who will answer your questions on what we are doing. Inspector Petrovsky of the local police is also here because animal control has become a security as well as a health issue. To the side, I see Semyon Irtenev representing the Kremlin from the Provincial Department, which has been of great support, and with him is one of my assistants Dmity Simovich. And most importantly, our musical group: "The Singing Mutts" are here to turn our dog experiences into musical favorites and memorable ditties to keep us in high spirits.

"I'm not here to review what we do, as that has been thoroughly covered in the local media," he went on. "Many members of the press corps are here today. My role is to listen and try to answer your questions. So, could you state your name and organization to be clear for the public and the media?"

A bearded man wearing a lumberjack-style shirt rose from the back. Definite NGO type, I figured. He could have been from central casting: spoke in an appropriate bass full of *sage gravitas* that got everyone's attention. If it was God, all eyes and ears were upon him in rapt expectation that he was about to make an earthshaking pronouncement that would be followed by thunderbolts and public wailings for justice. Luckily, the Mutts were here to do an accompaniment and keep things light and calm for now.

"I am Sergei from the Animal Welfare NGO. We've followed your doings in the media, and it appears that you are the latest in a long line of Russian Dr. Frankensteins, about to create a kind of new life and consciousness. I am sure that you are popular and have a wide audience. But we stand opposed to all this as unnatural."

"And well you should, sir," said Krastov quickly to prevent any more funereal drumrolls at the start. "Listen, sir, everything we do here relies on nature. We do not comb the slaughterhouses in search of dead pig brains to revive or transplant dog brains into humans as Bulgakov so graphically wrote about. Not at all, sir! Never swallow the Internet lies of the many scientific charlatans out there. We do not revive dead dogs. We have no top-secret projects, do we, Fyodor? You see the product of our work so far. Our well-trained and alert friend sits listening over in the corner. He is the result of scientific trial and error with additional mechanical processes and simple training exercises. He was a dog; he is still a dog, and dogs learn fast. But we discovered that they can learn even faster and to a much more advanced level than before. Didn't we, Fyodor?"

Fyodor stood and enunciated carefully and loudly to the audience, which stared up at him in stunned silence.

"You might think I'm not a dog anymore, a freak because I read books and can talk although, as you can hear for yourselves, more slowly because I'm still seeing my speech therapist for diction lessons. No, I'm still a wily trickster because I am at the core, like all dogs, a clown. I am still sly, obedient if it serves my needs, and am ingratiating if I can get treats out of it. I am still a normal dog and can steal things from your kitchens that you wouldn't even miss for days. I still like to go through garbage pails and drink out of toilets. Such behaviors give me a rush. In other words, I'm a lot like your favorite pet mutt, only I can explain my bad behavior.

Here the crowd laughed and were starting to warm up to Fyodor.

"I am not human, but I can do helpful things like provide patient understanding, induce calm and reduce conflicts between people, and show fierce loyalty to my master and his family. Right now, I am a dog that is on my way to achieving superior canine potential and still behave human-like. It's a balance. Can any of you out there say that you have achieved your highest potential and are still normal humans?

More laughter!

"I read that people in the City of Bucharest had to deal with 200,000 stray dogs back in 2007," continued Fyodor. "That meant 20,000 packs in a city about the size of Yekaterinburg that caused an average of 80 medical and rabies treatments per day. Like the average Russian, the Romanians have a long tradition of seeing dogs as poor but honest insurgents against a corrupt and oppressive state. It's part of the values and practices that make up our culture. We have been badly treated by a long historical tradition of brutal and insensitive officials. But my colleagues here are trying to manage this very serious city problem as humanely as they can—and they are certainly not fascist human or animal rights violators."

Applause and cheers from the crowd!

"Thank you, Fyodor. We like to talk about managing dogs and what they need. But how do we know? We aren't dogs. Fortunately, we have a dog here that can tell us precisely what they want and need. You, madam, please . . . your question?"

A bespectacled, rosy-cheeked woman in a brightly-colored peasant styled dress rose slowly.

"Alexandra Podtochin from the Coalition for Ethical Science. We are certainly impressed by Fyodor, and we wonder how he could be so perfect without major medical interventions and organ changes? It may be that we are stunned because no one has been in the presence of such an animal. We have all read about them in novels, but few of us have actually encountered one until now. So, with all the scientists out there who have been working on this for years, how is it you have hit upon the magic formula?"

"Thank you, Alexandra. We started with a rough objective and moved through trial and error to expand the basic qualities, which we identified in a local street dog. We may have been lucky. We are working with others, and it is going slow. One of them named Tsar, just died of cancers that were apparently growing inside of his intestines when we found him on the street. We've suffered setbacks and almost given up several times. The work has been tedious and labor-intensive. We still offer no scientific panacea; we created no bio-magic cells or new methods. We keep notes of our progress and setbacks like all scientists. As explained in these lab notes, we employ a mix of natural selection, environmental changes, and gene therapies—all to enhance natural processes. As Fyodor said, he will always be a dog. We just can't let him chase cars anymore."

Scattered laughter from the audience!

"We aren't breeding new kinds of dogs, though if we can breed Fyodor, maybe it will enhance future generations because we have set critical elements in motion," Krastov continued. "We have been using mechanical methods on dog organs rather on a case by case basis. Our method is to trigger their genes with minor medical interventions on the existing organs. Note how Fyodor's voice is much like his normal growl, but he can change tones just like before, depending on what he's thinking about. He still whines, wails, and barks like any dog. But words are attached to these tones now. We have induced behavioral changes such as he is displaying now. He can walk on his hind legs, read, and talk. He can't pick out any stylish or decent clothes yet, but we are working on it.

More laughter!

"In short, we are not the evil nature-changers vilified in the activities of Lysenko which were given Stalin's support. Lysenko, as you recall, was not a scientist but a charlatan groping for power. But research requires that we keep trying, and the Putin regime has supported our work—just as Stalin did not support Russian animal science years ago. Instead, Stalin's Communists supported charlatans like Lysenko and set the country back 100 years."

"Dogs, as you all are well aware, attach themselves to humans and, unlike cats, have high social IQs," said Fyodor to evident laughter from the cat-haters in the audience. "Russian animal biologists demonstrated years ago that because of this need for attachment, dogs may have actually helped humans evolve further. They evolved further by accepting the dogs in an interactive historical process: both parties gained. As my master, Dr. Krastov, will tell you, his theory is that they may have proven, with examples like me, that dogs are the evolutionary link to humans. We all know that apes stood up, fought in packs, and mostly fought wars between their colonies—basically tribal warfare. Apes evolved into something like humans. But we are obviously the link, not apes!"

"Looks like they have things pretty well under control, no?" I said to Anna.

Just as she was about to answer me, someone in the back stood up and shouted out: "Fyodor sounds like a lab nerd to me. Aren't you just creating nerds to replace dogs? That seems like changing nature to me!"

"Why should we listen to people like you?" Fyodor replied loudly in a distinct growl. "What do you really know about dogs or animals?

Maybe you have pets. But are they happy listening to you all day? I'd rather listen to a Rimsky-Korsakov Easter Concerto CD all day or even starve rather than hear your inane nonsense. You should be put down yourself, sir, for the benefit of humanity!

Laughter and taunts! "Bite him!" and "Throw your CDs at him!"

"I lived in the streets around here for years. Where were you then if you are so concerned about dogs and animals? All you have is a loud bark but no brain. Dogs suffer from owners and masters that are really stupid: they are cruel, insecure, venal, and frivolous people that want to keep control of dogs for all the wrong reasons. And for centuries, we have had to endure these people. People like you, it seems to me! I can tell you there are some nasty characters out there in the wilds that you don't want to growl at you or have attack your kids. They would make short work of both of us. You need to listen to the doctors here. They are trying to manage a problem of growing seriousness in the face of the competing pressures against them, such as, I suppose, your group. They are trying to create new types of dogs through training and environmental interventions. In my case, I'd say it worked. I just hope that many other dogs get the same chance I got."

Cheers and scattered clapping from the audience!

"Still, we think your approach to the dog problem is too conservative, legalistic, and buttoned-down. There are far too many strays, and my family and neighbors have to put up with attacks all the time," the shouter continued.

"And we would agree with you there, sir!" said Krastov. "We are working with the planning faculty at USU represented here by Doctors Anna and Nicholas to train our crews better. The only way to enforce policy properly is to have professionals who can judge what needs to be done on the spot. This is not something that Moscow or the provincial officials can deal with. We have to be accountable and responsive to the people here—to you. We need to respond to your complaints—now! You are not satisfied with current services, and neither are we. Some in this room would kill all stray dogs on the spot. Not a good idea at all! You've undoubtedly heard of the *velodog*? It's a small revolver that was manufactured for fast, personal use—for bicyclists to ward off attacking strays while they rode around town. Many other people here owned them and used them on their walks and family outings. Things were that bad here just a decade ago. I owned one of these guns myself. Now we take a more nuanced approach—triage if you will. The dangerous ones in our judgment—they still need to be put down. Right now that means most of them. That number will decrease. Others we identify on our field missions are tranquilized and become candidates for adoption or further training. From that pool or cohort, we hope to create more Fyodors someday. So far, there are few special cases such as him. But we need to find them. For instance, we need a Mrs. Fyodor right now. Don't we, Fyodor?"

"Not so sure about that!"

Laughter and shouting from the audience. "I have a neighbor in the next flat that could fit the part! But she would do better with a horse!"

"Hear! Hear!"

"It's still unethical. How can you play God and put down most strays?" came shouts from the back. I noticed a group of men standing. They were poised and ready for action, and I hoped that Petrovsky saw them. They were getting ready to make some disruptive moves. They wore football team jerseys, one of which said "Kyiv." They were clearly not animal rights supporters or even opponents. They probably didn't know or care what was being said here. To me, they looked like hooligans or hired thugs. I've been amongst soccer game hooligans and had always thought they were generated by the acute boredom of the game itself. I mean, what else is there to do after sitting two hours in the hot sun with a game at 0-0? Like the fans in the Simpsons show that started throwing punches to alleviate the boredom. But I was wrong; there were often organized toughs who liked to add to the intensity of the game. They disrupted events everywhere, and they caused a lot of grief. In this context, discussion time was over.

"No more killing!" "It's wrong! Stop the dog killing!" they chanted, probably from a prepared script given them.

Several of them came down the two aisles separating the audience, pushing several people standing to the side. They then rushed the stage all at once. I nodded to Ivan, and we jumped up to surround Fyodor. The crew and several others took up their defensive posts.

One of them came right at me like a footballer. Waving a small club and grinning straight at me, he then veered off and darted towards Fyodor, swinging wildly. I thought he had faked me out and was after Fyodor. But I got hit in the shoulder with one of his first swings. Then on the follow through, I got a punch in with my good arm that floored him. As he was about to get up, Fyodor bounded forward on all fours without his spectacles and bit him in the face and neck several times.

"Woof!" went he as he spit out drool, tongue flailing about. "I almost forgot to bark with my bite."

"Good boy! An extra book for you to read tonight!" said Ivan, as someone grabbed him and threw back his arm ready to land a punch. Fyodor jumped in the air, hitting the man in the side and knocking him off balance. He then grabbed the man by the neck and shook him like a doll until his body stopped moving.

"Wow! You must have been a real tough bastard on the streets!"

"I ran with the best of them!" replied Fyodor, dusting off his plaid vest with his paw.

The melee was going on in full swing now with Krastov and his crew fighting off several attackers in several locations of the auditorium. *Where the hell were Petovsky and his men?* I wondered. Right then, I felt a sharp pain as one of them got me on the cheek with a small club. I staggered back and went down. As I started to hit the floor, I saw none other than Cyclops approaching me. It was him all right, approaching me with his face looking like badly-baked bread with hischeeks puffed out like French popovers. All that emphasized his large, eye-like forehead pimple. He was like the Flashman character that kept turning up all over the country and at every event. Who the hell was he anyway? How did he get here? The stick pummeling stunned me for a moment. Then I saw Cyclops get up and with his club land a strong blow to the top of Dmitry's head, who happened to be near him fending off other attackers. The sound reminded me of the loud, hollow thump of a hammer hitting a coconut to break it open and extract the meat and milk. Down Dmitry went, and that blow looked to me like it might stick. I recovered, ran over and threw Cyclops backwards, away from Dmitry. That allowed me time to punch Cyclops a few times around the head and shoulders. To the side, I saw that several others were attacking Krylovsky, and that he, too, had been knocked down by several blows from one or more of the goons using their little truncheons. Apparently, he had not reined in the hotheads animal rights people after all! On the other side near the stage, I even saw Petrovsky smashing one of them with a clipboard he had brought with him to take notes!

After Cyclops finished beating up Dmitry, he spotted me and moved towards me with a club he had picked up. A man with a vengeful purpose, he was spurred to action no doubt by the recent memories of my escapes from him using my fists and pepper spray. I foolishly retreated into a corner of the auditorium away from the main fighting. He came at me and swung hard and missed as I stepped backwards. I was now boxed in by the wall behind me, the rows of seats to the side and the aisle upwards. Cyclops was waiting for me to take the aisle, which would give him a clear shot.

I had been cornered like this in amateur boxing bouts in the Bronx. My then coach was an odd little man, built like a steel robot that happened to be into Buddhism. He said it cleared his head and allowed his body to do supernatural things to get him out of jams. Coach fought like a pit bull, but had that far off look in his eyes as if he were taking cues from unseen spirits out there or perhaps inside of him. At first I thought he was kidding about Buddhism, then I saw him in action a few times and became an acolyte of whatever he had to teach. I was known as the Flying Russian Pigeon at the neighborhood boxing club, named after one of his techniques that I had mastered. Trying hard to recall those days now, as Cyclops approached slowly like a cat cornering a mouse, I spun around suddenly and faced the back wall. That surprised the bastard for just an instant. With my body erect and mind clear of all immediate distractions, I kicked off hard. I did two backward somersaults over him and landed a few yards up the aisle. From there, I sprang forward and ran ahead out of his reach.

Cyclops was also stunned, but only briefly as Andrey, standing nearby, got him a good one with his club. Down he went for the count. Now I got pissed. My frustrations, which had been building up inside for a long time since the theft of my wife by the rich slime bag in Elmira, released now at the sight of my new friends being beaten up by thugs. I was full of insane rage and went back down the aisle full steam in pursuit of the rest of them, recalling my youthful days of street fighting. Cyclops was already down, and I helped Petrovsky and a crew member collar him—like the rabid dog that he was. On the other end of the stage, a few scuffles were still underway. Both Anna and Ivan were fighting off some burly types that must have been part of the team sent to disrupt us. Those people were more than just random goons looking for a fight. But who were they? I went to the aid of Anna and Ivan, who were badly bloodied after being hit by clubs and fists more than a few times. To the side, I saw Vessie watching all this beside her stunned school chums that even featured her father getting clobbered several times. Vessie was also watching Ivan's attempts to protect Anna, but getting badly beaten up in the process. I picked up Cyclops' stick and went after them, clubbing all three of their attackers and receiving a few more hits in the process. I was knocked down several times.

As any street fighter knows, one feels no pain until the lights actually go out, which happened shortly thereafter for me. In the last instant, I recalled the old song lyric from "Stranded in the Jungle": "then something heavy hit me like an atomic bomb!" Then I smelled that peculiar nutmeg odor from being hit in the head, saw a few stars, and went down for the count.

———

Sometimes Semyon Irtenev had wild ecstatic dreams at night that affected him all day. He occasionally lost ability to concentrate. Other officials in his provincial office looked at him oddly—they often had to repeat what they had said to him several times and even then he listened distractedly with one ear. He had that far out look of the dissolute libertine in his eyes. At night, his head came alive with dreams that burned as clearly as scenes on a lighted stage. Just last night he dreamt that he was swatting hordes of large black flies—some of which bit into him. The more he swatted, the more of them surrounded him in thick, blackened waves. Of course, in the Middle Ages they had dream interpreters on staff, officials that were even appointed to ministries of dreams. The Tsars had several of them to tell them what the dreams meant and recommend daily course corrections, changes to appointment calendars, and other evasive actions if the omens sounded bad. Sometimes after a wild night of dreaming, he would wake up gasping, as if his head had been in submerged in a bucket of cold water.

But today was just another bright sunshiny day in Yekaterinburg, and Semyon was in his office daydreaming about his planned afternoon tryst with Anastasia. She had that curvy, fullish figure with shapely, athletic muscles that he dreamt about, especially the scenes where she twined around him like a python. Of course, he had to be more careful next time not to throw out his back during amok time. Some days he was bent and could hardly walk upright. The best remedy he knew was to stick to missionary position and hold the fancy stuff until he got back in shape. It must be noted that they were still in the rapid consummation of love stage of their romance. With Anna he had long passed that and was into the mild habit of conjugality, in other words physical boredom accompanied by emotional sterility and personal indifference. With people like him, successful higher-level provincial officials in Russia, this was not unusual. It accounted for the high incidence of men with mistresses and lovers that almost accompanied the superficial appearance of normal, happy marriages, families, and households. It was rare to find a mean between these extremes. And there it was. The light on the white phone that sat in back of his giant desk receiving private calls blinked brightly. The bell clanged away loudly interrupting his blissful reveries and bringing him back to cold reality.

"Damir, so good to hear your voice! To what do I owe the pleasure?"

Knowing that Damir Lebedev was the largest construction magnate around and a major supplier of city business services, he was especially ingratiating to him. This respect held in spite of the fact that much of Lebedev's business was sent his way by Semyon himself, who carefully arranged the bids to ensure that the City technical work specifications coincided precisely with his firm's products and capacities. They got right down to business.

"I hope you have been following the news, Damir; we have been faced with a forced work slowdown here. Moscow has cut off our construction funds. It seems they have overspent their budget on the Games, and there's nothing left for us but bread and butter issues like roads and bridges."

"Not to worry, Semyon, that's not why I am calling. It's another matter altogether." His tone was subdued. Not what he expected on this fine day before the late summer rains would intensify. The days would get colder soon, bringing ice, and presaging another nasty winter.

"What is it, Damir? Was it the food last time you dined at our house? Not sick I hope!"

But Lebedev was not in a jokey mood.

"It gives me no pleasure at all to tell you this. Tomorrow, you will be visited by an audit team from the Kremlin. You must know how dangerous these people can be in the best of circumstances. A visit from them is always stressful and bodes no good for anyone. You need to be prepared. From what I have learned, they have some films of recent crimes being committed by your associates that they can probably tie back to you. I have no details on names or sources, but the information on which their suspicions and allegations are based seems solid."

"But this is all impossible! Can you tell me more?"

"It's all I have at the moment, Semyon. And I am sorry, but I have to leave just now. You have to judge and act for yourself. As a wise man once said, the world is everywhere under the stars. I salute you and would rather that we not meet again anytime soon. That would be better than for me one day to see you and you not to see me."

"But Damir!" he yelled as the phone went dead. *Shit,* he thought, *this is bad . . .* His lungs sent nothing to his mouth; his hands tried in vain to link up directly with his brain and his palate, fingers, and spine—they were all totally numb. Now what? After an intense effort, the creaking, bickering components of his being began to communicate with one another.

"Anastasia," he called, "come in here a minute."

By his colorless complexion, she could see he had been handed some unfortunate news and that he looked scared, an expression she rarely saw in him. After he explained his predicament to her, she shifted into survival mode, from erotic smiles to scowls and venom. He almost didn't know who she was.

"Listen to me, Semyon! You simply and repeatedly deny everything, and it will blow over."

She had always been impressed and excited by his determined-looking face, his decisiveness, and his keen intelligent eyes. What she saw now was a cowering, frightened little man with a vacant stare looking at her like a lost dog waiting for a clear command to follow, a meek appeal for direction.

"Hey, why didn't I think of that?" he responded abruptly. "Look, these people play rough and will be sent here as the angels of death. I know how auditing inspection teams work as I've been on them before and have even sent them on surprise visits to handle my enemies in the past. Most of them don't know anything about accounting or auditing and are just there to make you run around looking for balance sheets and invoices. They are hired goons and often try to shake you down for payments. You pay them off. Then they go away!"

"I wonder if this will be so simple. What do you plan to do if you can't get rid of them? You can't hide anywhere; this is Russia. Do you want to face the threat of poisoned Bulgarian umbrellas anywhere in the world? I think not. Let's forget about it now and head for the hotel."

"Not today, Anastasia, zest and energy isn't there. I'm not in the mood for some reason."

She saw him as he really was—a cornered rat, the pathetic creature that she had to take orders from and provide sexual favors to. She suddenly felt humiliated, and this drove her to fury. Her face turned red, and she shrieked at him:

"You worm! I always knew you were all talk and no action." She slammed the door and left.

Worried, frustrated, and confused, he even tried to call Anna on her cell that night, but no one answered.

18   RABID NIGHTS

The familiar scenes ran through my mind like a grainy black and white trailer. I spotted something from the window of our train moving quickly across the steppe. Maybe a deer or lynx by the speed. No, it was that boy wearing his loose cap running ahead with a surprised, almost fearful expression on his face, as if a train were something he had never seen before. Yet his disheveled dress, ragged looks, and long strides expressed strength and the confidence of youth. I caught the beginnings of that defiant grin in that expression of fearful surprise. He was surely a tough one . . . maybe a Cossack or Chechen brave out for a run. His strides floated him on ahead; it was more than a run. Like a deer bounding and floating across a field. Behind him a few paces back ran his black and white shaggy dog, a ruddy, country type that was obviously use to these escapades with him. The peasant boy, if that was what he was, must have stepped in a ditch and fallen, as I could no longer see him though I pressed my face to the far corner of the window. The track was curving away, and the last thing I saw was the dog that probably had stopped to sniff around the scene until his master picked himself back up. I was that boy now. Who was the master?

The boy seemed to be coughing. Now he was stumbling around in circles like a confused insect and was having trouble getting up. I felt the beads of sweat studding my face and chest like scales on a crocodile. My breathing quickened, and I thought of the heart attack that finally killed my father. What an irony to die here, a half-national back in his old country . . . I squirmed around to try and get free of whatever was holding me back. But I couldn't. My strength was gone. Suddenly, some lights flashed. I opened my eyes to see several blurred faces looking down at me.

"You look like shit!" Andrey said helpfully. "Is this your way of avoiding work at the office?"

Anna was next to him, giggling apologetically but saying nothing. "All of you are sights for my sore eyes and body!"

"What's important is that you're going to be ok from the little melee we engaged in a few days ago," said Krastov.

"A few days ago?"

"Yes, you've been here that long and out of it. The doctors have patched you up pretty well given the amount of blows you received. It could have been a lot worse. But now we have a bigger problem."

"Pregnant maybe? Should we tell Anna?"

"Almost as dramatic and momentous. As I suspected, you have rabies. We talked of this before, after you were bitten in dog attacks and developed coughs later."

"So now what? Do you turn me into a full dog now like Fyodor?" I said, not wanting to hear any more of this. "Where are Cyclops and Dmitry?"

"Dmitry was killed by your pal Cyclops during the brawl. The one you call Cyclops is now having a chat with Inspector Petrovsky in a soundproof basement where they can drink tea without interruption. From videos turned in by Krylovsky, it appears that Dmitry also incinerated his pal Rat Face whom you had met several times. I'm sure you'll miss both of them!"

"The brawl … the two thugs, who were all those people?" I asked.

"We can never be sure about attacks like this," said Krastov. "From what I've learned from the Inspector, this group appears to be an older, bigger, hierarchical gang. We have a few of these types operating in Yekaterinburg right now. They typically fragment into cliques of hotheads, each with different agendas and paymasters. We saw the Cyclops character again, so we can assume there is some connection to Semyon's people. As for what to do about them, my view is that having police use the "iron fist" approach with violent types doesn't work. It simply creates more toughs. Why? Many see their friends beaten and humiliated like they were, maybe beaten by police and robbed by officials. All this works against trust in state institutions and the police and is counterproductive. Petrovsky agrees with all this, but he is just one local police inspector. We have to be more discriminating now in how we treat both dogs and humans.

"Fortunately, Cyclops was doing the discriminating for you and got rid of Dmitry after Dmitry eliminated Rat Face. Now you can breathe easier since the police have Cyclops in custody," Ivan said.

"We got lucky. I'm no policeman, but I've worked with them at times on call. The crime problem here almost solves itself. To avoid many innocent people getting hurt in the process, we have to enforce laws now, not just be nuanced with the tough guys to keep the public on our side,' said Krastov. "The soft academic crime sociology approach works in the medium term. But we have to deal with daily bust-ups like the one that just put you in the hospital."

"So back to my rabies. What happens now?"

"While you were out of it, I gave you the usual tests for rabies. We tested your serum, saliva, spinal fluid, and did a skin biopsy. Several of the tests are for antibodies to the rabies virus. You flunked all of them. So, I'm having you moved from here to my lab today. You have the virus, and it has spread inside of you."

They put me in an ambulance and drove me about a half hour to Krastov's full service lab. It was behind the animal control office, a place as expected, full of cages and howling, barking dogs. The non-descript brick building was common in the Soviet Union. Its inhabitants could be prisoners, students, patients, or veterinarians experimenting on dogs. Krastov told me later that he had done some of his more interesting and risky work on Fyodor's brain right here. It was a perfect, scientific hideaway in that it was sealed off from public scrutiny, and it was where the real trial and error work took place. Not something you could explain to the public at large with their propensity to look for sensationally incomparable experiences like Dr. Frankenstein's work or that of Nazi doctors working on Jewish prisoners. Even lobotomies were off limits, though they seemed to be coming back now with the more advanced technology and a kinder terminology to describe it. Such procedures are now called psychosurgery, which has a soft thera-peutic feel to it. No, Krastov's major canine body and brain repair and replacement work here wouldn't sell to the public at all.

At his full service lab, Krastov shifted back and forth between the rabies vaccine and Fyodor development projects. First, he went to work and developed Fyodor. It was a labor of tough love with lots of trial and errors. He hoped there would be other successes like him. If so, he could move to engineer security and military dogs, which wouldn't be much of a scientific challenge at all. But for now, Fyodor was a unique case. After he developed Fyodor successfully, he was stuck at the point where he could claim a bio-solution to strays and a remedy for the shortages of security personnel in the police forc-es and armies around the country. But he couldn't go forward and tackle the bigger problems because he lacked a good understudy. He needed someone he could train to handle the deadly pathogens and bring his lab up to secure standards. So he promoted Dmitry from crewmember to head lab assistant. But he was a "slovenly bastard," as Krastov put it, at one point pulverizing a promising sample of anti-viral cocktails that they had been perfecting for months. Dmitry left the machine on simply because he forgot about it and went on doing something else despite the noise, which, even with all the barking and other racket around, he somehow didn't notice. He lapsed into this kind of negligent activity all the time, and Krastov was getting pissed. Detailed, quick, and smart lab work was critical to developing an antibody drug to disable the rabies virus to try and cure those already infected—like he and his crew for instance. Then he shifted back to his rabies vaccine project. He was trying to develop a treatment that would keep the rabies virus from attacking the nervous system. That may have already happened in Krylov's case, which could mean a vi-olent, painful death for him. His vaccine had to be a quick treatment that could somehow reverse rabies in more advanced stages. No one had ever done this.

But what to do with this undisciplined and lazy "understudy"? Krastov mused that one day he might do a reverse Bulgakov—working like Dr. Bormenthal, but this time to transplant a brain from a dog into Dmitry's skull to create a more intelligent understudy. Why not? Maybe the dog's thoughts and instincts could add to Dmitry's intelligence and make something useful out of him. In any case, he had to do most of the work himself—testing his antibody samples on rabid dogs, of which there were plenty on the streets at present. Then he moved to testing it on his own crew and finally himself. And everyone was rabies-free, thanks to his own efforts in the lab, sometimes 18 hours a day doing his own research, then moving back to the Fyodor project.

Krastov was getting very tired and frustrated by doing all the detailed work that a good, trustworthy, biologically or medically-trained assistant could handle. He wanted to concentrate on the big things and leave the operational details of the lab to someone else. He was stuck. He also realized there could be no more spectacular events like the domestication of silver foxes into dogs: Belyaev and Trut did all that. Still, he knew he was definitely onto something here. Here he made a mistake, thinking that good, scientific workers were hard to find in Yekaterinburg. He was wrong on that point—USU has plenty of talented doctoral students and even junior professors eager for an exciting scientific experience in the real world. With the pressures from the Kremlin and the upcoming Games that had to be rabies-free, he thought that he had run out of time. On the other hand, Krastov thought he could try and develop some new products of his own that were not one-of-a-kind like Fyodor. And with Krylov as a new entrant into the mix suffering from rabies could be, he hoped he could make him a spectacular beneficiary of his new work. It would be his first test case outside of work on dogs and his crew in his lab. And it was a tough test because he knew that Nicholas Krylov had been living with the virus advancing for several months.

Krastov had already created an experimental drug long ago to deal with the rabies virus since they were most at risk from it during their work catching and killing nasty dogs every day. But he had never tested it on someone that had delayed treatment this long. Every day Krastov's crews were bitten in the process of tranquilizing, shooting, catching, and throwing dogs into wagons. The dogs just didn't sit there while they were under attack from his crews. The packs fought back. Even Fyodor had bitten one of them before he was nabbed. He apologized profusely and even wrote a letter explaining everything, which is still posted on the wall of the office. Most importantly, Krastov couldn't get approval for his new drug in a system that was too busy doping up its athletes on steroids and clumsily trying to cover it up. That in a country with a "medals over morals" policy for Olympic games. He should have pitched it for athletes that were bitten while hiking, jogging, or biking. So, he developed the vaccine pills anyway right here in the back of the animal control department in this lab and used it on himself and his crew. He knew it worked, or none of them would still be around. He also administered it to his friends such as Inspector Petrovsky, who was repeatedly bitten by dogs and criminals alike. And he gave Dr. Lubyansev several treatments. All to good purpose. They recovered, and now they covered for him!

"So what is this stuff?" asked Krylov, as he settled into the old leather chair in front of Krastov's desk. "I know some of the treatments in the U.S. are brutal and can take weeks. They feature stomach injections, according to people I know who have been bitten. Is that how this is going to work?"

"No. My crew and I have never had the luxury of down time like that. Dogs would have overrun the city by now, and the public would have run us out of town. And the disease is far too advanced in you to receive old-fashioned, anti-viral treatments like that. We have bigger plans for you."

He went to a cabinet and brought out several sealed packages of large pills and handed them to Krylov. "Are those for horses or people?"

"Does it matter if they work?"

"Has this been approved by the health authorities?"

"Things are simpler here. We approved them because we are the health authorities. Have you heard the one about two guys in the elevator? Power goes out, and they stand there in the dark looking at each other for an hour in hopes that the power will return and they can get out of there. But time passes, and they are still stuck there. Suddenly, one of them takes off his belt and lowers his trousers. He then squats down in the corner and takes a huge dump on the floor of the elevator. "Jesus!" the other one says, as he takes out a cigarette and lights a match to calm his nerves. "You can't smoke in here!" says the other. "It is prohibited!"

"As an ex-Peruvian ex-president named Oscar Benavides once quipped: "For my friends, anything; for my enemies, the law," said Krastov.

"I see ..."

"Good. Let's begin then." He called Leonid on his cell to assist him. In the back of his mind was to replace Dmitry with a new and improved version of Leonid. He believed that the leap from head of field enforcement to head lab assistant (and his only one) would not be that far for him.

"Leonid will help me on this. He has done this before, most recently with Inspector Petrovsky. I believe you met him once. He is especially knowledgeable as we gave him the pills and treatments, and they worked on him—several times. I can confidently say that he was cured, and none of it affected his singing abilities.

"Are you cured now, Leonid, or do you still chase cars?'

"You may have noticed him on the stage recently, dancing and singing right before you were clubbed and knocked out cold. He also has the best baritone voice in our Singing Mutts chorus. He is now going to administer the pills to you: one every four hours for two days. I am going to start with some sleep-tech prior to giving you the pills."

"What? Sleep-tech? Does that mean I am staying here?"

"It's for the best. You will be in no condition to go anyplace for a while. The idea of sleep-tech is to upgrade your "quantitative self" via sleep tracking and data analysis. It sounds flaky, but is simply Drucker's idea of improving things by measuring them first. It should boost your cognition, clarity, productivity, and mental health."

"All these benefits from getting rabies? If I'd known you could straighten out my head, I would have gotten rabies sooner."

"It's all part of the bargain—in Russian health care, we treat your whole measurable self, not just a body that got a bad virus. Or, and you must know this, outside the biggest cities and best clinics, the system treats no part of you at all. "

Sounded fine to me. The two of them worked on me after they had attached wires to my head from a monitoring machine. All very impressive. I've seen these pyrotechnics used for joint pains and thought they were really expensive placebos. Hey, I've been wrong before. Sitting in front of me with his laptop and notepads, Krastov played the role of the good therapist, asking and soliciting personal answers to his questions, which I tried to answer honestly. What did I have to lose? Leonid joined in between questions giving me inoculations and at least one large pill. Soon it became harder to focus on the questions and even harder to think of plausible answers. I must have started dozing off . . .

The pills slowly took effect, and I fell into a delirious state. It felt like the excellent, psychedelic, mescaline trips I had as a college student and later in life. I tried to think about all that but my train of thought became more clouded. Wild dreams kept coming in waves that tasted like mixed honey and lemon. The dreams were really sweet, but I could also taste rotten fruit. Everything around me whirled round and round. Then they became ominous and were more like nightmares. I realized that these people were out to get me—all of them: Petrovsky, Anna, working with Semyon, Andrey, and the rest of the faculty. Krastov was just their venal enforcer. Whenever I said anything, they looked oddly at me and whispered to each other without blinking. I dreamt that everything around Krastov was whirling round. Beautiful carpet patterns came before me in rapid succession. I yelled for them to wait, as I wanted one for the cover of my new book. I felt elated after all, a new book! What was it about? I couldn't remember.

"Leonid," I said, and the voice echoed in my ears. "I remember you were one of the best up there with the Singing Mutts!"

He smiled and looked at Krastov. "Dr. Krylov, we are in the middle of a pestilence here of contamination by stray dog attacks. Traditional control methods for lockdowns and quarantines used in pandemics won't work for dog attacks. Of course, that requires smarter city animal control services. It also required a biological fix of the type we are working on to improve dog species to such a degree that in the future, they will be treated as if they were human lives. As for our people, we need to keep them from getting hardened to the fact that their families and friends have been attacked. We want to prevent them from suffering in silence. We have to keep up the morale of the populace," said Leonid.

"Good way to look at it—health and humanity at stake here. And you are doing a great job, if I might say so," I said. "Your singing makes me happy. I feel buoyant when I hear you. I want to jump and dance, just like all the kids did. Like their pet dogs, they even sang along with you."

"Thanks Nick," said Leonid.

Now I was running, running without feeling the ground under my feet like the boy crossing the field from the window of the Transsib. Now I was giving a talk at an academic conference on something related to city planning. I kept forgetting my essential message, and several in the room started to hiss and laugh at me openly as they looked at each other and rolled their eyes in cruel mockery. They were dressed in academic regalia, some with their school colors as if for a graduation ceremony. The large room with gaudy red curtains was full of well-dressed people. I knew I had no pants on but pulled down hard on my t-shirt to cover up my testicles, which seemed to work at the time. I noticed then that it couldn't cover up my growing erection, which was embarrassing. Their giggling right in front of me was rude and became increasingly annoying to me. I was about to say something by way of reproach when I got the idea to get away from all this nonsense by running uphill to leave both the little town and the academics at the conference.

And when I was too exhausted to run any longer, someone grabbed me by the ear and twisted it. "Who's that?" I said.

"It's me, your wife!" a voice whispered into my ear.

"What wife?" I couldn't place her. Then after some difficulty recalling, I recognized that it was Laurie and said, "I thought you married your well-heeled pretty boy and sailed off to a private island somewhere."

I looked away from Laurie when I spoke, but then noticed that she had the face of a goose. I quickly looked the other way and saw another wife, who also had a goose face. I felt in my pocket for her familiar, perfumed handkerchief to wipe the sweat from my face and found yet another wife in it too. I dreamt another dream that my real wife was not a person at all but some kind of woolen material. Then it must have been sunrise because the light was powerful, and I could feel drenched in sweat.

"I heard you were dying, and I came as quickly as I could," said Laurie, who was standing by my bed looking down at me. Her expression was what I remembered, one of fatigue not empathy. The feeling returned that she had never liked me and simply waited for my demise. This was confirmed by the nervous cackles that accompanied her words.

"You know that when you left me abruptly, and I searched hard to find you here ... heh, heh!" she said. "Now was that very polite?"

"You came all the way to Russia and found me here?"

"Of course. I checked with the department, and they knew exactly where you were. And who is this?"

Anna was standing in the corner and moved forward. "I am Anna Irtenev, one of Nicholas' colleagues at USU."

"I'll bet you are! Heh, heh! Nicholas, I see you've been busy here!" as she looked her over while licking her face over lewdly.

"He and I are colleagues and teach here together," Anna said. "Nick, you can leave this place now, so let's go."

But I was still weak and felt paralyzed by the effects of the treatments and extended bed stay. I felt like a dog that had been hit by a car that couldn't move his legs.

Laurie came closer, put her face near, and threw a fierce grin at me. "You aren't going anywhere!" she hissed.

I knew then that I had to escape this place. It was full of jealousies, dangerous rivalries, and back-stabbings that led from the city to Moscow, from Semyon and Lebedev up to the Kremlin. The nightmares were a warning.

I kept trying to get up, join Anna, and get away from Laurie. I pleaded for help. Then I awoke and saw Krastov's face looking down at me. I was drenched in sweat.

"Welcome back," said Krastov. Leonid was standing right behind him, holding a towel. "You've been out for almost a day!"

They both worked quietly as if I wasn't even there, and I watched them. Leonid was handing him gloves and towels as he glanced at me and then quickly back to his measuring instruments. Whether he was really there or not, I began explaining to him in broken phrases that Inspector Petrovsky's daughter, Vessie, was studying animal cell biology at USU, and he should consider her for an apprenticeship at his lab.

"She likes dogs," I explained in all seriousness, as if that would persuade him.

"Good idea, Nick!" he said. "Since Dmitry was murdered, we need some new blood around here! No pun intended!" Leonid and he laughed loudly all of a sudden. "We need a sharper and better-looking replacement."

For some time, there was no talk, just those two moving about the brightly-lit lab and the sounds of electrical equipment starting and stopping.

"But there really is some unfortunate news," Krastov said to me. "During the melee last week, Fyodor was kidnapped, obviously by people who knew how to handle dogs. They had obviously come to cause a disruption and to steal him."

"I thought you said Fyodor well-protected."

"Not well enough it seems. Both Ivan and Krylovsky were busy being beaten up and coming to the aid of others such as Anna, who were also worked over pretty badly."

"What has been done to find him?" I asked.

"We have a chip in his neck for tracking. Of course, the kidnappers probably know this, which only increases the risk that something could happen to him. Petrovsky is standing by waiting for a ransom offer. But Ivan Kostov and Boris Krylovsky think they know where he is," said Krastov.

"Where?"

"I think you might be surprised!"

19   FINDING FYODOR

The two of them crouched outside the old three-story house out of sight. The outlines of the house and surrounding shrubs were clearly marked out by the moon. They had ended up watching the place thanks to Fyodor's collar chip that had led them there on a tip from Petrovsky. After first casing the surroundings and yard, they heard sounds coming from a basement widow and camped near there to investigate further. Since it was where Krylov lived and Sveta was his landlady, Ivan knew the layout quite well from his visits there. For more than an hour, however, nothing happened.

The French mystery writer Georges Simenon Semyon observed in one of his stories that when you watch fish through a pond of water, they remain absolutely still for a long time. Then for no reason, they twitch a few fins and dart off somewhere else so that they can do more nothing somewhere else. But this place had a bad feel to it. They both felt that sooner or later someone or something was bound to make a stir.

"We're getting good at this. I feel really qualified to hide in bushes, don't you?" whispered Andrey Kostov. "Only we're not just taking pictures this time. The two of them are inside with Fyodor, and we need to flush them out and get him back unharmed."

"So we have to wait, just like last time. We stake the place out," said Boris Krylovsky.

"What a waste! I don't understand why people can't follow the rules, and we could avoid all this. They must know that there will be severe consequences, maybe even jail time."

"What have you been smoking? Even our fairy tales here aren't that naïve!" said Krylovsky. "Have you been chewing peyote again?

Remember where we are—Russia, it's called. I see that you enjoy playing the rational man beset by the contradictions of laws and weak institutions. Who doesn't? It's an Olympian abstraction and keeps you
above it all. I wonder what you actually learn about real conflicts between people in your city planning studies? Are you still naïve enough
to think that states make decrees that simply command order and that
perfectly obedient behavior mechanically follows?"

"Not at all. We learn that ill-designed policies and clogged hierarchies prevent people from exchanging their entitlements."

"What abstract shit! You're not seriously telling me that officials
around here set things up for themselves and are corrupt, are you?
I would never have known that! Isn't that just telling me in more
multi-syllabic, abstract terms what I already know? What are entitlements, by the way, while we have a moment here?"

"Like having to exchange decent food for clean water."

"Could be. But it all sounds pretty abstract to me, like something
from an introductory politics course. Most people like me are torn between incompatible aims. Like trying to do this job now while avoiding getting us both killed. To do that I rely on instinct and experience
not some crap about hierarchies. See what I mean?"

"You're right, of course. But it is nice to remain above it all and avoid
getting my hands dirty. Complexity and multi-syllabic technical jargon
help with all that and impress the laymen. Ask any lawyer." said Ivan.

"I'm the one who should do the hands-off abstractions to deal
with my animal rights crazies! You've just come from one of our typical
wild-west meetings, and earlier we filmed a murder and waste being
dumped into the river to contaminate water supplies. And you wonder
why people don't obey the laws? Christ! Why not start with money,
power, and fear of reprisal, tribal loyalties, or maybe even a hopeless
cause like animal welfare? Think those are rational incentives? Maybe if
we live through all this, we can write an article on it!"

"What I really meant was why don't people learn?"

"Now that's a different problem. It has to do with the illusion of being smarter than the authorities—hubris. I won't get caught this time."

"But they always do . . . "

"Mostly, but it takes time, and you can enjoy the fruits of your ill-gotten gains for the short term at least. Think of it. A villa in Monte Carlo with a new Ferrari and some lusty women for diversion! We could have a hell of a time for a few years. The problem is we all get caught sometime, and because of hubris we plan improvements and work-arounds of our opponents next time. Quite futile really. To prove my point—we often find that our opponents here are part of our original group of animal rights activists. They splintered into lots of tribes loyal to their new leaders. I expect that things are so rational in your academic department at USU that all this rough and tumble must surprise you."

Andrey laughed hard at that one. "You must be kidding! It's a snake pit!"

Sudden gusts of wind came up, drowning out any voices coming from the house. They continued their intense exchange of professional gripes.

"I've heard you complain about the impractical USU bureaucracy and its lax controls on animal experiments," said Ivan. "The controls are needed to prevent Dr. Moreau types from cloning themselves over there. And USU's protocols and requirements for scientific experiments are rigorous and time-consuming. I know: I work there. You read Russian literature, so you must know from Bulgakov that even Dr. Persikov wanted those controls placed on people like himself to prevent scientific adventurism. Nobody wants to hurt dogs, but some of them are really vicious and would have to be put down anyway. The aim is to reduce strays and health problems like rabies and see what we can do about advancing the evolution of some dogs. So we left USU and moved off campus to Dr. Krastov's lab to get away from the bureaucrats; so far, it's worked."

"Ok, Ok . . . But your problems are really all institutional," said Krylovsky. "Just fill out the right forms, follow the process, and pres-to—a solution! You have to face varieties of officials that are mostly reflexively trained to say 'no' because that's all their job descriptions allow. They have petty, small-minded characters to perform this repetitive game. My problems require dealing with political advocates who play turf, ego, and power games full time. They are mostly loudmouth extremists, who all claim they care about protecting the lives of rats and other vermin as much as humans. What shit! Many of these groups are led by corrupt, ideologically confused, and incompetent people who believe they are idealists because they are loud and have people who follow them along. One group actually believes that strays are the returned ghosts of dogs sent into space that died up there! Now they want them preserved not controlled. Many of them are really quite stupid, and I get tired of listening to them. Nevertheless, my role has been to try and keep all the animal rights factions in line. At USU, you would call it a 'management role.'"

"I see your point. I couldn't deal with people like that!"

Without warning, a car drove up silently and parked nearby. From inside, Leo reacted first with a few loud growls. Fyodor knew what it was, but kept his snout shut. But the rest of the neighborhood canine chorus came to life, barking and howling.

Andrey could hear them all talking in loud whispers. "All right, let's get this over with, Pyotr. We can't waste any more time on this dog, celebrity or not."

"Right, chief. But if we screw this up, the Kremlin will let us know about it. They have their funny ways . . . We'll be lucky to end up cleaning out cages for Dr. Krastov," said Pyotr Kolokolov, the young sergeant who had accompanied Petrovsky.

"Never mind that," said Petrovsky. "Focus on what we're doing here. Let's move in closer and see what's going on. Get around back and watch any escape routes you can find."

Petrovsky had been dealing with hardened criminals for years, and he knew most of their habits. To figure out what they would do this time, he liked the challenge of entering new worlds that had been shaken up by some novel event. It was like predicting moves in a game, or working out a puzzle in advance. The events worked independently of him, and he had to keep up, to try not to be overtaken by them. Then he would attempt to enter that world as a stranger, an enemy, but also someone who wanted to learn from people's reactions to him. Any of them could be guilty, complicit, or simply playing with him. In this new world, he would investigate people who were mostly hostile to him to try and dig up clues and solve the crimes. That was his new world. His mandate now was to protect a celebrity dog that had already been kidnapped, and this threw a spanner in his plans. In the case before him, he had to deal with interacting dogs and people—a talking dog, a regular dog, a weird jealous woman, and her accomplice, who was probably a low level opportunist out for some quick cash.

All this was clearly more intriguing than the routine cops and robbers of his daily life. As a career cop, he had a deep prejudice against political investigation. But his problem was that in Russia everything was political, involving questions of who got what and who shouldn't be getting it. Once you started down the political path, the trails led in many directions, most of them dangerous and out of his jurisdiction or remit. But saving a human-like dog that could walk upright, talk, and was favored by the Kremlin—that was a new one for him. The powers that be swirled around him in all directions on this one. But he claimed that Fyodor's plight was in his remit as a Yekaterinburg cop, so he threw himself enthusiastically at the problem. Look at the characters that had already turned up! They could all be in a B movie.

Nearby, at the side of the house, Pyotr and Simon Petrovsky spotted Andrey Kostov and Boris Krylovsky, who acknowledged their arrival with visible waves. Pyotr took off around back to watch the escape routes; Petrovsky signaled to them.

"Wait a minute. Look over there . . . someone just came out of the house," said Petrovsky, over his cell phone.

Then they heard the sound of a bell ringing. It was like bell used in manor homes to call for dinner. But this wasn't a summons to dinner. Sveta stood some distance from them and appeared to be ringing a bell. She was waving a small candle-lit lantern around, creating a surreal effect.

"A curse on all of you!" she bawled. "Get away from here! I knew you were coming from my dream last night. You will not be successful in attempting to impede us from our purpose."

"Who is this nut, Krylovsky? Is she one of yours?" asked Andrey.

"More likely, just a camp-follower, trying to make money by kidnapping a celebrity dog. As for the curses, I read once that the Ottomans brought along pronouncers of curses to eliminate obstacles in front of their glorious troops moving around the empire to conquer and reconquer subject peoples."

"What's that got to do with her? Should we have brought a curse-giver as well?" asked Andrey.

"Don't know. What's her story? Why is she into curses?" asked Krylovsky.

"She's Nick's landlady, and apparently has a wild, jealous streak in her. We'll find out the details very soon."

"She's going back in! Must be thinking that her antics got rid of us . . . thinks the evil spirits worked."

They moved closer and heard more shouting and chaotic voices inside the house.

"Calm down, Sveta; you're scaring Leo and putting us all in danger."

"Shut up, Grigor! What do you know about danger? I've lived with perils for years, first with Semyon, who rejected me, and now with Krylov who ignores me."

"That's not true, Sveta. I've talked with Nicholas, and he adores you. He just has other interests right now. I'm sure you two can talk it out," said Fyodor from the corner where he and Leo lay on the floor.

Sveta contorted her face into a grimace and screamed insults at him.

"Shut up, you stupid dog," she hissed.

At this, Leo started howling, and a chorus of bellowing, barking, and screaming penetrated the air.

"What the hell is going on in there?" said Krylovsky.

"It's how a spurned woman reacts when cornered. We have to make sure she doesn't take it out on Fyodor," said Petrovsky.

Then they heard: "We need to silence this dog!" said Grigor. "He's upsetting all of us. He's going to get us caught."

"Please, Grigor, I'm simply telling you the facts. Leo is upset not because of me, but because he senses we have visitors. It's ok, Leo. Here, have a treat and lie down. Let me tell you how difficult my life was when I was a stray puppy running around the mean streets of this town."

"I said, 'be quiet, Fyodor,'" snapped Sveta.

The subterfuge fell flat. Petrovsky rolled his eyes and made a face that could speak volumes.

"Don't try and get sympathy from me. I'm a stray now, just like you were," said Fyodor.

"Come on, Sveta; we've heard all this," said Grigor.

"You haven't heard anything yet. And what do you know? You're nothing but an animal rights groupie, a reject who doesn't even like dogs."

"Hear that, Krylovsky?" said Ivan. "Whoever Grigor is, he is one of yours after all!"

"I've tried to survive in a cruel world of untrustworthy, fickle men. I've been Semyon's mistress for three years and look what I've ended up with." Here she waved her arms around, pointing to the useless and hideous ornaments in her rented flat in the house. "He won't even talk to me. Here, I'll prove it to you."

She whipped out her cell and dialed Semyon's private number.

"Semyon? Hello, Semyon? You're there. Speak to me!"

"What? You have your nerve! I served your every need for years. You can't just pitch me aside like an old dog. I even took Fyodor for your benefit, and now I'm stuck with two dogs to feed."

"What? Of course, I did it for the benefit of canine freedom not to be cloned and modified. But I did it for you, you bastard! You can't throw me under the tram," she hissed. "You forget that I know your superiors in the Kremlin!"

"You're wrong there, Semyon. You need to get real. The police aren't going to touch me. Putin and his FSB are not going to let anything happen to me."

"Ok then. Come and talk to me. I am waiting right here for you. No, I can't call Nicholas. He is getting rabies treatments from Dr. Krastov and has other things on his mind—like survival. Now you listen to me. We have Fyodor here and are going to kill him unless you give me some cash and make amends for your bad behavior. I won't stand for this anymore. That's right, I'm waiting here for you at the flat."

Leo was lying on the floor, trying to understand the harsh tones and shouts from this badly-scripted soap opera. The vibes were all bad, and he felt them. He carefully eyed Grigor and emitted a low, suspicious growl. Over in the corner chair, Fyodor glanced at both of them occasionally, trying unsuccessfully to show that he was not nervous.

"Leo, it's ok. You'll get your walk soon. Here, have a treat!" as he flipped him a small biscuit from his vest pocket.

Fyodor was following Grigor's increasingly agitated moves. His face and eyebrows twitched uncontrollably. His eyes darted around suspiciously, first at Sveta, then each of the dogs. He was confused and appeared ready to do something rash. Sweat beads covered his forehead. Now his eyes flashed hatred, and he clenched his large-knuckled fists as he spoke.

"This dog has wasted enough of our time. It's time we cashed in on him," he muttered and scowled stupidly at Fyodor.

"Be reasonable, Grigor. If you do what I tell you, you can all cash in. If you persist in this irrational, instant gratification type behavior, you will end up in prison or worse. And how exactly will you cash in on me if I'm dead?"

"Shut up!" he hissed. "We'll see who ends up worse, you half-breed cur!"

"All right, Pyotr. We've heard enough. Let's go in. Watch the back entrances and windows."

"I thought we were going to try the pretext first."

"What pretext?"

"We would post as tax adjusters and gain entry to measure the place for a random assessment and in the meantime survey the surroundings for the eventual raid."

"You've been watching too many afternoon crimys on TV. We have no time for histrionics or theoretical nonsense from police manuals. It's night time, and Fyodor is at risk. Even these people couldn't be so stupid as to believe that ploy. Everyone knows that few people pay taxes here, and those that do negotiate deals rather than rely on objective assessments. Sharpen up, Pyotr Kolokolov!"

"Sorry, Chief. Wait now... Here they come," Pyotr yelled into his cellphone.

The back door smashed open, displaying the large, burly figure of Grigor. He yelped in pain as a large dog in the form of Fyodor was attached to his arm. Still he ran forward, running with the dog, now attached to his leg, hitting Pyotr and knocking him flat. The dog took a few more chews of Boris as he ran by and finally let him go. Petrovsky followed all this easily, and as the man ran at him, he aimed his stun gun and fired.

Down went Grigor, howling in pain. His body shuddered a few times, then suddenly relaxed as he passed out from the drugged dart.

"Works well on dogs. Why not on humans?" said Petrovsky to Ivan, who had now joined him.

"It certainly does," said Fyodor. "That was a good outing. Reminded me that I can still be a real dog!"

"You can growl and spring with the best of them!" said Krylovsky, patting Fyodor and dusting off his frock coat. "I thought that canine aggression was bred out of you somehow."

"Ah, you've been reading too many sci-fi novels. I get real mad at cruelty inflicted by humans on each other and on animals. I will attack any of them with the best tools I have—my fangs and claws."

"Good work! We have a job for you with the police anytime."

"Not likely. My nature is still to love, to try and form special relationships with people or other creatures that I meet and others that treated me well early on," he explained. "Did you know that some of my best friends early on in my puppy days were the silver foxes and cats?"

"Why?"

"Because they accepted me into their packs just as many humans rejected me."

"So you trust those who trusted and cared for you early on?" said Andrey.

"That's right, and it worked both ways. Remember I was discarded by some family and became a free-roaming, hunter-gatherer, stray street dog. I was doomed for the pound and maybe the death cages until the doctor caught me—mostly by chance."

"And you trust him?" asked Andrey.

"Now I do. It took me a while to trust anyone after how I was treated. Most strays would tell you this if they could talk like me."

"And you hold no grudges? Most people would, then blame their deprived upbringing for their lives of crime."

"And they have a point. If they were 'rescued' like me before it was too late, they can probably return to their loving and trusting cores. Beyond some point, it is hard for most dogs or people to trust anymore."

"So, you can growl and spring like old times, but return to normal after the fight is over?"

"I have to remember how to set my teeth properly, drool a bit, and growl like a regular dog. I don't like to be irrational or aggressive. But you humans bring out the worst in us!"

"I've been meaning to ask you. With all this inside you, what do you dream about? I noticed you last week at the lab in your mock cage. You were snoring loudly, so I came over to have a look. Your eyes were rolling around and your paws were moving as if you were chasing something. You were in what is called REM or rapid eye movement sleep, which is when you dream. So what were you dreaming?" asked Ivan.

"Interesting that you noticed. I think in these dreams I am not chasing; I am running away from someone or something. But I couldn't tell you what. Maybe I'll find out someday and tell you."

20   THE KREMLIN SNAKE PIT

It was the late night shift at the central Yekaterinburg police station. With so many inert bodies pressed together in the pre-interrogation lobby for hours waiting their turns, the growing smell of body odor, damp clothes, and bad breath permeated the place and made it hard to breathe. As we noted before about this place, those marooned in the police station just sat there quietly. All the windows were still shut at 2 a.m. even though it was still hot outside, and this made it all worse. Some slept with their mouths open, drooling onto their shirts. Loud snores could be heard all over. There had to be fifty people in there, some wearing long beards, looking as if they had been waiting for years for their affidavits, permits, claims, or summons to be heard by some official. Few were ever approved, denied on minor technicalities to keep the state apparatchiks employed. It was a scene right out of Kafka where a basement full of people in a similar kind of place hopelessly awaited "justice"!

Into the room they came: Sveta and Grigor walked ahead of Petrovsky and Pyotr as Fyodor followed them. Petrovsky registered the sudden shock on the faces of those awaiting various kinds of judicial actions at seeing a walking dog, dressed in a plaid frock coat walk through the room. It was the best laugh he had had in weeks!

"Coming through!" he shouted. "Make way! Look at these people, Pyotr!" said Petrovsky. "Have you ever seen the lobby so alert this time of night?"

Typically, the suspects filed by, heads held down in shame, maybe even covered up with bags or sacks in case the media was taking pictures. The claimants would watch the nightly parade of their peers in bland silence. But tonight, the strutting, shaggy dog wearing a vest brought them to life.

Filing into a nearby interrogation room, one of Petrovsky's favorites because it had ventilation, the five of them sat across from a recorder. This time he had decided to interrogate both of them at once and have Fyodor sit in. Krastov had also been called in and would soon pick up Fyodor and get him back to safety. Meanwhile, Petrovsky stated the date and time for the record and pushed a button on a recorder to get the meeting going.

"Right now, I want to know what transpired and what your motives were. So I will ask Fyodor to lead off since you held him hostage there."

"You mean he held us hostage!" said Sveta. "Grigor and I had to listen to him prattle on for more than a day!"

"That could be. But how did he end up in your place then?" asked Pyotr. "You could have released him at any time. Isn't that so, Fyodor?"

"They first tried to overpower me at the recent animal rights meeting. But they failed and later took me from Dr. Krastov's lab to the house with a bag over my head. I was ready to get away from there anytime. A few days ago, Sveta came to Krastov's facility and told someone there that she had come to take me for a walk. Dr. Krastov and the crews were out on stray dog control missions. She told him that Semyon authorized it, and that Krastov knew all about it. That set off all kinds of alarms as we have to deal with loonies all the time at the lab."

Now Sveta became sly and detached. Petrovsky had noticed her peculiar mood changes before. He listened to her as she shifted from a weak, quiet voice to talking in a bold taunting way. But now she simply shrugged and looked at Pyotr and him with an aggressive smirk.

"They were both lies, weren't they? You simply tried to snatch him from the lab," said Petrovsky, looking directly at her.

"Of course, but the lab worker didn't catch it until I was out the door and in the hands of Grigor here, who threw a bag over my head and shot me with tranquilizer fluids that he brought with him for the kidnapping."

Petrovsky turned off the tape recorder. There would be plenty of time to take statements in writing and to get signatures. At this stage, he liked to be on his own with suspects, and he motioned for the others to leave. He nudged a packet of cigarettes towards Sveta and Boris.

"Why did you do all this, Sveta? You have never had any problems with the police before? You have no record."

She glared at Petrovsky. Then all at once she dropped her gaze and swallowed. "I was tired of being used."

"By whom?"

"By Nicholas Krylov and Semyon Irtenev."

"Krylov?" Petrovsky frowned and flashed a knowing grin at Pyotr. "You were his landlord. He walked your dog, Leo, regularly. He was only there in your house for the summer. You're not making any sense … I don't get it. What was your gripe with him?"

"I was being ignored by both of them and being put on the scrap heap. Hasn't that ever happened to you?" she said with heavy tears of self-pity around her eyes.

"Was it your idea to kidnap Fyodor? What for? Was all this simply to feed your wounded ego and get noticed by two imagined lovers? Sounds childish and reckless to me! Or were you put up to this by someone?"

"So, it's your idea, wasn't it, Grigor?" asked Pyotr. Grigor threw him a resentful look of suppressed violence. He gritted his teeth and tightened his jaw muscles. "The law says we can keep you here until you tell us what we want to know. We still do temporary detentions without charges in Russia. 'Temporary' can mean months, maybe years. That works for us, but can be unfortunate for people like you."

"Ok, I've heard enough, and it's late—or early," said Petrovsky. "I'm holding you two until we get some straight answers. Fyodor, come with us. Dr. Krastov or one of his assistants will be here to take you back to the facility. Unless you object, Sveta, I will instruct my daughter, Vesselka, to feed Leo as you are going to be here for a while."

She looked around, confused as if in a daze, a bad dream. She looked down at her lap in resentful silence and shrugged.

The next morning Petrovsky met up with Andrey and Anna at the Hungry Wolf near USU campus. It was nice to get out of the depressing regularity and smells of police headquarters. Meetings like these allowed him to recall that there was actually a world outside where people went actual places—not just to courts or prisons. He arrived there first and sat in a wooden booth near the back and waited for them. He absorbed the nice, homey feel that the Wolf had to it, with flags from universities around the world displayed around the interior. None of that really meant anything to him, as he hadn't been to university. But he liked the place. There were antlers from deer and elk, a few phony pelts from foxes and wolves, all slapped onto the dark paneled wood walls, which were covered with the rough odor from years of tobacco smoke. He was told by his younger officers that especially at night the atmosphere changed and was laced with the shrill, spellbinding tunes of a Roma musician's *zurna* pipe, accompanied by the quick beat of a large drum. He had also heard that the breakfasts were hearty. He mostly ate on the run, in police cars and during stakeouts or just in his office alone. But seeing the menu here, he looked forward to tasting some of the local breads and egg dishes. It was like visiting a foreign land!

He waved when he saw them enter, and Anna and Andrey sat down with him.

"We bring you greetings from Nicholas, who seems to have fully recovered from rabies, at least, and will be in touch shortly. Whatever treatment Dr. Krastov gave him, it worked. Unfortunately, Krastov could do little about his extensive bruises and sprained body parts."

"Can he still talk or is he into barking now?" asked Petrovsky.

"Around USU, we all bark. You make fewer enemies that way. And, this morning is on us, that is the department."

With that, they all ordered full breakfasts and dug in. "We'll have to do this more often," said Petrovsky.

"Probably not," said Ivan, as he was a regular customer of the Wolf.

"Let me fill you in on where we are and ask you about some missing pieces. Ivan, you know a lot about the raid on Sveta's place because you were there with Krylovsky."

"My hunch is she had the hots for Nicholas, but he clearly had other interests. He probably had no idea that she was after him," he said, winking at Anna who blushed slightly. "Sveta entrusted him with Leo for daily walks with the hope that activity would somehow bond them and could lead to further possibilities."

"But he hardly noticed any of this," said Andrey. "Obviously, he had his work at USU and grew interested in Anna."

"And what of Grigor? Where did he come from?"

"Where do most people like that come from? The sewer has plenty of them on offer. Meanwhile, there's Semyon. And that's where it gets unclear," said Petrovsky. "Somehow there's a link between him and low-level operatives like Cyclops and Boris. That's why we put both of them in the same cell. There is probably someone higher up that needs to use these types for their thuggery, such as Semyon, who recruited Grigor to work with Sveta. Whether she thought of the kidnapping, or whether it was Semyon and Grigor, doesn't really matter. They bungled a dumb operation from the start and are now in deep shit from those much higher up in the Kremlin because of their overt support for Dr. Krastov's work and specifically for dogs like Fyodor."

"Sounds about right," said Anna.

Krastov and Fyodor had just arrived back from the police station and entered the Animal Control facility when outside a car drove up, and two men got out. Suddenly, there was a violent commotion as the two began firing AK-47s at the building. Doors banged, and windows shattered, with glass fragments falling to the pavement and inside on the laboratory. Krastov dove to the floor and cradled Fyodor under him for protection. As some of the crew were on duty between shifts, they grabbed weapons from the cabinet and fired back out the windows. But it was too late as the men jumped into their car and sped off.

———

Sitting in his office at the police station, Petrovsky's cell rang. It was Pyotr.

"Bad news, Chief," he said. "Krastov and Fyodor hardly got back from here when their facility was attacked by more thugs using explosives and guns."

"Anyone hurt?"

"Doesn't sound like it. I spoke with Krastov, who said his crew was there and fought them off. But none of the attackers were captured, and they escaped in what may have been a van."

"All right, we have to give them armed protection around the clock now. I think we know where they went. I want you to come with me to Semyon's, and then we will pay a visit to them at the facility. Pick me up here at the Wolf in 20 minutes."

"More problems . . . Cyclops escaped from custody last night. He apparently had someone give him a uniform, and he slipped out. We lost him. Sorry."

"What stupidity! Are we really that bad? The force is run like a comedy police routine. We need to check the backgrounds of his supposed guards. But Cyclops' escape may mean that he may not be as low-level as we had thought. It looks like we let him get out using an old comic book trick. We should be proud that at least he didn't receive a file in a cake! All right, get over here as fast as you can."

"There was an attack on Krastov and Fyodor at the facility," Petrovsky told the others. "Nobody was hurt. But Anna, can you fill me in on Semyon's political links briefly before I head out? I should tell you that Cyclops got out and is on the run. Call Krylov and alert him as those two have developed an especially nasty relationship in his short time here. Also, I know this is delicately complex as well as risky, so I gather you don't want to accompany us!"

"No thanks! I don't mind risks, but I don't want to see him anytime soon. Still, I can tell you something about my husband's political ties.

"We have a hunch that this time, it's not Semyon or Sveta's people behind this. Nor is it one of Krylovsky's rival animal rights factions. Those are all too obvious and simplistic explanations. Something else is going on here."

"Something is always going on behind or above the scene in Russia," said Andrey.

"And we need to find out the primary cause starting from the bottom."

"Andrey—get Krylov over here if you can. I want him to accompany us to Semyon's."

"Is he in any shape for this kind of adventure?" asked Andrey.

"Maybe not, but at least he should be along. He can wait in the car if he wants."

"I'd like to blame it all on Semyon," said Anna. "But people like him are just flies in the larger spider webs of influence spun by the Kremlin. They may even be in webs outside the Kremlin's scope, but still driven by the need for power and recognition of the Moscow regime. So, my hunch is it's a gang rival to Putin himself. It might even be a faction within Putin's party United Russia that has been fragmenting lately, despite the glitz of Olympic and World Cup games on the world stage. Those events haven't made a difference to the lives of any working people here."

"Yes, Anna, interesting sociology of power musings, but what does any of this have to do with Fyodor's kidnapping?"

"My hunch is that Semyon already had fallen from grace thanks to several of his own dumb, greedy moves. Rivals have taken him out of the game. It doesn't make any sense that he would have anything to do with another attempt on Fyodor's life or Krastov's work. Even if he had wanted to, it would be too hard to arrange this quickly. He has few resources left to call on—if Cyclops worked for him, you already had him in custody. He wouldn't seek petty revenge that fast on a scientist and his prize dog. He also must have known that Krastov keeps a pretty tough crew on hand that doesn't mind violence at all. Grigor? He's hardly a prototype of the clever criminal—just another common street thug. No, Semyon's ouster from the top deliberately created a vacuum for leadership in the Yekaterinburg area. My theory is that now Damir Lebedev's faction wants to enter the picture and show it can fill the power vacuum—kidnapping Fyodor was a show of force."

"Who is Damir Lebedev?" asked Ivan.

"Lebedev has been a Semyon colleague for some time and a regular customer at the trough of public contract funds for his city construction works. Semyon arranges the bids and approves them. He is frequently invited to dinner parties at his house. Nicholas and I were at one of these gatherings together when he first came here from Bonaduz

College. He is well known as a powerful construction magnate that relies on contracts from the city and province. This is where Semyon has been of most use to him. But now, he can no longer provide such vital access, and my guess is that Lebedev made a deft move to disrupt things with the attack on Krastov and Fyodor. In my view, Damir engineered Semyon's ouster in the first place, and now he wants command of a rival gang in Putin's inner circle."

"Wow! All that's far above my pay grade. More importantly, it all sounds overly-complicated and pretty stupid to me," said Petrovsky. "That would mean Lebedev and his minions were directly confronting those who support Putin's pet projects such as the Fyodor experiments with Krastov. Lebedev may know city public works contracts, but through such rash actions he would be missing the big picture. Surely he knows that there is a bigger picture and that any grand moves like filling power vacuums would be very high risk. The Kremlin is ruthless and all-powerful. If Putin is replaced by some rival faction, the power structure still remains, and someone from his carefully cloned Moscow clique would simply replace him. No rival faction could intrude on this inner circle."

"I agree," said Andrey. "He would be making the same mistake that Semyon did."

"Ok, I'm getting a headache from all this. Thanks for your thoughts and for an excellent breakfast. I think we better get going and visit our friend Semyon. I'll let you all know if we learn anything new."

———

As described before, the road up to Leninskiy rayon wound its way up into the hills above Yekaterinburg through the thick forests. Pyotr knew the area, so Petrovsky let him drive on. They had picked up Krylov on the way, so the three of them had piled into the car and headed out of town.

"You ok, Nick? You seem a bit slower today than your usual self," asked Petrovsky, as he watched him move around the car.

"I'll be ok. Just a bit weak from getting Dr. Krastov's wonder pills and being shot with various anesthetics. I'm not 100 percent but close enough."

"Slow down, Pyotr. Let's make sure we get there in one piece. Remember this is a Lada police car and not a Ferrari," said Petrovsky.

"My grandfather had a dacha up here, so I know the way. My family used to take us up here, but that was when I was four or five years old," said Pyotr

"That's interesting, but maybe the roads have gotten worse since then so slow down. How did someone like you end up doing police work? Didn't you want to go to USU like others your age? Just a minute . . . I'm calling HQ to let them know we may need back-up. You did bring your weapon?"

"Of course, right here," he patted his side. "I liked outdoor sports—hunting and skiing, and didn't want to end up behind a desk. I got into USU and studied biology for a few years and dropped out. I can always go back if this doesn't work out. But I like interacting with different kinds of people, learning, engaging in a chase, investigating crimes. I've always liked a good rush. Desk jobs and labs usually don't provide that."

"I hope you stick around. We need bright, young recruits to give the force credibility. With well-known and acceptable corruption at high levels of this regime, we consider our little police force a bulwark against the rot."

Pyotr exuded the quiet confidence of an athlete, which fit his build. He was about 180 lbs. and wore a trimmed beard. He smiled as he spoke which added to his charm and elegance.

"I play amateur hockey in a club here. We were district champions last year, which was nothing special since there are 29 districts. But it is a tough league, and some of the players have gone on to national fame and even international stature on teams in Europe and the NHL in North America."

"Your surname is Kolokolov. Why is that familiar to me?"

"My grandfather was a crime boss here in the 1990s when Yekaterinburg was called the 'Chicago of the Urals.' He ran some of the local drug and prostitution rings."

"I remember him now—I had just joined the force. He was a king pin, and no one could nail anything on him. He was a famous Mafioso type around here. Did he ever get into dog-napping?"

"There weren't any famous dogs then. But there were plenty of valuable ones, overbred poodles and the like. Interesting question . . . Maybe some of his ex-associates are linked to these people here."

"No, probably not."

"I had to escape from these people and forge my own path. They all were headed nowhere except maybe to jail or wearing cement jackets in the river. My brother is a graffiti artist and runs the local festival here each year."

"I've heard of him too. I believe Andrei is his name, isn't it? He's quite famous in the art world. My daughter, Vesselka, always points out to me what he is doing. Not my thing . . . Modern art makes no sense to me, but she and her friends like it. I believe he is in the news as he frequently runs afoul of the Church and devout types who claim his artwork is blasphemous, isn't that correct? Sometimes Andrei's people even call on us for protection at their festivals!"

"He likes to stir up trouble because he thinks it sells his art."

"How so?"

"It's easy. Since the Putin regime plays up the spiritual foundation of its defense of 'traditional Russian values' against the decadent West from the church, Andrei and his people have run afoul of Putin too. He gets more good publicity, but it's very dangerous. I've had to steer a path between both wings of subversives in my family—criminals and artists."

"That's the interesting thing about local police work. We run across all types. You recall the local religious fanatic that drove his car, laden with gas canisters, into the local cinema showing 'Mathilde'?"

"Not really."

"It was about the love affair between a ballerina and the Tsar Nicholas II, who was murdered here along with his family. In the film, he was made an orthodox saint so you have to be careful now even of non-political movie content. It could turn into a mass murder."

"I do like outings like this where I get to meet interesting characters," said Pyotr.

"Well, you may just meet some of your old family friends and their enemies very soon. And you, Nicholas, we got word that your friend Cyclops escaped from custody last night. Be on your guard as he and his pals may still want to have a chat with you," said Petrovsky.

"Heartening news," he said from the back seat. "Nice to have close colleagues inside and outside the university."

"You back in shape after your ordeal with rabies, Nick? You were out for a few weeks and have been a bit quiet this morning," asked Pyotr.

"I'm fine. Dr. Krastov knows his stuff. In the freak medicine category, he'd give Dr. Frankenstein a run for his money."

After navigating a few more curves up the mountain, Pyotr Kolokolov slowed the car, and they turned into the drive with a large iron gate designed to keep out intruders. Hinting of neglect, the driveway was covered with torn branches and limbs from many wind-driven rainstorms. He found a box containing a speakerphone by the entrance, which he put to use and announced their arrival. Then they waited. What should they do if everyone had cleared out and no one lived here anymore? Suddenly, the gates opened slowly, allowing them into what was left of the magically gated kingdom of the Irtenevs.

They were shown in by an elderly servant and told to wait in the sitting room. Nick remembered Anton from his arrival dinner visit here months ago. He was a general dog body—gardener, servant, waiter, and caretaker. He was the kind of old-fashioned servant who had been around for years watching the family fortunes decline, but stayed on out of loyalty. While waiting, they surveyed the wood paneling and tasteful artwork adorning the walls. Petrovsky compared how a mid to higher level provincial official and councilman lived with his own life. It really was quite deflating. A while later, when they got used to the place being abandoned, Semyon suddenly materialized out of the woodwork and surprised all them. He came in silently, wearing an embroidered blue silk smoking robe, unshaven, and evidently recovering from an evening of heavy drinking by himself. It was a theatrical entrance right out of a bad murder at the manor horror film.

"Good morning, gentlemen," he said indifferently as if expecting them. "Can we get you some coffee or a bite to eat? Something a bit stronger perhaps to start your day properly?"

"No thanks, we just ate. Thank you for coming out to see us. We won't take up your time, but wanted to clear a few things up related to an event, which just happened in town. You may know some of the participants."

"Always glad to help our municipal colleagues in their work," he said in his best effort to be the bored host, still attempting to exude authority through indifferent, flat responses.

"Do the names Sveta or Grigor mean anything to you? It might interest you that they just tried to kidnap Fyodor, Dr. Krastov's special dog, and hold him for ransom. Any idea why these people might want to do that, and who could have put them up to it?"

Semyon stared at all of us calmly, as if reflecting on how focused his answer should be for the occasion. I noticed that his face shuddered slightly with small twitches. Then, he said, "Of course, Sveta, I've heard is Nicholas Krylov's landlady. He told me that himself. "Grigor could be anyone," he said, waving this thought away like an annoying mosquito. "I know you have the odd-looking thug known as 'Cyclops' in your custody. Ask him. But why they would try and steal a celebrity dog just after my public downfall is anyone's conjecture. It certainly has nothing to do with me. I've got other problems."

"Cyclops did a runner on us from the cell. We lost him, and he may be headed this way. Think that's possible?"

"Haven't seen him. You'd be the first to know," he said sarcastically.

"I'm sure. But back to our problem, which also might be yours. Is it possible that someone you know, someone that could easily profit from your current predicament might have put these people up to the kidnapping and later the attacks on Krastov?" Petrovsky asked.

"Snakes often slither in different patterns and strike very quickly when one of them is killed or injured."

"Any snake in particular?"

He took a swig of the drink in front of him. No mere coffee for this man. Anton had either given him schnapps or white wine, presumably from a standing instruction for his morning jolt. It all hinted at his current state of deterioration; his eyes were glassy and moved around slowly, unable to focus. Petrovsky had met Semyon before and recalled a keen, clever, flamboyant, rather pompous type who enjoyed being in charge. He had been confidently bombastic with his expansive recollections that held the attention of the entire dinner table with his guests. It seemed there were two Semyons: one talked loudly and puffed out his chest in an endless theatrical display. That role worked well at public gatherings. Then there was the other Semyon, who would suddenly forget to control his return to the quiet, shy, awkward self with its vacant stare. He surmised some of this reaction was due to his wife, Anna's, absence and the fact that he was living in a large, empty house alone with no plans other than to somehow avoid the coming abyss. It was also an insight into how quickly the effects of professional failure destroyed confidence and could mangle up one's character into nothingness.

All this was a special problem for people like Semyon, whose skills were box-checking, paper-pushing, and scheming new maneuvers for power within a governmental structure in which power emanated in all directions from the Kremlin and diffused itself among thousands of officials at the center and lower provincial levels. After all, he had lived in this closed petty world for years. Like being among scorpions in a bottle, he had populated a closed arena in which officials fought it out for the perks of power with no fear of accountability to the public. Like many others cocooned in the Russian state, his career depended on the vicissitudes of personality and the whim of higher officials and those at his level. At least local government officials had their own base and, at that level, people like Krastov and Petrovsky could actually exercise some technical skill to deliver services that would make a difference to people's lives. They usually didn't, but they did have the authority.

Officials at that level had to venture outside of their offices and actually face local residents. Different altogether from the massive government cathedrals in Moscow that only the elect could enter and from which they could expect nothing but a permit or license, usually in exchange for a bribe. Few saw any of these officials ever leave their cathedrals, and no one noticed anyway.

"How about your colleague Damir Lebedev?" said Pyotr. "Does he still visit?"

"Are all these questions because they have you investigating dognapping now?" he asked with a smirk. Now his confident side seemed to be returning.

"It might look like that to an outsider, but not to a knowing insider like yourself, Irtenev. Even this little dog problem has national significance now with the World Cup Games. Following the Kremlin script, we even had to take the Chechen terror angle to justify our investigations because that sells well in Moscow. We alerted several officials at the provincial level, and now I even have a few men guarding military and government installations to make it all look like security has returned. They drive around in trucks and tanks for the media to take pictures of them in heavy fatigues with guns pointed here and there. Muscular histrionics like these allow us to work without interference from higher officials. But there are really rogue elements here, and we want to know who they are."

"You would have to talk with Damir yourself."

"I knew you would help. There is one more item. Just after we nailed Sveta and Boris, and rescued Fyodor, Dr. Krastov and Fyodor were attacked at the local animal control facility."

"Come on. Do you really think I'm that stupid? I'm temporarily out of the power game at present, as you must have heard. I'm on injured reserve, but there are plenty of others who will take my place."

"Such as Lebedev?" proffered Pyotr.

"He was the bearer of bad news a few weeks ago, wasn't he? That can't have been a coincidence," said Petrovsky. "That must have upset you a bit."

Semyon took another swig and stared at them blankly.

"Well, so what? Bad news from any source is still bad."

"You know that we have Cyclops in custody—or had him briefly. You may also know we have the tapes implicating Dmitry and Cyclops in Ratface's murder. Not that anyone would condemn them for doing our work for us, but we also have Fyodor and his testimony as a key witness. Your name is written all over this, and with very little effort on our part, we could put you away now for at least an accessory or even part of the conspiracy to murder Ratface. That would put you on more than the injured reserve list. You might ponder that. If you have any information on the dognapping or later attacks, you would be wise to contact me and we can talk about it."

"That sounds like a threat. I don't know about the tapes. But no dog can convict me!"

"Of course, it's a threat. But we don't threaten—we promise. We promise that we will use the evidence we have against you for known and actual crimes. The threat, as you term it, contains an implied offer of leniency for cooperation. As you must know, the police commonly use plea bargains in special cases. As to the illegality of any testimony by Fyodor, don't be too certain. Like everything else, the law emanates from Moscow."

On that note, they all left and drove back into town.

21 THE FYODOR FOUNDATION

I watched the spectacle from the front row of the USU science auditorium. Sure I had to scratch my ass a few times, but I was able to
get behind my ears more deftly now since I had developed the new
flexibility in my front paws. My ears were still a problem though and
smelled like cheese mixed with bad breath. But I seemed to have fewer
fleas and ticks since the treatments by Dr. Krastov, which meant I wasted less time on scratching and gave me more time to think and read.
The only one who noticed my old habits there was Krastov, who told
me to stop it several times as the media would play up a vest-wearing
dog with spectacles that behaved like a street mutt when he thought no
one was watching!

"You're making us look like damned charlatans! Get a grip on. The
public might think you'll just revert to chasing cars right after reading
your Gogol novels. Can't have that!" said he.

It was an unusual gathering even by the money-hustling standards
of the university and research labs that all had to grovel for funding.
Fyodor had heard enough conversations between Krastov and visitors
from the city, the province, the Kremlin, and private firms to know
the arguments and pitches. He also knew all the counter-arguments.
Blah! Blah! They argued all day, sometimes interrupting his reading.
He wasted a lot of time on these people. Still he had to give them credit. Many of them were smart enough to show up and be seen, gorge
themselves on the free food and booze, show positive tendencies toward donating funds to Krastov and his university handlers, and then

disappear afterwards never to be heard from again. Presumably, they slithered back to where they came from.

Seated next to Fyodor, Krastov said suddenly: "This time, you run the meeting. They've heard enough from me." Fyodor was momentarily caught off balance, but then his amber eyes focused and he tightened his jaw, ready for a fight. He moved to the podium in front of the audience of about a hundred USU students, faculty, and representatives of invited groups, many of which were charities, foundations, and non-governmental organizations (NGOs).

Audiences used to watching animated films and cartoons packed with their favorite animal characters—chipmunks, deer, magpies, rabbits, and mice—would not be shocked by the appearance of a talking dog. Many there were dog owners who talked to their dogs regularly, shared their thoughts, and treated them as therapy partners for their problems. They were good listeners and rarely talked back. So it was the same when Fyodor took the podium and started moving his jaw muscles to emit words, slowly and methodically, on stage.

"There are some of you who think I shouldn't be talking because I'm only a dog: dogs shouldn't talk, and, in my case, a talking dog who must be a freak. Anyone out there understand barking?"

Ripples of laughter from the audience . . .

"I know there are people among you today who dislike my being up here talking like an expert. Like many of you, that I've seen come around the labs this past year, you'd like to stab me in the back. So let me stab you first! I may be a paranoiac, but I pride myself in good tactics!"

Stronger and louder laughter this time rippled through the auditorium.

"My presence up here reminds me of the old chauffeur joke which you've probably heard. A scientist was being driven to a conference of world famous scientists up in the mountains. As they drove on, the driver suddenly said to the scientist, who was in the back seat of the long black car:

'Are you going to give another talk on zoonosis today? I'll bet it's the one about how diseases can spread from bat droppings or bites to humans.'

'It might be,' the scientist said impatiently. 'Why do you care?'

'Hell, I've heard that so many times I could give it myself,' said the driver.

'Ok, if you're so smart, go ahead and give it.'

'You mean it?'

'It's all yours,' said the scientist.

They stopped the car and switched seats. The driver sat in back and the scientist wore his hat and drove to the conference facility."

"So there was the driver on stage, just like me, warming up for a lecture on zoonosis," said Fyodor . "He delivered his lines flawlessly and the audience was entirely pleased. Then during the Q&A period afterwards, a hand went up and asked him, how he could be certain that bats produced viruses in humans when there was no evidence from any of the bats that they had any of these viruses themselves?

The driver looked at the man asking the question for a moment, obviously stumped, and said: 'Thank you for that question. Hell, that's a good one and an easy one. Why it's so easy even my driver could answer it. At which point he turned to the scientist and said: "What do you think Pavel?"'

Rousing laughter this time with loud clapping!

"On the other hand, what worries me is that there are some of you who think you know more about dogs than I do. You view me up here as some kind of helpless victim and treat me as the gratefully dependent ward of your hearty benevolence. You think of me as a lab freak, a puppet, maybe even a monster to be exterminated like all my stray brethren out there on the street. I'm here to tell you that you are all way off base. I don't need your sympathy, and I welcome your scorn. Maybe you shouldn't be spouting so many opinions and should find more time to listen!" said Fyodor, throwing off his glasses, moving briskly away from the podium and strutting energetically around the stage.

"I know what you write about me, and I'm not flattered. But some of you attack Dr. Krastov and me physically, as if that would help the animal rights causes, if that's what they are. Some of you even had me kidnapped for money, as if that would help anyone beyond a narrow gang of thugs who would buy arms and drugs with the proceeds. There I wasn't the victim, but the target of mercenaries. And weren't those destructive actions helpful? Where does all your shallow thinking and violent actions get us? Do you want humane treatment for dogs or not? Do you know what that means actually? It means supporting officials that have to make unpopular, tough choices with limited funds and even less support from higher up officials. It means fewer dead dog carcasses dumped into rivers and shoveled into incinerators. It means more funding for dog pounds, and for the trained personnel and modern systems to enforce licensing and regulation of rabies vaccinations. It means funding for research that can create a new breed of dogs that can go forward and do useful things—guide dogs, security dogs, helper dogs for the disabled, and stray adoption programs and outreach. There are many ways we can contribute to humanity, but not if we are rounded up and slaughtered."

"Do you think all dogs could be as advanced as yourself? Aren't most of the dogs unfit for advanced treatments simply culled and put down just as any stray dogs?" asked a professor of biology from USU.

"Probably not. It's true that I'm a lucky dog that worked out. It costs a lot of money and takes time to do the trial and error science that allowed me to develop human qualities. You are correct. Dr. Krastov's team can only handle a small portion of the dog problem in Yekaterinburg. With more funding and supervision a much more comprehensive response could be made. And there are positive spinoffs for humans. I noticed that Dr. Nicholas Krylov was sitting in the front row earlier but has been called away on official business. A month ago, he had advanced stages of rabies from a dog attack, which in most cities and countries would have been fatal. Thanks to Dr. Krastov's research with experimental rabies drugs as part of his work, Dr. Krylov is cured. Many others like him could be for the first time."

"Back to your point about reducing the number of stray kills . . . You suggested that Dr. Krastov's advanced research can do this. Tell us how that magical result will occur," asked someone who identified herself from one of the local animal rights groups.

`"It's hardly magic and it won't happen immediately, you are right. In the short-term, more strays will still die, but over time, far fewer of them as our program goes into action."

"But what if no one supports your program, how will the street dogs be saved?"

Fyodor looked at her and didn't respond immediately, which threw her off balance. She had expected a verbal spar like in other meetings. Of course, those meetings led nowhere except more protests at more meetings.

"What do you suggest? I'm just a dog and can't think of anything practical here. Maybe you people can. Because otherwise, the answer is that they won't be saved."

"We think it's better to capture the dogs, vaccinate them, license them, and release them into controlled environments such as pounds for adoption," said someone from the back of the room.

"But every place with funding has tried this. Some of the special breed rescue leagues, which rely on foster families, take that approach, and it works well. But in most places without a culture of dog adoptions, the pounds fill up, and they must be put down as cruel as that sounds."

"We can't even get that far with the knotheads running this city. The mayor doesn't support us and looks the other way. We have suggested capture and moving dogs inland to places like Central Asia and Chechnya. The Spanish have moved many strays to Cadiz province to get them out of cities."

Scattered laughter could be heard from the audience. "Have you asked any people from these places? Technically, the Central Asians and Chechens are Muslim and view dogs as unclean."

Someone yelled: "We could ship them cleaned-up dogs!"

More laughter from the audience and now a few spirited boos.

"Other options have been tried abroad—such as official culls, as is 'done with deer' and contraceptive pills which work only in the long-term. The trouble is that the pills may be consumed by other species. And provinces to which dogs have been relocated complain about more dog crap, which dissuades tourists and is itself a health hazard."

"What have you done with your tail? Was it removed or do you keep it hidden from the public for some reason?"

"If you must know... It was mostly chewed off in a fight before Dr. Krastov's people captured me and turned me into what I am. But let me satisfy your curiosity."

Fyodor turned around and showed off his stump, which suddenly disappeared in a blur of enthusiastic wagging.

"Bravo!" shouted someone from the back.

Laughter and clapping . . .

"Your stare is intense. It's almost too bright—as if you could see right through us. Your ability to focus must be very developed. How did you achieve this and are there lessons for we humans?" asked someone from the psychology department.

"Didn't I tell you that I can read your minds as well?"

More laughter...

"Some people watch dogs sleeping, with eyes rolling around in their sockets like insane creatures of some kind that ought to be eliminated like vermin. That's called REM dream sleep. It is essential for brain repair, as I'm sure you know in your field of psychology. All dogs seem to have the REM dream sleep talent—even the most common stray mutt."

"I've tried to induce dreams or REM dream sleep. The only thing that seems to work is LSD," said someone from the front.

"Yes, you can take that route. I understand it works, but there are serious side effects. Dogs don't have to take LSD to have excellent dreams of chasing fox and cars."

"You noted the problem of allocating scarce funds for animal control by the city. How can you deal with that? We can't go forward no matter what we accomplish here without more funding. And as we know, Russian cities lack funds from Moscow and also from their own sources," asked Ivan in what was clearly a planted question.

"So we return to our original problem of funding," said Fyodor. "Let us now announce our proposed solution. For such a simple answer, let me turn it over to my driver."

Scattered laughter . . .

"First, the mayor has finally supported us," interrupted Krastov. "If I could jump in here and correct a few misconceptions. First, Bettina was not from the Kremlin's United Russia party and was elected, unlike most Russian mayors. But she supports us, as does the Kremlin—a perfect storm! What do they support? Our results here speak for themselves. Fyodor is a masterpiece of animal social cognition. Look at him over there—wearing his ill-fitting waistcoat. He carries a timepiece; he wears spectacles; walks upright, and his alert expressions reveal that he is cued into those around him. He knows how to hustle, whether it's for food or money. Don't ask him to do any manual labor though. With a bit of professional polish, he could be a CEO or CFO of a big company. In fact, that's what he's going to be: may I present the new CEO of the Fyodor Foundation!"

Krastov announced that Fyodor was to be CEO of the foundation and a board member. Humans as domesticated apes—Dmitry was only part way there. Still dragging his knuckles . . .

"How did you come up with all this?" asked someone from the audience.

"Fyodor came up with it himself after meditation," said Krastov. On cue, Fyodor came across the stage, lay down, and played dead with his paws in the air. "Fyodor has adopted the Zazen pose, a Zen Buddhist posture which allows him to regain inner harmony. Done properly, which Fyodor has practiced to include a serene breathing pace, this pose allows one to acquire enlightenment where before there appeared to be a dead end. In our case, there was no extra money around. Fyodor is demonstrating the posture of total renunciation here on the floor of the auditorium. He also gets some REM dream sleep in the process to re-energize his brain."

(Scattered applause …)

"So what will the Foundation use its new funding for? asked someone from USU.

"We've mentioned our planned activities before. Our objectives will be to finance work in humane reduction of strays and to make further scientific advancements to develop and to protect dogs like Fyodor that have been officially tagged as 'non-human species.' For the first years, our focus will be on new pounds, wider public licensing by NGOs and the City, and expanded placement of rehabilitated dogs with new owners. We will also focus less on bio-treatments and the creation of a new race of dogs, said Krastov.

"Listening to Fyodor you can picture what we have already accomplished. We know from previous Russian research in the 1930s–'40s that wolves evolved into more dog-like creatures. We already knew that dogs often take on the anatomical features and expressions of their masters. Look at your own dogs carefully, and you will often see yourselves in them. After domestic training and breeding, for instance, wolf snouts and those of tamed foxes became shorter and rounder. They became friendlier looking animals. So following the pattern, Fyodor gradually became more human-like. He needs to wears spectacles for his eyes—he is farsighted and can't catch things in the air. He walks on two legs, wears a tailored sport coat, and looks more like a middle-class professional than some humans, many of whom still drag their knuckles on the floor and get paid hefty salaries nonetheless." said Krastov.

(Laughter!)

"Dr. Krastov, you are a showman and a researcher, an excellent salesman for your work. But I fear that your research is incomplete. How can you really conclude anything about domestication of dogs from a sample of one—Fyodor? And what kind of evolution could you expect from an original sample of selected tame but nonetheless stray dogs? The originals were already ripe for training and evolution as you put it. So the domestication syndrome is hardly proven by your work."

"And you, madam, are you at USU?"

"Yes. I am Dr. Alena Kukekova, professor of paleobiology."

"You raise an excellent and well-known criticism of not only our work so far, but also that of the original work by Dmitry Balyaev. In his defense, let me say that given the political pressures, and the security and funding constraints on him and his team, it was lucky that they could get anything done."

(Applause)

"You have pointed to the need for more data and more research. We have a small, stratified sample, a prototype non-human person in

Fyodor, and a more important applied objective, which is to reduce or eliminate strays and prevent more health problems. Before Fyodor, I worked on an earlier stray, Tsar, I called him, who was badly torn up by cars and street fighting. I was still working with him, and he had advanced, though not as quickly as Fyodor, probably because of his poor health. Then he died of cancer. He gave me the inspiration to know I was on the right track. We have extensive notes from the cases of both dogs, and other veterinarians and researchers have looked them over. You are right, though; we have not demonstrated that the syndrome exists for all dogs because we have a larger applied purpose here—a better stray dog policy, that is, a model that could be used by all animal control departments in Russia and worldwide. The World Cup Games gave us the opportunity to go forward on several fronts, and the Kremlin supported us. So we are thankful for how it all worked out. To answer your concern, we hope that the foundation structure will give us the funding and freedom to continue. Colleagues in Russia as well as in the West are behind us in this endeavor."

"What can we do to prevent Fyodor and dogs like him from being attacked as stray mutts when they have clearly evolved? Can he meditate your way out of such attacks?" asked another professor from USU.

"Of course not. And I wouldn't need to," said Fyodor getting off the floor. "That's when we fight back with our natural tools against physical attacks for which we have ample fangs and claws to forge appropriate feral solutions. What we need and finally got from Dr. Krastov was legal protection. Without being a braggart, I am more than a dog now, and kidnappers realize our market value, especially if there are a lot of dogs like me coming on line. I am what the doctor has called a non-human person."

In private, Fyodor had been mulling over the dangers to himself and other dogs, which had become advanced over some time. Semyon's thugs, or whomever they worked for, knew that Fyodor had access to the tapes tying the Ratface murder back to him. The easiest way to prevent him from testifying or turning over the tapes to the police was to either kill or threaten their prize dog. He did want extra protection now since he was more than a just a prize pet dog and could think and talk like a biped human. Boris Krylovsky got a lawyer from the local PETA group to get the favorable court judgment. Krylov had been worried that PETA was simply a bunch of granola crunching virtue-signalers, and that they would be useless in real conflicts. He told Krylovsky and his lawyers that in the U.S., they protested eating crabs because of the inhumanity of boiling crabs alive, so why would there be much support for human rights for dogs? Prevent cruelty? Yes. But full human rights? Bit of a stretch … Krylovsky reminded Krylov that in Russia, they ate meat, especially crab meat, and that anyone interfering with that right would be cooked themselves. The trouble was, of course, that in rural areas, Russians also ate dog meat.

Nevertheless, the lawyer was effective and did get Fyodor protection. She argued that it was the modern trend, and that it was a needed protective cover for future animal biology work. The state attorney argued that dogs were not humans, and that they treated each other barbarically. He conceded that dogs should get protection from human cruelty because mankind was morally repulsed by cruelty but not because they were human. The PETA lawyer argued for a non-human creature category, effectively creating a new animal-like species. She won the day. That, at least, gave Fyodor some protection and legal immunity from bodily violence. Of course in Russia, revenge happens all the time among humans. So it could easily occur for a dog—a wayward car, poisoned food, a quick injection while he was walking—and Fyodor knew that. Krylovsky had the tapes and could reveal them anytime without Fyodor being alive or dead. Still, that didn't make it easier for Fyodor to sleep at night.

22   BACK TO LENINSKIY

It was a long way from Elmira. I had not been expecting such a wild ride for these past several months. I would teach a few classes, find a topic or two for research, along with some new data, and make a few contacts at USU for future Bonaduz students and faculty to work with. That would do it. I merely wanted to get away from my dead-end life and vapid ex-wife. Well, I did. Along the way, I met a talking dog, the pearl of Russian animal scientific advancement; got beaten up a few times by various gangs of thugs; made some close friends, and most importantly, seemingly found a long-term partner. She was someone who could fill the emptiness of my house and life. It was mid-August now, and I was due back there soon. I'm vertical again, strutting around rabies-free, thanks to Dr. Krastov. A few more lose ends here, and I hoped to be on my way.

I pondered all this as the three of us drove up toward Leninskiy the next morning. Was I becoming a convert to the old communist line that mandated an optimistic mentality—the classic socialist realists that saw science and medicine simplistically leading to a paradise on earth? Hardly—Fyodor (or Fido in English) was a solution to the stray dog problem here and to the success of the World Cup games. His progress was simply evidence of the best shot available, and it might or might not work. As for his medicine, because of Dr. Krastov's bizarre variations on standard medical practices, I was still here and not foaming at the mouth. And I certainly supported whatever he came up with.

The sky was filled with fog and some morning overcast, and we could no longer see the city down below the hills. The trees seemed thicker this time, and the heavier branches swooped low onto the narrow, winding road so that we had to be careful not to hit one of them. Suddenly, the windshield cracked with several thuds, and we skidded off the road. The webs in the glass suggested shots were being fired from someplace, and that we weren't welcome this time. Pyotr swerved the car, but we skidded and rolled over anyway. We were suddenly upside down, still skidding along the side of the road. The car skidded into a large tree trunk with a jolt that threw us forward like dice in a shaker. I got the back door open and crawled out of the car. I stood there in the forest and had a quick flashback. Shocks often produce these—I was in a wreck like this once in the Adirondacks, and after rolling out of my car then, my head spun around and around and I fell to the ground. I noticed then several brightly colored blue jays fluttering in a nearby tree. They had been surprised at our bad driving and were having a loud laugh about it. Here, I spotted a few ubiquitous magpies, whose day we had interrupted. Mainly, I was scared. We were under siege from at least one shooter. We were trapped here with no car and probably no cell phone service. Pyotr pried open his door and rolled out.

"Run for it. They could be anywhere. Get to the covered area over there!" bellowed Petrovsky.

I could hear Petrovsky calling for back-up on his cell. Except that it didn't work! He banged his the phone off the tree trunk and swore.

"Great! No cell service! No wonder they call us 'flatfoots.' We never catch anyone and are always outsmarted by these bastards."

Following Pyotr, Petrovsky had pried his door open and rolled out onto the ground. Pyotr motioned to me to keep down and to start crawling away from the car, which I did. I heard a buzz followed by a loud report. Several tree trunks near me were shattered, and splinters flew about. Wherever they were, they had a bead on us.

"We've got to get out of here! Semyon's place is just up the road or in that direction through the woods. No point in staying here. We're pinned down and sitting ducks. Move towards the house, and let's try to get a read on how many of them there are."

Crouching low behind separate trees, I saw Pyotr and Petrovsky draw out their police revolvers and heard them cock. I was several meters away in some bushes and took out Ivan's little two-shot derringer that I had borrowed from him. With this bare bones kind of arsenal, we were ready for anything.

We were spread out pretty well in the woods and advanced slowly up the hill from our separate positions. It was late morning now, and the summer time visibility had finally improved as the mist and fog had lifted. Then a large, bald man with clipped goatee emerged from the bushes nearby and quickly fired his pistol into Pyotr. Pyotr clearly didn't see him coming as he had emerged from behind him. It must have been the military 9mm-type pistol that fires as fast you pull the trigger. Pyotr must have been hit five times before he knew what had happened. I stood up and fired both shots from my derringer into the assailant. Petrovsky, also surprised, got him with his police revolver that was much slower and a smaller bore than the killer's. I ran towards the downed shooter and kicked the gun out of his hand to ensure he was out of it. I then grabbed his now discarded 9mm pistol and looked around for more of his mates. The bald-headed brute must have been 6'6" and 250 pounds. With his scarred face and goatee, he had the standard barbaric look of the low level street punk.

As we headed uphill, I noticed that Petrovsky was limping. A ricochet or a random shot must have hit him. He could still walk, but I saw blood on his pants leg. Despite what just had happened, it was otherwise quiet there, and we could hear birds singing, making the atmosphere even more surreal.

Our attackers must have enjoyed the show. Then there was a growl and what sounded like a fight going on up ahead. We couldn't see anything, but advanced toward the noise. In front of us was a large dog, attacking a man who was trying to hit him with his pistol. The man had apparently been waiting for a chance to pick us off when the dog surprised him. Whether it was a stray or perhaps owned by Semyon didn't matter. The point was to render the dog assistance quickly and worry about his origins later. The man was clearly occupied trying to get the dog off his arm, which he did several times only to find it then re-attached to his leg. He finally shot at it a few times, missing it because the dog had pushed him back each time preventing him from getting a clear shot. But he was too close to keep a steady aim. While this drama was going on, Petrovsky fired several shots into him. We moved away quietly since the dog could just as easily come after us now. But he stayed and seemed to enjoy chewing on the man's raw and bloody flesh, which only encouraged us to move faster. Why spoil his snack? He earned it!

I vaguely recalled the design of the house since my dinner there. The key was to avoid being seen as we approached. So far, I could see no servants or butlers. I gathered that they had been discharged now that Semyon was essentially persona non grata in the Russian government. But he probably still had some of his thugs hanging around, and we had to figure out fast how many of them were there.

I led the way as we entered through the back door of the house and toward the living room, where I figured he spent most of his time drinking to drown out his misfortunes. From outside a room in the back, we could hear heated conversation now.

"Give me the money now!" said the man, standing with a gun in front of Semyon, who was sitting with his head in his hands. "I earned it, and you pay up or there will be serious consequences for you!"

It was none other than my old arch enemy, Cyclops! He had somehow lived on and was still bullying, conniving, and scheming. He was like a bad dream that kept recurring for no reason.

"I've already paid you and your pals, now get lost! I told you the work is over. I've lost everything, and the regime is against us. There is no point in continuing, and I am going to confess all to the police."

"Ah, but you aren't. You will do no such stupid thing," said Cyclops as he raised his pistol and fired several shots into Semyon. He rolled forward and fell onto the floor with a thud in front of an oil portrait of one of his important relatives in the Russian army.

We entered with guns drawn. "Drop your weapon! You are under arrest," demanded Petrovsky.

"Right. Here it is," he said with a wily grin on his face as he hunched over, darted to the side, and fired a quick shot at us. He then slithered off somewhere. I had felt something graze my pants leg, but figured the shot missed. I got a quick shot off at him and may have hit him in the side. I ran out after him, but Petrovsky stumbled forward and fell. His pants were covered in more blood now, and he was nearly passed out when I left him.

I figured it was time to deal with this character once and for all. He represented evil in my simple worldview and had to be eradicated. He was not the type to train or try and rehab to somehow absorb the more exalted values of a better society. I'll leave all that to the sociologists. I was flogged toward the objectives all through life. Not the best method, but here I am. This guy is a perpetual criminal, a lifer, and has managed to hang on through an endless supply of new connections with bad allies. It had to stop.

I ran out the back door and toward a small shed where I supposed Semyon kept his tools. As I got close, I heard the repeated pop from a gun shooting my way. I hit the dirt again and low crawled to the side of the shed. I couldn't see him or even figure which way the shots had come from. He had me pinned down again.

Suddenly, I heard something move nearby. Cyclops was swearing, and there were loud growls as my canine savior apparently had attacked him while he lay in wait for me. Luckily for me, he had finished off his earlier snack and was looking for more, this time one of live human flesh and blood. Well, there's no accounting for taste. Figuring they were both busy, I ran towards the fight and spotted them rolling around in the dirt.

Cyclops was trying to kill the attacking dog. Rather than try and shoot him with my newly-acquired pistol as he moved around, I ran forward and surprised him from behind with a kick to the back of his legs. He turned, and I landed a nice punch to the ugly brute's face. That stunned him, but he still tried to aim his gun at me, which I fixed by clubbing him with the butt of his mate's former gun. He dropped his gun, and I kicked it into the bushes. Disarmed now, he tried to run for it again. I tripped up his back foot, and then hit him about a few more times with the end of the gun as he fell. Why not? No one was looking. He was the perennial bad guy—the personification of continuing evil, which kept turning up like a bad re-run. I punched him a few more times in the face, then kicked him in the balls and stomach for good measure. That was a refreshing rush for this fine morning. I then shot him in the leg so he couldn't crawl off again and headed into the house to find a phone or additional weapon. Suddenly, the dog got up and growled at me. Now why would he do that? A wounded Cyclops should have offered him a fine meal. Better to end all this bad drama—I gave the dog a quick shot as well. He dropped to the ground and after a few jerks and spasms expired.

I left the house after phoning police headquarters for assistance. The dog was lying there. I watched Cyclops get up and waited for his predictable next move. On cue, he got up and ran for the woods despite his leg wound. I fired four shots into him. That felt even better. I did feel bad about shooting the dog, but the idea of a stray running around with a taste for human flesh and blood gave me the creeps. Krastov might have been upset that we weren't giving him a chance for a comfortable rehab experience, but eventually I know he would have put him down too. At best any kind of rehab was a long-term solution, a potential benefit while letting him roam around was an obvious and immediate cost and risk to public health. It might make a good case study on ethical decision-making under uncertainty. Canine triage, perhaps, though not now. And the opportunity to wipe out two scourges in one day didn't come that often! I knew that somehow this human bastard would escape the law and be at it again. There was no one looking, and that made it all easier.

23   RUSSIAN STYLE HEALTH CARE

"Wakey! Wakey! Time to get up!" she announced.

Movement by something wrapped up in blankets nearby.

"Oh! Ho! Look who's here!" I managed to say.

"I came in earlier, but you were really out of it. So I waited awhile and heard your breathing change rhythms. Then I saw you move around a bit and came in!" said Anna.

She was wearing a loose, linen blouse and short skirt and bent over me in bed. I reached up and squeezed her hip with one hand and kissed her.

"What am I doing here?" I asked.

"What are you doing back in the hospital you mean? You've spent most of your time in these places since you've come here! Your favorite thugs beat you up again. This time you got a bullet flesh wound in your leg. Close call there! Don't you remember any of this?"

It was starting to come back, but I was more interested in Anna than trying to sort out painful recent memories. I reached out to grab her and almost fell out of bed.

"Steady on. This is a hospital, and everyone is in the next room—Andrey, Vessie, and Petrovsky. All your supporters who brought you in here after your latest scrap! You should get some kind of special duty pay—for getting beat up as a Dr. Krastov supporter, then as a cop for the Yekaterinburg police force. Let's at least wait until you get out of here in a few hours and then talk over dinner."

"I had this very fine erotic dream. I was doing the Ukrainian *hopak* squat dance while you were whistling, yelling out, and clapping beside me."

"You mean: "Hey! Hey! Hey!" she sang and clapped a few times.

"Right, you were hopping up and down to the cadence. I was bouncing around with my arms folded. Then I noticed we were both nude! We were managing to have sex while bouncing up and down to the music."

"They must have put Viagra into your anesthetic, and it reacted with the residual of Krastov's anti-rabies pills."

"Come on! Climb in here for a minute! Isn't that proper alternative Russian health care?"

"Down boy. We wait until dinner, and I have some surprises for you. See you in a few hours!"

I cried out in mock pain, but she had already gone.

I fell back to sleep and dreamed about doing the sexual *hopak* with her until the orderlies at the Yekaterinburg hospital woke me again.

"Time to check out, Mr. Krylov. This isn't a hotel," said the portly matron who was built like a tram driver or maybe a maintenance worker.

I got to Andrey's place around seven. I had been staying there for the past few weeks since I could hardly go back to Sveta's. As soon as I knocked, Anna opened her door. Beaming, she threw her arms around me. "Nick!"

No further words were needed. She was eager to see me—a good sign, I thought at the time. I caressed her cold arms and shoulders, and we engaged in a nice, long, sexually-charged kiss to open the evening. She looked smashing, stunning, strapping—all the best adjectives I could think of. We moved to the couch, and knowing my basic needs, she gave me a beer. She looked at me like we had already spoken about something and shared a secret joke.

"Quite some events today, wouldn't you say?" she said. "Then you've heard it? Terrible about young Pyotr! I'm sad about Semyon ... definitely not sorry about losing the rest of them."

"Semyon's demise must hit you hard! I'm sorry."

"It does. Even if he turned into a real bastard the last years, we had some good times. And we were used to each other's flaws. But while you were asleep, I got Petrovsky to sign my visa application to the U.S. Ivan witnessed it, as he will tell you himself later. Since Semyon is 'deceased,' and the coroner attested it, no need for his permission to leave anymore."

"Excellent work. I get more things done when I'm out of it in a hospital."

I looked her over. Tonight, she had on an even shorter brown corduroy skirt that allowed me to fully appreciate the muscles in her fleshy thighs and calves as she moved her legs around on the couch. The dimpled skin on her legs had a nice, caramel cream sheen that combined with their frequent adjustments on the couch, fluffing her skirt down, then up, then folding her legs under her, all moved me to a slow boil. Perfect healing medicine for someone in my state of physical and emotional debilitation . . . To set off her skin color, her hair had a deep, dark luster to it. I'd noticed this before, but hadn't had a good look at her in weeks. Tonight, she was wearing large, round Roma-style or Chechen peasant girl earrings. In the background was the low thump of a DVD full of some lively Afro-Cuban meringue rhythms. The piece was a slow, visceral, and repetitive chorus of drums, trumpet echoes, and solo singers from one of the many famous Cuban groups. Her presence and the music had stimulated the animal spirits in me. No murdering of silence with heavy metal or canned, mechanistic drug noise for me anymore. The right rhythms were as intoxicating to me as any drug or drink.

"You like this kind of music?" she said, blowing some more smoke from her cigarette behind her.

Standing by the doorway, she looked at me and let her hair fall in front of her face. It may have been accidental, but this little gesture sent my head spinning—I wanted her at any cost.

I moved over and kissed her neck, both cheeks. She planted her tongue inside my mouth and moved it around, then straight into my throat. As I had grown to expect from our experiences, there had to be a distracting knock on the door at this point. Right on cue, there was a knock on the door.

"That would be Andrey," I said.

After he arrived at his place and got settled in, I watched Anna in the small kitchen area on the other side of the large living room making a local dish of pasta mixed with lamb and spices. She talked and laughed with Ivan, while he poured wine on the meat and tomatoes, even helped cut the onions, and stirred some of the sauces. She handed him plates and silverware, and then glided around the kitchen doing a dozen little tasks. I admired her strong, decisive features. Several times, while cutting the meat into chunks with loud thuds, she threw back the falling locks of hair behind her ears. The sleeveless white blouse only accentuated the sensuous mixture of muscle and silky smoothness.

Later Andrey said, "Thanks to you both for inviting me for dinner, even if it is in my own flat." We all toasted to better days. "I mean, who else could I get to listen to me?"

"Plenty of people would want to hear your words of wisdom," I said. "For instance, I've wanted to ask you an obvious question since I learned about the stray dog attacks here. What was it like for someone like you, young, educated, professional, modern to live through the experience?"

"You know how the Romanians and Hungarians envied and respected the dogs as symbols of the freedoms they lacked. We younger Russians, if I could generalize here, took a different tack because this was a different context and era. We had no idea whether the problem of stray attacks would get worse or better. But we felt separated from it all in our downtown flats and in our middle class family cocoons. The dog problem, if indeed it was a real problem, was somebody else's and not ours. None of us knew anyone that had been seriously attacked, and so we felt superior to the problem and to the dogs. We simply didn't think about the dogs. They stayed as they had always been for us: pets, occasional curiosities trotting around town alone or with a few of their mutt friends. Nothing to get worked up about."

"What changed it for you, Andrey?" I asked.

"Maybe it was the number of attacks reported. Maybe it was that suddenly we knew family and friends who had been attacked. Maybe it was the coming of the World Cup Games, which put it on the agenda as a national disgrace to be eliminated. I often ask myself the same question. Let me read you something, and I think you'll understand what changed it for all of us."

He picked out a book he had been reading and quoted something for us:

They went on doing business, arranged journeys and formed views. How should they have given a thought to anything like plague, which rules out any future, cancels journeys, and silences the exchange of views. They fancied themselves free, and no one will ever be free so long as there are pestilences.

Just substitute 'we' for 'they' and replace pestilence in Dr. Rieux's quote from Camus' *The Plague,* and you might see what changed my views about the increasing scourge of dog attacks here. Something had to be done," said Ivan.

"I didn't know you read serious literature. I thought you only cared about city planning," said Anna.

"I was a literature major, specializing in Shakespeare as an undergraduate. The city planning study is intended to find a real job."

"You are full of surprises, Andrey! So, what was done?"

"Right around nothing. The Kremlin and its provincial minions were too distant to do anything except issue the usual plans and edicts. The local police were too heavy-handed to do anything other than treat the dogs like gangs and try to eliminate them by force. So the responses consisted mainly of occasional shows of force in the form of dog-shootings and round-ups. Unfortunately, strays breed fast and the net population levels of them stayed about the same."

"Until?"

"That's when Krastov came on the scene and made his move. Under Fyodor's wise council, he wrote to Moscow and the provincial officials he knew and asked for a hearing, which he quickly got. He presented a comprehensive and spectacular sense of the growing problem to them, explained his applied research, and then offered them a new way forward for the immediate problem and the long-term future."

"And they bought in?"

"More or less. They were skeptical and bureaucratic, wanting to delay things. But the force of events, especially the Games, all worked in Krastov's favor."

"Amazing, Andrey. We're always glad when you join us. And we like listening to you," I said. "You keep us thinking and on our toes, right Anna? Besides, it's your place, and we are your guests—not the other way round!"

"Right. And speaking of the police, at least one member of that iron-fisted community is not heavy-handed. I'm off to see Vessie this evening!"

"Great plan, Andrey, and good luck with her. Tell her to contact Krastov about the internship as I mentioned her to him."

Immediately after his departure, we returned to the sofa. Through all this I was holding tightly onto my napkin for some reason. Tossing it aside, I began easing her skirt zipper down. Running my finger along the furrow of her spine now, I felt the two dimples of her lower back. I realized she wore no panties. Not that this was unusual, but it fueled my adrenalin even more. Her hands found my back, stoking me in rough, massage-like circles until my thighs shuddered.

We moved off the sofa and into "my" room in the back. She lay back across the bed, and I moved in next to her. There I started with her neck and cheeks and licked my way from her shoulders and breasts slowly all the way down to her thighs. Both her knees were up now, and I took the opportunity to lick her bodily hairs, those that started at her stomach, spread like tough weeds down her legs, and then in between them. I worked down to the core spot, and began thrusting my tongue inside her. Hearing telltale groans and sighs, I replaced my tongue with the proper tool. God, it felt like it was a yard long now . . . I had to hunt for the end of it. Inside her now and pumping hard, she became wild, like a cat, shrieking, pounding on my back, but repeating 'yes' over and over to encourage me onward and inward. I kept thrusting and held on tight to this steed of finely tuned flesh. When we both came, in long surging spasms, it seemed like a perfect chorus of high notes. We moaned, sighed, and rolled around some more—then burst out laughing. Tears streamed down her cheeks as she cried out with joy. It happened with us spontaneously like this around two months ago when I first came to Yekaterinburg, in Sveta's apartment no less. The sizzle from that one still radiated through me for several days.

We must have fallen asleep together in the bedroom. I awoke in a sweat and noticed that Anna was not beside me. From the living room, I heard a different kind of music. It was still dark, probably around four in the morning now. I slowly got up and came out. The Afro-Cuban rhythms had been replaced by a softer, Middle Eastern village beat. In this kind of music, there was no singing, just the slow beat of a drum accompanied by what sounded like a clarinet.

She was dancing by herself in the living room, completely nude. I sat down on the sofa and watched. Anna looked my way, but it was clear that she didn't see me at all. In this trance-like state, she danced, shaking her arms and shoulders furiously. Moving about slowly in a large circular pattern, she skipped delicately about with her arms outstretched. I could hear her muttering what appeared to be a musical prayer or *zikr* as the Chechens call it. Moving now in ever smaller circles, she clapped her hands and stomped on the floor for emphasis. Faster and faster she went as her ecstasy mounted...

Suddenly, she dropped to the sofa and threw her arms back. One leg was over the back and one was on the floor. She reached slowly down between her legs and began stroking her pubic area almost imperceptibly, then quite vigorously. This was more than I could take. I was already aroused from her erotic display. Quickly, I moved her hand away, pinned both her arms behind her head, and furiously mounted her on the couch. Once again, she groaned and then screamed as I entered. With her arms back and legs stretched, she let out little yelps in almost perfect cadence with my thrusts. For the second time that evening, we both came. The odd thing afterwards is that when I looked into her eyes this time, she was still in a trance. As before, she looked at me like I was a complete stranger. It took about thirty minutes until her expression changed, and she looked at me in recognition.

"Hello, Nick!" she said.

I watched her carefully, almost clinically. "Where were you?"

"What do you mean?"

"I thought you had left me."

"Now you know . . . I take spiritual voyages when I am turned on enough. You did that. We did that . . . I'm back now."

24   BACK TO ELMIRA

Ivan drove us to Koltsovo airport, which was a newly-built terminal in Soviet post-modern, futuristic style. For a large hub industrial city of almost two million people, it wasn't very busy. As some said ironically: the future was just on the horizon, and it would come to them one way or another. After checking in, we went to the restaurant where we waited for the others to show.

While waiting, Anna looked worried.

"You sure you want to do this? Last chance to change your mind."

"It will be a new life for me."

"It will. You will be in a small town in a small university and be able to develop your ideas and skills. Elmira is a rather boring, infamous place. Its claim to fame, if there is one, is that the British writer Rudyard Kipling once met Mark Twain there in hopes that he could turn himself into an American writer. He failed because most Brits were already too similar to Americans to really become completely like them. You are distinctly Russian and could be a cultural voice explaining and comparing the customs, values, and practices of both countries. Let's see how it works. We can always come back here. I wouldn't mind that at all."

Then several of them arrived at once. It was Gyorgy from Perm and Krylovsky stopping by to say farewell. Gyorgy had an old book he wanted to give me of family history. He also had Pavel with him on a leash because he wanted to meet Fyodor in person, who had also just arrived with Krastov.

"I brought Pavel to say goodbye. I wanted him to meet Fyodor as an inspiration for him to learn how to talk."

"You sure you want him to talk? He might never shut up," I said. "Nadezhda not along?"

He rolled his eyes and grimaced. "I needed to get out of the house! Please, teach Pavel to talk, Fyodor, so I can have a companion!"

"We can sign him up for intensive training if you like," said Krastov. Petrovsky arrived with Vessie.

"Simon, thank you for everything. Since no good deed goes unpunished, I will try and bring Vessie over for study at Bonaduz, and you for a visit. You could join the campus police force."

"Sounds like an excellent retirement job."

"I also invited your relative Krylovsky for a goodbye chat," said Gyorgy.

"Sorry we couldn't talk more while I was here. But I was a bit busy as you know."

"I'm glad that you survived your stay here and are still vertical!"

"I will check around with the animal rights people and see if I can get you over there as well."

Ivan said, "Dr. Risanovsky sends his regards. He couldn't avoid an important faculty meeting so he sends his latest, autographed book for you."

"Sounds like a must read. Give him my regards."

Our flight was announced. As both of us were eager to start life over in a more predictable place, Anna and I hugged everyone and kissed them each three times as is the custom there.

It had been short, sweet, and I felt truly relaxed and satisfied for the first time in my life. I held her hand as the engines roared to life, and we started taxiing down the runway. We looked out the window at Yekaterinburg. An ending and a new beginning . . . We taxied into position and were thrown back by the force of the engines screaming down the runway to take off. I looked at Anna, then away. I always teared up leaving places and people who meant a lot to me. Almost on cue, I spotted something from the window moving in the same direction as the plane down the runway before liftoff. It was someone wearing a loose cap running ahead with a surprised but gleeful expression on his face, as if a plane was something he had never seen before. His disheveled dress, ragged looks, and long strides expressed strength and the confidence of his youth. He had that defiant grin on his face—probably a wily ragamuffin who regularly outsmarted the airport authorities and ran after planes for kicks. A tough one, just like I was once. He bounded ahead on long strides; it was more than a run. Behind him a few paces back ran his black and white shaggy dog, a ruddy, country type that must have enjoyed these escapades with him. Then I saw him down behind us and he was gone from view. He must have stepped in a ditch and fallen, as I could no longer see him though I pressed my face to the far corner of the window. We left the ground, and I could no longer see the airport or the runway. The last thing I saw was the dog stopping to sniff around the scene until his partner in mischief picked himself up.

AUTHOR'S NOTES AND REFERENCES

What got my attention was the estimate of 2 million stray dogs in Russia's 2018 Summer World Cup cities (June 14–July 15). It struck me as ludicrous that city authorities were only setting up temporary shelters during the Games and would likely just keep killing strays on the streets or later after they spent ten or so days in shelters just like they had before the Sochi Winter Olympics The earlier Russian plans didn't work, and now they were going to try it again. These events seemed ripe for fictionalization. The random stray attacks and spread of associated diseases as a result were like a pestilence for the citizens of Yekaterinburg. But here, unlike in the Oran of Camus' *Plague*, quarantines and lockdowns were not going to work. The city, the Kremlin, and Provincial governments had to somehow devise effective animal control regulations and coordinate implementation of them. They didn't move until the public pressures concerning the upcoming World Cup Games made them act. But they really couldn't act because of the hundreds of years of rigid formalism still extant in the values and practices of the Russian civil service, much of which is evident from Nikolay Gogol's short story "Nevsky Prospekt". The quote by Ivan later in the book is also from *The Plague*. My book may read like an update and revision of Mikhail Bulgakov's *Heart of a Dog* or perhaps his *The Fatal Eggs* and some of it should. Those superb works together with reports of the actual canine happenings for the World Cup games in Russia provided all the fuel necessary to get moving on this novel. I once urged my late brother

Cameron, who made films for the National Film Board of Canada, to make an animated film of *Heart of a Dog*, but he couldn't get his act together.

Heart of a Dog, the classic novel of turning dogs to humans, ends with tragic consequences. Similar novels have been written about animal vivisection to create humans, such as, H.G. Wells, *The Island of Dr. Moreau* and Mary Shelley's tale of Dr. Frankenstein's efforts to recreate life in a corpse in *Frankenstein* (New York: Bantam, 1981). Bulgakov's tale is infused with black political humor and is a fictional tragicomedy of veterinarians in service of the communist state. In Gogol's classic account of Medji, the clever talking dog who could also write in "Diary of a Madman," the narrator was more interested in what the dog could tell him about its lady owner (Fidele) than whether it could talk. Beyond such fantasies, it was refreshing to learn about a real story of jump-started evolution, turning foxes into dogs, which gave me the idea of trying to explain what veterinarians, animal biologists, and city animal control services in Yekaterinburg could possibly do in service to humanity. The reference to the Belitsa gypsy dancing bear farm in Bulgaria and the 'freedom research lab' project is from *The Dancing Bears* , Witold Szablowski's book about the captive trained bears, which is a compelling tale about the dangerous current nostalgia and fascination with tyranny around the world in many countries.

Useful historical background was gleaned from the guide I used when working on overseas aid projects in Armenia and Ukraine in the 1990s: *USSR The New Soviet Union* and the more recent essay on modern Russian political economy and history in the *Economist* (2019). Fascinating insights into life under the Soviets were provided by such sources as Karl Ove Knausgaard andby Paul Theroux, who provided some interesting descriptions of the Transsib almost 50 years ago in *The Great Railway Bazaar: By Train Through Asia* My knowledge of life under totalitarian dictatorships was enhanced by the many friends and colleagues met in countries such as Armenia, Bulgaria, Macedonia (now called North Macedonia), and Albania while providing technical assistance to national and local govern-ments for IMF and USAID. To round out the picture, I consulted novels such as Gyorgy Dragoman's *The White King* (2005) written from the tragi-comic perspective of an eleven-year-old growing up in Hungary. I would like to thank the late Simon Karlinsky, Professor of Slavic Languages and Literature for stimulating in me an interest in all things Russian from his course on Anton Chekhov at UC Berkeley during my time as an undergraduate there in the late 1960s.

DEDICATION

This book is dedicated to our fine family of loyal, clever, loving and playful Labrador and Golden Retrievers over many years: Gus, Chester, Benny, Daisy, Buddy and Beacon. It is dedicated to my wife Regula and sons Andy and Marty who grew up with and were raised by these amazing dogs...It is also dedicated to our black lab Beacon who inspired me to write this book. We "rescued" him from the Lab Rescue Committee of Potomac (LRCP) and he in turn rescued me from serious grief after a seizure suddenly ended the life of our white lab Buddy.

APA Publications (1991) *USSR The New Soviet Union* (1991) (London: Insight Guide),

Bulgakov, Mikhail (2012) *The Fatal Eggs* (Surrey: Alma Classics) (1968) *The Heart of a Dog* (New York: Harcourt, Brace & World).

Camus, Albert *The Plague* (New York: Vintage, 1991).

Dragoman, Gyorgy (2015) *The White King* (New York, Black Swan.)

Dugatin Lee Alan and Trut, Lyudmila (2017) *How to Tame a Fox and Build a Dog* (Chicago: University of Chicago Press).

Economist (2019) "Siberia: The Ironies of Freedom", December 21, pp. 111-114.

Isabelle Khurshudyan, Isabelle (2018) "Animal Activists in Russia Fear Repeat of Sochi Dog Debacle", *The Washington Post,* February 13, A8.

Knausgaard, Karl Ove (2018) "Out of the Past: A Journey Into the Heart of Russia" (*New York Times Magazine)*, August 18.

Gogol, Nicolay (2005) "Nevsky Prospekt" and "The Diary of a Madman" in *The Diary of a Madman, The Government Inspector and Selected Stories*, (New York, Penguin Classics).

Shelley, Mary *(1981) Frankenstein* (New York: Bantam).

Simenon, Georges (2015) *Lock #1* (New York, Penguin/Random House).

Szablowski, Witold (2014) *The Dancing Bears* (New York: Penguin).

Theroux, Paul (1975) *The Great Railway Bazaar, By Train Through Asia* (New York: Ballantine)..

ABOUT THE AUTHOR

When not writing fiction (and non-fiction) Dr. George Guess is a specialist consultant in public budgeting and financial management who helped reshape the transitional economies in the Balkans and Eastern Europe from 1992 until 2006. His ability to relate to clients in many different cultures helped him in his work asinternational consultant for USAID, World Bank and IMF, with project work in such countries such as Albania, Costa Rica, Ecuador, , Pakistan, Armenia, Myanmar, the Dominican Republic and Romania.

Dr. Guess received his B.A degree from UC Berkeley, and is the author of six books, including *Foreign Aid Safari: Journeys in International Development,* published by Athena Press in London in 2005, *The Dogs of Bucharest,* also by Athena Press in London in 2005, and *Democracy and International Governance* by Routledge in NYC in 2019. He is currently an adjunct professor at George Mason University in Fairfax, Virginia.